Fleshly bargain

"I know a young man—of a fine Southern family—who wants to join your organization."

The beautiful Jessie Lanier, herself an aristocrat, had come this morning to the bachelor quarters of Colonel Tyler, unbeknownst to her husband, to plead that her young son be admitted to the Klan.

"You must prove yourself, prove your dedication," said the burly, red-bearded man. Tyler was said to be high in the KKK, a crony of the leader, General Nathan Bedford Forrest.

Jessie understood and almost laughed in his face. He wanted to make love to her, to have her bribe him with her body.

Suddenly the risk of scandal, the danger of her situation began to excite her. She loved her full woman's body, and she wanted it to be touched and enfolded. She slowly opened her dress and caressed her breasts in a voluptuous movement.

She lifted her skirt and gazed at the big man in his threadbare uniform.

"Please . . . please undress me."

The Making of America Series

THE NIGHTRIDERS

Lee Davis Willoughby

A DELL/JAMES A. BRYANS BOOK

Published by
Dell Publishing Co., Inc.
1 Dag Hammarskjold Plaza
New York, New York 10017

Dell ® TM 681510, Dell Publishing Co., Inc.

ISBN: 0-440-06255-1

Printed in the United States of America
First printing—July 1982

1

On that cold day, large slips of paper printed in red were mysteriously scattered through the streets of Palmyra, Tennessee. Stray winds whipped them along the lanes and fields and they stuck to fences and trees and the front of buildings.

KU KLUX WILL PARADE TONIGHT!!!

Word spread to the countryside and a large, curious crowd gathered in the rasping darkness and smell of oil lamps along the street. People looked excited, a child here and there perched on a father's shoulder, all eager to see the show. They talked of the nightriders whose numbers were growing throughout the South. Few people in that part of the state had seen them and most wondered what they looked like.

"I heard they dress like devils," a man said. "They got horns and their horses are painted red."

"Why they get up like that for?" another said.

"Scare niggers, I hear."

"You don't have to tell a nigger nothing but a little hell to scare him."

"Not these times, old man." The speaker looked around to see if there were any negro militia in town, or Yankee

5

Loyal League agents who dressed in plain clothes. "They got us on the spit these days."

"My husband's cousin saw them parade through Goodspring last month," a woman said. "Told us they looked as smart as Heggie's Scouts. After they rode out, there was a big fire up on Hickett Knob that night. When people went up in the morning, they found a great big old cross, all burned and chars, and there was a notice pinned to a tree. It was printed big, all in red like this here, and it said something like this"—her voice became a loud hollow whisper:

"Thunder and Blood . . . Blustiferation and Hollow Hell and Fury . . . The Ku Klux Ghosts are everywhere . . . Niggers and Scalawags and Republican Radicals beware!"

"Your husband or his cousin sure know a good joke."

"It was so," the woman insisted. "Why, my cousin said that the horses' hoofs didn't touch the ground when them riders came in and then was lost in the trees. Just like a magic show."

Children ran in and out of the crowd. Eyes searched the darkness beyond the streets. An old woman sold corn cakes from a barrow. The mayor ordered men to light torches along the main street beyond the lamps. People huddled together for warmth. A group of negro men drifted into town slowly from across the railroad tracks and stood far down near the end of the street. None were from around Palmyra and they got suspicious, hostile looks from the crowd. It was three years since the end of the war, but people were still afraid of bands of freed slaves that roamed the countryside.

In the big Lanier house, a half-mile from the center of town, the family sat down to supper. Built in the Victorian Italianate style, the house sat on a hill that overlooked Palmyra. It had a mansard roof with cast-iron pinnacles as cresting. A grilled balcony ran along the south and west sides, and the bay windows in front had large panes of colored glass. The veranda had ornamented columns and carved and turned balusters for railing. The path up to the

house was wide, with tangled brambles of honeysuckle
and blackberry thickets. The house was hidden from the
road by long rows of tall poplar trees, but at the end of
the path it loomed big and white, with green and ochre
shutters. In daylight, sunshine streamed through the tall
windows into large, airy, high-ceilinged rooms.

It had been built just two years before the war, a gift to
Jessie and Everett Lanier from her father. Everett always
felt uncomfortable about the house, too big and lavish and
adorned, too far away from most other houses, and he
never felt that it was his own. It was a remnant of the
plantation way of life, a house bigger and grander than
anyone else's, a house for pretending aristocrats. And the
irony was that it had been built by men from the North;
there were few craftsmen in marble and stone and elaborate wood-carving in that rural society.

The family ate in silence until Matthew, the seventeen-
year-old son, said he wanted to see the parade. His father
told him to stay at home and they argued. Matthew
looked toward his mother.

"Let him go," she said. "There's little enough to amuse
him these days."

Everett, a spare-looking man in his late forties, touched
the stump of his missing left arm. It was an unconscious
gesture. Matthew knew that he did it in reflex whenever he
was disturbed or nervous.

"There's going to be trouble. I don't want him there."

"What trouble? It's just a parade."

"People down there don't know what's happening. You
stay home, Matt."

"You're making the boy into a calf."

Everett glared at his wife. "You didn't let Porter grow
much beyond that, did you?"

Matthew's older brother was killed at Malvern Hill in
the first year of the war, and his father's sour grief and
hate flared at any thought or mention of the dead son,
something about his mother pushing Porter into the war
when he was only Matthew's age . . . only a few weeks
after Everett left Palmyra with his own regiment.

At Malvern Hill, during the Seven Days before Rich-

mond in 1862, Porter was in a battery of Tennessee How-
itzers dashing into position. Opposite them were the
green-clad sharpshooters of Colonel Hiram Burden's regiment, all equipped with new Sharps rifles. As the battery
horses were pulled up, the Confederate gunners dismounted and unlimbered their gun. There was a sound
like a thousand snapping sticks as the Union soldiers
opened fire. The horses were hit first and went down,
flailing, wild-eyed and screeching. Porter and other artil-
lerymen tried to cut the beasts free and wheel the pieces
into position by hand. But every man was cut down by the
murderous fire. The one officer who survived came to see
the Laniers after the war. He told them of Porter's brav-
ery, and said, "We went in a proud battery and we ended
in a slaughter."

Adela, the daughter, hated the tension, the joy her parents took in flaying each other. She was only thirteen
then, but she remembered the night her mother brought
Porter to a Confederate officer she knew in Hatchie, said
the boy was eager to serve, and lied about his age. Like
every young Southerner in those years, Porter was full of
blood to go and fight the Yankees, and thanked his
mother. He was killed before his father knew he was gone
from home. It was more than a year later before Everett
returned, wounded, and found out that Porter was dead.
Adela broke the silence, trying to make the parade sound
silly and innocent.

"Oh, let him go, papa. It's just some fool men dressing
up."

"That's all it is," Matthew said. "They're just a social
club, a secret one. You said yourself we always had them
before the war. All they do is play jokes on niggers and
serenade ladies. Everyone says it's a great sight to see."

Everett could understand the boy's innocence, his eagerness. But he knew Adela was too smart to believe it.
She had some idea of what was happening in the South
. . . the Freedmen's Bureau and Loyal Leagues set up by
the Yankees, putting negroes into power to rule them like
a conquered country. There were vigilantes all over the

place. Not just the Ku Kluxers riding for "Southern honor"—but the Sons of Midnight . . . Pale Faces . . . White Brotherhood . . . Knights of the White Camelia . . . Order of the White Rose. But it was the Ku Klux Klan that captured everyone's imagination. They were the most violent, a cabal of mystery, and soon began to absorb the other orders. Let a negro farmer have a good crop and he was burned out. A woman who sinned was whipped half-dead. A negro teacher, a Northern clerk in the Freedmen's Bureau that helped negroes, a Southerner who pitied the ex-slaves and fed a starving family wandering a road, anyone who tried to change things was prey. Everett remembered a talk about the Klan with a judge in Alabama. "We are in the hands of murderers," the man said.

But Everett knew he protected Matthew too much, was too flinty and strict with him. Maybe the boy should see what the war had brought. He was growing up in a dying town in a defeated country. More battles had been fought in Tennessee than any other state except Virginia, and the land had been laid waste. The farms were blighted, a place without hope, the people restless, frightened of what was to come.

"Be home early." Matthew jumped up and was almost at the door when Everett called after him. "And keep away from that rough scum down there."

Jessie caught up with Matthew on the veranda. "I want you to see them. They're the ones who will fight our battle." She cupped his chin in her hand. "Porter's gone, but he was a hero. Never forget that. Your father's a poor cripple who's given up. You'll be the strong man we need."

Matthew didn't understand. Sometimes he thought that his mother was wrong in the head from everything in the war, losing her first-born, her father killed when he fired at a Yankee patrol foraging for food. She always talked like the 2nd Tennessee was still advancing up from Franklin to fight Joe Hooker's Union troops. Her hand grew firm on his chin, and her lucid hazel eyes burned from the glow of a lamp inside a front window.

"I hear they're mostly country men. The best the South

has." Jessie looked down the hill toward the lights in town fluttering between the trees. "They're the real Southerners. Town people, city people—they lost the war."

She did sound crazy. His father was from Memphis, a city man, but he was a captain of cavalry and had fought bravely until his arm was blown off at the Dunker Church at Sharpsburg, the terrible battle the Yankees called Antietam. Even after that, Lanier had volunteered to return to his regiment, but was refused. He was a lawyer and a former state senator. Jessie, two years younger, was a Kittredge from a famous plantation called Loretto in the southern part of the state. They met at a ball at Tolliver Shoals, and when they married she pleaded with him to take over the plantation and cotton gins from her father. But Everett insisted on living in town so he could continue his law practice. He wanted to live in Memphis, but she refused and he picked Palmyra in the northern part of the state. It had one of the South's first railroad lines, was near tobacco, cotton and coal country, and the Cumberland, Tennessee and Red Rivers. He thought it would be the next big city in the state. She hated it and always talked about going back to Loretto. But at first she was raising three children, then when the war came, she knew the dream was over. The Kittredge plantation was in ruins, the fields cut by gunfire—in the words of a Union officer— "as closely as could have been done with a knife." The Kittredge slaves, frightened and hungry, fled to the towns, never understanding that they were free.

Matthew had heard the story too often. How she sacrificed everything for her husband, that lovely and gracious life at Loretto, and endlessly described the mansion and fields, the look of miles of cotton in bloom, trying to make him love it as she did. She repeated herself, the same words, the same tears at appropriate moments. But Matthew sensed that she was an ally, would give him anything he wanted, help him when he needed it. He only had to pretend that the sad tale was fresh, that he longed for the life she talked about with sentimental longueurs, have sympathy for what she tried to convince him was no less than an immolation of her spirit and life. He knew it was less her love for him than the need to do anything that would torment her husband. She kissed him on the lips.

"Remember . . . under every grief and pain, runs a joy with silver twine."

He rushed down the road, crossed the small bridge over Elysian Creek, and stopped when he could still look down on the main street. A group of men stood at the side entrance of the Palmyra House. Some were town bums and drifters, but most were Confederate veterans who kept themselves apart from other people in town. They were edgy, gaunt, sullen men, most of them maimed one way or another. One had his jaw shot away at Chickamauga and Matthew could barely look at him. Two others had lost legs and hobbled and jerked around on homemade crutches. One man came out of the Union prison at Fort Seebert with ruined lungs and constantly gasped for breath in panicky spasms, coughs racking his body. Sometimes Matthew caught a glimpse of a revolver in someone's belt, always the same weapon, a big Navy Colt with a telltale cracked butt, as if they passed it around for courage like a bottle. Every town in the South had its haunted, gibbering, mutilated cripples who looked like they had truly seen hell. But one man in the group fascinated Matthew.

The left side of James Kortman's face was a scabrous patch of burn scars. People said it happened at the Battle of the Wilderness when a cannon blew up, but Kortman never talked about it. Tall and thin, he was a commanding figure despite the ugliness. He always wore a clean ruffled shirt, a black stock in the old fashion, a swallowtail coat, and striped trousers stuffed into high shiny Mexican boots. He walked the streets with an air, tipped his wide-brimmed black hat to women, always said something gently witted and flirting. His smile made his sharp face grotesque, pulling his eye and mouth crooked, but no woman who remembered the handsome man who left Palmyra for the war ever turned from Kortman as they sometimes did from other wounded men. Tennessee was the last state to go "secesh," but Kortman had run off to join an Alabama regiment a week after Fort Sumter was fired on. He was a

garish and enigmatic man, brought to Palmyra from the
West Indies as a boy by his father, and it was sometimes
whispered around that he had some nigger in him.

Matthew searched for Kortman but he wasn't around.
He often stood at the edge of the group, surprised that
they still spoke with beligerence, boasting how they had
whipped the Yankees and would do it again, talking old
battles, and how they could have won the war if it had
just gone on a little longer. He never made the connection
between these wounded men and his father. They fascinated him with their rough, swaggering talk, and he
looked on them as the real heroes, men who had undergone a special trial. He thought they were talking of
Southern ideals and honor, a way of life, but he didn't
know that the veterans were still obsessed by their love of
war. It was the one great lyric action of their lives, the
dirty secret of all warriors. Ragged and mangled, most of
them hated coming back to dark dusty stores and farms
with withered fields, and would fight again if someone
gave them arms and led them. They always made Matthew yearn for the suffering and glory he'd missed, the
past of the war years rustling with his regret.

A red rocket suddenly soared above the barren trees to
the east and the streets grew quiet. The crowd turned toward the woods at the edge of town. The first Klan rider
was coming over a low rise near the river. As he reached
the far end of the main street, torches suddenly blazed in
the trees, and there seemed to be hundreds of riders behind him.

2

THE leader was a giant figure cloaked in white, sitting in grim silence as his big mount came forward. He wore a tall, pointed, conical headdress that had horns protruding from the temples. Matthew edged to the front of the crowd. The white cloak fit the rider tightly, but was slashed up the sides to allow the legs freedom. There was a red band around the waist and Matthew noticed that the cloak had pearl buttons. Every rider wore the same cloak; they seemed to be well-made uniforms and not the bed-sheets he'd heard about.

The lead rider's eyes burned through slits circled in red to resemble blood, as was the slit for the mouth. A fantastic growth of hair spilled from his upper lip to the saddle pommel. White quills were stuck on the hoods of some riders and looked like long animal teeth. From the bulge in the head covering, Matthew could see that many of the men were bearded. There was a bloody heart painted on the white robes. The leader's conical hat had a large white cross and the KKK letters. The next morning a boy found a stick that made the headdress stand stiff and straight and had fallen out.

The Ku Kluxers came into town from four directions, their horses also cloaked in white and walking as slowly as

13

a funeral cortege. There was no word spoken. The column
leaders gave commands by blowing a whistle that had a
thin, high-pitched trill. A man in the crowd whispered
that it was "nothing but an old hunting whistle." Two columns met at the town square, the horses pawing and
blowing frost, and the leaders exchanged elaborate hand-
gestures. The march began and the nightriders passed
back and forth through the streets of Palmyra. Matthew
wondered if his family was watching from the hill. A
woman whispered too loudly that they looked like ghosts,
hellish creatures, and a rider brushed past her, staring
down, pulling at his horns. The woman fainted and the
riders passed in silence. There was little noise from so
many horses and Matthew realized they wore no shoes.
The only sound was the occasional whistle or clucking
noise, the rustling of robes flapping in the wind, the dull
pounding of the horses. The constant stream of riders criss-
crossed the streets and back again in the harsh shadows
of the torches. It gave the illusion that there were many
hundreds of riders. One man caught Matthew's eye. He
thought he recognized the backslope way the rider sat his
horse. Then he spotted the striped pants and Mexican boots
and was sure it was Kortman.

A man in the crowd dashed into the road on a dare and
lifted the cloak from a horse. He gave a surprised cry
when he recognized his own sorrel. The rider just stroked
the long hairy strings of his pasted moustache and rejoined
the column. The frightened man fled and the crowd began to cheer. Suddenly, the lines of riders seemed to thin.
They were vanishing into the dark woods, a last glimpse
of white in the cold moon and torchlight. Then they were
gone as silently and mysteriously as they had come. Some
boys started to run after them. Two Klansmen burst from
behind a line of buildings and placed their rearing mounts
between the boys and the woods. They had enormous
horns that dripped blood and stained their white robes.
Their hands were the bones of skeletons, both holding
flaming crosses. They threw them toward the crowd, a
warning not to follow, not to question. Some of the black

men started to laugh at the spectacle. A white man nearby warned them to be quiet. A big negro stood up to him.

"Hell, you ain't scare us. Them Kluckers ain't scare us. We got our own army now."

The white man shook his head. "I got nothing against you, nigger, but you hear what they did to some nigger militia?"

"You ain't do pigshit."

"They caught some of them nigger soldiers outside of Lenhart. They took them to a place and nailed them to the floor, stuck them good. Then they fired the building. I don't hold with it, you hear. But that's what them boys'll do, so watch your step."

Matthew was shaken by the exchange. The riders looked noble, like avenging white angels come to earth to fight for the South. They were smart-looking like an army, and all of them, he could tell, fine horsemen. He didn't believe what the man told the niggers. Men fighting for a cause wouldn't do anything downright damn crazy, even to niggers, no matter how much right they had, how much the niggers roused them. The man didn't sound from around Palmyra. There were troublemakers all over now, even his father said so. Men starting rumors just to stir people up, get them suspicious and fight each other, and not just white against nigger. Everyone said they were Yankee agents.

He stayed in town a little longer, then watched the negroes start back across the railroad tracks. He wondered where they were going, how they lived as free men. A week before, his mother gave food to a group wandering from the woods to the hill road. There was a terrible row after that. Everett was on his way home and saw it. He said she was making beggars out of them. They were free people and had to be encouraged to work. Three years after the war and she was treating them like they were still her slaves, playing the kindly mistress. Matthew thought it was funny. The poor niggers looked half-starved and gave them no trouble. His mother had grown up with slaves; his father, and nobody else in his family, had ever owned any, but he seemed meaner than she was. He thought his father was a hypocrite, always talking about how bad and evil slavery was, then treating the miserable poor niggers like they were nothing. He wondered why his father had fought in the war. Everett once told him that it wasn't to defend slavery, but the right of people not to have the government tell them what to do. The crowd began to thin and Matthew started home. He met Adela near the house and she took his arm.

"Papa's waiting for you." She felt his excitement. "What was it like?"

"Damn, it was something. You never saw anything like it. Never saw men or horses like that. They must have the best stock in the whole state. Jesus! Torches . . . wild scary dress, the crowd cheering. . . ."

She laughed. "Sounds just like a circus."

"Girl, what the hell would you know. They looked like an army. There was maybe a thousand of them."

"Any trouble?"

"No, they just paraded around town. Not even a damn whisper. Then they just disappeared."

"What do you mean?"

"I can't tell you if you didn't see it. They were there before you could hear them, and then they were gone, quick as a wink."

They sat down on the veranda steps. The tall girl took his hand. "I have something to tell you. You better know it before you go in to talk to papa."

"What?"

"He wants to send you to school up north."

"He's crazy. I wouldn't go there. What's wrong with Blount College up at Knoxville. It's the damn state school and it's good enough." He bit his lip. "What did mama say?"

"It's funny. I thought she'd get in a fever when he said it, but she didn't answer him."

"It's plain crazy. That's all I got to say. I told him I didn't want to be no lawyer."

"What do you want to be?"

"I don't know. Maybe a hunter."

She tried to suppress a laugh but her green eyes were full of mischief. "Great big hunter. You're the one who's crazy. Most every pig and cow and every kind of game in these parts was slaughtered long ago. You want to hunt buffalo, like in that book you read? More likely you'll hunt grubs and squirrel, root and rats. That's what some people have to eat."

"How come then we have pig to eat sometimes?"

She arched her eyebrows and smiled. "Because, dear brother, we're 'quality.' "

"There's a lot of big cats and foxes and wolves up in the hills north of here. Maybe bear too. Oakman told me he saw them."

"Oakman's just a sneaky little store-clerk. He likes to play big and mock you because you're his better and too dumb to know it."

"No, he swears it's true. Says he saw them when he went up there to see his family. Says a fellow could make good money from their meat and pelts."

"How come he's still working for three dollars at that mean old Mrs. Caulkins? And who'd buy them. With what, Yankee money? Not much of that around for us. Besides, those mountain people catch you up there, they'd make stew of a pretty young town fellow like you." She tucked her arms around her knees and stared into the dark trees. "Maybe papa's right. He says it would be a good idea if you got to know people up north. He says you could help us if you get a good education and saw more of the country than just down here."

"I'd run away before I went up there."

"You're such a hardhead. Just like mama. But I can understand why she feels that way." She turned to him, her face imploring. "Can't you see? It's all over. The war, everything that was here before. People that try and hold on to it are the ones who'll suffer. It's a different world now, but you'll never learn about it sitting and dreaming in Palmyra."

Matthew stared at the ground. "I'm going to join the Klan."

There was a long silence before Adela spoke. "What do

you know about anything? It's the way they look and the horses, all that prancing and parading around. It's the same reason boys run off with carnival shows. You think they're doing anything to help us? They're just making it worse, bringing Yankee troops in here again. All you did during the war was whine when we didn't have enough to eat."

Matthew pulled away. "You're a damned liar. Didn't I ask to go?"

"You were no more than fourteen, even at the end."

"But I asked to go. All papa did was wave that stump of his, and then he'd talk about Porter. Mama wanted me to go——"

"She'd throw you in a river of snakes if she thought it would get her back just one day of the old life."

"That's a hell of a thing to say."

"But it's true.

"She said it didn't matter how young I was. Said all the Kittredges were soldiers clear back to ancient Scotland, and I should go if I wanted. If you say no, you're a damned liar."

"Matt, try to see papa's side. He did his part. He wanted to save you. He wants to save us all. It near killed him when he found out Porter was dead."

"Porter! Porter! Jesus, that's all I hear."

Adela knew he was right. Matthew was smaller, slighter than his brother, with none of his earnestness and quick intelligence. His father made him feel that he was pale comfort for the loss of his first-born son. She tried to get him to think of the moment.

"The Yankees weren't bad right after the war. They came in here and helped us start to rebuild, and they gave food to nigger and white alike. Then those Radicals in Congress turned everything. Papa says they're doing terrible things now."

"The more reason for the Klan."

"It's the Klan that's making them do it. The Klan and mean spite. The more fight we show, the harder they're going to press." She felt exhausted. "Please, don't say anything about the Klan to papa." She rose and walked up on the veranda, her reddish-brown hair catching the light from the vestibule. "Don't say a word. I don't know what he'd do. Promise me."

He agreed and they went inside, Adela talking some nonsense to put her parents off. Matthew took a quick look at his father, who was reading by the fire, and nodded to him. He kissed his mother dutifully. She thought he was going to talk about the parade and put a finger to her lips. Matthew went up to his room and searched through a wooden chest at the foot of the bed. He pulled out a Walker Colt that had belonged to his Kittredge grandfather. He took aim at himself in the mirror and clicked the hammer. It might be too old, too much a curio now, for what he wanted. There was a knock at the door and he buried the weapon under a blanket in the chest. It was his mother.

"Judge Darcy came to see your father, all in a fluster about the parade. We can have a little time alone."

Jessie held Matthew around the waist for a moment, then moved past him and sat in a rocker. She was a woman incapable of doing anything without seeming to flirt. Matthew thought she was the most beautiful woman in Giles County, maybe the whole state or anywhere. She had strong features, warm russet skin, the long Kittredge nose, a wide mouth, and glistening, restless eyes. It was the kind of face that belonged on a ship's prow, too bold for most women to carry. She wore her auburn hair piled high and pulled to one side in a long drape of curls. She was known as a great beauty when she was young at Loretto, and only the strain of the war years had aged her a little. Friends joked that she was the only woman in the South who had kept her breasts and hips during the war. One woman said, "The women have no bosoms and the men are all string."

Matthew sat on the bed and she reached over and took both his hands.

"Tell me about it."

"What's this Adela said about me going to school up north?"

"It's just a crazy idea your father has. Don't think about it."

"I won't go. I'd rather die than go up there. I don't even want to go to Blount."

"You want to stay with mama?"

"I want to do something. I don't know yet."

"I won't let it happen. You can always do just as you want." She leaned forward. "Tell me about it, please. You're naughty; you enjoy teasing me, don't you?"

Matthew began to describe the eerie sights of the parade and her face became almost sensual, her cheeks glossing, her excitement mounting with his. He told the man's story about the way the negro militia were killed at Lenhart—*Did she believe it?*—then suddenly stopped. She thought he was trying to get up courage to say something and kissed his hands, murmuring "*Sweet boy . . . my strong man. . . .*" He was uneasy and pulled away. "What is it, darling? You know you can tell me anything."

"You don't hate niggers, do you?"

"No. I loved them. I grew up with them all my life until your father took me away." She tried to focus her last sight of Loretto that day. "They suckled me. They loved me best of anyone, even their own. I think of that so often, but it was so long ago. When I try and remember, it's all lovely and sad, like a golden sleep, and I pray I'll never awake."

"I don't hate niggers. I don't want to kill them. That man said the Klan killed and tortured niggers."

She went to the bed and pressed Matthew's head against her breasts, her eyes closing in languor for a moment. "But they have to be kept down. It's for their own good. They're just poor dumb beasts and the Yankees are tricking them."

"That's what eveyone says. They got to be kept down. And we got to keep the Yankees down, got to get rid of them."

She laughed. "You're beginning to talk just like a piney or swamper. '*Got* to keep . . . *got* to get . . .' We didn't give you a good Christian education to talk that way." She ran her hand through his sandy hair, then across the taut bony face. "I'm so proud of you. You'll be my St. George. You know what a man has to do. You were brought up a gentleman, to fight impure thoughts in yourself, and whatever's mean and unmanly and unrighteous." She kissed him excitedly. "There's no more glorious fate than to die fighting in a just cause."

She still thought of the war as glory, honor and cavalry charges. Cavaliers of the South, brave and dashing and handsome, riding away on sleek mounts as if to a knight's tournament. They were filled with ardor for the fight, escorted by loyal slaves, and longing to do great deeds and win honor for themselves and their ladyloves. Trumpets blew, bards recited heroic poetry, and all was ready for the exalting combat. But she kept the recurring nightmare concealed, never told anyone . . . the storms that were like fire, the shining knights unable to charge because their horses were bogged down and they themselves wallowing in mud to the groin, the splendid armor obscured as they fell, the armor splitting open and blood and entrails spilling out. The images were like festering wounds. Often, when she awoke, she realized that things would never be the same again, then stroked herself back to sleep with solitary love-making. But she never purged herself of the zeal and ferocity, the idea that the South had been betrayed.

"I want to do it, mama." He paused, afraid that what he'd say would shock her. "I want to join the Klan."

She pretended surprise, then quickly reassured him that it was the right thing to do. She had a feeling of intense relief, no longer afraid that he would dishonor her.

Matthew's face was eager. "You'll help me, mama, won't you?" He'd thought of going to Kortman, certain that he saw him in a column of riders, but was afraid he'd be refused, that the tall man would laugh at him. But wouldn't Kortman be surprised, even pleased, when he showed up to join?

"How could I possibly help?" She played the role well. The Southern woman, unworldly, helpless, indulged, adoring, petted and subdued.

"You know people."

She was afraid if her husband found out, but knew she'd do anything to help Matthew. She suddenly had a vision of Porter . . . the same age when she lured him, put him in a fever about fighting, pretended worship and seduction, nagged him to his death. But whenever she thought of it that way, she sometimes felt guilt, then quickly rationalized that he would have been taken soon after anyway, that she only did what any patriotic Southern woman did in those terrible days. She was able to see her own wildness, the ease with which she could send another son to his death for nothing but a memory, a way of life that vanished before her eyes. If only they had been left alone after the war. Things would have returned to the way they were. The Kittredge niggers didn't want to leave, she was convinced of it. They would have worked the place just as before, but now paid like a white man. She never quite remembered that Loretto was in ruins. That was the limit of her understanding . . . to put everything comfortably in place. She was bored whenever her husband tried to explain anything . . . politics, cheap cotton, why the South could never have won the war, the way it depended on only one crop, the North where many people worked in factories and were crowded into cities like rabbits in a hutch. . . .

She could never rant at him that way she wanted when he spoke to her about how slavery was wrong. That stump of an arm stood between them like some holy artifact. He was the one who had sacrificed for the slaves, and he was shrewd enough to know that the missing arm was like a phantom weapon that kept her at bay. When they argued, he waved the stump about, talking and explaining in a quiet, urgent voice until she screamed that she'd go crazy if he kept on. And every time she began to show hysteria, Everett had a satisfied little smile. He thought he could always punish her for Porter's death, because she never wanted to see the world beyond her own dreamlike life. But she was cannier, more energetic, than he knew, had learned and remembered much of what he'd taught her. Her nostalgia was only self-pity, and she tried to quell her bitterness by telling Matthew that the Klan started up because everyone was afraid of a revolution, a war between the races.

"Why didn't you go away like all those people after the war?"

"They were traitors. They ran to Texas and Mexico, some all the way to South America. They took their slaves—never told them they were supposed to be free—and thought they could live like before. Most of us made up our minds to keep this white country. We're not going to turn it over to the niggers. If we don't fight, they'll take over and rule. The Northern politicians, damned carpetbaggers, they told the niggers they could ravish white women and get away with it." It was always the best way to strike fear in a white man, the buck nigger in the bed. "You heard about the three they caught down in Hardeman County . . . turned out of jail after only a few days. One woman she killed herself because of that. Your father says the Klan is against the law. But they're the ones who're trying to see the laws are kept. They're quality men from the Confederate army. You can't trust rowdies and roughnecks."

Matthew needed no more convincing, but she continued to implore him. Jessie had come from the aristocracy, a proud people led by a warrior caste. They had believed themselves invincible and couldn't face the mortifying defeat. People like Jessie had created the myth that the Northerners were only ruthless and corrupt, intent on starving the white South into a subject country ruled by ex-slaves. Negroes were getting the vote, but nothing was done to prepare them for life as free men. There were negro artisans, small business men, farmers and teachers who wanted to help educate the ex-slaves, but the South resisted. Jessie never mentioned that war damage to buildings, bridges and railroads was being repaired under the Yankees, rations supplied, the first free schools set up for both races, negroes urged to return to their former masters and work for agreed wages.

She had to fix the other side of it, the misery, in Matthew's mind; make it more powerful and fearful than what she sensed was his boyish fascination with secrecy and rit-

ual, vague ideas, strange and strong men. She had tried in
passive, subtle ways to involve Adela with her secrets.
But her daughter was too blithe, too smart and open to
the world to be taught that narrow bitterness. Jessie heard
Judge Darcy call goodby, quickly kissed Matthew, promised she'd do what she could, then went downstairs.

When Everett left for his office the next morning, Jessie took the carriage to Aspen Hill to see Colonel Tyler.
He was a burly man with a pink bald head, a curly red-
gold beard, and freckles all over his forehead and nose
and the back of his hands. Tyler was surprised and
pleased to see Jessie and they made small talk for a while
until she was fairly sure of her man.

"I know someone who is interested in the Klan."

"Why, my lovely Jessie, the whole world is interested in
the Klan."

"Someone in Palmyra. This person is interested in their
good works."

"I admire them as well. What good Southerner
wouldn't?"

"This person is a good Christian . . . worships the
cross."

"As any son of Jesus should."

She had to take a chance. Tyler wouldn't commit himself.

"I want my son in the Klan."

"Why come to me?"

"I heard talk one night. Someone said something. Your
name was mentioned."

"Idle tongue in an idle head. That doesn't mean anything."

"It was because you served with General Forrest." She
was afraid to say more, perhaps had said too much already.

"My dear Jessie, if you would believe every rumor and
snip of gossip you hear these days, you'd believe that Jefferson Davis was the illegitimate brother of Abraham Lincoln—though the illegitimacy would be less stigma than
relation to that happily dead baboon."

Jessie smiled. He was being very careful, but she was

smart enough to play along, see what Tyler knew. She said nothing, didn't press. If the old soldier was the right man, he'd be eager for a recruit that Jessie Lanier recommended. Tyler had a servant bring some sherry and they drank and talked about friends. He rose and walked around the room, stopping in front of a calvary saber mounted on the wall.

"Does Everett know about this?"

"No. But he's loyal, wants his family and friends protected."

"Yes, he's a good man. But he reads too much. An educated rascal is the worst, meanest kind of rascal." She pretended anger for the insult to Everett and started to get up. Tyler eased her back to the sofa, apologizing. "Of course I didn't mean Everett. He was a fine soldier. I, myself, do not read any book unless it will help me to understand *the* Book. If a man wants a coat, he wants to get the best coat he can for the money. This is the law the world around. If we show men that Christianity is better than anything else, we shall win the world. Read the Bible. It teaches you how to act. Read the hymnbook. It has the finest poetry. Read the almanac. It shows you how to figure out the weather. There isn't another book that is necessary for anyone to read. It would even be better to destroy every other book ever written, and save just the first three verses of Genesis." He stared at her, the red fleshy lips and tongue smacking moist through the beard.

God, she thought, just a crazy old fanatic, but she persisted. "Isn't that what the Klan is doing, standing strong for white Christianity?"

He looked cunning. "They're doing more than that. They are going to show the Yankees that we won the war after all."

"How can that be, with all the suffering and shame."

"Because the Klan will hold the nigger down until it's too late for the North."

Jessie saw his eyes and knew he couldn't hold back any longer. "But how?"

"We have to have patience. Even under a federal system we'll get our way. No government can keep soldiers on every plantation, in every town. The North is getting rich. They have sold out to Mammon . . . Luke, Chapter 16, Verses nine, eleven and thirteen. Their army has disappeared. But if we hold out for a time longer, we'll have what we always had—cheap, servile labor."

"But there are no more slaves."

"Slavery be damned. It was the wrong way. We'll have the labor without buying them, spending great sums, and we won't have the social obligation that people like the Kittredges had to their slaves. Why do you think we haven't killed more niggers? We only kill and scarify the nigger officials, teachers, the farmers who make a go of it, proud damned niggers like that. We're going to need the rest of them, to work and breed." He pointed his finger at her like a schoolmaster. "Do you know how many federal troops there are to police the South and the whole Mexican border?"

She rattled her fan, as if excited on being told the number. "Why, no. But being a military man, Colonel, I'm sure you must know right down to the very last soldier."

"Twenty-five thousand, four hundred and fifty-seven!"

"Imagine!"

"Twenty-five thousand, four hundred and fifty-seven!"

"Why the Klan must have ten times that number."

"But there are a half-million of black niggers." Tyler began a little dance, drawing the sword from the scabbard and waving it, and sang a song:

"Oh, I'm a good old rebel, that's what I am;
And for this land of freedom, I don't care a damn,
I'm glad I fought agin her, I only wished we'd won,
And I don't ask any pardon for anything I've done. . . ."

He came to a stop in front of her. "Twenty-five thousand, four hundred and fifty-seven. You think they can stop us?"

Jessie pretended to be aligning the forces in numbers, so many federal troops, so many Klansmen, so many niggers, so many Southern patriots and diehards. She looked at Tyler, who was breathing hard, and thought he was just a dreamer of violence and death . . . so many towns in the South filled with addled old soldiers who could never rid themselves of the war, thought battle was "the real, highest, honestest business of every son of man," who talked as if the war was medieval legend, wore their brilliant sashes and swords that were useless before the cannon and machines and endless armies of the Union.

It was a moment when she was grateful for Everett. He, at least, understood his maiming, knew it had nothing to do with old myths, honor or Walter Scott heroes. He understood that the world was changing and would change with it. He was too sane, too sober, banked her passions, every passion, but he was one of the rare people who wasn't afflicted with the sense of everything past, lost, terrible grievances and regrets. Everything, she realized, that obsessed her. For a moment, she wanted to flee from the house. The Klan only existed to burn and kill and bring terror. And she was sitting in a dusty dark parlor, listening to a raving old soldier preach sermons of hate and blood, begging him to take her son, make him the same kind of man. But she had promised Matthew and couldn't fail him. She was only doing what the boy asked, only making the link.

Tyler was again the dignified ex-officer. He asked who the interested person was. Jessie was happy he's already forgotten. She wanted to make sure Tyler would help, afraid now to incriminate her son. She assured him the person came from one of the finest families in Giles County, was a Southern patriot, and would be of great value to the Klan.

"Before I can help you, there is a ceremony to test your sincerity. We are a movement of the plain people, the citizen of the old stock. We are emotional and instinctive—but these emotions and instincts have been bred into us for thousands of years . . . far longer than reason or intellect has had a place in the human brain." Tyler was looking at her differently and shifted his chair close. "These emotions are the foundations of American civilization. Reason and intellect cannot be trusted. The emotions can. This is a conflict between good and evil. The evil must be taken from you, so that the person you speak of is purified through you."

Jessie understood and almost laughed in his face. He wanted to make love to her, that was the bribe. She tried to bargain, get names and places, pretended that she didn't understand.

"There is no compromise with Satan," Tyler thundered. Then he touched her thigh. She slipped past him and went to the window. Wagons loaded with negroes passed the house. The wind blew dust-devils dancing along the road. The big elms in the front yard bent and branches scratched at the window. There were other men she might talk to, but if she refused now, she was afraid that he might warn them, concoct some story about the Laniers and make them victims. If she mentioned Matthew to others, he might be marked for her insult to Tyler. She thought he had to be very high up in the Klan, a crony of Forrest's she'd heard. She turned and looked at the bulky figure across the room, dim in the cold light, and felt no disgust at the idea. He was old but strong-looking, with passion enough about his own nightmares that might fuel another kind of passion. *And weren't they the same?* Even as a girl, she understood that people who took risks, the irrational people, were the ones who could thrill her. She no longer saw the snouty face, absurd beard, the forest of freckles. He was strong enough to break her. But she would only trade with him.

"First, tell me a place."

"A crossroads."

"Where?"

"Not far from here."

"And who is the man to see?"

"When you awake, the Grand Cyclops will be at your side. And all about will be the magnificent Night Hawks and Genii . . . Hydras . . . Furies . . . Magis . . . Monks . . . Sentinels and Scribes, Turks . . . the spirit of Ghouls. They will offer testimony to your purity, and that of the person you offer to the cross."

He sat beside her on the sofa and she leaned back against the pillows. She had never heard the names before. What did he mean? Was *he* a Grand Cyclops? Was that a Klan officer? He had given her secret names, she knew, and could be trusted, but she could never repeat them to anyone. Visiting an old bachelor in the morning, without her husband's permission, a servant who saw her. . . . If she mentioned the Klan, she'd be laughed at or vilified as a traitor to the cause. The anxiety, the doubts, began to excite her. She loved her full woman's body, wanted to be bollock to bollock naked, have the deliciousness of skin. The moment was always the same and always new, the instinct so strong it canceled memory. To lie still in the moment, in the heart of the flesh, the place of beginning and end, to snatch it out of time, to move still in all stillness of flesh, to taste that trembling moment again, to hold it, *and* to let it go, the small bird that she held, its heart hammering in the cup of the hands, flown into the air.

What did it matter anyway? In the war and its aftermath, everyone was dead or crazy in some way, everything was lost. It only mattered how one could redeem the loss and the dead, the dead, the staggering number of dead, the memories of those golden boys in endless rows of graves. Among much else, she thought and lamented, gentlemen would never be the same again. She looked at Tyler and thought she must not deny the vulgarity, her willingness and fatal delight in men. She slowly unbuttoned her dress and bared her breasts in a voluptuous movement. Tyler watched her as she caressed herself as if he was inspecting a rank of cavalry, eyes intent but cold, the threadbare uniform worn correctly, his head nodding slowly in approval. She lifted her skirt and asked him to undress the rest of her, begging silently for that mix of hard and slimy, the moment that was like death, tension leaving her body, in pain, and not in sweetness and pride. Then Tyler stood, opened his pants and began to masturbate, shouting:

"Vile, stinking Magdalene . . . rubbish and pig's blood. You won't tempt the Lord to your whore's hell. I would not touch your blood and stink!"

He was slobbering and suddenly collapsed in a chair.

Jessie covered herself with a pillow and felt sour and sly because she had him. He was possessed by religious demons too powerful for lesser ones, and had struck a cheap bargain. Jessie waited until the man's eyes flicked open.

"I came for information and did what you asked." She decided to challenge him. "You sad old man. I craved love, and you spilled yourself like a boy hiding in a barn. Your seed must be weak. Nigger seed is strong."

She thought he might hit her, but he seemed not to hear. He buttoned up methodically and was all business.

"Who is the person?"

"I won't tell you. But he'll go and join if you give me the truth."

"Tuesday night, when dark falls. The crossroads at Hope Mills. The road into the forest for a quarter-mile. He will see the ruin of an old mill. Beneath there is a cellar. Men will be waiting and watching. Have your man speak these words: 'Forrest has the sanction of Robert E. Lee. We are here yesterday, we are here today, we will be here forever.' He is to tell no one where or when he goes. He is to come unarmed and bring one Union dollar."

She knew Matthew was under-age, but didn't ask because Tyler might guess. "Is he to bring any papers, war service . . . ?"

"He is to bring only his white Christian person. The Klan is chivalric in conduct, noble in sentiment, generous in manhood, and patriotic in purpose."

She tried to erase any last doubts. "Will the Klan really help us?"

"Look about you, Madam. There are five thousand white people in Palmyra . . . and ten thousand niggers. The Yankees collect them in cities and towns and our farmers can't hire a hand. They gather them there to vote, to give them privilege."

He seemed anxious to get her out of the house and urged her to dress. At the door he put his face close to hers. "Never a word." He gripped her arm. "Never." She knew he wanted her to think the warning was only about the Klan. But he was just as afraid that she would tell a story about his advances . . . *to a married woman of his own class . . . the lewd feeble sex he forced her to watch . . . how degraded she felt*—and knew people would believe her. As he opened the door, their farewell was suddenly formal, like a customary social call, chatting openly and smiling in the event someone saw them. He remarked on his wishes for the health of her family, and Jessie knew it was a warning. She wavered for a moment, but said nothing and walked to the carriage.

She whipped up the horse, thinking that the Klan might be her protector, her salvation, but it was violent and once unleashed could strike anyone. In the chaos after the war, everyone seemed a little mad and treacherous. She had seen scalawags inform on neighbors and friends they suspected of too much Southern pride or obstructing Yankee business. One morning she saw a young man chasing a half-witted veteran through the streets of Palmyra with a sword, cutting the rusty buttons from the man's jacket. And no one had said a word or lifted a hand. Someone had informed on Mrs. Eveleigh, who had lost her husband and a brother in the war. She was arrested by negro militia carrying bayoneted rifles because her little girls were seen playing in the yard with something that looked like a Rebel flag. No one could be trusted.

3

Just before dusk on Tuesday, Jessie went to Matthew's room to make sure for the last time that he knew what to say and do. She cautioned him not to ask any questions, just follow along, then gave him the dollar.

"Turn out your pockets."

She took away the small Barlow knife he carried. She kissed him, said he looked manly and she would pray for him and the South, then closed the door quietly and went downstairs.

"Matt won't be down for supper. Poor precious boy is feeling sick."

Everett merely nodded, but Adela said she'd go up and keep him company afterward. Jessie kept her voice casual.

"Leave him alone. A good rest will fix him up. You're so full of the devil, you'll have him tossing all around the place." She pecked Adela on the cheek, a small affectionate gesture to ease suspicion.

When they sat at the table, Jessie couldn't help herself and glanced out the window toward the road. Then she began talking of a play the Palmyra Effodians were putting on, *The Betrothed Lady*, saying that it was lighthearted and humorous and would take people's minds off all the trouble.

"Wouldn't you like to go to Baltimore or New York one day and see the best professional actors?" Everett asked.

"No. I'll never leave here."

"Papa, you can take me."

"You'll get married like any decent woman and settle down," Jessie said.

Everett sensed the continuing tension between the two women. Adela was a mocking memory to Jessie—"*As I am, so you once were.*" But Jessie's presence was horrid to the daughter—"*As I am, so you will be.*" The mother's hypocritical worry for the young woman's moral, that is, sexual welfare, masked a desire to reduce Adela to the same state of passivity forced by custom and hedged by taboos . . . a prison she escaped only by daring scandal in mindless, stray passion.

"Mama, there's no one left to marry here." She often thought of the little German man who came to Palmyra after the war from Knoxville. He gave her piano lessons and, she joked, had ruined her bad nature by making her sweet and merry. She had been afraid of him. He was something of a salvationist and wished to save her with evangelical passion. But she was afraid of disappointing him and afraid of being saved. She firmly told him that she was mad and beyond redemption, and that he'd better leave her alone or he'd be in for something nasty. When she declared that she was full of the devil, he tried to seduce her, and she often wondered why she didn't let him.

Adela pushed the plate of hogback and greens away. "I can't keep eating this nigger food."

Everett gave her a sharp look. "I told you never to use that word in my presence."

"I'm sorry, papa. You know I don't mean anything bad. I just can't stand this town anymore. Take me someplace, a big city, just for a visit."

"We'll see."

Jessie's doubts vanished. She was right to push Matt. Everything was falling apart, families, people leaving Palmyra for the West, the damned Unionists. She had to stay and watch, save what they had.

"Maybe when we take Matt to a school up north," Everett said, glancing at Jessie. "Maybe we can all go."

Matthew opened the window slowly, crept out on the roof of the sun porch, closed the window and dropped to the ground. He went through the field back of the house, crossed pasture truning to scrub, and started north. There were still flecks of light in the sky as he walked, but when he reached the crossroads at Hope Mills it was dark. A humpbacked moon lay low over the trees. He went along the road into the forest, each step expecting someone to stop him. He'd walked what he judged was a quarter-mile, stopped and looked around, but saw no old mill. He heard someone coming up the road. He turned, expecting to see a robed Klansman, but it was a young man, roughly dressed, probably someone from back in the woods. They said nothing to each other. The other man walked a little further, then turned off the road into the woods. Matthew figured a country man could find his way in the dark and quickly followed, his heart hammering. He was surprised that the Klan had no guards out. Anyone could get in there with no trouble if they knew the meeting place. They came around a bend and Matthew saw a line of about twenty Klan riders through the trees. A man on foot came through the line. He seemed eight feet tall as he came stomping toward them. The Klansman stopped a few yards away and spoke in a voice that sounded as it came from the tomb:

"Horrible Shadows . . . Enter the Devil's Den!"

He beckoned them forward. The line of riders parted and they passed through as a third man came in from the road. The Klansman took them through weeping beech trees whose branches dropped to form a tunnel entrance to the old mill. It had been destroyed by fire years before and only one wall of jagged brick was standing. Matthew and the other men hung close together. The Klan escort was met by another robed figure. They exchanged an intricate handclasp and began talking. Matthew thought it sounded like little boy's or baby's nonsense.

"Ayak?"

"Akia,"

"Capowe."

"Cygnar?"

"Kigy?"

"Itsub."

"Sanbog!"

Later he found out what it meant:

Are you a Klansman?

A Klansman I am.

Countersign and password or written evidence.

Can you give number and realm?

Klansman, I greet you.

In the secret, unfailing bond.

Strangers are near, be on your guard.

The three recruits were taken down a long steep flight of crumbling steps into the dark cellar. Hands forced them into chairs. Matthew heard nothing, but was sure the place was filled with men. A voice rang out:

"Light the light for Lord Jesus Christ and the White South!"

Torches hung in brackets or jammed into niches in the wall suddenly blazed. A group of men in robes and masks sat on a platform before an altar at the far end of the cellar. On the altar was a Confederate flag—most Klan dens liked one tattered with shot in battle—a Bible open to Romans XII, an unsheathed cavalry sword, and a container of the initiation water, which was sprinkled over new members to rid them of "alien" defilement. A small fiery cross burned behind the display. It was supposedly the way Scottish clans summoned their highland members. Klansmen were strung out along the walls. Matthew thought that many men there must know him. A Klansman on the platform rose. He wore an elaborate linen robe, starched and ironed, with a great bloody cross on his chest, a peaked headdress with three curved horns, but there was no fantastic nose or moustache and beard, no false tongue and frightful teeth.

"The password to glory?"

The three recruits were separated and each was told to speak into the ear of three Klan officers. Matthew whispered the message without faltering . . . *"The General has the sanction of Robert E. Lee . . . We were here yesterday, we are here today, we will be here forever. . . .* Later, when Matthew discovered the Klan lied about Lee's approval, he regretted soiling the name of that saintly man.

Matthew was called forward. He stood in the harsh flicker of torchlight and faced the inquisitor. The Klansman spoke again.

"I am the Grand Cyclops of the Devil's Den."

The voice sounded a little familiar, but Matthew warned himself not to do any guessing.

The Grand Cyclops pointed to each man on the platform.

"These are my trusted Nighthawks . . . the Grand Magi . . the Grand Scribe . . . the Grand Monk . . . the Grand Exchequer . . . the Grand Turk . . . the Grand Sentinel . . . the Grand Klud. . . ."

Matthew thought he recognized the tall stooped figure of the man called the Grand Klud . . . the Reverend Lancey, their own Methodist minister. Klud, he thought must mean the Klan chaplain; every army had one. The Grand Cyclops waved toward the body of men in the cellar. "These are my ghouls. If you are false, your life is in jeopardy. You now know the secret list."

The Klud handed the Grand Cyclops a cross and a Bible. He touched Matthew on each shoulder with the cross and gestured for him to place his hand on the Bible.

"Are you a Christian?"

"Yes, sir."

"Are you of proper heritage?"

"I am Welsh and Scotch and English, and my mother says old Teuton and Norman stock." He never believed it, but thought is sounded impressive.

"Have you ever served in the Union Army?"

Matthew tried to sound heartfelt in his denial, indignant. "No, sir . . . No!"

"Are you a member of a Freedmen's Bureau or a Loyal League?"

"No, sir."

"Are you a Radical Republican?"

"No, sir." He thought the questions were stupid. Why would he be there if he was that sort, and wouldn't a Yankee spy swear to anything?

"Are you opposed to nigger equality, both social and political?"

"Yes, sir."

"Are you in favor of a white man's government?"

"Yes, sir."

"Will you fight for the enfranchisement and restoration of all rights to Southern white men?"

"Yes, sir."

"Are you eighteen years old?"

Matthew thought it would be his only lie, innocent enough. "Yes, sir. " But if anyone knew him, they knew his age. No one said anything and the Grand Cyclops continued:

"Do you recognize the majesty and supremacy of the Divine Being?"

"Yes, sir."

"You swear all this on the Book?"

"I do." He wondered how close he was to being a Ku Klux.

"This is a society of Chivalry, Humanity, Mercy and Patriotism. Our purpose is to protect the weak, the innocent and the defenseless from the indignities, wrongs and outrages of the lawless, the violent, and the brutal . . . to relieve the injured and oppressed . . . to succor the suffering and unfortunate, especially the widows and orphans of Confederate soldiers. We protect and defend the Constitution of the United States and all laws passed in conformity thereto. We protect the States and the people thereof from all invasion from any source whatsoever . . ."

Matthew thought the speaker was high-born, the voice cultured but firm, like a military man accustomed to command. Who in Giles County? General Albert Blanton. He warned himself again; he would know soon enough. The Grand Cyclops droned on to the end of the speech.

"Do you agree and swear to abide to all the rules and regulations, to do the bidding of your superiors without fear or question?"

"I do."

"Should you ever betray or reveal any person, anything learned, you will suffer the most horrible death. Night buzzards will pick your heart clean of red hot spears. You will suffer the garrote and sword, the tortures of Beelzebub."

"Yes, sir."

At a command, the robed and masked figures in the cellar paraded in front of Matthew, stopped before him, eyes piercing from the red-rimmed slits, each man staring for a brief second or two. The Klansmen returned to their places and the Grand Cyclops spoke.

"Do you have the dollar?"

Matthew held it out and the Grand Exchequer came from the platform to take it.

"Kneel. Raise your right hand and embrace the Book with the other." The Grand Cyclops held the point of the sword at Matthew's throat. "Have you spoken the truth?"

"Yes, sir."

Water was sprinkled on Matthew.

"When next you address me, you can speak my title." The Grand Cyclops kept the sword pressed to the flesh, his hand never wavering. "Is it your wish to join this sacred society of the Invisible Empire in the Realm of Tennessee?"

"Yes, Grand Cyclops."

"Do you promise to abide by all rules and regulations?"

"Yes, Grand Cyclops."

"Offer your life to our cause?"

"Yes, Grand Cyclops."

He called to the Klansmen. "Is there a nay?" The ranks were silent. He tapped Matthew on each shoulder with the sword. "Arise, Ghoul."

Matthew suddenly realized it was done. But no one came forth to congratulate him as he imagined, the convivial scene of brothers in arms. The other men had to go through the same ceremony. Matthew thought the tall one he'd met on the road was a farmer or logman. The other, middle-aged and pasty-looking, he took for a tradesman, a storekeeper in one of the villages around Palmyra. He, however, was from quality, certain that his idealism and morals, his eagerness to right wrongs, were superior. He had a Klansman at each shoulder as he dreamed of battles and strong comrades . . . a cleansing . . . like the Crusaders of old, the defenders of Christianity against the infidels. All his life he had been taught the endless stories, the myths and legends, of medieval chivalry and daring and gallantry; inspiring images from poems, books, ballads and plays that were too often out of touch with reality. He had reveled in the romance of it, but never learned of the butchery and greed and betrayal in the guise of being a warrior for God and fair ladies.

The initiations were over and each man removed his hood. At first Matthew saw no one he knew except Oakman. Then the officers on the platform revealed themselves. The Grand Cyclops *was* General Blanton. He knew almost all of them . . . Fred Currier . . . Colonel Tyler . . . Lyle Hoagland . . . Israel Buckner. . . old Graham Petit, who came over and spoke to him.

"Your mother was very brave coming to me. She told me of your spirit. We agreed not to let a few months stand in your way. Everyone is needed now."

The last man to unmask was Kortman, his face twisted in a grin. It gave Matthew confidence. They were from the best people in town, and he had heard that in every state the Klan officers were that kind. But he was snobbish and caste-ridden, disappointed with his first glimpse of the rank and file. Many of them looked like hard trash, swamper, pineys from back in the mountains, freighters; one that he recognized worked for the railroad. But it was that way in any war. The able, the intelligent, the aristocrats commanded the ordinary. And he felt sorry for himself because they were all equal in the Klan.

A Ku Kluxer who was a tailor in Lutesville took a uniform from a trunk. Matthew put it on carefully, surprised at its weight, had imagined them as gossamer to ride the wind. He could walk freely and liked the look of the red lining that flapped open with every stride. The tailor said it would need no fixing. A man fit a conical headdress on him, and when the front mask flap fell over his face and he peered out of the slits his heart beat fast. He had never known such a moment. The man said that a thin stick kept the hat peaked. The uniform cost five dollars and could be paid off at one dollar a month. Matthew was told that he had to get his own weapons—revolver, carbine, dagger or knife, and whip. He was given instructions: how he would be contacted for a meeting or a raid; how to carry his uniform concealed until he reached Hope Mills or a rendezvous place; where horses and weapons were supplied if he had none. General Blanton, one of the heroes of Fredericksburg, spoke to the three new men:

"You are subject to military discipline. Drunkeness is fined. Fornication with women not your wife, or whores or niggers means a court-martial." He had a mean look. "That's a death sentence."

Matthew wondered why anyone who wanted to keep the niggers down would have to be told not to lay with them. But he knew that white men took nigger women all the time, a fact of life in the South. Maybe the Klan would change all that, make the race pure again, both races. He once heard his father talking to Lyle Hoagland about the mulatto bastards in town. Hoagland said it was a perfect system.

"The nigger man is in fear of his life before he'd touch or even approach a white woman in the wrong way. If he's such a wretched, dirty beast, that means his women are even lower, and they're picking for white men who can't get the same kind of thing with their women. It's like fucking in warm dark mud." When Everett showed disgust, Hoagland laughed. "You should have been a minister. But you have no worries. You have the handsomest woman in the County. She raises everyone's blood." Everett thought it was the ordinary thing to say of a man's wife, but Matthew could see that he was flattered and even laughed a little.

Matthew thought it strange that no whiskey was passed around. Blanton didn't say a man couldn't take a drink.

Get this many Tennessee men together anyplace and there would be a lot of drinking and a couple of good-natured fights. He had seen himself sitting around with good men, telling stories, boasting about his father and brother who fought bravely in the war.

"No celebration?" he asked a young tow-head named Billy Laidlaw. "Seems if you go into a special society like this, there should be some kind of celebration."

"You heard the General. No fornication, no drinking, no stealing, no gambling. That's for niggers and Yankees, and that's what we're trying to stop. You're a Christian, ain't you?"

"Of course. But that don't mean a man can't take some pleasure."

Billy winked. "There's ways. What church you go to?"

"Well, we were Presbyterian. Now we're Methodist."

"That's good enough. But we're river Christians, most of us."

Baptists. Matthew always thought the Methodists took all the joy out of life. But the Baptists were the worst. And he had been wrong about Reverend Lancey. The Klud was a Baptist preacher from Wyatt. Billy began talking about the old American stock and Matthew looked around. There were mostly raw country faces, descendants of those people who had struck through the Alleghenies, down the Ohio River, through Kentucky, or came in from the Carolinas through the west of Virginia. Even in the best days, they were a low class, looked down on by quality whites. They came from dead, dreary, spiritless places that stretched across the South. Fundamentalists who found solace only in the Bible; petty, impotent people who lived untouched by any beauty or mystery. He recalled how he always feared them, strange ragged figures, the slattern women, from hill farms and mountains and forest, how his father had spoken of them with contempt.

"Trash . . . ignorant . . . worse than a good negra who'll give you his word and keep it, or do a good day's work."

The meeting ended with a blessing prayer by the Klud. Matthew rushed back to town with Billy Laidlaw, wondering how long he could keep the secret from his father. He thought about telling Adela. He had to have an ally in the house besides his mother. He was told there might be times he would be away until early morning. Sometimes, Billy said, they had as many as a hundred riders. There was talk that they were going to join with Arkansas men to raid the Loyal League building in Memphis, where negroes were given free passage on Mississippi boats. For an instant, he thought of coming right out with it to his father. There might be a commotion and a lot of ranting, but in the end he couldn't deny that Matthew was doing the right thing. But the closer he came to home, the less insistent it seemed. It could wait until a confrontation was necessary, or inevitable.

4

MATTHEW climbed to his room, but it was awkward carrying the uniform. His boot scraped along the side of the house and he hung at the top of the sun porch until sure he wasn't heard. He went through the open window and immediately folded the uniform neatly and placed it beneath his mattress. The conical hat was opened, stretched flat, and hidden behind a bookcase. He looked out the door and listened carefully before he examined his revolver. The door to his parents' room opened slowly. His mother came along the hall with a lighted candle in an ornate holder. She started into the room but Matthew stood at the door.

"Did everything go well?" she whispered.

"Yes." He gestured for her to leave.

They heard Everett calling her. "It's Matt. He wanted me." She touched her fingers to her lips and pressed them against his. Matthew was sick of her kissing and touching. He wasn't going to be treated like a calf anymore. He was Ku Klux now and could be his own man. Jessie wanted to talk more, but he kept the door open only a little way to block her. She muttered something that sounded like a prayer, then returned to her room. He took out the old Walker Colt his grandfather had used in the Mexican

War. He had to get a better weapon. Federal troops had tried to confiscate all military weapons in the South, allowing only old muskets, but there were thousands hidden away . . . French and English and Austrian revolvers and rifles brought over during the war, the beautiful Enfield a friend's father had before the Yankee's grabbed it, the new Colt and Remington and Smith & Wesson handguns, cavalry carbines, and heavy caliber rifles from both armies. The Jew peddler would be through Palmyra next week on his regular trip. He could pick up a bowie knife without anyone asking questions or knowing that he was armed with a real sticker, not that Green River junk. There were whips hanging in the family stable. His mother would give him money for the weapons. He thought that he was still dependent on the women in the family for everything . . . to buy guns and knives, to keep secrets, to protect him. But he rationalized that he would be their protector and they were only preparing him for the duty.

The next morning he came down to breakfast as his father was leaving.

"Where are your books?" Everett asked.

"Left them at school."

"I want to see the headmaster one day soon. And there's something I want to talk to you about."

"Sure, papa. But not today. We got all that powerful Greek translation."

"Which are you doing?"

Matthew panicked for an instant, then grinned when he remembered a name. "Epictus."

"*Epictetus.*" The father gave him a rueful look, shaking his head. "Now, how in God's name can you translate anything if you can't even remember a Greek name!"

Matthew walked with his father down the road toward town, then left in the direction of the school. He ducked behind a tree and watched until Everett turned the corner of the red brick bank and headed for the courthouse. Matthew ran back up the hill to the stable and saddled their horse. His father rode away to the war on the splendid chestnut, but it was getting old and he warned himself

to ride easy. Billy Laidlaw had told him about a gunsmith
in Seebert who outfitted a lot of Klansmen. He gently
spurred the horse across the pasture and reached the trail
that ran along the foot of a ridge. He figured he could be
back in school for the mid-day break, when his father often strolled past as if taking a casual walk. In Seebert, he
walked the horse along the main street looking for a gunsmith's sign, but saw none. He asked two old men sitting in
front of a livery stable if they knew Hooper Atchley. One
man rose and limped over, fixing his shrewd, rheumy eyes
on Matthew.

"Why you want to know?"

"I was told to see him."

"By who?"

"A friend."

"What for?"

"You know."

"I don't know nothing, you strip. What the hell you
doing here?"

Matt leaned down and spoke in a low voice. "I want to
get a gun."

"Hunting gun?"

"No. A soldier's gun."

The old man looked at him for a long time. "Federals
took Atchley away."

"Why?"

"They figured he was selling new guns, not just fixing
old ones." Matthew didn't know what to say, but the old
man began to help him. "Young strong fellow like you, he
don't want no old Kentucky gun." Matthew nodded. "Hell,
there's guns thick as weed around here. Just have to know
the right place to look. You got to be the right kind of man.
You the right kind?"

Matthew was puzzled, but he knew all old folks liked
Christian talk. "I'm a good Methodist."

The old man spit. "I wouldn't give pigshit to a Methodist." He took a long look at the horse. "This here mount is
getting old, boy. Gonna have to shoot him soon."

"I'd never do that. My father rode him at Sharpsburg
when he lost his arm. And my brother who was killed at

Malvern Hill loved this horse. His names's King Bruce."
Matthew took a chance. "Colonel Tyler over at Aspen Hill
surely admires this horse."

"King Bruce, huh? Good name. Fine name." He rubbed
the chestnut's muzzle. "War horse, huh?"

"Maybe good for another war."

"What the hell would a damned pup like you know
about a war." He waved toward the other man. "Me and
him we killed the Mex' in one war, and then we killed
the Yankee bastards in another."

"I hear about a war now on the Yankees and niggers."

The old man rubbed his jaw, glanced at his friend, then
grinned, showing stumps of teeth. "You go see Atchley's
sister over to Delina. Name's Flora."

Matthew rode the five miles to Delina and found the
woman. She was enormous, maybe six feet and two
hundred and fifty pounds, he thought, and she stank of
pork fat. She took him around the back of the house to a
root cellar and led him into the cool darkness. She lit a
lamp and Matthew was amazed at the rows of gleaming
weapons on the wall.

"Show me your money."

Matthew took out twenty dollars. There were Deringers
with three sizes of barrels, an Elgin cutlass pistol that had
a knife-blade under the barrel, Springfield .45-70 caliber
rifles used by the Union Army, Winchester 1866 carbines,
Sharps cavalry carbines and rifles, Henry .44s, Spencer
carbines. She had some old Walker and Navy Colts, but
most of the handguns were the best and newest . . .
the Smith & Wesson Schofield .44, the .44 Remington,
the Smith & Wesson American, double-action British
Beaumont-Adams revolvers, the 10-shot French La Fau-
cheux, a .42 caliber Le Mat grapeshot pistol that had a
folding dagger blade and a set of brass knuckles that
pulled out as a handle. There were many others, but he
liked the heft and look of the Schofield. The woman said
he knew guns, that it was rugged and accurate . . . "A
couple of boys in Missouri that's robbing up on banks and
railroads, they use it and the .44 Remington."

He wanted a Deringer too, thought it might be smart to have one of those "stingy" guns, just in case. He said he'd take the two handguns and a Henry carbine.

"Sure you don't want the Spencer?"

"The Henry's better, isn't it? It's a repeater."

"I hear a Sharps gun like that was found with John Booth when they killed him in that barn."

"No, the Henry."

"You ain't got enough. All you get for twenty dollars is the Schofield."

"I can come back with the money. How much more?"

"Fifty dollars."

"Can I take the guns? I promise I'll come back tomorrow. My name is Matt Lanier from Palmyra."

"How in hell do I know that's your real name? You could be a Federal for all I know, except you're too sweet-looking. All you say the same. I been stolen on too many times 'cause I'm a trusting woman." She moved closer to him. "I'm a loving woman too, and I could be real nice to a sweet-looking fellow like you. You ever fiddled?"

She pushed her big shapeless breasts into him. He could barely stand her smell. She had small mean chicken eyes almost hidden in her fat face. She grabbed him and said if he wanted the guns real bad, he could have them and she'd throw in ammunition.

"I don't have the blood poison, sonny." She reached for his groin. He tried to pull away but she was too strong. "You been trying them cat-wagon girls?" She was talking about prostitutes who traveled the countryside in boarded wagons. "Come on, I'll give you the guns for twenty dollars and that nice young gun you got down there." Her rough hands stroked his face and hair. "I like to fiddle-fuck with a sweet-looking sonny like you."

Matthew knew he'd never find the fifty dollars by the next day. He had to have the weapons, and couldn't risk another trip to Delina. He let her play with his penis through his pants. It felt good . . . if only he could shut away the look and smell of her.

"You promise I'll get the guns?"

"I wouldn't trick you, sweet sonny." She began to breathe hard. "Christ, I got a nice big hot hole for you . . . come on."

She unbuckled his belt, pulled his pants off his hips, and rubbed his penis in her sweating hand. She led him to a pile of hay in the corner. He was ashamed, but he wanted the guns too bad to think more about it. She started to lay down and he felt sick when he saw the coarse wrinkled flesh as she pulled her cotton dress up and rolled the dirty long bloomers below her knees. She began to sound incoherent as she pulled him down and kissed him.

"Blow the lamp out," Matthew said.

"Do it, damn it . . . God, I want to fiddle you."

Matthew turned the lamp down until she was only a dark shapeless mass. For a second he thought of running out but returned to her. She held a breast to his mouth and made him suck the big nipple. He began forgetting himself when she shoved him inside her. She heaved and twisted, making choking sounds, cursing him, telling him he'd be her sweetheart, her sweet sonny all the time. He had a quick orgasm and lay in a stupor. She rolled him back and forth, clasping him tight with her powerful arms and legs, the smells of dry hay and port fat and sweat mingling with the smoky lamp and cellar dirt and decaying squash and pumpkin until he felt he would smother. He was soft inside her, but she kept thrusting her massive body up to him until she screamed and choked him with kisses, rubbing her breasts in his face.

After only a few minutes she rolled him on his back and began to kiss him again, whispering obscenities, epics of filth, reassuring him that she'd give him a time he'd never forget. Her rough tongue lapped down his face and chest and she shifted her body. But now even the rustling when she threw her dress off excited Matthew again. Her mouth was boiling and hungry, and he grabbed the big hams of her ass until she straddled him with surprising quickness and rocked him to orgasm. She felt like a ghostly hammer in the darkness and stayed on him until she quivered with strangled little yelps—"Fiddle and fuck, you sweet little bastard!"—then suddenly collapsed and blacked out. Matthew couldn't move her and waited until she came to. She caressed his face.

"You come back to Flora tomorrow. I can teach that rooster cock of yours a lot of things." Matthew didn't move and she laughed. "Never see a real woman naked?" She put the dress on and turned the lamp up. She sat down heavily, a stupid gluttonous smile on her face. Matthew dressed and brushed himself off. He promised to come back soon.

"You can trust Flora. I ain't got the blood poison." She looked at him with admiration. "I sure fiddle and fucked, but I ain't never had one like you. Real gentleman, I can tell. You be Flora's sweetheart and she'll give you all the guns you want. Make you a big man. I know what you want 'em for."

"I just want to protect my family."

She began to tease with a song—*When Nighttime comes to Ole Nigger Town*—and sniggered. "You're born of the night and vanish by day. . . . Why you dumb little sweet sonny. How did you get to Flora? Only the Ku Kluxers know to come to me in Delina for guns. You're a long way from Palmyra, Matt Lanier, or whatever the hell your name is."

He grabbed the Smith & Wesson and put it to her head. "You say a word, you old cow, and I'll come and blow you to kingdom come." He liked the sound of that.

Still laughing, she rubbed his pants. "Sweet big prick. Hell, that's what I want. I can do you good. I can even get you a shiny nigger to fiddle." She saw his look. "Sonny, all you quality is been fiddling niggers. Bet your daddy has one hid away. You should have the same. I wouldn't be jealous with my sweetheart. I like the look of a nigger woman. I would sure like watching you and a nigger hole . . . see she wouldn't do nothing bad to you."

He put the Deringer in his pocket, jammed the revolver in his belt, started for the stairs and low slatted door carrying the Henry, then stopped and threw her the twenty dollars. "I'll get the rest to you. And don't forget what I said." He leveled the carbine in a menacing way.

She lazily rubbed her stomach, then suddenly glowered at him and snatched a Colt from the table.

"Fancy little Ku Kluxer, ain't you. You dumb little snot-prick. Your guns ain't even loaded. You say one more bad word to Flora Atchley and she's going to tell 'em all, every Kluxer from here to Texas, how you throw down with an empty, how you gave your name, and tried to cheat them guns. You say two bad words—and any head-blowing around here, Flora's gonna do the blowing. Now drop that carbine and Deringer, and get the hell out of here!"

Matthew ran out and mounted, warning himself never to make that kind of mistake again. He'd have to toughen himself, and wondered how he'd act on his first raid. Riding home, he watched the sun and knew it was too late to return to school. It didn't matter anymore, he'd have to face off with his father sooner or later. Everything was upside down, he thought. If his father was against the Klan, then he was the enemy, and felt a shiver that he could think anything that bold. But he had to be his own man. His mother was always pushing him this way or that, even made his decision to join the Klan seem like her own. He reached inside his jacket and felt the revolver. What good was school anyway in bad times. Even his father said there could be another rebellion. Only this time it would be fought at night, in secret, and no mercy shown. A man once told him that his regiment fought nigger troops for the first time in the war at Fussel Mill and trapped a company in the weeds. They felt pity when they saw the terri-fied faces and took them prisoner, when if it had been Yankees, white men, they would have massacred them. It was the one thing in the war he regretted, he said, that he hadn't put those niggers to the sword.

On the road Matthew met a rider on a big splotched bay. The heavyset man hailed him and they stopped to talk.

"You a Delina man?" The stranger took his hat off and ran a hand through thick graying hair.

Matthew thought he'd play it sly. "Yes, sir, and proud of it."

"Know a woman name of Flora Atchley?"

"Sure do. Big fat woman."

"Don't know this country too good. I'm an Arkansas man."

Matthew wondered why someone from across the Mississippi would come to Delina for guns. He was about to give a Klan recognition signal, but thought he'd have to be careful.

"Long way to come to see an old fat woman."

The man smiled. "Ain't the fat I seek. Got goods to sell. Wagons are coming up tonight. She's ordering more every month. My son generally works these parts." Matthew gave him directions to the Atchley house. The man gave King Bruce a tap with his crop. "Good-looking red you got there." He said goodby and rode on.

"You say hello to Flora for me," Matthew called. "Name of Johnny Fiddle." He was laughing, but when he glanced back, he saw the man halted in the road, staring back at him, hat held high as shade against the sun. Matthew thought he'd been stupid for joking . . . the man had to be a powerful Ku Kluxer to be running guns into Tennessee. He gave his horse the boot and started fast for Palmyra.

A week later Billy Laidlaw passed by the school and said there would be an operation that night. After supper, Matthew slipped out his bedroom window, went to the stable and stuffed his uniform in a large saddlebag. He led King Bruce at a slow walk on the grass alongside the road until he reached the trail to Hope Mills. He looked back toward the house. Someone was carrying a lamp up the stairs, and there was a light in his father's study. He didn't care any more if his father disapproved. He might be dead that night. His passion for melodrama made the scene vivid . . . his flag-draped body carried into the house, mother and sister sobbing, his father full of rectitude at first, then repentant, bending to kiss the dead boy's brow. There was a sensuous pleasure at the image and he felt that this would be the greatest night of his life.

He made the rakish mount he'd practiced so often, a quick bent-knee leap to the stirrup with his left foot and a slow graceful swing over the saddle. He spurred the horse and reached Hope Mills along with a big group of riders. They dismounted, the horses pawing and snorting, donned their uniforms and walked to the cellar. The officers were already on the platform and the men stood in silence, but unable to hold their excitement, shuffling and moving restlessly.

At a nod from the Grand Cyclops, Kortman rose. He was the Grand Magi, second-in-command, and planned all the raids.

"There's a nigger blacksmith name of Jim Parton over at Caledonia. He needs smarting up. He shod horses for us. But a good nigger told us that if Parton thought a man was Ku Klux, he'd mark the shoe with a bent nail or some other way. After a raid, he'd go out on the road and see if that special horse was rode and tell on us. We were going to take care of him anyway, but he did something else . . . told a white man he wouldn't shoe any horse until he got paid in advance. Nigger said the white man owed him money. The nigger, he bought a house the Yankees took from a good white man. People in Caledonia say Parton got too much money for a nigger. We'll teach the black son of a bitch a lesson he'll never forget. Other niggers'll learn from it." He held up a Boston newspaper. "And we'll teach the Yankee papers. They play us like a joke, say it's all play-dressing up and 'scaring darkies' like they draw in the picture. We'll show 'em tonight."

Matthew wondered what they would do to the nigger. Maybe just scare him bad, make sure he treated white men with respect.

"Make yourself look bloody," Kortman said, his voice rising, " 'cause there is going to be blood tonight."

Men dabbed more red around the slits in the hood and streaked their robes. They twisted paper and cotton together to make fierce horns. Daggers were shown in scabbards strung high on the chest, swords clanked, revolvers stuck in belts on the outside of the long robes. Kortman turned to the Klud who came forward and raised his arm for the benediction:

"Holy Klan . . . Christian Knights. By bloody moon

and gloomy month, mark well your foe, Jim Parton. Nigger blood and nigger shit. Our purifying drink is made of
distilled hell, stirred with righteous lightning of heaven,
and sweetened with the gall of our enemies. . . ."

Matthew thought it sounded crazy. He never heard any
preacher talk like that. Usually they shouted about dam-
nation and sin and all that, but this Baptist sounded like
the babbling old men he saw around the courthouse
square. You couldn't give reason to ignorant men, his father said, no matter how patriotic they were for the South.
Maybe the pineys and the hill farmers had to be stirred up
that way. Kortman gave the order to mount up and Matthew rushed up the cellar steps. Kortman walked his horse
to him.

"You ride with me. You got to learn things."

Fifty men rode through the woods toward Caledonia,
came out on the road at a gallop, then went back into the
woods when they saw the negro's house. Parton had
worked hard that day, and when he came into the house
he went without food and lay down on a trundle bed.
Three of his children climbed into bed with him. Sometime in the night he heard a dog bark and fell back to
sleep. Then he felt his children shaking him, saying they
heard noises out front. Parton looked out the window. A
long line of Klan riders came through the trees into the
clearing and stood quietly about twenty yards from the
house, a little way off from the blacksmith shop.

"Damn Ku Kluckers," Parton muttered to his wife. He
told her to take the seven children to the back of the
house. He had been a slave for all but five of his forty-
three years, and prized his freedom too much to be scared
of what he called "trash." He liked to talk about the day
he heard that "Abram Linkum" freed him. "I made up my
mind I go and get my share. So I slipped away and got
through the lines and join the 54th Massachussets Colored . . . fought in three battles."

At the end of the war he gathered a few tools and set
up a smithy in the back of the shack where the family
lived. All the plantations used to have their own smiths,
but now they were scattered. The owner had to pay for a

smith's. work now and they found it cheaper to come to Parton. He was making money and able to buy the confiscated house. But he was generally well-liked around Caledonia because he was a good smith, intelligent, and whites sensed that he was a strong-willed, courageous man. He was courteous, but not humble to whites, and most of the local white men seemed to like him for that. He never played the sassy nigger, had a quiet wife and clean children who went to the new schools.

The trouble began when a father and son named Anson owed money for work he'd done. They had run up a big bill and always put Parton off whenever he asked for his money.

"I tole 'em I couldn't work just for scoring it down, so I quit doing their horses. Folks around here I always got along good with starts to talk to me about me being too smart for a nigger. But I kept right on. I tole them I was a free man—not born free, but made free by a miracle from the Lord—and I wasn't going to do no man's work for nothing. People had a lot to say about it, but it didn't hurt my trade none. I just went on getting all I could do, and most of the time more than that. I knowed I acted independent. I knowed there wasn't a better blacksmith in the county and I was gonna get my children the education. Well, I feel that way that I had things just as good as I wanted. When there come an election, I had my say, and tole the colored they was free and could do the same. That's bad talk around here. The white folks they don't mind us getting on if they have a mortgage on us, so the earning goes in their pocket. And they don't care about us voting so long we votes like they tell us. That's the white man idea of freedom for a nigger.

"I got a warning from the Kluckers about smart niggers. They tole me to git. Well, I heard about these Kluckers and allowed that they was just some trifling boys that fixed up and went around to hellify niggers. So I said if the Kluckers want anything from me, they better come and get it. I got a gun and I was a soldier who used that gun. I didn't believe about them Kluckers coming straight from hell and drinking the rivers dry. If they come to mess with me, I allowed some of 'em would go to hell before it was over."

Just before the Klansmen showed themselves there was a series of hoots and clucks and moans and screeches and groans. Parton knew what it was and wasn't surprised when he saw the riders emerging. He walked out the door. To another nigger, Parton thought, it would chill his blood. Giant white horned figures sat in silence atop ghostly white horses. Ghastly noses and tongues and fangs showed from the slits, the long hair that spilled from hood to pommel stirring in the night wind.

"What do you want?" Parton shouted.

Kortman edged his mount forward. In a horrible groan that rent the night, he asked for water. Parton went to the well-bucket and returned with a brimming dipper. He knew what they were going to do, had heard the tale too often from other negroes, and was shrewd enough to play his role. The ghostly figure roared, "Damnit, nigger! Didn't I say I was thirsty? Bring me a full bucket!" Parton bowed and scraped and rushed the full bucket, over a gallon of water, and lifted it to the rider. He seized it, threw his head back and drank deeply, making loud gurgling sounds and smacking his lips. Parton pretended to look amazed that a man could drink that much. Then Kortman drank two more buckets. Parton knew the water was going down into a goatskin hidden under the man's robe. He'd heard about niggers who'd fled their homes after that.

Kortman smacked his lips again and moaned. "Aaaah . . . I've ridden a thousand miles tonight and I was powerful thirsty. That's the best drink of water I had since I was killed at Shiloh!"

Patron knew he should show terror, then beg for mercy from these spirits of Confederate dead, leave home and work if they demanded it. But something strong and stubborn in him made just stand his ground and look up at the rider.

Kortman's voice became threatening. "Beware, you shit nigger. Work for the white man like he asks. Obey all white men. Stay off the roads after dark. Stay away from

Yankee hellishness." He leaned down and jabbed the stock of his whip into Parton's face. "We're watching you. You bend another nail or insult a white man again, we'll come back and take you away with us. Down . . . down . . . down . . . to the fiery pit of Hell!"

"Only Hell I know is the one my preacher tell me about. That the same Hell?"

Kortman lashed out with the whip. He gave an order and four riders surrounded the negro and herded him to the blacksmith shop. They ripped his shirt off and tied him face down on his forge. A Klansman named Hickman, a former overseer on a plantation, came forward with a short stout whip. He lay into Parton's back methodically, cutting the flesh with a symmetrical cross-check pattern of welts, his trademark. There were dozens of ex-slaves who bore those notorious scars.

Matthew was alongside Kortman during the whipping. Parton didn't cry out once and he thought that was one brave nigger. He tried not to feel sorry for him; it had to be done. He shut his eyes as Hickman kept flailing away, his skill impressive. It was said he could flick the eyelash off a man. Parton was untied and brought out. He was forced to watch as Klansmen dragged his wife and fourteen-year-old daughter from the house, tore their clothes off and raped them. Then the Klansmen broke up everything inside the house and formed ranks again.

"You learn respect, boy?"

"Yessuh."

"You never gonna bend a nail again?"

"Yessuh."

"You never gonna ask a white man for money in advance?"

"Yessuh."

"You gonna forget about voting?"

"Yessuh."

"All right. Be a good nigger and you won't have any trouble." The voice was a moan again. "Shake hands on it."

He thrust out his white arm. Parton was frightened that the man had a revolver concealed in the loose sleeve, had just been tricking him along all the time, and was going to blow his face away at close range. The pain in his back was like fire and he didn't think he could raise his arm. He pretended that he didn't want to touch no dead man's hand.

"Damn you, nigger—didn't I offer to shake your black hand."

Parton slowly offered his hand and found himself gripping the bony, fleshless claw of a skeleton. There was a lot of laughing and hooting. Parton wanted to kill them. Not because they whipped him—though all his life as a slave he had felt the lash only once when he was a waiting-boy—but because they treated him like he was less than a man. He was supposed to cringe and run in fear, do nothing when they ruined his women. He dropped the claw.

"Now, get off my land!"

Kortman pulled a knife and made the sign of the cross an inch from Parton's nose. The negro heard his wife and daughter shrieking in pain and terror, the frightened crying of the other children. He knew what the Ku Kluxer wanted, and bowed under the knife. Kortman gave a signal and the riders disappeared into the trees, the ghostly hoots and clucks and whistles mixing with the cries of the children.

Parton took his family back inside the house, locked the door and pulled the trundle bed up against it. His wife bathed his back with salt and water, the age-old remedy for the lash that drew out some of the soreness. After they cleaned up some of the wreckage, Parton lay down with his wife and daughter and tried to comfort them. They began to drift into sleep, Parton swearing that he would fix up a finer house, with everything a prosperous white man had. The whites had driven the Indians out and sent them off West . . . Cherokee, Creek, Tuscarora, Chickasaw and Yamani. And they were trying to drive out any niggers who wouldn't work humbly, wouldn't sign a contract for work that made them just like slaves again. He was a free man and they weren't going to drive him out. They'd have to kill him first.

Kortman held up the column in the woods. "I don't think we did that nigger good enough."

"You want more whipping?" Hickman asked.

"I want more damn respect. He wasn't scared. That nigger got too much guts in his belly. You can whip that kind of nigger into straw and he wouldn't bend. He's gonna show off that whipping like he was proud of it, and he's gonna tell other niggers how they shouldn't be scared."

Matthew thought he understood Kortman's fear . . . that the Klan could be made to look foolish if they let some proud buck get away with something. He wanted to say something fierce.

"That nigger needs some more doing."

Kortman whirled. "Shut up, you little pork-ass." He turned to the others. "Well, we're just going to blow the guts out of that nigger's belly."

They walked the horses back to the clearing. The house was silent and dark. They found a pile of logs that Parton was going to use to build a new kitchen. Six men dismounted, grabbed the biggest log and ran at the door. There was a splintering, crashing noise as the door came down on the bed. Klansman ran in over the door and crushed the wife's skull. The girl screamed and fought her way out. Parton was trapped, his leg caught between the bed and door. Two Klansmen pulled him out, but he struggled and broke free for a moment. A group of riders boxed him in, their mounts crushing him. Men punched him in the face and ribs and he fell to the ground. They tied Parton to a log and Kortman walked his horse around it. He drew a double-barreled shotgun from the scabbard under the horse's covering and cocked both barrels.

"Get the nits out here!"

The fourteen-year-old had sent the other children fleeing to the woods, but she stayed hidden.

"I want them to see you blown to Hell. Just so they could tell about it."

Kortman brought the shotgun up. He saw the look in Parton's eyes. The nigger bastard would never bend. Kortman pulled both triggers. Parton's body was driven against the log.

"Take the damn rope off him."

Matthew felt a shiver go through him. It was the first time he ever saw a man killed and his nerves were jumping. If Kortman thought the nigger needed killing, he was sure it was right and no use feeling sorry. He only felt bad that Kortman had lowered him in the eyes of the others. Hickman whispered something to Kortman. They argued for a while, then Kortman nodded. Hickman searched the house and found the young girl. He mounted and pulled her up behind him. Matthew wondered what they were going to do with her. He didn't hold with killing a young girl . . . even a nigger. Billy Laidlaw whispered that Hickman liked young nigger ass, and no one was ever dumb enough to say anything to his face.

Parton was still alive, crawling to the house as the Klansmen rode off with his daughter. He was weak from loss of blood, his chest smashed and half his face blown away, but he reached up inside the fireplace and pulled out a rifle. He dragged himself to the window and lay the weapon on the sill. The riders were turning into the woods. His daughter's back almost shielded Hickman but he took careful aim at the man's head. He fired and fell to the floor. The bullet slammed into Hickman and he fell off, taking the girl with him. Kortman rode back to the house. He drew his revolver, smashed the glass and saw Parton lying beneath the window. He pulled off four shots into the dead man's head. The girl ran into the woods and Kortman said to let her go. It would be good for her to tell about it. They lashed Hickman's body to his horse and galloped away.

Two days later there was a funeral for Hickman in a town not far from Palmyra. It was said that the dead man had been kicked in the head by a mule. The undertaker who buried him said the corpse was already laid out when he got to Hickman's house, and some men insisted in putting it into the coffin. When the undertaker was putting the cover on, he got a chance to put his hand down on the corpse's head. Afterward, he always told the story with a sly grin.

"If that man was kicked by a mule, it must have been a

remarkably *tall* one, and it had to be the only mule in the great state of Tennessee whose kick looked like a hole made by a .57 bullet. I ought to know. I seen hundreds of them in the war."

After the riders disbanded at Hope Mills, Matthew rode home with Billy Laidlaw. "You ever see that before?"

Laidlaw nodded. "Once. But that was a white man shooting at us. It sure shook me when Kortman started back for that nigger. I knew he was gonna do it."

"I thought the nigger was scared off the first time. He was going to show respect after that whipping."

"Nobody knows what a nigger is thinking. But Kortman knows as much as any man." They looked at each other . . . *the talk about Kortman and nigger blood.* "He knew what he was doing. That nigger'll never sass another white man."

"It's sure funny how a fellow like Kortman can be so easy a man in town and so mean when he rides. He didn't have to take me down like he did back there."

"Aw, hell, what's the difference." Billy patted Matthew on the shoulder. "That was a rough way for your first ride. It's mostly beatings and like that. Sometimes it's a lot of fun."

"Don't worry about me." He was afraid Billy would think he had a soft stomach. He wanted to believe that Kortman was right. Niggers had to be taught respect for a white man. A nigger didn't as much as tell a white man he didn't trust him, which is what the nigger did. But he had to be fair. That buck was one brave son of a bitch. He thought it would take him a long time to understand men like Kortman. They loved the war, and they loved killing after so many years at it. He'd listened to men from his father's regiment when they came to Palmyra every year to visit. They always talked about the war, how they hated it, but they were too ashamed to talk about their lust for it. He heard talk about the "beauty" of action later recalled in the Lanier parlor as awesome, astonishing, painful and glorious, an ecstacy that was shared by comrades in arms and was their dirty secret. Many were men who volunteered over and over again for risky missions, rode with cavalry raiders. Once, when he asked his father why men would constantly take such chances, Everett said it was "to escape the monotony and stupidity of war, not its terrors."

The two young men rode the rest of the way in silence and separated just outside of town. Matthew stabled the horse, rubbed him down and fed him clover. He had to get his own horse. There might be a time he needed King Bruce in a rush and someone in the family would be riding him. He felt uneasy because what he thought would be a patriotic adventure was something different. He had sworn away his life and had to obey any order. His life had already changed. He was riding with hard men, the kind he rarely talked to. From what he could see, most of them had nothing to lose. They had nothing before the war and had nothing now. Maybe they were afraid the Yankees were making the nigger their better. They'd kill easy, he thought. But what if he had to kill a nigger? Could he do it?

He knew people like himself had the most to lose and couldn't ask other men to fight their battle. Even his father had killed for a cause, though he could never make the connection between a hell-for-leather cavalry captain and the spare, quiet man who spent his evenings reading the Greek philosophers. Watching Kortman was the worst thing. The scarred face mde Matthew think of him as someone specially marked by the war, that because of his hideous wound Kortman had learned to be gentle.

But he was just being sentimental, self-pitying, because he wasn't sure of anything any more. He was almost convinced that maybe he was too much like his father. To be a good Ku Kluxer, he had to learn to be careless about life, love danger, not qualify or try to reason everything out. And the worst—or the best—he was still too bewildered to know—was that he had to learn to beat and bully, torture and hang and kill if he had to.

5

HE had to talk to someone and saw the lamp in Adela's room. She answered his soft knock.

"Where have you been? You look like a stinky pissraker."

Matthew was always surprised by his sister's language and found it funny. He often wondered about her. Did she make love to any of her beaus? Even some of his father's friends were too familiar with her, always offering a ride in a carriage, taking her to a show when a traveling company was in town, sometimes suggesting that she visit their place of business. Everett was never aware of their flirting, but she took pleasure in encouraging them, a bewitching girl who seemed to live with her own rhythm. She offered them some kind of spindly promise, made them press for a moment alone with her. Matthew was sometimes shocked by the eccentric things she did, not to defy or annoy people, but simply because she had a different center, a wayward outlook on life. A friend of his father's said that she was the kind of creature who, glimpsed once, could ruin years of a man's life, make him want to go home and murder his wife.

Matthew loved her, and knew his love was ludicrous. But even talking to her was different than when he was

ers think they're helping us. They're just going
worse. We'll have more Yankee troops in here
ny, if this kind of thing continues."

ht the Kluxers were good Southerners. Don't
he negra down?"

nothing to do with keeping negras down. It's
er and land . . . and money, who has it and
for it. When the war ended the government
to be easy with us. We got our own men back
nd they started the Black Codes. Poor negras
off than when they were slaves. Either they
y and homeless, or they worked for white men
ges. He had to contract his labor a year in ad-
egra blacksmith or shoemaker had to buy li-
hans were apprenticed to their old masters until
eighteen. Negra needed a pass to walk on the
s the Freedom's Bureau that helped them, not

y're trying to make the negra our better."

ard what happened at Memphis and New Or-
hundreds of negras murdered by white trash,
t was played up big in the Northern papers.
es saw things like that . . . and the way we
l up life like it was before the war. They went
mish us. It started mostly with two men from
sets. Thaddeus Stevens is a Congressman, the
aid 'The proud traitors will be stripped of their
tates.' Other is a Senator named Charles Sum-
the one who said the South committed suicide
ceded. They're the kind of Republicans called
at brought the military rule. We're a conquered
vided into military districts like in the war. Un-
ls rule us like kings. They can do whatever they
re are no civil courts. I have to defend people
ilitary tribunal."

telling me all the good reasons for the Klan."

re killing the Klan does, the harder the Yankees
o pinch us."

a lot of politicians and swindlers come down
up north just to do us?"

with other girls. She never evoked boredom, made every
moment together seem a pressing want. Adela made him
aware of his passion, his capacity to adore and please because she often treated him like a beau. Other times she
was quick to establish barriers by her teasing or simple
dismissal of him as too callow, just a dreamy young rough-
neck who she helped out of scrapes. But when they were
together and close, she gave clarity to mysteries, comple-
mented or improved his fantasies.

Growing up with her lovely presence stalking the house,
he was taught by indirection the complexities of sex. She lent
excitement, gave and broke promises that only he inter-
preted as such, taunted him, glorified him, and tormented
him when she went out walking with a strange young
man. And he loved her wistfully, gratefully. He was sensi-
tive to the tremors between men and women, and however
young, he sensed that with his sister he would never have
to experience the litany or fury of parting, the sin of boredom, or the suicide of deep affection. His mother, he
knew, demanded his love only because she feared her
power with men was failing, that age had made her unat-
tractive. She wooed him with favors and flirting as Adela
never did. It was his mother who convinced him that any
connection was like the germ of corruption entering the
soul. She wanted to rule him, ruin him for others.

He was at that point in life when he felt strong and capa-
ble in the presence of others, stored up emotional credit,
because he once sensed that in the end, when it came
down to a moral courage he lacked, he'd throw himself on
the mercy of others. Because of his age and the position of
his family, people would always make allowances for him
because his life was an amiable presence, a stock of juve-
nile braggadacio and hail-fellow anecdotes. Except for
Adela, he felt isolated in the family, the town. It was the
isolation that often filled him with terror, the feeling that
if there was no one to witness his strength, share his
dreams, he had none. It was an emotional physics that
threatened to crush him if he lingered too long at the
point of contact. Adela was the one person he could confide in. She saw through his intricate ruses, his sometime

charm and evasiveness. Often she saw through him with precision and made eerie revelations to him. She once told him of his passion for her and said she understood, but he would grow away from it. She stripped away everything in an artless, often sadistic honesty that further infatuated him.

She put her arm around him and kept asking what was wrong, but he shook his head.

"What's the matter?"

"Nothing."

"Tell me. How can I love you if you don't trust me?"

"I do. You're the only one I trust." He tried to pull away but she held him tight. "I can't talk."

"You didn't steal in here for nothing." She laughed. "You're such a baby." She took a scented handkerchief and wiped his sweaty, dirt-streaked face. "God, you smell. You took King Bruce for a little night ride." He nodded. "I bet I know where you've been."

"Aw, me and Billy Laidlaw went over to some whores in Wyatt." He tried to look at her but she was angry and he stared at the floor. He knew that look of hers, the variation of her eyes in every mood. When she was mad, they had an instant opaque quality and looked like emeralds, then they bleached out, almost dissolving into yellow pinpoints.

"Where's your funny hat?"

"What are you talking about?"

"You know damn well. " Her face softened. "God, how could you be so dumb. Now you're caught."

"We just went with some whores."

"Why did you come in here then?"

He started to answer but she put a hand over his mouth and gestured toward the door. They waited but no one came.

"Poor little dumb brother . . . a Ku Kluxer." He tried to deny it but she shook her head. "I heard mama say something to you. I couldn't make sense out of it then, but I do now."

He thought it would make her proud of him, but she

---

made him feel stupid and he
right thing to do."

"What happened, whip some
"I can't talk about it."

"You came to me because you
minute I saw you. I promise I wo

"You do and I'm a dead man."

"Maybe I ought to blow your
someone's going to do it sure."

"It wasn't what I thought it w
time, trying to keep from laying
killed someone." He saw her look
assure her. "No, I just watched. I
to happen. It was quick."

"You thought it was going to
prancing around on horses, flags
ing. Don't you know what's happ
papa, you'd know. It's another w
of war."

"I know it."

"Oh, shut up! Papa's never to k
how we can keep it from him I do
out, or worse." She knew better t
ticulars. "Just go along with the
right." She hated herself for tryin
but she was afraid of what he'd
ened . . . just a high-strung boy
what her father called "gore and g
and thought how contrary it all v
comfort, to involve her, maybe to
that she approved. She wondered
the dead man was.

Three days later, the Palmyra
count of the deaths of the blacks
wife in nearby Caledonia. Adela
his head as he read the paper. Sh
motioned for him to talk to his fa
walked over and sat down.

"You read about that negra getti

"Ku Klu
to make it
soon, an a

"I thou
they keep

"It's go
about pov
who work
was going
in power
were wor
went hun
for spit w
vance. A
censes. O
they wer
road. It v
us."

"But th
"You b
leans . .
scum. Th
The Yan
just picke
hard to
Massachu
one who
bloated e
mer. He's
when it
Radicals
country,
ion gener
want. Th
before a

"You're
"The n
are going

"Didn'
here from

"It's true. They fixed it so there would be more negra voters than white. They're using the negra vote to get power for themselves, not because they love the negra. Negra can't read or write or understand anything because they were slaves. It's our own fault. We did nothing to educate them . . . too damned proud. People like your mother's family lived like lords in Europe."

"But if things are so bad, then the Kluxers are helping us."

"You know who most of them are?"

Matthew's heart pounded. He misunderstood, thought his father could identify local men. If he knew them, it wouldn't be far from knowing his own son was one of them. Adela was listening at the door and wondered why Matthew was stupid enough to keep mentioning the Klan.

"They're poor farmers, mean little clerks, people who came out of the hills to loot the planters because they were always jealous . . . and kill negras they hate. And they do it because their own lives are so miserable and hard."

"I hear there are people of family in the Klan."

"That's right. Who are the officers? Who leads? Everyone knows General Forrest is their Grand What's-His-Name, as much as he denies it to the newspapers. They're trying to get back their place in the world, the power they lost. They're afraid. And when you're afraid that way, you'll take any desperate way out . . . all in the name of Southern honor. Damn bunch of masked cowards."

He saw Matthew's puzzled look. "Son, you don't know how bad it was for a few years. You're from a good town family and you were too young. It was a life that meant just not dying. But in places like Texas that was never invaded by Yankee troops, masters still hold slaves. That and the rest is the kind of thing that brought the Reconstruction Act last year and the Occupation. Tennessee was the first state the Yankees took over." He smiled. "You could say we were last for the war and first after it."

"Didn't the Yankees occupy right at the end of the war?"

"Yes, but they were correct. They didn't take any private property. A lot of land was sold for unpaid taxes and they gave some to the negras. But they were usually fair, gave most of the selling price to the old owners."

"I hear a lot of good families went north. At least the Klan stayed to fight holy injustice and disgrace."

Everett was amused. Only hotheaded boys and pompous orators used words like that. "What could they do here? It was all ruins. They were educated men. They went to cities like Baltimore and Philadelphia, even New York and Boston"—he had a sly grin—"Yes, those dark lairs of the devil Yankees. They went to make a good life, a new life. You know they call Baltimore 'The poorhouse of the Confederacy' because so many of them are there." He paused. "By the way, no Ku Klux will tell you about the millions of dollars the government and private men in the North sent down here, the food they sent us."

"But didn't even Lincoln say the negra and white couldn't live together?"

"That's right. But he thought it would do as much good for the negra as the white man. His mistake was that he freed them but made no plans about how they'd live, earn their bread. Maybe he would have if he lived." Everett took a deep breath. "It wasn't Ku Kluxers who killed him, but it was the same kind of thinking."

"All I see is negras roaming around, sassing. . . ."

"What did they know? Being free meant no more hard slave work. They took to the woods and roads, came to towns. Man gets used to one kind of life, it's hard changing, especially when you're hated and treated lower than a good horse, when no one shows you the way. Well, the politicians were smart. They showed the negras the way, only it was for the white man's gain."

"But don't we have negra politicians ruling us now?"

"Matt, you're thick. The Freedmen Bureau helped them, but had no idea to give them the vote. I told you what brought it down on us. But even before there were Ku Kluxers, there was the same kind of thing . . . killing and burning and terror. The same kind of trash were burning schools and running white lady schoolteachers from the North out of town. They said education would spoil the negra. What they meant was he might get too smart to work for starvation wages. It's always money, son, and mean little people wanting to keep them low so they can feel they're better than someone."

The boy was beginning to tire him. "And it isn't negra rule. They don't *rule* any state government. They're twisted around by Carpetbaggers and Scalawags. But negras don't pass any laws against their former masters. They don't slaughter like they were slaughtered. They have their own churches. Most negras in office fought to educate themselves. They're no worse than the ordinary run of politicians. The negras white men hate are the ones who show some brains and get-up." He tapped the paper. "That man and his wife, killed by cowards. Sounds like he was a good family man, church man, best smith around they say. A negra trying to get up in the world."

"I don't say they should go around killing them."

"They killed him because he was a bad example for other negras to see. That if a man works hard, he can make something of himself."

Matthew couldn't believe Kortman would gun a man down just for that. The Klan had scared a lot of niggers out of Giles County. Parton took a bad beating and might have gone too, or at least learned some respect. No one would put two barrels of shot into a man for just working hard. He understood some of what his father said, but was still confused.

"I can see the Yankees doing all their thieving and helping negras. But Scalawags are traitors because they're from the South."

"Most of them do it because they want work, so they join the Republican Party. A lot of them are scoundrels, sat out the war. But some of them did it because they were Unionists. There are men called Scalawags who believed slavery was bad, and they wanted to help the negra."

"They're just many dogs . . . stinking villains!"

Everett laughed. "Some people say they're just poor whites who were held down by the planters and think they can do better if they join the Yankees. Others say they're betrayers of the white race, and they're doing it just to get their mealy share of the spoils. But there are a lot of important men, Southern patriots, that you could call Scalawags. General James Longstreet, one of Lee's commanders, a hero, said that we were conquered and should accept the Union's terms, and try to raise the negra. James Orr, the fieriest secesh man in the Confederate Senate . . . and Del Aspinall, the biggest slaveholder in Mississippi. They have the right idea—go with the Radicals so we can control their action and stop their mischief. Aspinall believes the negras should get more help . . . a man who had thousands of slaves. He says the Republican Party is the one that will give them protection."

"But you admit there are Scalawags who are crooks and scoundrels."

"Some men are getting rich. They're looting and taking bribes. Joseph Brown, the governor of Georgia in the war, already owns a railroad, and he's involved in a steamship company, coal and iron."

"Why would a Southerner hurt his own country?"

"Well, we gave a lot of trouble to Unionists down here during the war. Not every man wanted it. Right here in Tennessee it was split just about down the middle whether we'd secede or not. A lot of people here believed in the Union."

The more Everett talked, the more bewildered Matthew was. He thought the talk would give him a simple idea of the troubles, confirm his own action, but his father hardly talked about the Klan. Too many facts, too much windy stuff about politics and money and poor whites and good niggers. But he was sure of one thing. It didn't seem that his father made the Klan look so bad, whatever he said. If all those things were wrong, then who would look out for them, protect their women. He was sure he didn't hate niggers. But wasn't that what it was all about, what caused the trouble. *The niggers* . . . and keeping the South a white man's country. In his stubborn passion, he let everything his father said slide by.

The conversation drifted off, almost as the boredom,

the hopelessness of each understanding the other, was evident to both. When Matthew rose from the chair opposite, Everett gave him a cautioning look, an imploring look for him to try and understand. He lit his pipe and looked out the window. He couldn't tell the boy that he was sympathetic to the ex-slaves, had tried to help them . . . to learn, to live better, to vote properly and not at the whim of some politician. He never told anyone in the family that he had already been warned by the Klan because he talked around town that they were thugs who would hurt the South—a note stuck in his office door with a dagger . . . *DEAD, DEAD UNDER THE ROSES, THY END IS NIGH!*

He had met one of the men who started the Klan at a ball at Loretto, John Lester, and later served with him in the 2nd Tennessee Cavalry. They lost touch when Everett was invalided out, but Lester came to see him after the war and told him about it. It began so innocently, out of restlessness and boredom, out of a need to provide some escape from the drear and suffering, some joy, in a somber hill town called Pulaski near the Alabama border. . . .

There were six men in the law office of Judge Edgar Dyess that Christmas Eve of 1865: John Lester, Lucious Kennedy, Samuel Crowe, Frank McCord, Henry Stewart and Ned McAusland. Later they would tell people that they never had any other idea than to form a social club, try to liven up the town and have some innocent fun.

"We might have called it 'The Jolly Six' or 'The Thespians,' and it might never have taken that turn," Lester once said. "But before the war Southern men always liked to have secret societies. That's all we were trying to get back."

That holiday eve Lester was looking out the second-story window at the barren hickory trees along the deserted main street. There was little in the stores to buy and storekeepers would only accept Union scrip, whining that it wasn't their fault, they couldn't give credit to the whole town. The men, all officers in the war and some college-educated, talked about what a poor Christmas it would be. They reminisced about past holidays when peo-

ple went from house to house to drink and feast and cele-
brate, when the stores were crowded with townspeople
and farmers from miles around. There would be damned
little enough to eat this Christmas dinner. Wind rattled
through chinks in the old ochre-colored frame building.
The other men sat close to a potbelly stove, smoking, passing around a jug of homemade whiskey called "Busthead"
for Christmas cheer.

"Jesus Christ!" Lester slammed his fist on the window
sill. "Sometimes I wish the war never ended." He knew
the others felt as he did. They went away to war roaring
boys in a parade, the women gone wild and throwing
flowers and jumping to the saddle to kiss any man. They
came back ruined men to a ghosty town, and had never
rid themselves of the lust for battle.

"Eight months. Damned nothing to do," said Crowe.

McCord grunted. "This is the only place I can sit for
even a few minutes without wanting to tear someone's
head off." He spit on the reddish-iron glow of the stove, a
sizzle of steam dropping on his torn and cracked boot.

"Look at that," Lester said.

The others crowded around the window. A band of
freed slaves were walking in stray aimless groups up the
main street. They looked ragged and tired, some women
carrying two children or a big blanket bundle filled the
family's possessions. The men looked wary, wondering
what these townspeople would do. They had been driven
from Diana.

Thousands of niggers like that . . . looking for the
Promised Land the Yankees promised them. He couldn't
help feeling sorry for them. They no longer had the protection of their masters, no one to feed or clothe them, just
dumb ignorant beasts wandering the countryside, begging
scraps of food, bending proper and "Yassuhing" and "Yass-
mamming," their gaunt dogs foraging in backyards and
along the roadside. A white woman gave them a quarter-
loaf of bread and the man who looked like their leader
tore it into bits, trying to make equal shares. Lester noticed that they fed the children first and the adults went
without.

He wanted to forget it all. Right after Appomattox, he thought of fighting on as a guerilla, forming a company to go into the woods and harass the Yankee troops, fighting until they killed him. When he couldn't raise enough men or horses and guns, he thought of going west, or to Mexico or some other Latin country. They were always having 'Wars of liberation' and revolutions and could use experienced officers. Many Confederate veterans had run away to South America, mostly Brazil and Argentina, and were getting rich, slave-owners again, some of them generals commanding their own private army.

But when Lester's father died, he had to care for his mother and sister, along with his own wife and child, and put the wild idea out of mind. He tried to think of something he and the others could do, something that would make everyone forget their misery for a while, the war and destruction, the farms laying fallow, the noble sentiments all turned to bile. Some people still couldn't give up the dream, the magnificent houses, the grandeur and power and formal pleasures of their former lives . . . a lot of them crazy people sitting behind shuttered windows up on the hill or out in the country, half-starved while they dressed in their best and ate cattle corn off cracked Limoges china and dirty damask tablecloths . . . men who killed their women and burned their great houses to keep them from niggers and Yankees, and then committed suicide with antique dueling pistols.

Lester had fought from Pittsburg Landing to Vicksburg and had seen terrible things. But sitting around useless was the worst thing. Every day the same, trying to get some work, grow a little food, make a dollar to keep his own family from starving, long trips by foot to other towns in the hope that there was food to buy. Not much better off than the niggers. Maybe worse off when everything was finished. Pulaski was dying. The countryside and the state and the whole South was dying. First Lincoln, then President Andrew Johnson spoke of an easy peace, bring the South back into the Union quickly. One was dead, the other a drunk that his party was trying to impeach because he wasn't hard enough. But he had to say it, the

Yankees had kept their promise so far, and there was talk of good money being sent down to help build up the farms and towns. Political power was back in the hands of people who had it before the war, and what was the difference if they set up this Freedmen's Bureau to help the nigger. But men came back from Washington with rumors that bad things were stirring.

"They're going to let these niggers vote sooner or later," Lester said, "That's what the damned Congress is talking about."

"And maybe take it away from us," McAusland said. He pulled out a Deringer he kept hidden in the back of his belt under the coarse woolen shirt. "I'd like to blow someone to hell."

McCord drew a knife, "You blow 'em and I'll cut 'em up."

"Enough of that talk," Lester said. "Put those away. Yankees catch you with them and you'll wind up in Fort Donelson for sure." He watched the negroes pass out of town under a gibbous moon, bent against the harsh wind. *Poor niggers.* "Maybe we could do something to cheer people up."

"We could go over to Morehouse and get some of those whores—if someone had a dollar," McAusland said. "That would cheer me up a load. But them bitches is as bad as the store people. They want Yankee money for that poor snatch."

Lester laughed. "Ned took a Yankee .57 in the thigh at Franklin and his cock was still standing stiff as a ramrod. Horny little bastard, you forget about the whores. We need something to cheer up our mothers and girls."

"How about a club?" Kennedy said.

"Sure," Crowe said. "That's a good idea. Remember 'The Roundheads' that used to come over from Carolina? 'The Yorkshire Cavaliers' . . . 'The Highlanders' and 'The Knights of the Round Table.' They all had a hell of a lot of fun, all that hocus-pocus and jabbery talk, and the costumes and uniforms."

"A secret society," Lester said. "A lot of passwords and hell-raising. We can scare the dickens out of people. It'll give us something to do and it'll perk up the women. You know how they like to see a man in something fancy." He tried to visualize a costume. It might make them all feel more important, make the women respect them more when they saw their men being lively again. Before they left for home, they agreed to meet the day after Christmas.

At the meeting, a lot of flamboyant names were offered, but they couldn't agree. Kennedy said that Crowe had a good idea.

"The Greek word for circle is *Kuklos*."

"Hell," Stewart said, "that's nothing grand like 'Knights of the White Camellia' or 'The Sons of Midnight.' We be a laughing stock."

"We don't say it that way because we don't want anyone to know. We call it the Ku Klos."

"Ku Klos? Maybe Ku Klux," said Lester. "Sounds better, more mysterious."

"It ain't long enough, don't have no roll to it," said Stewart. "It don't sound grand."

McAusland repeated the name slowly. "Well, no one would know what the hell it is."

They discussed it for a long time before Lester thought he had the answer. "We're mostly Scotch and Irish here. We come from clans. How does that sound . . . *Ku Klux Klan*."

Crowe had a big smile. "Sounds just like a gun being cocked and fired . . . *click, cluck, clack*. . . ."

"Sounds like some foreign babble or child talk," Lester said. "It's perfect . . . secret. No one's ever going to figure this one out."

They were excited as they tried to decide on names and ranks of members, then broke for the night. At the next meeting the six men deliberately created nonsense terms. Lester, the leader, was designated the "Grand Cyclops." Crowe, his assistant, was the "Grand Magi." There was also a "Grand Scribe," a recruiter called the "Grand Turk," two guards known as "Lictors," and two "Night Hawk" messengers. The ordinary members would be called "Ghouls." Initiations for new members were good-humored, prankish affairs, despite the macabre names and trappings.

Disguises and regalia were the essence of every secret society, but there was little left in Pulaski to use. It was McCord who suggested they raid the family linen closet. Pillow slips became hoods, sheets became robes, and tall conical hats they remembered from children's parties added the final touch. Each time they met some member added a refinement: the dabbing of fake blood, the sweeping moustaches and beards, horns, protuberant noses and lurid teeth, secret signs or crosses painted on the robes— until the society had devised the costume that would become notorious. A "click" or "cluck" or whistle became their signal. They added a secret handshake and ways for members to identify themselves to each other. Pleased with themselves and their appearance, they rode abroad at night to play practical jokes and serenade the ladies. When they outgrew Judge Dyess' office, they met in Colonel Sylvester Martin's house. When that became too small, they looked around for a new "Den" as they called their meeting places. McAusland found exactly what they needed. Beyond Pulaski, on the crest of a long ridge, was the shell of a building battered by a terrible windstorm years before. Only three rooms were left standing in the rubble of brick, but there was a large cellar. It was a desolate place, ringed by dead trees, their branches blighted and bare the year around.

Whenever new Klan Dens formed—men were joining by the hundreds each week—they tried to find lonely places, scabrous-looking country where no one ventured. Even in daylight, the stream of negroes clogging the nearby road always hurried past the ruined building. Now the rubble became haunted with ghostly white figures who came and went on death-pale horses. One night McAusland reported something strange.

"Every other road is filled with niggers day and night. But you don't see them passing this road."

They began to ride the back roads to scare negroes, and, Lanier once insisted, that was all. Bring the niggers to their senses by giving them a warning with what was just a prank. Then it seemed logical to think of themselves as police, protecting whites from "marauding herds of niggers." Before the war, iron discipline was enforced on the slaves by patrols, a system of local constabulary policing each area to make sure that no nigger was abroad without a pass, and that no secret meetings took place. The planters always feared another slave rebellion like the bloody one led by Nat Turner earlier in the century, or like the revolution in Haiti. At first there was no violence. Then, slowly, the terror began. Negroes were the obvious prey, whipped and driven away. But the Ku Kluxers began to judge and punish the morals and political opinions of whites. They whipped seducers and adulterers, burned out "troublemakers" and merchants they thought were profiteers, rode through town to intimidate people, firing shots into darkened homes.

One night a stranger came to a meeting at Hop Mills, a dark-eyed, burly, grayhaired man. He was talking to Kortman when he spotted Matthew and gave him a searching look. Matthew became aware of him and suddenly remembered . . . the hard-looking man he'd talked to on the road to Delina who had turned back to look at him, as if marking his face. He wondered if Flora Atchley had said anything to him. But the man made no sign that he recognized Matthew. General Blanton introduced him.

"This is Isaac Catlin, a brother from Arkansas. He is building a strong organization in that state, and is their delegate to the second Nashville convention. He will join Lyle Hoagland, our man. When they return, we hope to have exciting news of new operations. They will speak to General Forrest."

General Nathan Bedford Forrest was the Grand Vizier of the Invisible Order of the Ku Klux Klan. He had been installed the year before with his ten Genii at the Klan's first national convention in Nashville. Below him in descending rank was a Grand Dragon of the Realm and his nine Hydras, a Grand Titan of the Dominion and his six Furies, a Grand Giant of the Province and his four Goblins, and a Grand Cyclops of a Den with the officers origi-

nated by Lester and his friends. Forrest, 48, was an imposing man, 6 feet 2 and 185 pounds, broad-shouldered with
lean muscular limbs. A handsome man with a dark beard
and piercing gray eyes, he was the Confederate cavalry
officer most feared by the Union Army.

In his earlier years he made a fortune as a slave trader,
looked down on by Southerners who did business with
him. But he bought plantations with his profits, and when
the war began he raised and equipped a battalion of cavalry at his own expense. In time, he became a hero in the
Western theater of the war, sweeping across Tennessee
and Mississippi with 6,000 men. Always at the head of his
troops, he was wounded several times and had 29 horses
shot from under him. He also committed one of the great
atrocities of the war. In April, 1864, his men took a strong
point called Fort Pillow atop a bluff overlooking the Mississippi above Memphis. It was garrisoned by 550 men,
half of them negro volunteers. Forrest massacred the negro troops. There were affidavits that they had nailed them to
the floor of the barracks which was then set afire—a bar-
barism later used by the Klan—buried some alive or shot
them in cold blood as they pleaded for mercy. Forrest was
also accused of violating a flag truce in order to make the
attack while a surrender was being negotiated. There were
charges of a later "death march" during which the fort's
officers were killed. Forrest never bothered to deny the
story. But it seemed that he was no crazy hater of black
men. He had freed his slaves in 1863.

After the war, he told his men to disband, go home in
peace and obey the law. He settled in Memphis and became president of two insurance companies and later the
president of a railroad. However fierce in battle, he was
described in private life as a mild, temperate, considerate
man. When the Klan convened at Nashville in 1867, they
turned to Forrest for leadership. He never admitted that
he was "Grand Vizier," and years later, before a Congres-
sional investigation of the Klan, flatly stated that he never
"saw the organization together in my life, never saw them
out in numbers or anything of the kind." He claimed that
his only knowledge of the Klan constitution came from a

copy he received in the mail. But he made a series of fast trips throughout the South, and wherever he went Klan activity grew and Klan terror spread where it had never existed before. In 1868, he gave a remarkably candid interview to a reporter from the Cincinnati *Commercial* who came to Nashville:

"I loved the old government in 1861. I love the old Constitution yet. I think it is the best government in the world. I am opposed only to the Radical Revolutionists who are trying to destroy it. I believe they are the worst men on earth . . . men who would stop at no crime and want only to enrich themselves."

"If Governor Brownlow of this state calls out the militia," asked the reporter, "do you think there will be resistance?"

"We will look on it as a declaration of war—because Mr. Brownlow has already issued his proclamation directing them to shoot down the Ku Klux, and he calls *all* Southern men Ku Klux."

"Why, General, we people up north see the Ku Klux as an organization which exists only in the frightened imaginations of a few politicians."

"Well, sir, there is such an organization, not only in Tennessee, but all over the South, and its numbers have not been exaggerated."

"What are its numbers, General?"

"In Tennessee there are over forty thousand. In all the Southern States about five hundred and fifty thousand men."

"What is its character?"

"It is a protective, political, military organization. The members are sworn to recognize the government of the United States. It says nothing about the government of the State of Tennessee."

"Is the organization connected throughout the state?"

"We gather lists of names that are forwarded to the grand commander of the State. We want to know who are our friends and who are not." He refused to give the name of the commanding officer, but said "I intend to kill the Radicals if the militia hunts Klansmen. Every Radical

leader is a marked man. They want the consequences to
fall on the negroes, but they can't do it. When the fight
comes, not one of them would ever get out alive."

"General, do you think that the Ku Klux has been of
any benefit to the State."

"No doubt of it. Since it's growth, the Loyal Leagues
have quit killing and murdering our people. There were
some foolish young men who put masks over their faces
and rode over the countryside frightening negroes. But orders have been issued to stop that. You may say that three
Klan members have been court-martialed and shot for vio-
lation of orders not to disturb or molest people."

"Are you a member of the Klan, General?"

"I am not. But I am in sympathy. I know they are
charged with many crimes they are not guilty of."

"What do you think of negroes voting?"

"I am opposed to it under any and all circumstances.
But I am not an enemy of the negro. We want him here
among us. He is the only laboring class we have. More
than that, I would sooner trust him than the white Scalawag or Carpetbagger."

The interview, however frank Forrest was at times, was
evasive. But every Klansman, from Forrest down to the
newest recruit, had sworn never to reveal any secrets of
the organization. He tried to give the Southern point of
view:

"The Klan is for self-protection. There were a great
many Northern men coming down here . . . Negroes
were holding night meetings, were becoming very insolent. Ladies were ravished by some of these negroes, who
were not punished." He admitted to membership in a society called "The Palefaces." The great fear of people at
that time, he said, "was that they would be dragged into
a war of the races." When asked what class of men were organized to prevent this war of races, were they rowdies
and rough men, Forrest replied, "No, sir, worthy men who
belonged to the Southern army. The others are not to be
trusted. They would not fight when the war was on them,
and, of course, would do nothing when it was over."

The first convention at Nashville drew up a set of bylaws called "A prescript of °°°". The order was deemed so secret that its name should not appear in print, and three asterisks or stars were always substituted, even in the bylaws, for the words *Ku Klux Klan*. The Prescript, a small yellowbacked pamphlet of 24 pages, was printed secretly in the offices of the Pulaski *Citizen*. Frank McCoed had become its editor.

6

THE Klan spread from Virginia and the Carolinas west to
Arkansas and Texas. Its popularity was used by enterprising
tobacco, paint and hardware companies whose prod-
ucts bore the Klan name. In some places negroes formed
Klans of their own to retaliate, but they were soon broken
up. Other men with no Klan connections found it easy to
don a Ku Klux disguise and commit violence. Often they
were motivated by the desire for personal vengeance, to
settle a grudge, then blame the Klan. It was believed that
the Radicals were guilty of using Klan disguises to burn
and harass negroes and whites, stirring up sentiment in the
North and South against the night riders. It was a time
when no one was sure who was friend or enemy.

Newspaper editors aided the Klan by publishing notices
of meetings, and printed warnings directed at Republican
politicians. The editors disclaimed any connection or sympathy with the Klan. They informed their readers that the
notices or warnings had been found tacked to the door or
slipped under. The Palmyra *Register* editor said he refused at first to print them, then found a coffin at his door
one night. He said he didn't know what to do, he had a
family to protect. But when his printer was badly beaten,

he printed the next notice that was stuck to the door with
a blood-encrusted dagger:

*THE KU KLUX KLAN ARE KALLED UPON TO
KUSTIGATE OR KILL ANY KULLERED KUSSES
WHO MAY APPROVE THE KONSTITUTION
BEING KONKOKTED BY THE KONTEMPTIBLE
KARPETBAGGERS AT THE KAPITOL!!!*

A week later there was a grisly poem that the editor apol-
ogized for. He said he had been taken out and whipped
when he first refused to print it. He said it would offend
polite ladies and frighten the young. "I didn't mind the
whipping. I could stand that, it was only pain and I knew
I'd get over it. But they told me they'd kill my wife and
children if I refused to do what they asked." People saved
the poem, pinning it up in a place where they could see it
every day. Mothers used it as a threat against unruly children, reading the poem to them, warning that the Klan
was on the watch for bad boys and girls. The men in the
Palmyra Den thought it was smart, showed people what
they were made of.

> *We're born of the night but we vanish by day,*
> *No rations have we, but the flesh of man—*
> *And love niggers best—the Ku Klux Klan;*
> *We catch 'em alive and roast 'em whole,*
> *Then hand 'em around with a sharpened pole.*
> *Whole Leagues have been eaten, not leaving a man,*
> *and went away hungry—the Ku Klux Klan;*
> *Born of the night and vanish by day,*
> *Leagues and niggers, get out of the way. . . .*

Matthew didn't like most of the new recruits, all the
rabble and riffraff, cutthroats, base and common men.
They were fierce and turbulent, whipped because they
loved to see pain and suffering, or killed simply for the
thrill. Killings like the murder of Parton had been rare,
but now the violence mounted until it was a fever. . . .
Negro tenant farmers run off the land by the Klan after

they laid in a good crop . . . a negro crippled in both legs because a white woman said he insulted her with a "How d'ye sis" . . . a white man killed because he married a mulatto girl who the Klan thought was too dark; the girl was murdered because she had married so white a man . . . the school burned because they said Southerners could educate their children at home the way they always did . . . a negro named James Le Roy had his tongue cut off and put in his pocket, then was hanged, accused of slandering a white woman. His only sin was that he was a very lightskinned man who could read and write, and was always troublesome on election days by preventing frauds on negroes . . . an Irish-born man who taught a negro school every day and a white Sunday school near Marion. The Klan took him one night, slicing off both his ears, cursing him for being "a nigger teacher that taught Sunday school and that's the worst damn thing in a white man's country." They whipped and cut him again, warning that he had three days to get out of Dickson County, but he escaped under fire, taking wounds in the shoulder and neck. He taught school the next day, then swore out affidavits against fourteen men. A United States Marshal with a military escort came to Marion to arrest the men. But they were never found and nothing was done, and the teacher was later gunned down at a railroad depot.

William Blackford was a doctor in Murfreesboro. He was a Union man before the war, but after the secession was tried for disloyalty and was saved by influential friends. He served four years as a surgeon in the Confederate army without commission, refusing to take a loyalty oath to the Confederacy. Under Reconstruction, he was elected a judge. The Klan threatened him repeatedly, but he ignored the warnings and was shot in the back on the road one night.

Abram Colby, a 52-year-old member of the state legistature from Palmyra, was taken from his house one night by thirty men and beaten until the Ku Kluxers thought he was dead. It took Colby almost a year to recover, but his daughter had died from the shock of witnessing the beating. Colby was an old friend of the Laniers and Matthew had to go along one afternoon when the family visited him. He went to live with a son in Stewart County and put his house up for sale. He went back to Palmyra once to get some keepsakes his wife had left in a hiding place behind some bricks in the fireplace. Matthew was in the party of Palmyra Ku Kluxers that followed him, locked him inside and torched the house. Behind the mask Matthew's face was an agony as he listened to Colby scream and burn to death, though one man said they "heard a shot and thought the bastard blew his brains out when he knew he was gonna roast".

The Klan paraded one night in Clarksville 200 strong. Six men suddenly broke from the ranks and rode up to the house of a white man named Ives and emptied their revolvers into the windows. Ives had been warned and sent his wife, children and servant along the corn rows into the woods. He stayed hidden in the corn crib near the house with a rifle, ready to kill some Ku Kluxers if they tried to burn him out. Ives watched as the frustrated Klansmen rode to the house of a well-known negro, but the man escaped. They turned for the house of Allen Gordon, another white man. When they found him gone, they raped his wife and ten-year-old daughter. The grabbed the bedcords and went down the road to the house of John Chavis, said they were going to hang him because he had fired at them when they were there before. Neighbors shouted that Chavis slipped out only a few minutes before the riders came. He was never seen again. Some people thought he ran away to the North, but most said the Klan killed him and threw his body into the river or buried it deep in the woods. A year later, a skeleton thought to be the remains of Chavis was found in a swamp not more than a mile from Clarksville.

The most brutal mass slaying took place in Perry County. Joe and Mary Brown were thrifty, hardworking negroes who had paid cash for a cabin and thirty acres. A white man wanted it but Joe outbid him by twenty dollars. He had no idea that he had offended every white man around. Instead, he felt pride that "a poor nigra turn

loose with only his claws at the end of the war could beat
a white man who been his own master since he was man-
grown." The couple lived with Mary's mother and younger
sister, two children, and Joe's crippled father. They
worked hard on their own place and occasionally for a
white neighbor and were full of hope.

One night Mary started out to visit a friend in the bend
of the river below her place. Instead of going the long
way around, she cut across the fields, walking along the
high brush close in to the river. About a half-mile along
she came on two men holding guns. They moved back
when they saw her and stood watching. Their faces were
black, but she spotted the white skin beneath their shirt
collars and around their wrists. Mary was frightened, but
knew the best thing was to pass them by as if she had
seen nothing. They watched silently as she passed. When
she was out of sight, she gathered up her long skirt and
ran. When she reached her friend's house she was gasping
for breath, almost laughing at her own panic.

She suddenly heard two shots from the direction where
she saw the two men. Then she heard two more shots. She
went back and saw the two disguised men examining the
body of a man. He was a deputy U.S. Marshal and she
knew him by the name of Casson. He had come across the
river in a small boat and they ambushed him as he
stepped ashore. She thought it wise not to say anything. A
short time later, a white woman neighbor asked Mary
what she had been telling about two young men—naming
the two Mary saw at the river—killing Mr. Casson. She
said she never said anything like that and swore on her
children. Two days later, some neighbors told her six-year-
old son to tell his parents that they could not live there
any more. If they did not leave the place in three days
they would be killed. Joe didn't take it seriously, thought
it was "some damn trash drunks trying to scare a little
niggra."

The Klan came at three in the morning of the fourth
day. They broke down the doors, tore the chinking from
between the logs and shoved gun muzzles into the cabin.
The family was taken out and Joe Brown was stripped

naked and thrown to the ground. A Klansman stood on the
negro's head while the others beat him with long reed fish-
ing poles and hickory whips. Then each member of the
family was stripped and beaten, even the six-year-old and
the crippled father. Trace-chains were linked tight around
their necks and they were dragged around the yard behind horses until the masked leader gave the order to stop.
He walked over to Mary.

"Who you see down the river there the day Casson
was shot?"

Naked and bleeding, she struggled to talk. "Bailey
Smith and Frank Hancock."

"That's why we came to whip you."

"I never say the names, white boss. Not till you ask.
Jesus make me know better."

"We'll kill you. Goddamn your black nigger tit."

She was picked up and kocked down, her nipples cut
off, and pistol-whipped because she kept denying that she
told the authorities, trying to get to her children. Then the
Ku Kluxers brained the seven people with clubs and
choked the life out of those still living.

But the chaos and plundering by Northern politicians
continued. Over 200,000 negroes had been given the vote
in 1867, and at least 300,000 whites had lost it or were
disqualified from holding office. The Radicals made sure
the black man was in the majority. The cost of a state
legislative session rose from $100,000 to $1 million under
the Radicals. Millions of acres of land held in trust by a
state was sold at five cents an acre—to selected purchas-
ers. In Arkansas, a negro politician billed the state and
was paid $900,000 for repairs to a bridge that had origi-
nally cost $500 to build. If a politician lost $1,000 on a
horserace, the legislature voted him for faithful and effi-
cient service for the same amount. Millions were stolen in
the manipulation of railroad bonds. Negroes were sold
land formerly owned by whites. All this was added to
grievances that occurred right after the war, swindling
that Everett was never aware of when he lectured Matthew. Treasury agents had confiscated $30 million worth

of cotton. Little of the sale money went to the government, the bulk of it stolen by the agents. And they were greedy for more. A planter was forced to sell at very low prices or see the cotton confiscated and get nothing. Tax collectors swarmed in to collect from property owners who were bankrupt. Farms and plantations were forced on the block by the tax collectors, then purchased by them at token prices. The rule of the Radicals was reinforced by the army troops, negro militia, and the constant strengthening of the Loyal Leagues that became little more than plundering militia. It was fertile soil for violence.

By the spring of 1869, the Klan was an army that occupied a territory as large as Europe. It was striking hard, but people began to fight back. Four Klan riders approaching a negro cabin under a bright moon were fired on and two men killed. The white robes that had been so effective at the start, as an apparition, a ghostly presence to superstitious negroes, were now too familiar and had become a liability, too good a target at night. The Grand Vizier visited his Realms, the states, and suggested that all Klansmen wear red or black robes. Matthew was disappointed when the Palmyra Den changed to red. He thought it made them look like any other mounted body. In the beginning he had thought of the white as purifying.

He was tired from the constant night raids, the nervous strain of sneaking in and out the house to keep his secret from his father, never knowing if he could ride King Bruce or have to rush to a livery stable to get a horse, watching or being forced to take part in the same unstinting brutality, occasionally taunted for his reluctance. He began to be haunted by the faces of victims, filled with gnawing guilt. It didn't seem that the Klan was doing much good. The bigger and more powerful it became, the more violent it became, the more resistance it met. People were arming everywhere, the militia was growing, big patrols always scouring the countryside, and there was the threat of Federal troops being pulled in by Governor Brownlow. There was talk in the Klan around the state that they had to go after the important men, cut at the heart of the Reconstruction authorities. They were talking about wholesale assasinations. It was like declaring war all over again against the Union. One night when Matthew arrived at Hope Mills, he saw Blanton, Tyler, Hoagland and Kortman talking quietly in a corner of the cellar.

Blanton said they would have to stop John Douthit, accused of being a Scalawag. But this operation would be different. To kill him at night, when he was alone, with no niggers to witness the execution, would do no good. A Democratic convention was being held in the courthouse the next day to nominate candidates for Giles County. Blanton read from the Palmyra *Register*:

" . . . Since the military usurpation took away from the people of the South the right of self-government, and made them subservient to the will of the degraded Niggers, and their infamous Carpetbaggers and Scalawags who unite with and lead them, the honest people of Giles County have had no voice in their government. They have now rightfully concluded that the time has come when they will make one more effort to control their affairs. . . ."

Kortman took over the meeting. "We hear Douthit is going to spy on the Democrats for the Yankees, help those niggers to vote. He's going to be stopped."

Matthew thought that Douthit was a man who had stood aside during all the turmoil, like his father. He had never heard any talk about the man working for the niggers. He was thankful that his father seemed interested in the problem only in a remote way, a talking way, unwilling to go against the majority of people in the County. What could Douthit gain? Matthew always thought the man was ripe with the Klan. Douthit was a big powerful man in his forties who had commanded a Corps for General Lee at the Battle of the Wilderness, attacking Union troops at the Orange-Fredericksburg Turnpike, his troops charging out of the thickets to break the enemy breastworks. He was a quiet man around town who never said a word for the niggers, Matthew thought, one of the men he idolized when he was growing up. Kortman picked the men to accompany him to the courthouse—Matthew, Billy Laidlaw, Hoagland and Grover Morehouse, all men from good family who wouldn't be suspected. But Kortman in-

cluded two new men, toughs named Cissel and Thevenow.
They were from up in the hills, a place where people were
called "Honey Creekers." A Klansman who knew them
said, "They're cousins, but one of them could kill the other
and don't need no snuff to do it. Killing's their pleasure."
Kortman turned to the rear of the platform and Matthew's
heart hammered when he saw Issac Catlin walk from the
shadows.

"Catlin's come cross river special to go," Kortman said.
"He's got the same trouble and wants to see how we do
things. That's a real honor for Palmyra."

The next morning the eight men were seated in the
courthouse when Douthit walked in. The Klan had
warned him to stay away, riding up and down in front of
his house, scattering people off the road, then left a coffin
with a notice stuck to it with a bloody dagger. Douthit
knew he was in danger, but contemptuously sniffed the
dagger and muttered "Pig's blood." A friend of Everett's,
he told him that he thought the Klan would get him before the struggle was over. But he was cautious enough to
rarely show himself on the streets, especially after dark.
Friends had tried to keep him away, but he insisted on
going, said he was needed, that the convention was going
to be a showdown to see who really ruled the County. The
morning he came to court he was heavily-armed and carrying a large sum of money, intending to put it in the bank
the next day.

The courthouse was filled with men who hated Douthit
and they gave him harsh looks. But he walked to his seat
with calm, took out a book and began making notes. The
speakers—General H. I. Pettibone, Edward Harper, and the
Honorable Braxton Liddel—stirred the crowd with fiery
speeches, then turned their attention to Douthit. They
scourged and valified him, but he just had a quiet, scornful
smile and continued taking notes as if he was sitting in his
own study. A companion whispered that they should
leave, the crowd was getting out of control. Douthit shook
his head.

"You can go. I'll stay to the end. I have to let them

know I'm not afraid to do it. And I have to know what the opposition is planning in the campaign."

He wanted to speak to some politicians who had approached him about a compromise ticket for the County. Douthit had supported Democrats in a previous election for sheriff and other offices, saying that it wouldn't be wise to put ignorant and incompetent men in such places. He said poor men owed slavery a great deal, the fact that they were kept ignorant, and they had every right to hate it as much as if they were niggers.

The two men who spoke to Douthit about the ticket said they wanted to see him privately. They met in the County Clerk's office and the door was locked. The eight Klansmen were in the room and Douthit greeted them politely, had known most of them a long time and asked Matthew about his father. He was surprised to see Cissel who had served under him and shook hands, then faced the group.

"Well, gentlemen, what do you want of me?"

Kortman later said the damned bastard looked as cool as if he was sitting on his own veranda drinking a lemon punch and being fanned by a nigger boy.

"There seem to be enough of you to do as you please," Douthit said, "so I'll ask your will and pleasure."

Howard Gillespie, one of the Democratic politicians, took a paper from his inside pocket.

"We want you to sign this."

Douthit examined the paper. It was a statement that said Douthit, as the suspected leader of the Radicals in the area had brought all the troubles to Giles County in the past few years. He had roused the niggers, burned barns and houses and blamed it on the Klan, stolen money, and was creating revolution under the direction of Radicals in Nashville.

"If you sign it and agree to leave the state in ten days, we'll let you and your family off safe and sound."

Douthit had an abusive smile. "You might kill me, but I won't sign any such paper."

Kortman glanced at Gillespie who understood . . .

*they didn't want to kill Douthit, but they had come too
far to back out now.*

"There's nothing else you can do," Gillespie said. "Sign
it right now or die like the dog you are, you nigger fucker.
Then we'll take care of your family."

The Klansmen were getting restless. Why argue with
him? The traitor wasn't going to sign, the kind of a man
who turns insanely stubborn with principle and pride.
Matthew knew that this time he wouldn't be able to avoid
anything, as he often had in the dark windy nights that
made the swirl of riders a confusion. He looked at Laidlaw
and saw that he was frightened too, his face pale and
tight. It was going to be murder in cold blood. Douthit
began shouting and Hutchenrider, the other politician,
tried to pacify him.

"Don't pay no mind to Howard. You know what a hothead he is he don't get his way. Now this is just a little
political squabble. We're reasonable men, we can make a
deal. Sign the paper, John. It don't mean a damned thing.
We just don't want any more trouble. We'll give you more
time to leave. Even send you off in grand style." He
paused for a long time. "Don't force us to extremes."

But Kortman couldn't hold back any longer and
grabbed Douthit's arm.

"You son of a bitch. You teach the niggers to vote. We
know all about you. You steal our money and give it to
them. You give them advice on how to fight against white
men. We ought to kill you for just that."

Douthit suddenly knew the men were a Klan execution
squad, leaped back and pulled a revolver. But Thevenow
caught his arm and Cissel slipped a noose around his neck
and jerked back. Douthit tried to reach for the gun in his
boot and Catlin punched him. Laidlaw motioned to Matthew and he joined the others in forcing Douthit to the
floor. Matthew kicked the gun out of his hand. Maybe
he'd sign it now that he saw they meant business. He
never believed they'd kill a well-known man in daylight in
a crowded town. Dozens of negroes were standing around
outside the courthouse, waiting for Douthit. Thevenow

pulled Douthit to his feet as Cissel drew the noose tighter.
Catlin was raging and shoved his gun into Douthit's face
but Kortman stopped him.

"This is our show. He did us bad, not you." He turned
to Douthit. "You got five minutes to live. Prepare yourself."

Douthit maddened them with his nonchalance. "I suppose I am allowed to pray." Without waiting for an answer, he kneeled and prayed for his family, his friends and
neighbors, then directed a prayer at each of the ten men
standing around him. The praying was getting a little too
passionate and Kortman gave the noose a jerk and said he
didn't want any more of that.

Douthit pretended to go limp with fear, then broke
away and tried to get to the window, but was pulled back.
Catlin grabbed a piece of firewood from the box and kept
slamming it across Douthit's leg. There was the sound of
snapping bones. They threw him on a long table. Douthit
saw that it was all over and groaned. They turned him on
his back and Cissel and Thevenow held his arms and legs.
Kortman pulled a knife, looked at Matthew, then turned
to Catlin.

"Can't deny a big Arkansas man. Here, you want blood,
get it."

Matthew couldn't help himself and shut his eyes as Catlin plunged the weapon into Douthit's throat. Blood
spurted and began to fall on the floor. They caught the
blood in a bucket and later let it out the window to men
on the outside. "Come in handy," Kortman said. They
cleaned up until there wasn't a drop of blood or any sign
of a struggle in the clerk's office. The body was jammed
into the woodbox and covered with logs. They planned to
bury Douthit under the nigger schoolhouse after dark,
then claim the niggers did it, maybe get some of them
hanged.

"Well, the son of a bitch is as dead as Julius Caesar,"
Catlin said. "I admire you boys. You don't need strangers
from another place do your work like I know in some
Dens." He thanked Kortman for the honor of the execu-

tion. "You come to Arkansas I'll get you some nigger tits to cut."

Kortman's look was murderous. "What the hell makes you think I'd torture a woman, nigger or no? This one here, he needed killing."

Gillespie kept shaking his head. "I thought he'd sign it. He was a smart politician . . . could have found a dozen ways to get out of it."

Kortman thought Gillespie was weak enough to talk if pressure was put on him. "This was your damn idea. You know why he didn't sign it and I got respect for it. It had nothing to do with nigger votes. You're right in one thing. What the hell difference if he signed a paper. But he was a Southerner, damned if the devil wasn't, and you can't run a man like that to do something he don't want to do, can't run him out of his house and town, damned if you can."

Matthew was surprised by Kortman. He didn't think the man could be fair to an enemy, make something rational out of a murder and give tribute to a dead man. Maybe that's why he let Catlin do it. He was still shaken because he thought that Kortman was going to make him kill the man.

"I was no friend of Douthit's," Gillespie said, "but I wish it was done some different way, not trapped like a coon and killed in cold blood."

"Hell, why didn't you say it before. Cissel here could have taken him in a fair fight." The thick-necked man looked proud as Kortman clapped him on the back. "Whole County's yelling for someone to get rid of Douthit. Now we do it and you put on the sad old widow face. It ain't too damn encouraging for us who take the risk. Maybe the next thing you do is go and tell on us . . . like you and Douthit were just talking some politics and we came and did him in."

Gillespie was quick to reassure him that he and Hutchenrider were as guilty as anyone and they had to stick together. They waited until dark and left by the window, then mixed with the crowd around the courthouse.

* * *

When Douthit didn't return home by suppertime, his wife called to some passing negroes and asked if the meeting was over.

"Yes, mama. Long time now."

"Did you see my husband, Mr. Douthit?"

"No, mam."

The woman suddenly began to sob and became hysterical.

"They've killed him! I knew it! I pleaded with him to give up and leave here. Why didn't he listen to me. Oh, my God, they've killed him!"

She collapsed on the steps and the negroes carried her inside the house. A neighbor was told about it and went through the town asking if anyone had seen Douthit after the courthouse meeting. One man said he saw him in a certain place, another saw him somewhere else, a third remembered a friend of his saying that he saw Douthit heading north out of town. Reports spread that he was missing; then people began to say that he had been killed. Douthit had a tremendous hold on the negroes, and those on the street who had heard the rumors became frightened and prayed. More negroes crowded into the street and there was a loud keening sound of mourning, moans, threats and curses shouted as the crowd surged toward the courthouse. They never questioned that Douthit was dead. He had been marked for death for a long time because he had helped them.

"Come on," shouted one of the negro leaders. "The body is in the courthouse or around. Them murdering Kluckers hide the body."

White men who had been at the meeting, but knew nothing of the murder, gathered in small groups down the street and talked quietly. They said nothing hostile to the negroes, offered no aid, but didn't ridicule the idea that Douthit was dead. Afraid of what might happen, they began to drift away as the excitement grew more intense. The crowd swelled and within an hour or two almost a thousand negroes surrounded the courthouse. A group went in and searched every unlocked room. The custodian said keys to some of the rooms were lost and some men

wanted to break the doors down, but the leader said they
would be lawful and led them out. Some white people
came through the crowd, Douthit's companion in the
courthouse and Judge Darcy at their head.

"Now what's all this commotion?" Darcy said.

"We know Mr. Douthit he dead in there," a negro said.

"Nonsense. Mr. Douthit told me he was going to Dunboro tomorrow. Maybe he decided to leave tonight."

"That right," said one of Douthit's negro aides. "He tole
me he going there."

"He probably just wanted to get a good start so he
could do his business bright and early and return to his
family."

"He didn't tell his wife," Douthit's friend said. "That's
not like him. Poor woman's going crazy. Last time I saw
him he went off with Howard Gillespie. We should talk to
him."

Darcy stroked his silky beard. "You know John
Douthit." He tried to reassure them with a smile. "He
doesn't talk much except when he gets up on the stump
and then you can't shut the windbag up. He probably just
up and went to Dunboro."

"She thinks he's dead."

The negroes said that it was true, that the Klan had
murdered him.

Darcy had the same fear but he was trying to prevent a
riot.

"That's nonsense. All of you go home now." He touched
the shoulder of some of the older negroes. "Now Trask
. . . you Sam . . . you should all know better . . . this
is folly. You're old friends and neighbors, I want to save
you from trouble."

"Judge, sir, you be no friend of mine," said Trask, a
man in his late sixties with skin like fine parchment. He
fixed his yellow rheumy eyes on Darcy. "And we be no
neighbors, Mr. Judge Hugh Darcy, less you call it neighbors with me slaving for your family from the day I was
borned until I was made free."

"You were always treated well, Trask. I had my eye out
for you all the time when I was big enough. Even now,

I'm trying to teach you the right thing." Darcy hated talking that way, but he was trying to keep passions down.

"You can teach me where they put Mr. Douthit. That all the teaching I want off you."

A young negro stepped between Darcy and Trask. "Judge, you talking to the wind. We gonna find Mr. Douthit, dead or alive, and likely dead."

Fires were lit and a line of guards was put around the courthouse. Clambering from one window ledge to another, a few men tried to peer into locked rooms, but their torchlight bounced off the panes and they only caught a momentary glimpse of a patch of floor. It was getting late but the crowd grew bigger. Negroes were coming in now from all around the County, on horse and mule, packed into wagons, many walking toward the fires that were like beacons.

White people watching from their windows were afraid the crowd would begin to riot if Douthit didn't turn up. Men went for hidden weapons, locked their women and children in a back bedroom, a storehouse or cellar, and stayed wary . . . *niggers were barbarous and emotional, a herd of dumb beasts that could suddenly break and stampede, rape and kill, slaughter every last one of them.* But the negroes stood quietly most of the night, doing everything by the law. They didn't approach or talk to any whites still on the street or go near their houses. They searched for the missing keys everywhere, but no locks were broken and there was no violence. But they were sure Douthit was inside, dead or dying. They called out his name and were met by utter silence.

Kortman and a few Klansmen were still hanging around the hotel. He watched, angry with himself for not taking Douthit's body out with them. Then he realized that there were too many negroes by then. It was stipid to kill a man like that in a public place in the daytime. He wondered how Gillespie could have convinced Blanton to do it. He had argued with the General but was told to follow orders, then had to put on a brave show when he organized the execution squad. But he'd been crafty and knew they could throw the blame on Catlin, a stranger, if it came to a showdown . . . *walked in on private political talk and killed a Palmyra man in cold blood, and for what reason other than he was crazy, Kortman couldn't say.* That was the way he rehearsed it in his mind, and didn't feel a traitor or ignoble. He looked out at the crowd again. Klan murders were often done to terrorize, but he saw that the negroes weren't cowed this time. Instead, it had given them courage.

The negroes waited and watched through the night of a warm spring rain and no one slept. At first light, the crowd began to move restlessly around the courthouse. The sun was coming up fast when a young man mounted on another's shoulders and looked inside the County Clerk's office. They had searched it the day before but found nothing. Shading his eyes with one hand, he scanned the dim-lit interior. Nothing seemed out of place . . . a desk and three chairs, a high wood cabinet, a Union flag, a small bookcase, pictures of former mayors on the wall, a long table and a firewood box. He was about to jump down when he thought he saw something—part of the brim of the beige felt hat Douthit always wore sticking out between logs in the woodbox. Two logs had fallen to the floor after they left the Clerk's office the previous evening, dislodged when they ran through the halls, desperate to find Douthit. He looked again and was sure.

The crowd lost all restraint about breaking in. Husky men kicked and battered the door until it splintered and flew off its hinges. They rushed in and saw Douthit's body doubled over in the woodbox under the logs. They threw the wood aside and saw the noose cutting deep into the neck. As they carried him to the table a man spotted the stab wound in the throat. There was no blood anywhere in the room. But Trask, a plantation butcher in the old days, said the knife had cut an artery and that made a lot of blood. Douthit's open eyes bulged, as bloated and popping as a frog's.

7

It was still early evening when Matthew came home from the courthouse that day. He looked in the study to the side of the hall and saw his father sleeping in an old horsehair chair. Matthew watched him for a few moments and knew he was having bad dreams. Everett's mouth fluttered and twitched. It had happened too often to him since the war. His mind escaped the hobbles when he was conscious, when he made stoicism a virtue, and swiftly yielded to a frieze of images that unloaded hell—a vivid scheme of battle, nightmares of what had happened to his command . . . the girded silence of cavalry on foot slipping through a dark mist, leading their horses with one hand over the animal's snout to keep it quiet . . . then the squall of gunfire and green clumsy legs sprawled along the blossoming trees . . . figures in long perspective . . . The muffled clap of an explosion, then Everett suddenly staring at his arm lying a yard away in a bush, and he had felt nothing more than if he had been punched or hit sharply with a stick . . . the methodical way he took the severed arm in his good hand and carried it back to regimental headquarters until he fell unconscious from loss of blood. He re-viewed the deaths and mutilations in slow-motion with terror-filled images of gigantic Yankee soldiers playing the deft, deadly butchers.

Matthew went up to see Adela. It had become a ritual whenever he returned from a night ride. He never told her anything about what had happened, and she never pressed him, sensing that he could shed a little of his guilt and anxiety by being with her. He needed the familiar surroundings, her softness, the smell and charm and memories of her room and person to make him feel human again, ordinary. His mother stopped him on the stairs, always eager to hear about who had been punished or driven away. He tried to pass her without a word, but she took his arm and made him nervous as she always did by smoothing his hair, chatting about how filthy her boy was. He was suddenly afraid he might have blood on him. She wanted him to be a thug and murderer in a righteous cause and still look like he was a young gentleman returning from a lawn social.

"Where were you?"

"No place particular."

"Was there any excitement?"

"No, I was fooling around with Kortman and a couple of those boys."

"Why do you have to be with people like Kortman?"

Matthew stiffened and he stared at her, puzzled because she knew how important Kortman was, angry that she was putting on those damn social airs of hers, snobbery that was just an old response, still pushing him about their class, how important they were, and how he should avoid riffraff.

"What do you have against Kortman? Seems his father had money and a high place in town."

"He's a rowdy, that's all. I thought you would be riding with gentlemen."

He wanted to tell her that Kortman was a damn sight more than a rowdy, a cruel bastard who could murder easy. He started to laugh. God, she was crazy. He had rid himself of most of the sentimentality by now, and he'd had to see a lot of meanness and blood and suffering to learn it. She seemed to be stuck back somewhere in the

first days of the war . . . when young bloods from the
plantations rode off adorned with flowers in their hats
and epaulets, bright yellow sashes girding the splended
tunics, swords waving, riding the best horses in the
County, the big mounts rearing in lordly combat thrusts
with their front legs, as if they were medieval warhorses
trampling archers and soldiers on foot, the men shouting,
drinking toasts, boasting how they would be home in a
few weeks after licking the Yankees good, then riding off
silhouetted against the sun in a great whirl of pale dust
. . . like a painting, he always thought.

"I want to see Adela on her birthday."

"That's tomorrow. Come with me to your room."

Matthew pulled away and went up the stairs. Jessie
watched him until he went through the girl's door, a
clamped, jealous look on her face. Adela greeted him casually, trying to make the visit seem innocent, a chance
encounter, as if he was passing the door and absent-
mindedly walked in just to exchange some local gossip.

"Mama's going to drive me crazy."

"What is it now?"

"Still that talk about gentlemen and rough men. She
was the one who helped me get into this. Sometimes I
think it was her idea. She knew who the men were. Now
she suddenly starts in about Kortman, how I shouldn't ride
with him." He managed an ironic little smile. "He could
have killed me for that. I've seen him do horrible things.
He's either crazy for any kind of blood, nigger or white, or
else he was always just mean. But I don't remember him
that way before all this."

"You always looked up to him. You always talked about
him, hung around the hotel so you could be near him. It's
nothing bad . . . he fascinated a lot of people. You were
probably too young, but do you remember what he looked
like before he was burned like that?"

"Maybe, I don't know."

"I'll tell you. He was the boldest-looking, handsomest
man you ever saw. I was about fifteen when he came
home once during the war, and I had ideas about him in
those days. But mama always kept me away, said it wasn't

right—'seemly' she always said—for me to talk to such a man."

"What was he like then?"

"He had a way about him, always dressed in the finest clothes from New Orleans tailors. Rose Duncan remembers him better than I do from before the war. She said that everyone thought he was just too flashy a man, too easy with the women. But he was quiet too and he liked to read poetry she said. A year or two before the war he came home from Sewanee college, before he went off to Blount, and there was a lot of talk about him and a professor's wife. They're still *always* talking about him and someone's wife. He was going to study medicine, but after he came back from Blount, he just played around until the war came."

Matthew tried to sound sly. "How come you know so much about him?"

"Something you'll learn, little brother. If a man has a hold on a girl, there isn't anything she wouldn't do to be around him and know all about him."

"You ever see him alone?"

Adela curled up on the bed and looked at him for a long time before she spoke.

"I could tell you a secret . . . two secrets you can call it. God, how I've wanted to tell someone. But I think you're still too much the courtly young Southerner. You'd want to do something stupid about it . . . talk about avenging honor and pork like that."

"I wouldn't. I swear."

He had no idea of what she would say, but her teasing talk had made him forget all about Douthit, made his nerves tingle with the possibility of a secret that might link them closer. He looked at her in the half-shadow of the lamp, the russet hair and green eyes, the elegant way she draped the nigiligee about her, and thought she wanted to challenge him with something dangerous. *For whom?* Often when he saw her like that, he thought of stories about bad blood in families, sisters and brothers caught in an attic room, mothers and sons murdered. He felt as if he was at the edge of dark swampy woods, afraid of taking a false step that might take him back into the dismal trees, but aware that he had to be bold to save himself. He had never seen her look that way, afflicted, tense, wishing to confess or do something because it would be solace.

"You let me talk to you, and I trust you. Don't you trust me?"

"I don't trust anyone." He saw tears. "Wait a minute." She went out on the landing and listened, crept halfway down the stairs and saw her father still asleep. She heard Jessie walking around her room. She returned to Matthew and locked the door.

"Maybe it's fair to tell you. It would explain a lot. Maybe if you knew something terrible about this family, you'd have something to hold over our heads. You wouldn't be at our mercy." She saw his look. "Yes, you are. Even if you're a big Ku Klux. It isn't papa. It's something mama and me know about each other. So far, we just talk past it. It's never mentioned. But don't you see anything strange about us?"

Matthew shrugged. "It's like she's jealous of you."

She patted him on the head. "Maybe little brother isn't so dumb. Why do you think she's always hugging and kissing you, makes you walk out with her, always cooing and talking about how loving her son is to her."

"I'm sick of it. She makes it like I'm her beau."

"And she treats papa like he's an old piece of furniture. Didn't you ever wonder why?"

He looked as if he didn't much care. He was too young to understand the passions she would tell him about. He would suffer, but Adela was determined to speak about something that had been hidden too long. If everything was disintegrating, she wanted to prepare him, make him strong, make him understand the lure of one person for another: the slope of haunches, the way bones were hinged, the look of eyes in a face, the excitement that killed reason, glints and hues, the length of limb, the smell of hidden lewdness . . . the way men preyed on women like foxes on rabbit, the way women wanted to taste something of a man's freedom and strength, the way they were

prey that willed their own capture, the fascination of ruthless people. She almost held back at the last moment.
When she looked at Matthew before she told the story,
she experienced for the first, terrible, never-to-return time,
the sweet and destructive joy of pity. She was going to
have to break his heart, destroy any illusions.

"I don't want you doing things for us in the Klan because you think we're the fair flower of Southern woman-
hood, I don't want you to have any false memories of this
house."

It was at a cornhusking the first year after the war.
There was a good crop and everyone was happy that there
would be something besides the gristly hamback and
greens they called skunk cabbage because of the smell.
Half the town was celebrating at Dewey Hatton's cornfield. Kortman came and stayed on the edge of the crowd.
His scarred face made him mysterious to Adela, but vulnerable, melancholy, less remote than the cavalier she remembered. He had been strange when he first returned.
He had a long beard—to cover something of his maiming,
everyone said—though there were bald patches, and wore
only a scarf over his uniform in most weather. On bitter
days he put on a hacked-off piece of rug, rigged like a
cape on his shoulders, and held in place by laces and
flaps. He held his tall figure straight, the bare head of
thick rumpled hair slewing this way and that with his long
strides. Kortman still had the sharp, hungry profile, but
the arrogant look was dissipated in pain.

Then, within a month, he began to wear good clothes
again, the clawhammer coat, a low-crowned and wide-
brimmed panama straw, a cream-colored waistcoat of silk
or cashmere, flawlessly clean shirt and simple black stock.
His tight striped trousers that flared at the bottom and
had a sling to catch a heel were years out of style, but
Kortman wore them stuffed in his boots. Adela went out
of her way after school to pass him on the street and they
flirted innocently. She met him once at a social, but he sat
in a corner most of the time, looking glum or bored, and
she didn't want to approach him. But she watched while

the others danced and swore that he was talking to her, pulling her to him.

During the husking, Adela said to him that it was remarkable that so many niggers had come to help. Would they be given a share?

"I don't want to live on black sweat any more," he said. "I wouldn't want to live at all that way. It was a terrible mistake and we paid for it."

She later remembered that he said it, and never understood what had changed him, made him a Lucifer in his own dark hell. Many times she thought it was the scars that made him bitter, but knew it was just melodrama. Other men had been marked much worse and came back the same. He was like an actor who storms and rages onstage in a villain's role, then strolls into the wings and drops the mask, becomes reflective and solemn. It had to be something deeper. Was it because he was so far from what he was intended to be. . . ?

"Selling and buying people like they were stock . . . that was the old way."

"But you sold Shaddy," she said, referring to a young Kortman smiled. "Do you feel sorry for Shaddy, or were

"That was different." He shifted his feet, agitated. "Sometimes, you have to do things you don't want to do."

"But you wanted to."

Kortman smiled. "Do you feel sorry for Shaddy, or were you jealous of her?"

"The hell with you."

"How old are you?"

"Going on seventeen."

Kortman pulled her to him. "You know what was going on. Every bullhorny bastard around here was doing her. Shaddy had to go someplace where I knew the people, knew she'd be taken care of."

"She was carrying?"

"And no one knew who the pap was. She wouldn't say. Probably didn't know."

"Might have been you."

"Listen, you smart little rusthead. There are two things a gentleman shouldn't do. Fuck a nigger woman or a sin-

gle woman above his station." He was amused because she
was trying to look casual. "I haven't done either."

"Not from what I hear."

"But I might just do one of them today."

They began to stroll toward the woods. He liked her
because she showed no shock, no snotty, pouty face like
another woman would. The tall coltish girl was smiling,
her pale green eyes had a crazy shine, and her hair
glowed red in the low sun slipping down between the
trees, tipping out in a squashed fiery ball on Whitlock
Mountain. He pulled her deep into the woods and they
embraced. She pressed against him, murmuring "*Wicked
man* . . . wicked *man* . . . . She began to kiss him pas-
sionately, touching his face. He stopped her hand short of
the scars, but she forced his hand away and he relented,
allowing her to caress the ravaged flesh. She kissed and
licked it, then reached for his pants.

"Where the hell a strip like you learn that kind of
thing?" He put her at arm's length and looked at her and
laughed. She had a mocking smile. Kortman thought she
would be all kinds of trouble, that he was making a mistake.

"Could you love me?" she pleaded.

"You'd be a bad choice." Then he thought it was a mistake to speak of a bad choice in love, since as soon as a
choice was made, it could only be bad.

"You could come to love me."

"I don't think so. I like you. I want you. . . ."

"Even if I didn't love someone to begin with, and I
did what I want to do with you, I know I'd come to love
him after a time. I'd have to," she said as if willing it.

"Maybe we're talking too much." Without even touching he could sense the wetness between her legs.

She stood under a far outriding branch of oak, her ravished face and a few wisps of hair turned away the last
searching light.

"I'll confess something," she said. "I think about you all
the time. I think about making love to you. I wanted you
for years. You made me wet and hungry when I was just
getting my woman-blood. Someimes it's only after years

that you get some shape on things. Sometimes I'd find my fingers reaching out, and I'd wonder what they were reaching for, and then I'd realize they were reaching for your skin. I often have a dream, that we're like two marchers in a parade who strut off on their own, leave all the ranks behind, and skip around in the deep dirty grass and poison weeds."

He didn't understand the metaphor, the fable she'd made up on the spot. But he knew it was a ferocious attraction for both of them. He tried to say something, but his voice sounded so awkward and crabbed that he felt bells should mock the still air. She had hunted him with cunning, and he was going to make love to her right there in the grass and weeds and deep shadows of the woods. What they might have could be madness, but a lunacy so ordinary it bored him. She was a little crazy, or stupid. No, not stupid. But in the end, despite her proud and furious passion, she'd stir in the worst sentimentalities . . . the sacrifice to aristocratic piety . . . kill him with guilt. The role didn't fit him. But he wasn't going to wait patiently for her to grow into a woman. He'd risk the scandal, wait for some halfwit obsessed by honor to ambush him for soiling a 16-year-old.

Her face looked triumphant, then languid as she leaned against a tree, both hands pulling through her hair, her eyes drowsy. He kissed her, fumbling between her legs, but she broke away, her voice strangled. *Not here. Not like this. I swear I want you, but not like this.* She ran her hands over his face, talking urgent nonsense to distract him, until he began to laugh. But there was no more resistance. She bent so nicely to the ground, he thought, smelling the sweet breath of her thigh, and began to make love to her . . . making plans for his escape. However obsessed he was with her at the moment, he couldn't give her any power, and he was rough with her, shrewd enough from the start to know that one might kill the other in time if they stayed together. Her lean springly body was locked around his, the eyes and hair vivid smears against her face. Her eyes rolled back and all he could see was the disordered nest of reddish hair and the distorted perspective of chin and lower lip and nostrils. Her breathing began slowly mounting in tempo until she pleaded with almost spastic hands. *You're so smart . . . just like this . . . perfect, perfect . . . .*

It was his own flaw that made Adela fascinating to him. Every woman he'd known was prey to his elaborate ruses, gingerbread constructions of charm and evasiveness, and a quick intuition that kept him a step ahead of being unmasked. He thought it ironic that the burned face had helped him, made sympathy quicker. Women excused ordinary weaknesses easier. He barely had to convince a woman that he could never live normally and they capitulated, later leaving in a quiet, despairing, romantic sorrow.

But from his few encounters with Adela, the way she talked that day, he knew she'd seen through him from the start, sometimes making eerie revelations to him about himself. He'd always lived with a disease that crippled any hope of permanence; whoever he was with, wherever he was, he wanted to be with someone else, someplace different. It was the reason he had welcomed the fever and excitement of war, the imperative to stand or run, the confusion and fear of battle. She stripped away his rage and contempt for the world with an artless honesty, and rejected the idea that she was too young . . . artists are born to their art.

They made love again until they were exhausted, but it was like formalized mimicry of the first moments. He thought she was trying to make him overcome his morbid self-pity by her wild surrender. He remembered his first look at his burns in a piece of broken mirror . . . ugly strips of parched flesh, like lava oozing from a crater wall, covering the left side of his face, the eyebrow burned off and his eye and lips tugged out of shape, the way he pulled and felt the pain like distant fire, fearing that he would be the town monster. He stared down at Adela. Her beauty and wit, her quick show of desire for him, made no difference. That lust of hers would make everything life or death. She was the kind of girl who wanted life to be a long, happy, dreamlike excitement, imposing her own cadences. She once explained it to him.

"I love parties, socials, balls. Not for the people. They can die for all I care. But it's a new world for the evening, like a play where no one knows the ending. You know it's only pretending, making yourself up to be someone else just for a little while."

He remembered being puzzled, had never heard anyone, least of all a young girl, talk that way. She saw his confusion and said he was dumb. "Don't you see? We know we're supposed to be a lot of wonderful things . . . full of joy, interesting, passionate, beautiful. But most people aren't. Look at the kind of drab people in town. But at a party you can pretend you're all of those things, at least for one night."

Kortman suddenly smelled dead animals in the woods, the sour stink of weeds. He rolled off her but she grabbed for him.

"Please! Come back!"

"Get up."

"Please . . . get back inside me . . . fill me that way . . . ."

"What the hell do you think I am, a goddamn bull."

"Please . . . ."

"You crazy bitch, get up!" He squeezed her arms. "It was Shaddy. I loved Shaddy. But my father wanted me to be respected . . . said he'd kill her if I didn't quit. I offered to take her west where no one knew us, maybe people wouldn't care so much. Then he told me that Shaddy was my uncle's brood. It was bad enough her being half-nigger, he said, but she was my cousin. I said I didn't care and made him promise to keep her until I got back. Then I got a letter from him that they were going to sell her. There was nothing I could do, that's what I thought then. I didn't sell Shaddy. My father did. But there was so much talk about her, I took the blame. People thought if he sold her, she might be carrying his child. Those bad things I told you about her . . . it was all lies."

Adela was shaking. "But you must have bedded half the women in town."

"That was a way of hiding things. When I came home

looking this way, I didn't look for her, thought she wouldn't want me. But I know different now."

"I'd be the same for you."

He shook his head, tried to tell her that they had shared nothing but pleasure, and no two people's pleasure could be the same for long. "All the time I'd be looking for Shaddy. I'm always looking. But even if she was gone for good . . . dead. . . ." He kissed her breat gently. "You're going to be too much for most men . . . too proud, too smart, and the worst is you like what you think are bad men. I was able to love someone soft. You're dangerous game to trap. Take it from an old hunter."

"You know what Rose Duncan says about you . . . says you're a gambler trying to be a saint. What does she mean?"

He liked that, had always trusted to luck and circumstance of the moment. But he thought that if you trust to luck, you're impotent. Because if you lose, you can blame the world for its indifference, its cruelty. He admitted that he was afraid of failure, humiliation—his face was the ultimate humiliation and he had failed at everything but being a good soldier until he began to ride with the Klan—and his defenses and fears often made him ridiculous. He suddenly grew tired of berating himself. After a time no emotion seemed to matter, he thought; it became a way of passing time, or making time pass without going mad. It was only the *idea* of, say, happiness or its absence, that distressed him. But if he had lost everything, he wanted somehow to make amends for the loss.

He warned himself not to trust that noble voice, working off his demeaning self-hate in a sloppy travesty of being a redeemer, saving the South. He didn't know what he was. Too many parts of him had been left in different places and times, like a foreign country to him now, and he saw that however far and fast he fled, how much he squandered himself in violence, he could never manage to escape from anything. He was caught on endings, and instead of regenerating himself with something new, he was always stuck in the haunting Southern past, where all endings vanished forever. And no one guessed the absurdity of the heart he was encumbered with.

Long after that day at the husking, Adela thought she understood something of his turmoil, sensed that Kortman had a hunger for involvement with something beautiful and desirable. But it had little to do with sex. It was an attempt, desperate at times, to hook into the warming density of a world beyond war and blood, beyond the isolation she thought he felt because of his mangled face.

But she never knew, no one did, how he was really hurt. He had been taken prisoner at Petersburg, Virginia, late in 1864. But he hadn't been wounded in "glorious battle," as people said. He was an anonymous victim among thousands in a terrible disaster on the Mississippi river.

On april 24, 1865, the steamboat *Fatima* put in at Cairo, Illinois, carrying cargo and about 100 passengers. Captain J. C. Guthrie was to pick up Confederate prisoners, freed and going home. Guthrie hoped there wouldn't be too many men. He had a legal limit of 376, including his crew. But he knew he'd have to stretch the rules a little. The big sidewheeler eased into its berth, smoke and sparks shooting from her giant twin stacks and whistles blasting in the night. Almost before he tied up, Guthrie saw endless lines of men walking toward the *Fatima* down a torchlit road, shouting and singing and joking. As the first men broke out on deck in the glare of the boatlights, he saw their feverish, gaunt faces, many pocked with disease sores, crippled, arms or legs missing, starving and sick men.

Guthrie asked a Union officer how many men he was expected to take. The officer said he had orders to get them all down-river to Tennessee, Mississippi and Louisiana for discharge as soon as possible, and Guthrie would have to take as many as the ship would hold. The crew tried to maintain some order, but the ex-prisoners filled the hurricane deck, then the lower deck, and soon were pouring on to the boiler deck. They jammed into every corner of the streamer: hull, cabins, Texas deck, even the pilothouse. As

Guthrie watched, helpless, the engineer told him that the boilers were leaking. He thought he could use this as an excuse not to continue the journey, but when he heard the shouting, he thought he'd have a riot and ordered a repair gang to work on the boilers. They were fixed and when the *Fatima* cast off and left the lights of Cairo behind, there were about 2,300 people aboard—seven times more than the boat was designed to carry.

For a time the *Fatima* traveled slowly, but with no sign of trouble. On the evening of April 26, she steamed into Memphis. Some passengers debarked and cargo unloaded. Another leaky boiler was discovered but the repair gang fixed it and there was no delay in the midnight sailing. The *Fatima* crossed the river to take on coal. The engineer said one of the four boilers was acting up again. Guthrie ordered makeshift repairs and gave strict orders that only the crew be told. The *Fatima* headed back into the river. The current buffeted the big steamer and the wheezing, tired boilers fought to push the abnormal load against the choppy water. About 2 A.M., a master's mate on a river gunboat, lying just above Wold Creek near Memphis, saw the lights of the *Fatima*. Then he saw the lights disappear behind a group of islands known as "Paddy's Hens and Chickens," then turned to scan the river below the city.

Moments later he was stunned by the force of a deafening noise—the *Fatima's* leaking boilers had exploded under the mounting steam pressure with a blast that split the sky and was heard nine miles back in Memphis. Red-orange flame boiled and soared into the sky, lighting up the river for miles around with a stabbing column of fire. There was another convulsive roar that broke the steamboat apart. Hundreds of sleeping soldiers were thrown into the dark cold water, and with the flailing bodies went great chunks of twisted machinery, railing, deck beams and cabin furniture. Hot coals rained out, sputtering and hissing as they hit the water, smashing into men trying to clear the steamboat.

Fire broke out on board and snaked into the middle section with furious speed. The *Fatima* began to list and a stampede of men leaped into the water to escape the in-

ferno. The superstructure of the ship collapsed and there
was a huge hole in the hurricane deck. Kortman was in a
mob of screaming men trapped by fire and falling timber.
He felt his face flaming, the flesh melting and dripping,
and leaped into the river. Some of the men in the water
were too weak to fight the cold current and gave up and
went under. Kortman didn't know where shore was—the
river was three miles wide at that point—and swam in aimless circles until he felt his strength giving out. But he
made it to shore, stumbled inland, and was almost
drowned in the flooded countryside. He reached high
ground and watched boats steaming toward the burning
Fatima.

The great twin stacks shuddered and crashed to the
deck, pinning men until fire silenced their shrieks. Sec-
tions of the stacks smashed into men trying to stay afloat
in the river and killing them. A strange cry, like a primitive death chant, broke out among the men trapped on
board. They had escaped death in a dozen bloody battles,
survived the prison camps, and now there woud be no re-
lease. The *Fatima* turned into the current and the wind
blew the fire toward the bow where the last survivors
were singed off like flies on a wall. She was carried close
to shore and struck a small island. The fire began to die,
but there was a sudden loud hissing and a gigantic column
of smoke and steam and the *Fatima* sunk.

Survivors were spotted all along the river downstream
from Memphis and rescued. Parties searched the flooded
lowlands, and every available boat from Memphis and
other river towns put out to pick up the dead and dying.
Mile after mile of the river gave more terrible evidence of
the tragedy: bloated bodies—it was the time that Kortman,
despite his pain, noticed that women floated face down,
buttocks up and awash because that was the fattest part;
men floated face up, just sky-staring—carcasses of mules,
pigs and horses, caps and shreds of uniforms, severed
limbs, headless torsos, bits and pieces of the doomed
steamer, and everywhere the smell of death and decay.

Kortman was one of 542 men and 2 women rescued
and taken to hospitals in Memphis. About 400 died soon

after. For many days a disaster barge went out every morning to search for the bloated corpses. At night, a somber group watching at river edge, it returned to Memphis with its grisly cargo. Then the river was combed for the last time. About 2,000 men had died. The disaster received little attention. The nation's mind was fixed on the end of the bloody civil war. The Union Army wasn't anxious to publicize the accident with a new President in office, and the influential eastern newspapers ignored it with only mention in its commerical column about the great loss to the steamboat's owner. But while he recovered, Kortman thought he had been kept alive for a reason. He had nightmares that the Yankees had put them aboard to slaughter them. He would make someone pay for it.

They returned to the cornfield and Kortman left Adela without saying a word. She walked away with a pretense of ease, that it meant little to her, glad she hadn't nagged him to stay. A few minutes later she saw her mother talking to him, but she turned back to the crowd. Lanterns hung from poles and tree limbs. Then musicians were over at the side, one real fiddle and a makeshift fiddle with horsehair strings that gave a ghastly note, a man who beat on an overturned tub, a man with clap-bones that were lengths of beef-rib held between the fingers to snap and rattle with the music. Negroes were gathered in a big circle, with the whites on the edge. Balanced on a heap of unshucked corn was a big fine-looking old negro, blue-black and shining in the face, with a long black coat and a red neckerchief, and a voice like a melodious bull. He tossed down the corn still to be shucked and yelled out songs to be sung, and his voice rode over all the other voices and music. He was the "Corn General." And all the time jugs of whiskey went round and round.

When the last ear was shucked and divided, the negroes receiving a fair share, the Corn General let out a whoop. Men rolled out two barrels and placed a springy board across the tops between them. A man and woman got up, facing each other, and began to dance at a clattering pace while the board bounced and the crowd yelled and sang:

Step it Jabby, step it higher
Old Tennessee never tire
Heel and toe, ketch-a-fire!

Then with elaborate apologies they grabbed Everett, lifted him high above to crowd, jubilating and shouting. Adela was afraid for her father, afraid of his balance on the board if he tried to dance, his embarrassment. But he seemed to be enjoying himself as they bounced and jounced him, and to her surprise he was laughing, probably a little drunk. It was the first such celebration she could remember in years, not since the first great victories of the war. Everett was passed from hand to hand as the negroes sang:

Ride Ole Massa
Ride him high
If he give me whiskey
I be drunk till I die!

A woman near Adela said, "Did he give them poor negras whiskey to make them work all this time?"

"They didn't have to come to the husking if they didn't want to. They're free. It was a party and corn for all . . . white men worked."

A negro girl broke in. "It prove we be no slave no more that a massa can make work with drink."

"No," Adela said. "He just wants them to have a good time."

A gaunt, swart, untidy man spoke in a clear cold voice. "Was your father a good master? If so, he was the most dangerous."

"My father never held slaves. He always treated black folks good."

"Master or no master, good man or not, the man who treats negroes with kindness is their worst enemy. Indulgence rivets the shackles. His affection corrupts their hearts." Then man's splay-jointed fingers pulled a Bible from the pocket in the tail of his coat. "Love must be scourged in the truth we find only in the Book."

His accent marked him as someone from one of the border states, Kentucky or Kansas. They were often the quickest to punish Southerners because they had been treated so harshly themselves by Confederate soldiers and guerillas. Kortman was attracted by the people crowding around Adela and pushed the man away, calling him a "damn jackleg preacher." The stranger walked off into the darkness, quoting scripture. Kortman tried to comfort her, but she pushed him away and rushed off.

Jessie saw her husband still dancing and fooling with some old black men he had known since he came to Palmyra. They were laughing at his clumsy attempts to dance, his stub waggling in time to the fiddles, and held him upright, but careful to be respectful. It was the only time Jessie had ever seen him drunk and garrulous. She watched until Everett passed out and was placed on a pile of corn to sleep it off, then took Kortman's arm and asked him to escort her home. He didn't at first believe what he was going to do. But her look told him he was right. Without any curlicue evasion or manners he suggested that it might be safer in another town, then softened it by saying casually that there were some Yankee soldiers in the area who might have been attracted by the noise and lights. She looked over at Everett.

"Is Cumberland all right?"

"Just right. I know a place."

"Wait," Jessie found old Miss Dyess and said she would take her home, that she looked poorly. Kortman thought Jessie was smart, a ready excuse, and a dimwitted crone who maybe wouldn't remember whether he was along or not. They dropped Miss Dyess off at her house a few yards from the Carlisle-Cumberland crossroads. Kortman whipped the horse around up the Carlisle road and stopped in front of a ruined old house. Jessie asked who owned it.

"That's Lily Pittman's place."

"A friend of yours?"

He had a malicious grin. "You might say it. That's the town whorehouse."

"No. Not there."

"There isn't a better place. You want it that bad, this is the place to hide." He looked at her. A maddle-aged lady, but, he had to admit, as handsome a woman as he'd ever seen. Adela was young and tart and tall and lank and smoky passion just blossoming; this one was golden ripe. He thought she might be the kind of woman he'd heard about and never believed . . . excited by broken or disfigured men.

"We'll have to get back quickly. Can this woman be trusted?"

"Don't worry. She'll never know you. Lily ain't been out of the house in twenty years . . . about the last time it was painted."

The gate sagged and the path was overgrown with weeds, except for a narrow portion in the middle that was worn thin. Jessie held back, but Kortman put his arm around her and touched her breast.

"No one here knows you. Even if they did, they've seen quality here before."

"Not a woman."

"What the hell's the difference?" He was impatient. "That's part of their business, keeping their mouth shut about what they see." He started to whip the horse up.

"No. It's all right."

He thought she had come with him because she saw him going off with Adela, didn't want to stop them because she wanted something to happen. Maybe bad blood between them. Jessie, from what he'd heard, was a woman who'd once had her pick of men, traveled in Europe, her daddy's favorite, a mean teasing beauty, and maybe not much different now. She'd lived in a mansion along Shoal Creek at Loretto that had imported marble, crystal chandeliers big enough to light a town, and mahogany chairs with satin oval backs that had once been in a French king's court. That kind couldn't stand ending up with her looks fading, married to that pious cripple, a daughter at least as striking as she ever dreamed herself to be, and smarter, wittier and more spirited. He thought that it must tear her joints apart every time she looked at Adela.

A woman like that could be driven desperate to keep

from growing old and bored in a town like Palmyra. It was just another place ragged from the war . . . the great web of railroad lines that were only a vision, the population that never arrived, once-busy stores boarded up or in ruins, coal and timber that belonged to the Yankees now, a town stuck in yesterday. The only sign of the city that Everett had promised her was the Opera Hall where no theatrical company came to play any more, no conventions of bibulous fellows from the societies, the plush curtain torn, the windows crusted with dirt, the stage boards used long ago for warming fires, too magnificent for the town even when it was built.

He'd seen too many women that Jessie might become, faded widows or women who married a cousin for a roof and bread. They lived in small cluttered houses down lanes overhung with big hickory and elm trees, behind drawn curtains and closed shutters, thinking their life finished but dressed properly in bombazine with old-fashioned bell sleeves, black velvet wristbands with a mosaic clasp, bonnets of velvet and corded silk. Their eyes beseeched passing men for a taste of love, rooted in dreams by sentimental songs like *"Lorena"* and spasmic fragments of the past that were still vivid. And Kortman was never surprised when one of them was found in an upstairs bedroom a suicide, her throat cut, appropriately, with a pair of delicate sewing shears. Maybe that's what Jessie was afraid of, why she showed no patience, or softness or charm, to seduce him.

They were all victims of the romantic illusions the South had died for. He had been in the wrong kind of rebellion. The past had to be destroyed. Southerners had hated working the soil, unlike the German and Scandinavian immigrants beginning to fill up the West—and had niggers do the dirty work . . . too many of them wild Celtic men who were prodigious drinkers, thought themselves perfect knights, hunters, heroes and poets, not farmers and bankers. They were easygoing but proud, clannish but ornamentally polite and hospitable. Their wild charges during the war . . . nothing had changed in a hundred years . . . the same way they died at Culleden in 1746. War . . . nigger fuckers . . . sex and death and honor. . . . And they made nothing but adornments and doll-like children of their women.

Lily Pittman greeted Kortman warmly, but never looked at Jessie. They passed a room where three women were eating. She led them to an upstairs room overlooking a shed where they kept the milk cow. The bed sheets were filthy and the smell from the shed carried into the room. Mrs. Pittman closed the window.

"We'll be getting busy soon. You can go back down the back stairs."

After she left, Jessie started out the room. "Not here, not a place like this. It makes me sick."

Kortman grabbed her. "It's good enough for the whores."

"But I'm not a whore. I'm a Kittredge—and you're lucky to have me. But not here!"

Maybe she's right, Kortman thought, but she wasn't going to play fancy with him. "Get your clothes off." He opened the big wood closet. She saw pink and red and purple nightgowns with feathers and fringe. "Put one of them on."

She refused at first, but he thought he knew what she wanted. He took her face in his big hand and began to squeeze until the tears came.

"You do like I tell you, damned whore!"

The pain unlocked her. She put on a red gown, pretending to be modest, all the time saying she was doing it for an ugly, cruel son of a bitch. She pulled down the front and exposed her breasts as she lay on the bed, her eyes heavy and lewd. He fondled her, then suddenly found himself thinking of Shaddy. His memory was eccentric, hoarding random moments and fears of the old days. She kissed him lavishly and pulled him down on her.

"Love me. Can you love me?"

Damned hypocrite to the bargain, he thought, mewling about love. A woman that wanted to be debased took her excitement any way she could, was grateful for it. But she wanted everything on her own terms. He was inside her and she kept clutching at him, when he began to punch her wildly and her cries brought Mrs. Pittman to the room. She said for them to be quiet, she had customers downstairs. They dressed quickly and left by the back stairs, past the cow shed. She asked him to carry her but he just laughed. Jessie began to cry, muttering that she didn't know why she had come with him, and begged him never to speak of it. He promised, but later told Adela. The carriage rattled along the dark road, and Kortman dropped off just out of town. Jessie was in bed before friends brought Everett home. She sent Matthew for Doctor Tallichet to tend her bruises, said she had been attacked on the road by a nigger but beat him off with a whip.

8

"It wasn't just me," Adela said. "It was mama too. I thought she was up to something that night when she kept talking and touching him. Then I didn't see them around any more."

"You were no more than whores."

"Ah, poor sweet brother. We were worse. At least a whore gets something back."

"How did you find out? How do you know it's true about mama?"

She gave him a sidelong glance. "Do you think if a big buck was close enough to attack her, she could beat him off?" She took a deep breath. "Kortman told me. He said it was he that punched her and gave her the bruises, that she insulted him, made him crazy. He said he took her to Mrs. Pittman's place in Cumberland. You know what it is?"

"You didn't have to tell me all this."

"I did. I wanted you to see that people do bad things because they want to, have to. It's not just about the Klan protecting fair white ladies from nigger rape. My God, papa told it all to you. Things like killing Douthit. That's the kind of thing it's about. But you don't think that's going to help us? Lord, they're going to bring more Yankee troops in here and then there'll be another war."

"I didn't like it, but the negroes would rule us if we didn't."

She pitied him because, despite his misgivings, he was still defiant, stubborn, trying to assure himself that he hadn't condemned himself to an outlaw life for nothing.

"Why did mama go with him?"

"Because papa's too upright, too stingy with his passion, same reason she's gone with other men. The only time I ever saw him joyful was that husking night when he got drunk and danced. But he seemed ashamed afterward. And I think he knew mama did something that night. It was never the same in this house after that. Sometimes I think mama helped you get in the Klan just to make papa miserable if he ever found out."

"That don't tell my why she went with Kortman."

Adela thought he sounded more jealous—of who, she didn't know—than angry, too easily ensnared by strong people.

"Didn't you hang around him all the time, listen to him and the other soldiers . . . made him your special hero because he came home with medals . . . and that face? And because he never lost his pride, still struts around town like he's the handsomest beau around.

Matthew knew she was right. Kortman, much more than his father was the pathetic stub and out of the war so quick, gave him the version of the war he wanted. When he saw Kortman at the Klan meeting that first night, he was certain he was doing the right thing.

"What made him turn like that? He likes to hurt to kill."

"I don't know. I told you how he was when I was so young and walked around mooning after him. He was kind . . . so kind to me, flattered me. He could make a young girl feel like a woman, but keep her at a distance so she understood it was just an innocent game, so it wouldn't be dangerous for her."

She looked out the window. A storm was coming up. The sky was an eerie mixture of shadow and thin rays of light that appeared and vanished. Tendrils of lightning split the low clouds and the rain was already visible to the southeast. The sky suddenly went white, then a strange glossy pink color, as a segment of storm dropped out of the sky like a dead leaf.

"Maybe it had something to do with that girl Shaddy. I told you about. He went everywhere to look for her. I think he had this idea she was wandering the road, starving, like a lot of niggers. Maybe he thought she was longing to be with him, the way he thought about her. Then, maybe a year or so later, he found out she ran away up north with another white man. He went crazy for a time. Maybe that's what turned him."

"How do you know?"

"Dave Trimble used to drink with him. He said Kortman would talk about it all the time, said if he could get up north, he'd kill her and the man. He made it sound like he would just take a train to New York or Philadelphia and walk down the street and there they'd be for him to shoot. I feel sorry for him."

"Is that why you went with him?"

"You don't understand what love is, or even the way a man and a woman want each other. You don't find that in the cat-wagons or whorehouses. Once in everyone's life, someone makes a fool of you. But you have to be smart enough to expect it. And enjoy it for the time it lasts. But he's killing himself over a woman. Maybe that's why he doesn't care what he does."

She thought she understood Kortman now, and would always have to guard herself, that she'd never be satisfied with an ordinary man, a good man as the would would see him. She wanted her heart touched too deeply, to explore hidden places. She despised women who settled for less than they desired. Her mother—full of tricks and schemes because she married wrong, sick with memories of Lorretto, nervous and possessive because she felt unloved, or worse, that she couldn't love. And she and Kortman had put their faith in the Klan to insure their salvation, reinforce their spite and hate. They were people hanging on to something dead, like mad old women who kept their man's moldering corpse in a dark house and slept alongside it. To hell with that, with people who made their own ugly fate. She felt happy at the revelation and thought she could free herself and Matthew.

"Go to school up north where papa wants you to go. I could come with you. It's the best chance to save yourself."

"They'd come after me wherever I go. They have ways you don't know."

"You believe in this Invisible Empire? You think they'd ride right after us if we were on the Nashville and Chattanooga, changed at Richmond for another train north, then follow us right into Harvard College and kill us? They're just country brutes."

He started to protest, but she shook her head to silence him, tired of the same blustery speeches. All he'd been left with, after all the talk, was the "shame" of his mother and sister, afraid that everyone in town knew about it and laughed at him behind his back. It was funny to her. He was the one in the family who suffered least from the war, and was the only one who talked blood all the time. When it came right down to it, he was just a bullheaded boy. Like most of his generation, he felt guilt and frustration because his young animal energy was never tested.

In the last year of the war, when the Junior Reserves, only a year or two older than Matthew were called up, he begged to go, but Everett refused. He was going to nurse that "shame" and "scandal" and forget everything else. He would tend it, make it bloom into some urgent lie until he did something stupid about it . . . maybe, she thought with a bitterness that surprised her, kill Kortman because he was the base seducer, when it wasn't that way at all. It was useless. Matthew didn't understand that everything in the world now was bent crooked. She became determined to dam up her love for him. She couldn't save him. If she tried, she'd doom herself. He was going to die one way or another, at the hands of a nigger that fought back, a Yankee soldier, a Ku Kluxer turning on him, maybe Kortman himself if Matthew was hothead enough to confront him.

* * *

The day after the killing of Douthit, a negro named Pompey, who worked for Tom Chatterton, went to Trask's cabin. He said that Hutchenrider had come to the house late at night and told him what happened in the Courthouse. Pompey was hiding behind a door and heard Hutchenrider mention names of Klansmen who did the murder. He had come to Trask because he was the only negro who denounced the Klan openly. He constantly urged other negroes to organize and resist. "Aint no one gonna make you free from them Kluckers, true free, 'less you do it yourself." It was because of Trask that negro men had started to fight back. Raids had been less frequent and furious in past weeks and everyone praised Trask, said he was showing them Kluckers.

Arthritic and unable to work any longer, he lived in a decent small house among white neighbors. Since the death of his wife six months before, he mostly sat rocking on the small porch or tended his fruit garden. Many white friends had given him cuttings of peach, apple, apricot and cherry trees. He learned to bud and graft in a rude way, and had plants everywhere about the place. In the springtime, the house was half-hidden by the trees and snoy blossoms. Chinese honeysuckle climbed over the trellis-work that ran from the door almost to the gate and leaden with waxy white flowers that had a spicy smell.

The day he spoke to Pompey was the regular prayer-meeting at the negro shcoolhouse. Trask arrived early in the evening and saw some white men in the audience. They were strangers, but he made them welcome. They sat in the back, and when the meeting started they began to guffaw and make a disturbance. Trask walked slowly on two canes to the pulpit and looked toward the white men.

"We glad to have white folks come to our meeting. Always think it do us good, and them too. It certain ain't hurt no one, cause the good Lord'll bless us all. But when white folks come to laugh at our weak prayer—that hurts the man. We got no learning but we tries our best. And when you laugh at us, we think we might have done better if we ain't been slaves all our lives to the white folks."

The men grew quiet for a while, then began to act up again. A couple of times Trask raised his head and stretched forward on his canes, as if he would speak. But each time he thought it better to wait. Finally, he couldn't endure it any longer, rose and walked toward them. When he came within two or three steps, he took both canes in his left hand, raised the right and pointed at them, standing rigid and silent. At first, the strangers tried to mock him, but Trask's angry eyes silenced them. Then the old negro coudln't hold himself. He began to curse them and told how the Klan had killed a good white man. The hushed audience became frightened when Trask shouted the names of the men who were in the courthouse. He told the story of the murder in detail, as Pompey told him he heard it from Hutchenrider's lips, his voice ringing out in the bare piny schoolroom. There was a cry from one of the strangers as he ran for the door, and the others followed in silence. Trask seemed to be in a spell. He was lying back on a bench, panting and moaning. Pompey rushed to him.

"Lord, Uncle Trask. What you do? What you *do?*"

Trask seemed unable to understand, then his eyes opened and he pulled himself upright. "What I done? I hurt your feelings, boy?"

"You know who one of them men was?"

"What's wrong? What I done?"

"The one on the end. He turn and look at you just before he go. The square-build man. That the one I tell you about . . . Catlin, the Arkansas man. Hutchenrider he say he high with the Ku Klux. That why he here. He the one break the bones on Mr. Douthit before thy kill him, then he help pull the rope."

Trask seemed resigned. "The the Lord use his serveant Trask." He remembered the man, the one who mocked the loudest. He knew that kind of rough white man, had been under their heel all his life, men who made a simple movement a threat, with the animal creak of leather in boots and belt and holsters and whips.

The terified people rushed from the schoolhouse and the news spread around the cabins. Pompey stayed with

Trask until he was sure the old man felt ready to go. He assumed Trask would go into hiding.

"Where you going, Uncle?"

"Why I going to bed, then in the morning I go to my garden like I does every day. The Lord blessed me with that fruit and flowers."

"I could trust the Lord a whole lot better if I was across the line and out of ole Tennessee by tonight. You better come."

"You crazy, Pompey? I live all my life here. Where I gonna go?"

"Then I say goodby to you, Uncle. I gonna get out of here sure."

A week went by and nothing happened. Pompey was gone, but Trask was seen every day working around his place. Negroes were heartened that the old man could denounce white man and live. Negro men came in from the fields after dark on Saturday. Cornmeal and greens and a rare side of bacon was put away for Sunday supper; even the poorest family tried to make the sabbath meal special. Clothes for church had been washed and ironed. By midnight the cabins were dark and quiet. A spatter of rain passed, the moon broke out from behind dirty clouds, and squinch owls racketed.

Then the negroes heard shrill whistles and the sound of horses moving slowly. They looked out the windows and saw a Klan rider in front of every cabin and at each lane and the crossroads. In the field beyond they could see a big band of men, more Ku Klux than anyone had seen before. The Kluckers had come for them, they whispered, and this time there would be no escape. Some men went for their guns, but in most cabins families pressed together in bed, feigning sleep, as if the abominable riders were a nightmare that would vanish.

The silent watch continued, each masked rider sitting his horse as if he and the animal were marbled ghosts frozen in motion. Five minutes . . . fifteen minutes . . . thirty . . . and the riders sat their mounts in silence. Then a whistle sounded on the Shiloh Road. The night riders, about 300 strong, a gathering of many Dens, turned northeast and moved off in long silent columns toward New Providence. People rushed from house to house to see what the Ku Klux had done. Everyone seemed safe and they thought it was just a showy warning. Then they came to Trask's house. The door was open, the house empty. The straw mattress had been thrown to the floor and the hempen cord it rested on was gone.

"Maybe they take Uncle Trask out just to give him a scare for all his talking."

"They lay a hand on that ole man, he gonna die."

"Even them Kluckers wouldn't hurt a cripple ole man."

They searched for Trask for a while, then a negro went to Judge Darcy's house. Darcey sent him to the Lanier house and Everett joined a search party. A man brought in a red coonhound and let him smell around Trask's house. They looked in deep ditches and swamps, favorite dumping ground for the Klan, walked both banks of a creek for two miles and as far west as the Yellow Fork River. Carrying torches, a group headed by Everett broke into the wooded hills with the dog. They were working out of a ravine at first light, when the dog began to strain at the leash. He led them along a shallow outcrop and through the trees to the knob of a small round ridge.

A mutilated, partly-decomposed body hung from the limb of a lone tree that looked like a gibbet, swinging in the high wind, some long-forgotten lynched man. The top flap of his skull fell forward over his face. His eyes had been gouged out and the ears, nose, tongue and penis cut off. The feet were burned. A deep sword cut had opened the stomach and what remained of the maggoty intestines spilled over the groin. There was the scabrous, putrified smell of decayed flesh. Some negroes fell to their knees and sobbed and prayed. Everett couldn't contain himself and tears came. Other white men turned away in shame, wiping their faces with dirty sleeves or a bandana. They thought they'd seen the worst battle, but even the toughest were stricken that men could do anything like that, even to a nigger. They cut the body down and buried it and washed themselves clean in the river. Everett was hopeful they'd find Trask alive . . . maybe he was scared when the Ku Klux came and hobbled off to a hiding place.

But when they returned to town, they saw his body hanging from the low limb of an oak near the courthouse. The town was filled with a dread quiet, few people on the street, and those going to church crossed the road to avoid passing the dead man. Everyone had loved Trask, and people often said his garden was the only beautiful thing left in Palmyra. Everett wondered why the body hadn't been cut down, where the marshal was, then realized that everyone, white and negro, was afraid to be accused of any connection . . . of doing the hanging, or treating an old nigger body with too much respect. He thought that if he ever had any doubts about fighting the Klan, they were gone now.

Adela broke down when he told her. She and Trask had been special friends and she often visited him. He always said she was "sweet and fresh and pretty like the morning flowers," taught her to garden, chided her when she rode King Bruce too fast and far on a summer day, saying she was "too hotblood and highbred for to go slow." She often brought him plants, especially the bundles of sweet-potato slips he planted in a bucket and sprinkled with fresh water. She loved the garden, felt enchanted in it, far from the drab world. She spent hours talking with Trask, believing in his wisdom, fascinated by his tales of the old slave days, so different from the way her mother told it. When his wife died, he seemed to lose his hold on life. Adela tried to comfort him, her heart twisted, saying that he'd live a long happy life yet in the little house.

"It them Kluckers make me feel trouble," she remembered him saying. "I use to dream in the slave time when I was young. Many the time I think about being free. I wish all the time for a place like this here. The the Kluckers come and then I lose my woman. Trask thing the Lord don't care that he trouble me a heap. But there was one piece of scripture I keep in my old head. That's where the Lord said to the ole fighting man Joshua: 'Be ye strong, and very brave.' There's more, but I disremember. I heard your papa talk it and read it to me one day. God bless him!"

The old man often laughed when he saw how easily she could make King Bruce and other animals bend to her will and charm and soft singing voice.

"Young men better watch their step. You gonna get them just as easy. They gonna gyrate and gyrate over you. No man stubborn like a horse."

That night Everett asked a friend named Ferris Taylor, who lived near the courthouse, what had happened.

"I saw the Ku Klux stop in front of every house, every street and road crossing, like picket guards. And it wasn't just the negra places. I heard no word, only whistles. They came like we were dreaming and they left mist goes off the swamp. I thought we were going to have to fight for our lives. They looked like an army. But they didn't bother the whites. I went to my back bedroom on the second floor and saw them around that low-branched oak not more than forty paces from the courthouse. After a while I heard something like a 'click-cluck' or two. I saw a match burn and then the body comes swinging down from under the limb. I knew there was a hanging, but didn't know who. Then I saw some men come out and talk to the Ku Klux. There were lights in some offices in the courthouse and a few houses. I thought it strange because it was so late. But the town was still as the grave. Looked to me like a lot of folks expected them to get rid of old Trask and were staying low."

Everett thought that what he'd feared had come to pass—the town could be taken over by armed, disciplined men, immune from the law, with friends and sympathizers in almost every house. Even the Yankee troops on occupation duty would have trouble stopping them.

"Why wasn't the body cut down before we came?"

"We thought about it. But the truth is it didn't seem a safe thing to do. We knew they like people to see their work and thought they might still have some sharpshooters around. I tell you, Everett, I saw as much in the war as any man. But I'd rather charge up the round top at Gettysburg again than be the one that bunch rousts like that."

Everett insisted on an inquest, but the report of the sworn jurors said only a male negro known as Uncle Trask, age about seventy, was hung in the township of Palmyra on April 26, 1869, and died of a broken neck, the perpetrators unknown.

What had happened to Douthit and Trask, Everett knew, to hundreds of men throughout the South, could be done to him or Darcy, or any man who was less than fanatic about resisting the Yankees. And not a Klansman punished. When he complained, the answer he generally received was, "If people are killed by the Ku Klux, why do they not kill the Ku Klux?" He tried to believe that it was no longer the responsibility of Southerners. Federal troops would have to put down this second rebellion. In any case, his ineffectiveness didn't matter; he knew how puny his power was, however respected and influential he appeared. He could do nothing to save anyone. A sense of impotence weighed upon him. During the war he hated and feared the Yankees. Now they just seemed perverse, spiteful humans, as frightened and contemptuous of him and other Southerners as he had been of them before.

The Yankees were hated, but they weren't the deranged sadists who had done the job on that strange negro. Not even local Klansmen, he thought, would do anything like that. He knew the leaders, everyone knew the hierarchy that ruled the local Den. It was the town's grisly joke. But men like Blanton, Hoagland and Tyler would never allow or encourage a mutilation. Not unless they were all going mad—his heart began to pound—or they were no longer in control. Would Forrest know everything that local Klans were doing? Everett suddenly remembered the description of a strange man, the heavyset man with the broken nose, who had been there when Douthit was murdered. From someplace in Texas or Arkansas, he heard. Maybe that's the way they went after the Indian, but negroes were part of the fabric of Southern life, as much a part of the land as their old masters or any white man. The man had been seen in town the past few days and Everett tried to remember his name.

The morning of the inquest, Everett and Darcy came

out of the courthouse and passed a crowd. One man named Miksell said loudly that Trask was a good enough old nigger, but it served him good what they did to him because he talked too much. Darcy quickly turned and faced him.

"You're all eternal cowards. If you're Ku Klux, then you're the worst cowards in hell." Everett started to say something but Darcy pushed him away. "Can't you learn? It's all gammon, nonsense you're doing and talking. I've been a slaveholder, and I may believe the negra is inferior. But I learned that the abuses and cruelty had to stop."

"To hell with slaves," Miksell said. "We never had none like you proud bastards. You're the ones who did them bad, and now them and the Yankees is doing us bad."

"If you're a Kluxer, I'll tell you that we could have it easier if you stopped all this outrage and murder."

"I ain't no Kluxer, but I hold with them. Why do we get all the shit the Yankees give us. We were rebels in arms. When we surrendered, the Yankees promised us no punishment long as we obeyed the laws. That meant we would have our own say in how we have a government in the state. Instead, they treat us like some Portugee bandits, put military officers to rule us. They put bad things on us. Yankees come down and they get place an power by niggers voting and renegades like you and Lanier there. They steal from us, tax us to give schooling to the nigger, take our land . . . everyone owes money. It's the damn others make the Klan ride."

"That's the saddest part of it. You don't even understand that the Klan uses the excuse of a lost war for organized defiance. You talk about a Yankee tyranny or a negra rule. Christ Almighty, man, they're thirty thousand Ku Klux in one state, forty thousand here, twenty thousand somewhere else. Even Forrest claims half a million. That's a greater army than the Rebellion put into the field. The Ku Klux *is* an army. But they kill without honor. You gain honor through risk. They hide and kill at night."

The crowd started to break up, but Everett was surprised when he saw Darcey, a spindly, consumptive man, grab Miksell and spin him around.

"I'm ashamed of Southerners like you. When we met the Yankees in battle, there was always one satisfaction whoever got fanned out . . . always our own folks who did it, and we were proud of the job. I tell you there was many a time when I could hardly tell which I was proudest of—Reb or Yankee. I saw both sides stand under bombardment or meet the bayonet as cool as if they were at the opening of a cotillion instead of the last gallopade. I thought then that if the worst came, as I always knew it would, we could have pride in our conquerors." Darcy was coughing and growing hoarse. "The Klan kills deliberately. They take their victims by using overwhelming numbers. They rouse them from sleep at midnight, then leave their ignorant, childish signs on the dead. Did we tell you about the negra we found? Remember the Jew peddler?"

His name was Joseph Mendel. Every six weeks he came through the countryside around Palmyra, carrying two packs with notions, pots, patent medicines, trinket jewelry, cloth, miners' pants, glassware, toys, harmonicas and Jews-harps, perppermint candy, hairpins, and the like. Each trip he brought in something special for a customer, a shiny violin or a pier glass mirror. His route took him from Kentucky thorough Tennessee and northern Alabama. A small, sturdy man, he wore an oversized coat and a soft straw hat pulled down on his head.

When he accepted a drink or meal from a farmer's wife and took his hat off, she was surprised to see a good-looking young man with curly black hair matted by sweat. He had a long bony nose, restless and curious dark eyes, a thin face with prominent cheekbones and pointed chin burned by sun and wind, and was rarely seen without a smile. The farm women, glad to have company, joked with him, and he teased them in his strange accent about how much younger and prettier they looked since his last visit. He often got into friendly discussions with the men about religion. They liked the "Israelite," as some called him, and thought him better than a Catholic; the Jew peddler was no threat to their bony fundamentalism. Sometimes Mendel found a preacher who knew Hebrew and they played the game of exchanging Bible quotes:

"A friend loveth at all time, and a brother is born for adversity . . . Proverbs 17:17."

"Man goeth forth to his work, and to his labor until the evening . . . Psalms 104:17," responded Mendel. "It's good you study Hebrew. It's the language of holiness."

At night when he lay under a tree, lonely and cold, his muscles stiff and sore, he lit a candle and wrote his thoughts in a book . . . if he died in some forsaken place, people would know of Joseph Mendel, that he had lived a hard, often dangerous life, always on the edge of failure, but continuing with optimism and good cheer with the hope that one day he could open a store. One night in a snowstorm, he wrote:

"Winter came suddenly . . . and not far from here I was forced to stop because of the heavy snow. I tried to spend the night at the house of Mr. Shepherd, but his wife said she was afraid of a stranger, and would not sleep well. Oh God, I thought, is this the land of liberty and hospitality and tolerance. Why have I been led here? The worst blizzard I have ever seen was raging. I talked to this woman for a half-hour and said it would be a sin to turn me out. I was allowed to stay in the barn. When Mr. Shepherd came in at dawn, he said there was breakfast waiting in the house. The woman made me a very good meal. I had to eat the flesh of pork, but she was very kind to me. She begged to be excused for the night before. She said many terrible things were happening, and everyone was afraid of strangers. I think she means this strange Ku Klux Klan. I gave her a wristband of velvet and she thanked me and said to visit her on my next trip."

Mendel sometimes wondered why he didn't give up the life. It wasn't just the fatigue and weather and loneliness. Local laws were passed to protect merchants and he had to pay a fee if he visited a village. He was often thrown in jail because he could not pay. He could speak fair English and that was no barrier as it was to many peddlers (though, he often laughed, there is an international sign language of trade). He had to face rough treatment and jokes from town louts who heard that Jews were allied with the devil. Peddlers were robbed and murdered, their bodies found along some rural road. One night Mendel wrote a melancholy entry in his diary:

"A peddler's life does not allow a man to observe the smallest commandment. We wander about this great strange land by the thousands, start out young and strong men, then we waste in the terrible summer heat, lose our health in the icy winters. We completely forget our Creator. We no longer out on the phylacteries. We don't pray on work days or on the Sabbath. In truth, we have to give up our religion for the pack on our back."

One day a farmer near Sycamore Creek came in from the fields and found his wife raped and murdered. Riders gathered at the farm, and at first it was thought that she had been killed by negroes. They used the creek as a guide on their way north along a well-traveled route to the Kentucky line. Word reached Palmyra, twelve miles away, and some men, including Hoagland, Buckner and Cissel from the Klan, rode out.

"You see any niggers pass here?" Hoagland asked.

Evans, the farmer, shook his head. "Maybe three days ago. They don't give us no trouble. Sometimes they're hungry and do work around the place for a meal."

"Anyone else? Any strangers?"

"The Jew peddler was here yesterday. But I know him." Evans picked up a thimble and needles and thread from a sewing basket. "Sold her these. Gave her a stick of peppermint candy. She liked it like a child."

"He leave right after?"

"No. I always let him stay in the barn, feed him."

"You see him leave?"

"Hell, I was putting in hay with a hired man in morning dark."

Hoagland glanced at Buckner. "Maybe it was the Jew."

Evans looked troubled. "I don't know. He been coming here for a year or two. Always got a funny story, always tried to pay for his supper. I liked the fellow."

"You don't think a good Christian would do your woman like that. Only a nigger or Jew."

"I treated that Jew fellow decent. He wouldn't do no damn thing like this."

"Hear he was a good-looking young fellow."

A signal of dull wisdom flashed on the farmer's face. "He was always joking around with her."

"You see. It was the dirty Jew," Hoagland said. "Which way he take when he leaves here. He always goes the same way?"

"Over around Washburn. That's a long way." Evans seemed eager now. "Man with a heavy load like he carries wouldn't be too far up the road."

Evans joined the posse and they caught up with Mendel at a farmhouse six miles away. When they rode up, Mendel saw some men he knew and greeted them. Two riders bulled him against the side of the house and men leaped off and grabbed him. He tried to fight them off, but they punched him to the ground and kicked him, men pinning him with boots on his arms and legs. They tied his hands behind his back and there were cries to string him up. Buckner sent the woman into the house and warned her not to say anything. When they pulled Mendel to his feet, Evans spit in his face and punched him. Everything in the Jew's face was loathesome now.

"She was a good woman, you fucking Christ-killer!"

"What are you talking about?" Mendel shouted. "What is this?"

"Hang the son of a bitch!" Evans said.

"No," Buckner said, "there's a better way. We got to teach these foreigners a lesson." It was the same lamentation, that inferior people were muddying the old American stock. "People got to see this one after we get through with him."

Hoagland grinned. "Yeah, we'll deliver him right to the Headquarters of the Yankee Military District."

A noose was put around Mendel's neck and Hoagland took up the slack of the rope. "You walk fast or I'll choke your Jew neck off." He turned to the other riders. "You scatter home. We'll take him in."

"You're no sheriff," a man said. "Where the hell you taking him?"

"The right place . . . Hope Mills."

The others grew quiet and the man no longer objected. They all knew it was the Klan place. Buckner gave the frightened woman a last warning and said she should thank them for saving her from the dirty Jew. They watched as the three men rode off, Mendel struggling to keep pace, stumbling, grabbing the rope to keep from being strangled.

"What's this all about?" the woman asked.

"The Jew peddler raped and killed Evans' woman."

The woman sniffed. "That tallowy, wet-eyed, sad old thing. More likely, she would have tried to get the Jew into her bed. Sure as pig ass tastes sweet, she wasn't getting it from Evans."

"How the hell you know, woman?"

"Cause men like to boast. I hear him and my Moody laughing about him piddling around every cat-wagon that passes on the Brascoe Road."

A man sidled his horse close to a friend's. "Seems like a young fellow like that'd want soft hand and sweet titty."

"He never give no one no trouble."

But they didn't want to go to the Yankees. Better to stay quiet. Let the Klan do its work. Maybe they were just going to give him the tar and feathers and run him north when the murderer was found. A rider glanced down at Mendel's packs. They were open, the goods and trinkets in neat piles on the canvas.

"What do I do with this?" the woman said.

"Put it away safe," the rider said. "Maybe he'll be back for them."

She looked up. "You know different. They're gonna kill that poor fellow."

"Well, I'd take Buckner's talk serious. Forget you saw anything. They'd burn you out, or worse."

"That sad slack-titted old woman . . . you gonna let that Jew die?"

The rider started off and said over his shoulder, "Better him than me, lady."

The Klan gathered in the cellar at Hope Mills. When Mendel was brought before the tribunal, the masked in-

quisitor spoke calmly, said he'd be given a fair trial. But
when he tried to speak in his defense, men in the ranks
began to snort and shout. They were the nasal, poor-white
trash voices he had come to recognize. He thought they
were much like the peasant voices of his youth in Poland.
Ignorant and mean voices, the sound of people who lived
hard lives, the poorest people who slept in hovels, people
who were religious not because it lifted them spiritually,
but because it promised deliverance from their misery.

"I have always tried to be honest. I would not do what
you say I did. My religion—your own—forbids such a
thing. I even studied English in my village in secret. I
dreamed about coming to America." A nerve pulsed in his
temple. Would they know that only four months after he
landed in Boston, he had been taken into the Union Army.
Would they kill him for that? He had never been bothered
by the Klan before, though many times sleeping outdoors
he saw them ride the countryside. One night he cried
when he watched them whip a negro, then half-drown the
man in a creek. He had found the negro farmers kind.
However poor, they shared their food with him, grateful
that a white man would take the hard way to their cabins.

The inquisitor spoke softly and respectfully at first, and
Mendel thought they would let him go or at worst give
him a beating and run him out. Then he realized the man
was clever, kept him off-balance until he became fearful.
The inquisitor was even hideously gentle at times, probing
all the little hair cracks. He thought he should stand up to
them, refuse to beg for mercy. He wasn't afraid of the
pain they might inflict. But though he had always been
alone, it was the isolation that terrified him.

One of the guards near him suddenly crashed a fist into
his face. He reeled toward a corner and men were on him,
punching him in the ribs and face. He felt a sickening
snap as two ribs broke. He tried to tuck his head into his
chest, but a blow caught him in the mouth and teeth came
loose. He tried to swing his bound hands and heard himself moan as the teeth spilled out. He was choking on
blood when they stopped beating him.

"Take him out!" It was Tyler's voice. "You know what to do."

They put him on a horse and the band rode to an abandoned lean-to in the woods built over the entrance to a large cave. They burned him with cigar butts while a kettle of water was heated over a fire. The scalding water was poured into his mouth, nostrils and rectum, then they stomped him. He was half-dead when they dragged him outside to a tree. They threw a rope over a limb and attached it to the wrist-bindings. At the moment when he felt his arms being torn from their sockets, they dropped him to the ground and flogged him with blackgum switches. A man rolled Mendel over and pulled down his pants, said he had a devil's prick—look, they could see—cut it off and dropped it in the fire.

"Maybe we should have cooked it first and made him eat his own Jew meat."

They rode off and left Mendel to bleed to death.

Darcy faced the crowd. "Why, damn you, most of you are Ku Klux." He turned to some women. They don't look like it, but they are—nearly every man you see here." Everett knew he was right. There weren't more than five or six men he didn't suspect. "They're all good church members and respectable. But you see them with their masks and robes on . . . they look savage enough then." Darcy seemed exhausted. There had been little hostile response all the time he talked, and no one made any threats when he left. Everett helped Darcy and felt the older man trembling. He knew both of them were in danger, but Darcy in particular. He tried to convince him to leave town for a while until people cooled down.

"Go to your farm." He saw the dark look in Darcy's eyes. It isn't running away. Too many brave, stubborn men have ended up dead. These people are like wolves. Give them a taste of blood and they go wild for more blood. It was our mistake—not taking them seriously from the start. We thought it was just another tinpot fraternal order created by brains half-cracked from the war. But it's a hellborn cabal. Maybe they could have been stopped then. Please, you're a sick man. There's been too much excitement. The rest will do you good." He left unspoken what Darcy knew . . . after today he was marked for death.

"I'll go if you promise to come down on a visit."

Everett agreed and the two old friends shook hands.

"Remember," Darcy said, "how we loved the law, saw it as the path to a complete civilization. Now it's used by every villain for his purpose."

"Tell old Jack to lock up tonight. I'll see you off in the morning."

9

EVERETT went to his office after leaving Darcy, much of the time staring out the window at the main street. He was appalled by what had happened in recent weeks, and had little faith in any comforting illusions. It had to do with time and seeing the future implicit in the present. Things would get worse. He thought of Jessie and felt an ironic sadness. When he was young he was grateful for the outrageous good luck that he had found her. But now he believed that she was more corrupt than he could guess. In those moments he wished he could control her, or that part of her that he imagined was dissolute, unfeeling and without any moral limits.

He left the office late and walked the deserted streets, his hand resting on the revolver stuck in his belt. The town looked peaceful in a night lustrous with stars. He had chosen Palmyra to live in as much for its name, and what it evoked in him, as its one-time commercial promise. Everett was a man in love with the ancient world. Palmyra had been named for a city in Syria thousands of years old. He knew its history as he knew that of Giles County. Tradition said that it was founded by Solomon and appeared in the Bible as Tadmor, the city of palms. Palmyra was captured by the Arabs and sacked by Tamerlane. It fell into ruins and was forgotten, but its great temple dedicated to Baal and other remains showed the Oriental splendor of the city at its prime.

Everett passed the Opera Hall, standing solemn and shadowed across the square from the courthouse. He wondered if one day people would examine it for knowledge of another Palmyra. Only ten years old, it was shabby, little used since the first year of the war. He and other leading citizens had raised money to build "a temple to the arts." It had been too ambitious, too grand from the start. The lobby had a colonnade of mirrors and fireplaces, lighted by glass lamps between the columns. There was a coffee room and private boxes, a pit and gallery that held 800 people. The ceiling was painted as dome, with panels of light purple and gold mouldings. The boxfronts were decorated into panels, blue grounded with white and gold ornaments, a crimson festoon draped over each box. The interior was lighted by glass chandeliers. Great actors had come there . . . Edwin Forrest playing *The Last of the Wampanoags*, Edwin Booth as *Macbeth* and *Richeliu*, Joseph Jefferson and Dion Boucicault. There had been classical music performances and moral lectures. But Palmyra people, except for a few cultured families, demanded more popular entertainment, and before it cloesd, there were singers from Memphis and Louisville performing all the comic and sentimental songs of the day . . . *The Dinner Horn, I Must Go to Richmond, Following the Drinking Gourd, Blue Tail Fly, The Old Armchair, Listen to the Mocking Bird* . . . and the haunting *Lorena*, a hymnlike love song that was a favorite of both Union and Confederate soldiers. He remembered young swains serenading ladies with the song *Jennie*:

"*I've wealth and I've rank,
I've lawns and I've deer,
I've mansions and grounds, but all these without you,
What are they to me? What are they to me?*"

It was those foolish delusions, the sentimentality, the worship of the Romantic that had defeated the South and brought it the misery it endured now. It was the fault of people like the Kittredges and Bowdens and Kimbroughs and Petits, who loved in splendid arrogance, never realizing that there was a mass of poor whites who would one day take their revenge. The Klan had been the dream, the army, of aristocrats in the beginning. Everett remembered Dwight Petit ranting that first year the Ku Klux rode:

"Again and again, it's been proved that it is war, and only war, which forges a people into a nation, and that only great brave deeds, wrought in common, can forge the strong links which bind them together. We are only continuing the war. . . ."

But now the Klan was an army of people who wanted their share and were willing to kill to get it. The people he knew, the class he and Jessie came from . . . they were like a family seated at a dinner table quietly eating while their whole world fell down about them. They had all their values wrong, trusted too much in their divine right to live on the backs of others. He sensed that there was a great chasm in history now, whether you were grown before the war or not. The world, time . . . it had slipped . . . jumped forward three decades in one. The world was becoming modern, rational, while the South was permanently out of joint.

It had been hard at first to discover that Matthew was in the Klan. But it was no surprise; even Darcy's nephew was a member. It had split families and towns, created a secret half-world where men were one thing by day, another by night. In the beginning he willed himself to think that his son's absences at the time of many Klan raids was just coincidence. *Who knew where young men went at night these days?* But he was certain now. There was a change in Matthew, a look of constant misgiving, hours of brooding in his room as if he was waiting for something to happen or pondering a problem, a nervousness that made him talk banalities, afraid he might give himself away unless he made his youth and foolishness and ineptness obvious.

Even when Everett began to suspect, he was afraid to search Matthew's room, afraid of a confrontation that might tear the family apart. He had a father's obligatory fear of a son's injury or death, but any father who lived in those times could accept the possibility. His real concern was for the boy's motives. Matthew had never been mean-spirited and he couldn't imagine him ever hurting anyone. His wife and daughter had to know something was wrong. Why hadn't they said anything to him? Were they afraid of what he might do, or were they in sympathy and helped him. Jessie perhaps, but, he hoped, not Adela. He rubbed his head, trying to drive away the feeling that he was being betrayed, then began to blame himself for everything. He posed as a rational man in an irrational time. But he thought that he was wrong, that only people of passion would survive, whichever side they chose, zealots like the Klan or courageous men like Darcy.

Turning up the hill road he saw a horse browsing in the front yard. It was a Yankee mount with a blue and yellow saddle blanket, the Union cavalry's McClellan saddle, a carbine in the scabbard. Adela and Jessie were talking to an officer in the parlor.

"This is Captain Daniel Catlin, papa," Adela said. "He's come to save us good Presbyterians."

Everett was annoyed. "Don't mock, girl. It might come to that."

The officer rose and shook hands with Everett. He was in his early thirties, a goodlooking man with light brown hair and a hawkish face, tall and lean—Everett recalled how the cavalry of both armies liked men with that look; horsemen took it as an affront to a splendid animal to put a short stubby rider on its back, though that changed quickly enough when the armies became masses and the elite had been killed off.

"I've been ordered by Governor Browner into the county. The Klan here is no worse than any other part of the state, but we go where they steep up their raids . . . where there are raiders. I have a company of regulars to enforce the law, along with a company of negro militia. They're the natural terriers for this hunt."

The anti-Klan laws had become a farce. No one obeyed them, and no Klansman had been punished or convicted by courts. The law stated that any person belonging to a secret organization engaged in night prowling "to the disturbance of the peace," or sheltering members of such organizations would be punished by a fine of not less than $500 and imprisonment for a minimum 5-year term, and was to be "rendered infamous." Informers were to receive half the fines if ordinary citizens, three-fourths if public officers. There were also levies on a county permitting Klansmen within its borders, $500 to $5,000 to be used for school funds. There were civil damages ranging from $10,000 to $20,000 for victims of Klan violence. When the laws were made, General Forrest ordered the Invisible Empire to dissolve, bury or burn its regalia, and destroy its ritual and records. But no Klan Realm took it seriously. It was a ruse that would no longer make the Klan responsible for violence and crime reported in northern newspapers.

The officer's deepest eyes fixed on Everett. "We're not here just to show a presence. We will have the laws obeyed to the letter. Palmyra is the new Headquarters of the Military District."

"We've had other troops in here, but it did little good. It's no secret, sir, that you haven't the soldiers to stop the Klan."

"Some officers did their best, but too many made only token efforts. The Klan has to be crushed. I've heard white men, Southerners, say that they're in the hands of murderers, that the Klan carries elections by the bullet and the noose. Negroes who want to fight are stripped of their weapons by white sheriffs. But they will fight now. We're arming them."

Everett thought it was foolish to create a black army, putting the fat in the fire. But he said nothing.

"I was told," said Catlin, "that you were a man who had influence in Palmyra and could help."

Lanier took a piece of paper from his pocket. "Read this." The note was handwritten and had skull and crossbones at each corner:

DEAR, DEAD UNDER THE ROSES.
X MARKS THE SPOT WHERE YOU DIE.
AS PROUD OF LUCIFER YOU ARE—
AND HOME TO LUCIFER'S HELL YOU'LL GO!!!

"That's only the last one. There were others."

"Those scrawls mean nothing. If they want to kill you, they will. Pinkerton detectives say those are sent mostly to people they're afraid to touch." He smiled. "It shouldn't frighten a man like you."

"No, they're laughable. If anything, I'm more determined." He knew he was only putting on a show for the women. "I just hope you understand the kind of man you're dealing with. They play the tune on one string, like the one the old cow died of. Only it's not the cows that are dying. These aren't outlaws like those Missouri boys. You can't chase down the Klan. They're everywhere. Walk down the streets here. Try to pick out a Ku Klux. But I'm sure you know all this."

"The government is going to enforce every law. If this continues, the President will send an army down here."

"That weakling Johnson? He's the one who bent to Stevens and the others who did this."

Catlin laughed. "I know Southerners don't exactly care for the man—but I'm talking about Ulysses Grant. He took office last month."

Everett was embarrassed. He was as bad as the rest, he thought, so fixed on villians, on the injustices of the Reconstruction, so obsessed by his narrow corner, he had forgotten."

"Well, his election didn't stop them. They're not afraid of him. They know he could never raise a big army again so soon. And there are many soldiers fighting in the West. If anything, they stepped up their raids, just to prove their power, their contempt for the government, for anyone who tries to stop them."

Adela brought in tea and corncakes and the talk became light and social. Everett kept his eye on Jessie, watching her try to charm the officer. But Catlin often fixed his glance on Adela. He had never seen anyone like her . . . quicksilver and rust plush, bright and alert, and, he could tell, restless. He had the image of a splendid filly that he watched gambol in a paddock, wondering at what moment she'd leap the fence, because he knew it was inevitable. He was told there was a Lanier son who was out with friends.

"You know how young men like to roust around town," Everett said. *Where was Matthew?*

Catlin smiled. "I miss that."

"Forgive me, but you don't sound like a Northerner."

"Born in Ohio. Then my family wandered to Missouri. When the trouble started on the border with Kansas, we just went on to Arkansas and settled there." He saw the surprise. "I was a Unionist. I never held with anything else. My father was a man who wanted to own land and slaves. The war ended all that. He runs a hardware store in Piggot last I heard."

"What did he say when you went Union?"

"He never knew, all luck to me. I was scared of him in those days. He's a good man, but he had a streak of mean and rough I didn't want to tangle with. Right after they fired on Sumter, I said I was going to Crittenden, where they were forming a cavalry regiment. He gave me twenty dollars and said he was proud of me. My brothers didn't go at first and he gave them hell. I got out of there real quick and that money bought my passage up the river to Cairo and a railroad ticket to Chicago. I joined the 24th Illinois."

"Where did you see action?"

"First time was that first bad day at Antietam.

The day at the Dunker Church, Evertt recalled, the wood beyond. The day came in gray, a slow drizzle, then a pearly mist that lay in the hollows around Sharpsburg and shrouded the fields and woodlands. It came with a crash of musketry, backed by the deeper roar of cannon-fire that mounted in volume and intensity until it continuously jarred the earth beneath the feet of both armies. The Yankees under Joe Hooker came out of the West woods, his three divisions in line abreast, driving the Confederate pickets southward onto high ground where the road ran past the square white block of the Dunker Church. That was Hooker's objective.

There was a glint of bayonets and the boil of smoke

from the cornfield and Hooker began to take heavy losses.
Six of his batteries came up and began to flail the standing
grain that September day with shell and cannister. The
Yankees had three dozen field peices and heavier long-
range guns. General Hood thought his Rebs might have to
fall back across the Boonesborough Turnpike to Antietam
Creek. The artillery poured in a crossfire from the ridge
beyond the creek. Captain Lanier, riding a handsome
gray, waited with his regiment of cavalry back of the Sun-
ken Road, watching the carnage. Haversacks and splintered muskets began to leap up through the dust and
smoke, along with the broad-leafed stalks of corn and the
dismembered heads and bodies of men.

The Yankee infantry started forward, their battle flags
swooping and fluttering, falling and then caught up again.
As they started to break the Rebel lines near the Dunker
Church, cavalry came in behind the shrilling infantry
through the mist. It was the 24th Illinoise. The red flags
of the Confederates staggered backwards, and still the
bluecoats came on, driving them through the blasted
corn, until at last they broke and fled, their ranks too thin
to rally. The Yankee cavalry came in with swords to finish
them off. But a thin column of men in butternut uniforms
emerged from the East woods to flank the Yankees, try
and hold until reinforcements could be brought up. The
cavalry commander saw a chance to turn the battle and
sent Lanier and his men forward. He was galloping toward the Rebs when a shell exploded to his front. He was
thrown, but thought he'd escaped injury. He rolled over to
cover himself against the fire and his face sunk into the
blood of shattered of his left arm. He saw the arm lying
nearby, the palm turned up and the fingers curled as if
still gripping his sword. The sun was burning through,
first dull metal, then brassy, and all he could see was the
whitewashed brick Dunker Church, dazzling against the
trees still in full late-summer foliage. A wounded man near
him, a bullet through his colon and oozing excrement,
cried, "The sun's going backward . . . night will never
come!" Everett remembered picking up his arm, thinking
that these Dunkers were strange Christians . . . their

church had no steeple because they believed a steeple represented vanity. And when he thought that, he wondered if he was going to die . . . he had heard so many strange utterances from dying men.

Everett nodded to Catlin, his eyes shining because they had shared that horror . . . September 17, 1862, 26,000 Rebs and Yankees killed on that terrible day. Everett wondered how often in the future men who had fought against each other would meet, just old soldiers telling tales of the war. He felt love for Catlin, not hate. Men who pit themselves against each other in war, in any dangerous undertaking, understand the pain and misery because they shared the same fate, and those who passed through the terror were forever changed. Only generals spoke with fury about the enemy, and it was the politicians and the people at home who hated. He wondered if he should tell Catlin.

"We've met before."

Catlin looked puzzled. "Sir?"

Everett touched his stub. "The Dunker Church."

Catlin didn't know how to react, then saw Everett smile. The two men embraced.

"You were very brave. We had you heavily outnumbered. It was touch and go for a time."

"No," Evertte said, "that was the Southern way of fighting. Suicidal. I was lucky. I was out of it. I wasn't a warrior and I never had a moment's regret. I've heard hunters spilled from their horses curse their fate worse."

"Well, you remember the old soldier's cry—'A man won't sell you his life, but he'll give it to you for a piece of pretty colored robbon.'" Catlin had gone through the war from Shiloh ("Pittsburgh Landing" to the Rebs) to the invasion of Tennessee, where he was wounded at Tullahoma. Like all ex-soldiers, he wanted a link, a reassurance of those bloody days. It made the memory less of a nightmare than he never waked from, but only another gory tale told in a tavern. He wanted to believe that he had seen Everett writhing on the ground as he charged past the Dunker Church. But there had been hundreds of shattered men, screaming and fouling themselves. Still, they had been within yards of each other because he remembered the last burst of his own artillery fire that broke the Reb cavalry charge.

"What did you do after the war?" Adela asked. "Did you stay in the army?"

He shook his head. "I was restless, went to sea for a time. Then I came back to the army. I couldn't go home and I didn't know what else to do."

"Where did you sail?"

"Mostly Africa. Funny, but the ship I signed on was still slaving."

"Where?"

"Rio Pongo, the first time. Everywhere between Cape Verde and Cape Saint Maria. Sierra Leone and Liberia, where freed slaves were setting up a country . . . Monrovia and up the Bay of Benin where the Benin flows in. But the negroes there were bad for slavers. Eboes. They'd get the skulks or sulks, or the vapors, and swallow the tongue. The Windward Coast and Bonny River and Ananaboe, Gaboon, Gambia, Calabar . . . I've seen them all."

"Were you ever in a storm, a bad storm?"

"The first time coming into Benin, a squall. Clouds lay over from the northwest solid like a bridge span, color of a dirty sheep belly." He found himself talking like a sailor again. "Then sea and sky turn a shiny white and purple, and the rains come all at once, like you had kicked the bottom of a barrel, and the barrel sky-high and you under it. The rain just tromped the ship in the sea. And the lightning, it never let up, red sheetfire and stab all around."

"Why didn't you leave the slaver?"

"Hell, we were ass-deep—pardon me, ladies—and where would I go? I would have sat in that godforsaken country and died. It was full of negroes trading their own off. They cut throats and drank blood like it was buttermilk and chopped off heads, heel-hung in a slaughter place. I knew it would be my last trip on a ship like that and went along peaceably." He had a faraway look as if remembering something stirring. "Those slavers were Baltimores, lightweather flyers. They carried sail that could pick up the faintest new sea breeze. They moved like a dream. A dead calm, and they'd leave a chasing British cruiser like a cow staked out on the common."

He was trying to intrigue Adela, thinking she'd like a rakish man. But from her quizzical expression he didn't know whether she was fascinated by the strange places and people and adventure, or repelled because he had worked to carry slaves so soon after fighting a war to free them.

"That skipper he ran his ship clean for the poor negroes," he added quickly. "They had to be laid on the lave-shelfs, but he gave them turn room, and all day, gang by gang, on deck for air and dancing and a hosedown with seawater. Every other day we hosed down and holystoned the slave decks till they looked as white as ginned cotton and sprinkled them with vinegar. We made them wash out their mouths with lemon and gave them chewsticks for their teeth. They were fed like the crew, fish stew or dried shrimp with palm oil and beans with biscuits cracked up in the mess. That ship didn't smell, and that skipper landed his cargoes with not one of them dead." He said nothing about the women they kept on deck at night to lie with, looking up after his lovemaking to see the topsail drawing across the stars, steady and full with the trade winds.

"You haven't seen your father since 'sixty-one?" Jessie said.

"I wrote him a letter from Cairo that a negro took to him by hand, trying to explain what I did. I wrote after that, but he never answered. Then at Mechanicsville, I found my brother Tom in a prisoner pen. He said the old man had forgive men and welcomed me home whenever I wanted."

"Did your brother come through safely?"

Catlin laughed. "Nothing could kill that devil."

"Do you have any other family?"

"Two sisters and another brother. There's a breed slave, a half-Shawnee name of Simon Hooper, we always felt was part of the family. He stayed with my father."

"You see," Jessie said, "many slaves stayed with their masters. They knew who loved and cared for them best. They didn't run away."

"That's more than you can say for the Kittredge slaves," Adela laughed. "From what I hear, they skedaddled out of Loretto so fast, grandpa didn't know they were gone until two days later." She pointed to a large Louis XIV mirror. "You know, mama's mighty proud of that. Her family brought that over from England to Virginia over a hundred years ago, and then to Carolina until they butchered all the Indians down at Loretto and decided to build a mansion that fit such elegance. A million negras polished it every day. Looks kind of silly in this house, though."

She saw Catlin looking at her as if he understood everything at once. A man like that, she thought . . . maybe a man like that. Everett said it was late and rose. Catlin politely asked if he could escort Adela around his encampment the next day; she'd see that Yankee soldiers weren't the devil. He turned to Jessie.

"I would spare your feelings. The soldiers are good fellows, but a rough lot."

"Then why would you ask my daughter?"

"Someone of your quality might take offense. But young people are never really shocked. They like it in fact."

"Jessie seemed placated because he treated her with delicacy and respect. But Adela knew it wasn't that. She liked him, liked people, especially men, who had the good sense to laugh at something funny, say something funny that ridiculed hyocrisy and stuffy ideas. Everett understood and thought that Catlin was a shrewd fellow. He had cut Adela right out of Jessie's hands and she never knew it. A slick fellow, maybe different than the other Yankee officers. Darcy and Ferris Taylor would have to meet him.

As Catlin was leaving, Matthew came in, looking shaken. He greeted the Yankee officer and went to his room. Adela walked Catlin out on the veranda and said she was looking forward to the next day. Their hands touched and lingered, but she was thinking of how strange Matthew looked. When Catlin rode off, she went to her brother.

"What's wrong?"

"Nothing."

"Come on . . . I can see it in your face."

Matthew broke down. "I've seen them do awful things, and I went along with it because I had to most of the time . . . because I thought it was for a good reason. But tonight they killed white women . . . cold blood."

"Who?"

"Some whores over at Cumberland."

It began because the Baptist preacher was sermonizing at a meeting that the whores had to be driven out. They were an affront to decent white women. He groaned and screamed about sin and the devil to pay if they didn't heed God's commandment to hellify the stinking, vile creatures. His eyes rolled and his face and body twisted, his voice rang through the dank cellar at Hope Mills. He had a vision, he shouted, that all would be hellfire if the countryside wasn't scourged. He cursed those present as whoremongers, said his command had come from higher up than General Forrest himself. God had told him to burn and burn and burn the whores.

Matthew said he didn't think Kortman and the others meant any real harm. There had been a brothel at Cumberland as long as anyone could remember. The whores kept to the house, and every Christmas Eve Mrs. Pittman sent food around to poor folks. It was no secret that almost every man from miles around had been there at least once, a ritual for the young, and it was like a big mock shivaree when a whore came out a door holding a smirking boy like a newlywed.

They rode over late in the evening, when the house was busiest. They were in Klan uniform and when they came to the house a man named Louis Chandler dismounted and knocked on the door, holding two Smith & Wessons. The negro maid opened the door and screamed. Chandler brushed her aside and shouted for Mrs. Pittman. She came out of the parlor and stood with her hands on her hips.

"What the hell is this?"

"Get them whores out!"

"Listen you ghoulie or ghostie, or whatever the hell you be, Lily Pittman runs her business like she wants."

Kortman stayed back, certain she would know him even under the mask and robes. But other men ran upstairs and flung open ever door. Each man thought the Klan had come for him and cowered in bed.

"Get the hell out, you fucking whoremongers!" Chandler shouted.

The whores grabbed anything handy and covered themselves. One named Maggie Barton joked that "the damned Klan come here for free goods, and the hell with them." The customers ran out, chasing their horses that the Klansmen had whipped away, or tried to right their overturned buggies. Chandler, Thevenow and Cissel herded the girls into the parlor and Mrs. Pittman tried to calm them, saying it was just some drunken fooling. A dozen men stood watching with cocked revolvers. Kortman was about to call them off, when Maggie Barton saw him standing just beyond the open front door. She recognized the light leather Mexican boots with the high shine; only one man in the county wore anything like that.

"Jimmy Kortman, you sonofabitch. You come here for cow ass or cat pussy? No one would fiddle an ugly bastard like you."

She thought he would laugh and unmask; they had spent many nights together. Kortman was silent. He pulled a shotgun from under his robe and walked forward slowly. She misunderstood, thought it was a game, and laughing she held her negligee open to show her breasts and cunt and began to wiggle.

"You want meat like this, or you want to go out back to the shed and suck the cow's milk tit? I hear all you Klan fuckers like that."

Kortman blew her face away. He gestured toward Mrs. Pittman and Chandler grabbed her. The big woman fought and scratched, but Chandler and Cissel pushed her down in a corner as the whores ran to the other side of the parlor. Chandler jammed two revolvers in her breasts and fired. She sat wide-eyed, staring at the spreading blood-stains. Cissel shot her in the groin, then a runty man named Crabtree said he wanted some of the old bitch. The others stepped aside. Crabtree held his weapon with a wavering hand, his skinny face pinched. He put the barrel against her temple and fired, and in that instant Mrs. Pittman gave a ghastly moist sigh and toppled over.

"The rest of you get the hell out of here," Kortman said, "and don't ever show your whore face again." He remembered the preacher's command: *"Purify . . . burn and purify."*

They spilled lamp oil and set the house afire. The women didn't run at first, standing near the road to watch the flames. One tiny whore known only as "Schoolgirl Elsie," the one Mrs. Pittman kept for old men, turned from the burning house to face the Klansmen. Her voice was high and piping:

"You goddamn weasels . . . I seed every one of you here. I can smell you. I know you all." The others tried to quiet her, but she kept raging. "We ain't niggers. You ain't gonna kill white women and get away with it. You ain't got the right!"

Kortman mounted and started for her. An older woman tried to make peace.

"She ain't right in the head. She's only fourteen year . . . only fourteen year. She come right from Goodspring. Her pa sold her to Lily cause she was no good to him. All she know is to lay down and fiddlestick herself all the day."

But Kortman knew the little whore was too smart, too observant, if anything. He stowed the shotgun in its scabbard, calmly pulled his revolver and shot her. Cissel leaped from his horse holding a carbine. He jammed the barrel between her legs and kept pumping it.

"She sure got the big fiddlestick now! yelled Crabtree.

They rode away at a gallop, laughing and hooting.

Adela hated Kortman, hated herself for being so stupid. She wanted to kill him. He was like a dog with the froth now, mad, a killer because he had the taste of blood and couldn't get enough. She thought that one night he would find a reason to kill her or Jessie. The killing now was without stealth or guilt. It was the Klan's pleasure. She couldn't understand Kortman . . . as deadly as he was sensual . . . *and the other way around.* She suddenly thought of Daniel Catlin and thought she would be safe with a man like that.

Matthew was sobbing and she thought of the times before the war. They had been clever children, Porter the natural leader, and competitive. In the garden each had his or her special climbing tree; and each one of their family quarrels took place because they wanted what was best for themselves. It was early one morning, and they were looking out of the window in the boy's bedroom at clouds beautifully colored with the light of a winter dawn, arguing fiercely over which cloud belonged to them, Porter and Adela paying little attention to Matthew's cries. Sukie, the black woman who had brought them up, came into the room while they were still fighting, and told them never again to take things belonging so much to heaven as their own.

Sometimes in those happy days, there would be a delicious hour before bedtime; dim lamps burned on the landing, and turned low in the bedrooms, curtained to a firelight glow. It was between six and seven o'clock, when their parents were dining, and Sukie and the maid were doing the downstairs rooms for the night. At this hour, the children had the run of the upstairs rooms and played hide-and-seek or other games. Then, tired and almost ready for bed, they would be allowed to go down to the dining room to join the grownups for dessert. They would be given a biscuit or a piece of fruit, and a sip of wine before bidding their parents goodnight.

She remembered Sukie's herb garden, how the old woman taught her to use Broom for a toothache, Comfrey for a sore throat, Sage for insect bites, Rosemary for eczema and bruises, Thyme for headaches, and the many teas she brewed. There were tears in Adela's eyes. It all seemed like a foreign country now. She was too young to have to throw herself back into the past to find happiness.

Once, she had gone to a Baptist camp-meeting with other curious girls. The preacher had paid them special attention because they were Presbyterian and Episcopal visitors, and thought he was being kindly, concerned, when he warned them:

"You will soon pass from girls to young ladies. No human misery will be spared you."

She wondered if the world she once knew was irretrievable, and the thought provoked sharp pain. She felt like a scrawny pretender in a violent game, ill-armed, a vicious plucking at her heart. She put her arms around Matthew. He was young and had made a terrible mistake. If he could escape the Klan, he might learn what the new world after the war was about, never fall prey again to antiquated and morbidly romantic ideas about chivalry and honor. But he might not be allowed that chance before someone killed him.

"You have to get out. Even if you run away."

At first his look was imploring, then became rueful, as if he knew his fate. "You joked about it once, but once a man joins he don't get out. It's true, I've seen them get men . . ."

"Even if you went north?"

"I told you——"

"Papa knows a lot of people in Memphis. He could get you on a boat." She kept giving him alternatives, the run in the night, a wondrous escape, but he kept shaking his head.

"They got people watching everywhere. I couldn't get on a train, or even take a ride out of town without someone telling."

She was afraid that his shock at the Cumberland raid would lessen each day, and he would, as he did before, begin to forget, feel no anguish or guilt about the murdered women.

"Do you really want to get out?" He nodded and out his face in his hands. "Then if you won't take the chance of getting away now, there's only one way. You ride with them. Be as rough as the next man so they'll never suspect you. There are ways, I'm sure."

She thought that in time she could confide in Catlin, get

him to arrest Matthew and send him to a Federal prison up north. It would be arranged, as if Matthew surrendered on his own, and they woudln't be too hard on him, take his age into account. But she was too pleased with herself, never thought that if they had a confessed Klansman in prison, the authorities would try to get information from him. Was Catlin a decent man, or would it have to be the barter of sex for a favor, a dangerous favor for everyone.

She was making the decision for Matthew, trying to wrench him from youth and wrongheaded passions. Forced to witness murders and whippings and fires of destruction, there was no woman's lending hand to comfort him by its mere touch. The Klan tried to ride like ghosts, but the violence was no illusion, no phantasm of a dark night. Matthew had a dim future, she knew, either way. And when he discovered what she did, he'd hate him. But that was better than letting him die on some lonely back road with a bullet in his head.

10

THE second night after he returned to his farm at Burdette, Darcy saw Klan riders brandishing torches, circling in the road about a hundred yards from the house. When they left, he found a death warning to keep from meddling in the murders of Douthit and Trask. He knew it was hopeless, no witness—Trask dead and Pompey gone—at least none willing to talk. He had been given names, but knew it would never stand up in court even if he could get the suspects arrested.

The next moring a stranger came to the house. Darcy was careful and held a revolver on him. The man came forward with his hands up.

"My name is Evan Cornelius. I'm from Stoddard. I used to live in Palmyra."

"What's your business?"

"I can't keep still any more, Judge."

"About what?"

The man flicked his eyes at his raised hands and Darcy said he could lower them, but kept the gun on him.

"I thought about going to Texas, but I knew it would follow me."

"What are you talking about?"

"Trask. I can still see his face."

"We all feel sad about the old man."

"He used to play with me and teach me things."

Darcy was exasperated. What good did all the mewling do? People could whimper and cry, talk a lot of nice pieties, but no one ever risked their necks to help. "Why did you come all the way out here to tell me that. Then, almost in the instant the man said it, Darcy knew.

"I know something about the hanging. A heap more than I wish I did."

Darcy took a chance. "Are you in the Klan?"

"Joined a couple of years ago when I was studying to be a minister at Mr. Hoyt's school. Almost everyone in that school was Ku Klux. I belonged to Den number four. The sherriff was a member and was one of the officers. He was what they call a South Commander. My uncle was one of the officers too. I was on three or four raids and it just seemed good fun at first. . . ."

Darcy didn't press him, let the young man take it at his own pace.

"I took an oath, but I never figured on anything like killing old Trask. I ain't been able to sleep since that night."

"Did you come to tell me about it?"

"That for one thing."

Darcy was amazed. No one had ever betrayed the Klan, or if anyone had tried, he was a dead man before he could talk.

"You know what you're doing?"

"I gave it a lot of thinking, Judge. I heard about you giving them fellows hell."

"What happened that night? Who was there?"

"My uncle told me that Den number four in Stoddard got a decree from a Cheatham Den to make a raid in Palmyra. That's the way they do it now. A Den hardly ever does anything on its own now. The Klan got too big. They send a decree to another Den, or two or three others, and the Dens that get it have to execute it."

"What happened that night?"

"We met a squad from another Den and I acted as guide because I knew Palmyra. We went into an old pine-field and put on our uniforms. Then Watson, who was the East Commander of the other Den, he asked me if I knew where old Trask's house was. I said I did. He said that was the man they wanted. It was voted it should be a hanging. I couldn't get out of it by that time. When we got to the west part of town, Watson ordered the pickets out. We went to Trask's house and there was no lock on the door. Watson struck a match inside and there was Trask on the bed, sleeping like a child. We took him and I was glad he couldn't see it was me that he taught how to fish. They tied him up and put him on a horse near me. He never said nothing after we waked him, only some chattering like 'Come Lord Jesus, come quick!' "

"They take him to the courthouse then?"

"That's right. I was feeling mighty bad all the way. When they began to do the hanging, I rode away near the courthouse like I was looking out. But I didn't want to see any more."

"What did you see?"

"I couldn't help looking back after a while. When I did, someone drew a match and held it up, and I saw the face of old Trask as he hung on the limb. I've been seeing it ever since."

"You know the names of the men who did it? The Palmyra men who ordered it?"

"I got to answer that?"

"Do as you choose," Darcy said; his voice purposefully harsh. "You've already confessed enough to convict you."

Cornelius named fourteen men that he could remember, bitter because "They got me into this trouble, and a lot of other good young fellows."

Darcy knew most of the names. "You'll have to answer a charge of murder."

"I'm guilty. I don't deny it. I don't want to dodge or run. At least I'll sleep tonight. I just ask one favor, Judge."

"What's that?"

"Don't send me to the Palmyra jail. If you put me there, I'll be hanging on the same limb before two days are gone."

Darcy knew he was right. He wrote a letter to the Commander of the Military District. "Do nothing to arouse anyone's suspicion. Go home and do the same as you do every day. You will be arrested and held by the Yankees. The Klan won't get to you. All they'll know or think is that someone informed on you. They'll trust you to hold to your oath." He admired Cornelius for not begging for some mercy because he was risking his life, and added a postscript to the letter. "I'm recommending that you be given good treatment in custody. When the trial comes, I'll see that you receive some leniency."

"I thank you, Judge."

"Do you know anything about Douthit's murder?"

"No, sir. I swear."

Darcy looked out the window toward the road. Two young negroes were driving past in a wagon. "Are you armed?"

"No, sir."

Darcy went to his bedroom and took a revolver from a chiffoniere drawer. "Take this. I want you alive." Cornelius jammed it into his belt under the short corduroy coat and left. Darcy watched him until he cut southeast off the road toward Stoddard. He went into town soon after and sent a telegram to Everett, asking him to come to Burdette and accompany him to Cheatham County.

On the appointed day, Everett left his office for the depot to catch the 6:30 train to Glenville. He would have to change trains for the southbound to Mobley, the nearest stop to Burdette seven miles away. Darcy would meet him there and take him back to the farm. Everett figured it would be after nine before they reached the house.

Toward sundown, Adela was sitting on the veranda. Jessie and Sukie, now a very old woman who still helped out occasionally, were inside preparing refreshments for the Palmyra Ladies Literary Society that met every Thursday. The sun was glowing like a great paper lantern on the western highlands, when a horseman came in sight down the road. He came to the gate at a trot, stopped, and looked at the house. He seemed to be searching for certain feature that would identify it as the Lanier's. When he was satisfied, he gave a loud "Halloooo" Adela walked to the steps.

"Here's a letter," the horseman said. He held an envelope up for Adela to see, and when she started down, he threw it over the gate and cantered away. Adeal picked it up. It was addressed in a coarse, sprawling hand to:

> Captain Everett Lanier
> Palmyra

On the lower lefthand corner, written small, she noticed something else:

> Read at once

At first she felt no urgency. Then she thought that she didn't know horse or messenger. The rider was a boy about fifteen, and it wasn't too strange that she didn't recognize him. She was struck by the hesitant way he approached and inspected the house, as if he didn't even know the town, the biggest in the county. And there wasn't a boy that age within many miles who wouldn't know the Laniers and their grand house.

But what roused her curiosity about the letter was that she didn't recognize the horse—a handsome iron-gray with a white mane and brushtail, a bigchested animal with a strange, slanted rump and a beautiful action in the canter. One of the best horsewomen in the state, she had seen that in a glance. Her love for horses made her notice any animal on her daily rides, and that horse was from nowhere near. Everett always joked that she knew twice as many horses as people, because she usually noticed the horse and not the rider. The writing in the lefthand corner was different than the other, as it it was disguised. She thought her father might be in danger and quickly broke the seal. She tried to read, but the short twilight was failing and she went inside and read it by a lamp near the door:

> Captain Lanier—a raid of the K.K.K. has been ordered to make Judge Darcy pay the extreme penalty tonight (the 29th inst.). It is understood that he has telegraphed you to visit his home. DO NOT DO IT.

*If you can by any means, give him warning. It is a
Big Raid and means business. The decree is that he
shall be tied, placed in the middle of the long bridge
across the Hatchie, the planks taken up on each side,
so as to prevent a rescue, and the bridge set on fire.
I send this warning for your sake. DO NOT TRUST
THE TELEGRAPH. I shall try to send this by a safe
hand, but fear that it might be too late. I dare not sign
my name, but subscribe myself your*
UNKNOWN FRIEND

Adela stood frozen. Even if her father wasn't included
in the decree, if he was found with Darcy they'd kill him
too. She never doubted that the warning was real. She
looked at the mantel clock: 6:35. It was too late. Jessie
came out and saw the letter. "What is it?"

Adela never understood it later, but her instinct was to
keep the warning from her mother.

"It's just a note from that Yankee officer." She tried to
sound frivolous, but was wondering where Matthew was.
Jessie just gave her a sly look and returned to the kitchen.
The letter said that the telegraph was under Klan control
. . . they'd know her father was metting Darcy. She ran
to the back porch.

"Willie! . . . Willie!

Sukie's grandson answered from the stable. "Ma'am?"

"Saddle King Bruce and bring him around quick."

Jessie heard her. "Where are you going? You said you'd
help entertain."

"Miss Adela," Willie shouted from the stable. "You
know this hoss crazy. He been smelling mare pass by."

"Bring him out or I'll give you a hiding."

"Yes, Ma'am." He thought she'd never handle the horse
this time. He never liked the strain of Arabian in King
Bruce, always said "Furrin-bred hosses is all crazy."

He threw open the stable door. The powerful chestnut
gave a short vicious whinny and leaped, his ears laid back
on the sleek neck, teeth bared, and thin bloodred nostrils
distended. He went for Willie who hid behind the

stable door. The horse pranced around the small stable-yard, then stopped suddenly and stretched his head for the bit, quivering in every limb with the promise of a run.

Adeal ran upstairs, put on her riding clothes and stuck a revolver in the waistband under the short jacket. She wrote a note to Matthew . . . maybe Willie could find him around town . . . didn't let herself think that he might be on the raid. She tried to remember the country between Palmyra and Glenville and Mobley. She had never crossed it at night, but thought she knew the landmarks well enough to make it safely. Rushing down the stairs, she tried to remember the train schedule her father mentioned. When she went outside, Willie was holding the restless horse, Her heart dropped. He had put the side-saddle on.

"Damn you, Willie! Not the goddamn hookleg! Get a regular saddle!"

The horse was mad to run and began to buck when Willie led him back to the stable. He muttered to himself about quality ladies that would curse that way and ride a man's way, and thought that all white people were crazy, just like their horses. He resaddled quickly despite the skittish horse and brought him around. Adela gave Willie the note and told him not to say anything to anyone, but to look all over town for Matthew. She gathered the reins, found the stirrup, mounted and shouted "Let him go!"

Jessie and Sukie stood on the back porch and watched as Willie freed the horse. King Bruce reared and pawed the air, leaped once on his hind legs, then stretched into a gallop under her crop, pounded across the field and headed toward the Glenville Road. Adela heard the train whistle a far way off. For a moment she thought of Catlin and his troops. But there was no time. And she had a horse that could outrun any army mount. The two women watched horse and rider until they were gone in the shadows. The secrecy, the haste, made them think Adela was rushing off to a lover. Jessie said she'd raised a slut to go off in the night like that, with no shame.

Sukie laughed. "That child sure got the blood to get

someplace fast." She kept looking into the darkness. "Sure wants to get someplace fast. . . ."

Adela felt the horse's power and knew once she whipped him up, she'd have trouble pulling him in. His head was leaning and stretching and he almost controlled the bit. She kept her eye on the road so that if he swerved or shied she wouldn't be thrown. He had galloped about five miles and she thought his heart would burst if she didn't slacken or give him a rest. They came to a river and King Bruce went down the long slope at full gallop to the ford. She tried to rein him in, but the horse kept shaking his head and held his stride until he reached the water. He paused, threw his head up at the rising moon, then stepped high into the fretted waters, throwing up small jets of silver spary at every step.

Adela lay across his neck, patting and praising, and was able to control him while he made his way through the deepest part of the channel, turning him left and right, and once all the way around just to make him obey her will. He shook the water off, wanted to gallop again, but she walked him to the top of a hill and veered a little to the west, sure she would avoid any more water. It was growing cold, the wind banging in from the highlands. She reached back and searched with her hand for the hooded waterproof, grateful to Willie that he remembered to jam it under the cantle. She smiled, thinking how scared he was when she scolded him. She would reward him when she returned . . . might even part the curtains when she got undressed. She often saw him standing in the yard, half-hiding behind a tree and looking up to catch a glimpse of her naked. That took a lot of courage and he must want to look real bad. Poor nigger boy. She'd give him the treat. She pulled the waterproof over her head, gathered her hair into a bun and put it under the hood.

She cut across a long valley and picked up the road. King Bruce shied and she dug her spurs into his flanks, but he refused to move. She slapped him hard with the stinging reins, then regretted it and her voice was carressing. The horse moved in tight nervous circles, fighting her, but she finally prodded him into a trot. She'd gone only a short way when she saw what had disturbed the animal. Off to the right bent across some rocks was a body. She went close and saw it was a white man, congealed blood trailing in brittle clots from a wound in the skull. She galloped off, her heart hammering, thinking the man had only been killed a short time before. Once or twice she slowed to examine what landmarks she could make out, decide which road or trail to take. She thought she knew just about where she was . . . the stand of forest to the northwest, a smear against the sky . . . the sound of Cedar River to her left. She took the horse through the trees, startled by an owl's cry, then moved across reedy ground where wild hogs started from their hiding place, darting and snorting. One was close enough to snap at the horse's leg, but Adela beat it off with the crop and King Bruce streaked past.

She pulled up at a fork in the road and thought she was lost, was losing precious minutes. Then she saw a high ridge with an Indian profile scoured out of its north end . . . *Quapaw Nose.* Adela turned the foot of the ridge to save a few miles, then picked up the road. Suddenly she thought she saw a red flaring in the north sky . . . a fire raging on the bridge . . . her father and Darcy burning to death. But she knew it was too early and she was a long, long way from the Hatchie bridge. It was fatigue, a sudden blink, her mind faltering. She galloped through an avenue of oaks at a crossroads where she remembered stopping once with her father at a giant tree felled by lightning. He had said that it was halfway from Palmyra to Glenville.

Whenever the road took too many turns, or Adela reined in to look for landmarks. King Bruce went into a swinging foxwalk until she spurred him again. He showed no signs of tiring as they went through tall pines that climbed halfway up a ridge. She came to a place in the middle of a rolling field where the road branched out in four directions. There seemed to be no difference . . . each bordered by scrub pine and running moonwhite and straight into the darkness. She went a short way up one road, hestitated, looked at the stars to try and orient her-

self, swung back to the road on the extreme right, then
heard a sound that made her freeze—a whistle shrilling to
the left . . . three times . . . then a reply from the road
to her front.

She knew they were Ku Klux whistles, signals, was told
about them by Matthew. She stroked the horse's neck,
afraid he might skitter at the sudden noise, but he stood in
the patch of moonlight as still and solemn as a monument
battlehorse. Adela couldn't wait much longer. She had
only two roads now to choose. She heard the drum of
hoofs on the road to the front, then on the left and right
roads. She realized she had stopped right in the middle of
a rendezvous point and moved into the dense scrub pines
that grew between the roads. There was only one choice
left and she thought she heard Ku Kluxers riding from
that direction.

She saw the first horseman, turned back toward the in-
tersection, drew her weapon, leaned over King Bruce's
neck and peered through the low branches. She kept
stroking him, whispering for him to keep still. The inter-
section was filling up with masked riders. Three men
came into the road to the right of her and her horse gave a
low whinny. But there were so many animals about, neighing and snuffing and whinnying, they paid no attention to
it. She remembered the flask of whiskey that was always
in the saddlebag, poured some in her hand and leaned to
rub it on the horse's nose to keep him quite. A rider was
speaking to the group:

"Gentlemen, I am East Commander of Den number five
of Robinson County."

"I am from Den number eight of Cheatham."

"And I of Palmyra Den number two. We were ordered
to report to you."

When Adela heard the Palmyra man, she prayed that
Matthew hadn't been called that night. Perhaps with so
many men from different counties he wasn't needed.

"Is this Bellsburg's Cross?" asked the first man.

"The same."

"I was told it was four miles from Glenville."

"Nigh about that."

"We leave the road about a mile and a half from this place to get to Mobley?" asked the Robinson man.

"Yes, and cross to the river road."

"How far to that road?"

"About five miles."

"It's now near eight o'clock. We have time. How many men do you have?"

"Thirty-two from Cheatham."

"Thirty-seven from Palmyra."

"I have forty-two," said the Robinson man. "Do your men know the work at hand?"

"Not a word."

"Are we safe here?"

"I've had pickets out on the road since sundown. We had just come from the south not ten minutes before you signaled."

"I thought I heard a horse on that road."

"Has the party we want left Burdette?"

"A messenger from Mobley says he's there to meet the Palmyra man on the Glenville train."

"And they will return to Burdette, to his place?"

"Yes."

"Does the decree cover both men?"

"No."

"I don't half-like this business, and won't go across exact orders," said the Robinson man. "What do you think?"

"Shouldn't we say the decree covers both?" replied the Palmyra leader.

"I can't do it. You know the rules. When a party is made up from different Dens, it makes one Den that can regulate its own action. We can vote on it."

When he spoke to the riders, he only mentioned Darcy's name, but said there was a Palmyra man who was not in the decree who would be with the Judge. Should they take both men?

"Who is he?" asked a Palmyra rider.

"Lanier . . . what do you Palmyra men say?"

"He's the scalawag scum that was there when Darcy talked us down after we got Trask. If Darcy knows the names, so does Lanier."

"His son rides with us," said another Palmyra man.

"Is he here tonight."

"Out on the picket."

"Keep him there for the night with a couple of men. Tell him he's to cover us going and coming back."

"Let's get the hare before we cook it," said the second Palmyra man. "We been warning Lanier a long time, but we never ruffled his hair. Maybe there are high-up people don't want him touched."

Adela recognized the voice, Austin Phillips, the railroad agent. It sounded like he was trying to save her father. When the vote was taken, only Phillips objected.

"First we know, we'll all be running our necks into hemp. And from out won people. Follow the decree. If you say no, I'm getting the hell out. Stinking business, killing a man who has a good Ku Klux son. That's not Christian."

"Move a pace and I'll put a bullet in you," said the Robinson man.

"Phillips drew his big Navy Colt and cocked it. "You go to hell. Either we do it right or we don't do it."

Most of the Palmyra riders began to side with Phillips. Adela slowly went up the road that the Klansman said led to Glenville. She kept King Bruce in the deep shadows along the grass and felt the horse tugging to run. He was rested now and she thought it was the moment to break away. But she saw a Ku Klux sitting his horse quietly far out on the picket line. The rider was facing away, but turned as she approached.

"Who's there? Halt!"

It was Matthew. She wanted to call to him, tell him their father was in danger. Her mind ran fast. What could he do? If he rode in and caused trouble, they'd kill him so he wouldn't talk. And she wondered if he had the courage to try and stop it. He was the last barrier and she had to get past. If she worked in close, she thought she could just wound him, but if she killed him, better that way than the Klan or a Yankee firing squad. Adela eased King Bruce forward, the horse trembling with excitement under the tight rein.

"Halt or I shoot!"

She thought she was close enough now and spurred into a charge.

"My God!——" Matthew cried as the big chestnut was on him. Adela fired and the bullet slammed into his left arm near the shoulder. His startled horse reared and Matthew went limp. Galloping down the Glenville Road, Adela heard shouts and three shots. Pursuers were swarming out of the pines. Another shot sounded, like a distant cough, but she had lost them.

Matthew returned to the crossroads and told the leader that a rabbit ran across the road, spooked his mare and his pistol went off. "I couldn't hold the reins and she like to take me to Memphis before I could pull her up."

"Is it bad?"

"Well, the arm's no good for now, I guess."

Phillips was detailed to accompany him back to Palmyra to a doctor, while the others started for Mobley.

The train pulled into the Glenville depot. Porters removed the luggage and passengers were taken by horse-bus to the two hotels. The station agent was in his office when he heard the sound of a fast-running horse. He glanced out the open window. A girl with long hair flying was riding through squirts of steam from the engine and came to a skidding stop, shouting:

"Mister Lanier . . . Everett Lanier!"

The agent pointed to a carriage turning into the Glenville House. "He's going to wait for the southbound. . . ."

"Papa! Papa!"

Everett looked out the carriage, jumped down and saw Adela riding toward him in the streaked shadows of the street lamps. She pulled up, looked at her father, then fell into the road. When she came to at the hotel, she told him about the Klan raid.

"Rest easy," he said. "Darcy's in the hotel restaurant at this moment. He decided to come all the way up to meet me and notified the station agent to tell me. That's his carriage. I think we should all return to Palmyra."

They stayed the night in the hotel, but she didn't tell him about Matthew. In the morning, they drove back in

Darcy's carriage, King Bruce tied on behind. When they arrived home, Matthew was in his room, his arm bandaged. Everett and Adela went in and he had a sheepish smile, said he got hurt a dumb was fooling with Billy Laidlaw's gun. Everett left after reassuring him that everything was going to be fine. Adela started to say something, but Matthew broke in.

"That was a hell of a piece of shooting." She was surprised he wasn't ranting, that he could be that casual. "You aim for the arm?"

She laughed. "No, the leg."

"Damn." He laughed too. "What if you killed me?"

"I figured better your own blood than a Klucker or a Yankee."

"What the hell were you doing out there?"

"Trying to save papa and the Judge."

"What are you talking about?"

"You didn't know . . . they were going to get them at Mobley and burn them on that long bridge that goes out to Burdette."

"You'er crazy."

She showed him the letter. "They're such dirt. They were going to kill papa even though it was only supposed to be the Judge. I heard them take a vote on it, and at first the Palmyra men were for doing it, and you riding with them. Only Austin Phillips put up a commotion."

"We were told we were going to Mobley because the nigger militia were getting too strong there. We were gonna get some."

"Haven't you done enough. Can't you see by now what it is?"

"I'll tell you the truth. Whatever they did, I never killed anyone. I whipped some, but I never killed or even shot anyone. It's because when they start a raid, there's so much running around and mixup, everyone trying to prove to Kortman and the others how much they want blood, I could always make it look like I was doing something. But I never did anything real bad." He looked out the window. "Funny . . . Kortman always seemed to watch out for me. If there was sentry duty or messenger duty, he picked me . . . like he was trying to keep me away from the bloody stuff. Maybe——"

"It had nothing to do with me and Kortman, or mama." She tried to sound light. "Maybe he thought you're too small and skimpy." She saw the petulant look. Despite everything he'd seen and hated, he was annoyed because she didn't think he might be man enough. "You still don't understand. I'm trying to get you to see that you're too gentle and decent, and you put on a sour face. God, when are you going to stop dreaming?"

"Well, you're telling me I'm not a man."

"You're not—not for that. That's not what a man is anyway. You don't have to be a brave man to be violent, you just have to be crazy with your fears. You're so damned confused, you're going to get yourself and the rest of us killed. You've got to take a stand. That's what a man does."

"Maybe I could get away. Go north to school like papa wants."

She looked at him with scorn. "It's too late for that now. Then they'd really go after him, just out of meanness. They hate him anyway. And you think those Ku Klux gentlemen would leave me and mama alone after that?"

"Maybe Kortman——"

"Kortman be damned. I only told you about him so you would know what's going on . . . maybe face things. But you're too stupid. He's not out to save anyone. You think because I made love to him once, he's going to have any mercy on you or any of us?"

"What can I do?"

"Do what I tell you. Papa can't even face talking to you about it. Just go along for a while. Maybe Catlin can help."

She couldn't tell him that there was something terrible in her at night when she was alone. She had weakened and gone with Kortman again. She began to feel sick and thought it would pass, then thought she was pregnant. It was a shock, not because she was naive, but because she was faced with a crisis, had never thought anything like that could happen unless she willed it. She evoked the

kind of surprise when the body took insult, the sudden
feeling of vulnerability, the loss of control, the mere fact
that anything that hard and bitter and marvelous could
happen to her. She had done things other Lanier and Kittredge women were killed for. And she couldn't blame Jessie this time. It was her own nature, coarse and greedy
when it came to certain men. If she was pregnant, she'd
have to marry someone. The idea came almost too easily.
Why not Catlin?

He often came to the house as if visiting Everett, but she
knew it was because of her. He always stopped to talk and
she found him pleasant. He was decent and civilized, and
as long as he was in town, her father was safe. After those
first tales about sailing on a slaver and the exotic places
she found him boring. But he began to court her with an
old-fashioned probity and ardor that amused her. They often rode out into the country and she thought he would
try to make love to her, but he never did. A good man,
and, she thought, everybody hates good men, especially
women. Sometimes he moved her to lava flows of bitchi-
ness.

When she suspected she was pregnant, she seduced him
in a hotel in Gladehill, but still playful enough to make
Catlin sign the ledger *"Duc Du Guise and Lady Swelling-
breast,"* and they laughed going upstairs. In the room she
dreamed of a stronger presence when she was in his arms,
mesmerized by a phantom lover who would enslave her,
make her anxious only to please him. As they lay on the
bed in the late afternoon, Adela put her face in her hands
and began to cry, filled with self-pity. She knew how dangerous it was to wish too desperately for a different kind
of man. It was hot in the room and she opened a window.
She smelled the spring twilight and felt a poignance like
pain. The room looked repellent to her now. He tried to
comfort her, and she thought it would be a hideous trick
to make him think he was father of a wretch born of Kortman. But it was no time to keep from deceit, think she
was being immoral or simply unfair. Catlin would get
what he wanted, and she would do her best to love him.
But she felt sour and sly and abruptly asked him to leave,

knowing it would make his anxiety greater, afraid he hadn't pleased her, make him ask something sooner than he thought proper.

"Wait, just a few minutes. I want to talk to you."

"This place gives me the itch. I think there's beggar lice here."

"Adela, do you love me?"

"Why do you think I came here?" She pretended to break down. "You think I'm just a whore?"

"No! No!" He jumped from the bed and embraced her. "Never. I hoped you came because you felt the same way I do. I love you."

She tried her angelic-tender look, touching his face softly. "I love you too, Daniel."

When they kissed, she felt a surge of guilt because he did love her. She hated herself, wanted to tell him the truth, but wasn't certain any longer. He wasn't the kind of man she had been warned against, catlike and predatory and utterly charming. He could never intrigue her. But she felt a soft emotion that denied her shrewdness. She broke away from him and walked to the window with her limber stride. Now she smelled tar barrels burning, the odor she connected to voilence or times when the Klan paraded. She could never feel passion for Catlin, not the way other men's flesh struck her with fresh anguish. She knew she was Jessie in that way. She could do shameless things, but she needed a safe harbor, a cave, a fortress, a nest to return to. There was a moment of tension as she and Catlin stood like combatants. He kissed her roughly now and ran his hand over her buttocks. She was burning to make love again, but pulled away and told him to dress.

"Will you marry me?"

"You'll have to ask papa."

Catlin smiled. "I already have. He said if you'd accept me, he'd be very happy."

She pretended to be the innocent, said that men were just too smart and teasing for her, and looked peevish because she had been tricked.

"You're not angry that I spoke to him. I was surer of

him than I was of you . . . I needed that courage before I asked you."

Her smile was radiant, as if grateful for his passion. "I'll marry you."

"When?"

She had to be certain she was pregnant. "I'll tell you in a few weeks."

He thought it was only the indecision and excitement of a young woman; there were preparations to be made, the wedding dress, distant relatives invited, all the proprieties observed. When he agreed without a murmur, she wanted to tell him how sweet and good he was, and what a damned fool he was. . . .

In the weeks before she was to make her decision, Catlin was often away because the Klan had stepped up their raids, and she found herself hoping he'd be hurt, wounded just bad enough so she wouldn't have to set a date. One night when Sukie was in the house, Adela took her upstairs to her room.

"I've got a bad secret. You promise you won't tell anyone, Sukie?"

"Child, I never hear nothing or tell nothing."

Adela knew it was true. Sukie knew all the family secrets . . . the thieves and cads and mistresses and slavers. She had wept for Porter like he was her own, and secretly blamed Jessie for his death. She knew Adela's wildness, the men who hated her because she refused to love them, how her father had become a frail hostage to Jessie. She long knew Matthew was in the Klan, but protected him fiercely. She was that way not because she felt the faithful retainer any longer, the slave who had stayed behind when others ran—but because she was a Kittredge, then a Lanier, and felt their blood was her own.

"I think I'm going to have a baby."

"I seed signs, but I don't say nothing. It ain't you been swelling up. But there's a look I knows."

"Sukie, I have to make sure, or I'm going to make a bad mistake and hurt everyone."

"Lay down and open your legs naked."

Adela tucked her skirt under, took off her underdrawers and spread her legs.

"Crook 'em, child."

Adela bent her knees and Sukie put a pillow under her. She rolled her right sleeve up, washed her hands with brandy from a small flask she carried in her apron—both of them laughing when she produced it—then gently put her hand into Adela. The alcohol stung a little, then she felt Sukie's hand pressing against the wall of the uterus. She tried to watch for any sign in the black woman's face, but Sukie was concentrating, probing and pressing.

"It soft, child."

"What? The baby?"

Sukie laughed. "No baby there now, but the wall is soft."

"What wall?"

"I don't know the name, child. We calls it the birthing place. What take the seed and make the baby."

"The womb? What does it mean if the wall is soft?"

"There's a birthing coming. But it's still a long way off."

They smiled like conspirators, and Adela felt safe in Sukie's hands, sure she could do something. "Everyone thinks I'm such a quality lady."

"Not your mama."

Adela put her arms around the old woman. "What were you like when you were young. Were you bad like me?"

"I was a slave then. I had four husband because the work kill them off. Big good-feature men. I like a man in the nightbed."

"Even now?"

Sukie gave a throaty giggle. "Well, there's still a man around what like a fat old Aunt Sukie." She suddenly looked serious. "But Aunt Sukie smart. She don't give no man no power to hurt her."

Adela knew what she was trying to say. She could handle clever, careful men, romantic men, she could captivate anyone with her beauty and charm and clowning. But there were others she was loony with. Men like that defined her. She clasped Sukie tighter.

"What am I going to do?"

"Sukie can kill it."

"What?"

"I can do it for you. In the old days, sometimes there was a mare or cow they didn't want to birth, and I watch the way they do it."

"Is it dangerous? Will it hurt?"

"It chancey. And it hurt for a spell."

"Did you ever do it before?"

"In the old days sometimes. When a master he lay down with a nigger woman and he don't want no baby. But I ain't done it for a long time. You trust Sukie?"

"Yes. God, I have to have it out. I don't want it." She had a sudden vision of a monstrosity, a scarred and violent infant. She knew it was crazy, but couldn't free herself from it. She began to laugh hysterically and Sukie put her hand over Adela's mouth. "Shush your bellering, child, you gonna wake the dead."

"When can we do it?"

"Night after next, your mama and papa is going to Nashville. She want to see a show, and your papa he got business with the governor. They gonna stay at the Maxwell House until the next day. We could do it then. But you got to think about it strong."

Adela felt a wretched sorrow flooding her. But she couldn't be sentimental, even for Sukie. She had to risk it. If she lived, she was free again, wise enough now, she thought, not to make the same kind of mistake. If she died. . . . She cut it out of her mind. Sukie had magic hands, long and thick and strong, without a tremor even at her age. Sukie would free her. She could put Catlin off. Tell him that she was too upset to begin a marriage with all that was going on. When he got rid of the Ku Klux, that's when she would marry him. It sounded reasonable to her. He was fighting, out most nights hunting them down. He could be killed or badly wounded. She didn't want to be left a widow. If they were married, he might become too cautious, and it was the cautious men who were killed. Didn't she hear that about the war from her papa. And she deluded herself that it would sound sensible and right to Catlin.

11

IT wasn't as bad as Sukie said. First she gave Adela a little whiskey.

"That the sugar-tap whiskey. Ain't no strong like the corn, but it make you feel good."

Adela lay near a window, smelled honeysuckle that made her think of twilight. Sukie was muttering, warning herself to be careful and not hurt her child. Adela felt a sharp pain for only a few seconds and Sukie stood upright with a flaplipped smile, her few snaggly teeth gleaming in the bright lamplight.

"All done. You see that old Sukie knowed something."

"You mean it's all over?"

"That's what I see and what I know."

Adela was happy enough to dance, but when she tried to rise, she felt weak and sore. "How can I be so tired?"

Sukie had a cunning smile. "Not the same kind of tired like when you took the seed."

"No . . . nothing like that."

"Just a little rest. They won't be home till tomorrow night. By the morning after, you feel like stepping high." Sukie gave her another drink of sugar whiskey and took a swallow of brandy. "I sure like that furrin whiskey." She meant a place that she vaguely knew was Europe, far across an ocean.

"That's not whiskey. That's what you call brandy."

"My number five husband he gave it to me, rob a store."

"I thought you only had four husbands . . . all worked to death at Loretto." Maybe, she thought, it was true what everyone said about niggers. No matter how good they were, they could never tell the truth. Maybe Sukie had never killed an unborn before, maybe she was lying then. But she was angry with herself because she doubted the good old woman.

"I never told about the number five husband. No one really know about it. I marry him against the master wish cause he from another place. After we was freed, he live outside town here cause the Kluckers was always giving him trouble and the like. I go down there when it safe. Didn't want him here cause the family they be in trouble. His name was Ogden. Mighty fancy name for a fieldhand, but he come from the Chatterton place and they always give their hand name like that. Ogden Tolliver." She slapped her thigh in amusement at the florid name.

"What happened to him?"

"When the Kluckers get strong, he and some colored men they was the ones start the militia. The governor he give them the old guns what the Reb soldier use, so they got them old muskets to protect them. Ogden he was a leader like a real soldier, even if he be an old man. They only meets when they hear Kluckers is coming for colored folks. They hide in the cabins, and that's when they find out who a lot of them Kluckers was cause a lot of them was killed.

"They find out Ogden is one of the leaders, so they take him to Robinson County and hang him for a sass to a white lady they says. One colored got away and he tole me they tries Ogden in the woods. Then they scratch his arm to get some blood, and with that blood they writes, 'He hang tween heaven and earth till he am dead, dead, dead, and any nigger who take the body down he get hunged too.' Ogden he hung eight feet over the road, with that writing right over his head. Nobody'd bother with that body for four days until the sheriff come and take it down. Mister Chatterton he a Klucker, but he hear about it and give Ogden a Christian grave. How you figger that?"

"I don't know. Everything's so crazy now. Everyone carrying a gun. You don't know who to trust."

"Seem like you trust someone too much."

Despite the dull soreness and fatigue, Adela had to smile. She loved how bold Sukie was, said whatever she damn pleased. It was as if she had seen so much of life, gone through so much, suffered and worked and loved and saw death until she had no fear of anything. When negroes got the vote, she went right down to the courthouse. There were some white men hanging around, telling the negroes not to vote. Sukie said, "Well, I am going to the poll if I got to crawl." When a white man asked her how she was going to vote, she asked right back, "How you going to vote." The white man said, "I'll vote as I damn please." Sally opened her parasol against the sun and said, "I'm going to do the same thing."

She told Adela the bad things that happened "when them Kluckers break out. Some colored they started to farming. If they make some good money, the Kluckers murder 'em. The government builded schools and they burn 'em. They go the jails and take the colored men out and knock their brains out and break their necks and throw 'em in the river. Then there was some niggers so dumb they don't know they was free even after they saw the Yankees riding around here for three years. I ain't talking about what I hear, I talking about what I seed."

They were the same grisly tales that Adela had heard a hundred times. She was tired of the terror, the killing and burning and all the rest. She wanted to learn woman wisdom from Sukie.

"You want to know the man who did it to me?"

"You mean the man you *do it with.*"

"You want to know?"

"White folks do as they pleases, niggers do like they can."

"Maybe you can teach me."

"I don't know what I can teach you. You a devil I loves. In the old days, people *raised* children, took care and watched like a good crop. Now they just feeds 'em and lets 'em grow up. The old training was the best. Seems like nowadays people don't like their children.

"It was Kortman."

"Whooh . . . that scarry man?"

"Yes."

"Mean a man as God ever wattled a gut in. He make a lot of bastard nigger orphans." She looked at Adela, curious how she could bed a man like that. She thought of her own husbands, all fine-looking men. "Ain't up to me to say nothing." Then she began to cry softly. "I should just give you a whipping."

"I know. Like you used to say when I was a little girl and did some mischief—'Hit you a striaght lick with a crooked stick.' "

Sukie wiped her eyes. "Didn't do much good as I sees."

"I'm not bad, Sukie, I'm not. But even when I was young that man used to put me in a fever. Those burns didn't change it. It made me feel sorry for him, made him more interesting. Even when I found out he was in the Klan. I hated him for the kind of things he did, but I still wanted him. I was with him three or four times. After the first time I hated myself. I promised I'd never go near him. But I did."

"You learn anything?"

"The only thing I learned is that I don't want to marry the Yankee." She told Sukie why she went with him to the hotel in Gladehill.

"Now you got no birthing, you don't want the man."

"No, I want to be free."

"Don't talk 'free' to me!" Sukie said with anger. "He look a good man."

"That's the trouble. I think about living all my life with a good, kind man, and I get terrified."

Sukie was impatient, confused with a white woman's contorted emotions, didn't understand that kind of talk. She knew that all her flie she had to be cunning and

quickwitted just to survive. And when she found a man
who would feed her and love her, she was grateful that
she wasn't alone in the world.

"That Catlin man ask you to marry?"

"Yes. I accepted. Then I knew I couldn't do it. That's
why I came to you."

"You takes one thing and then you calls it another. You
just like a nigger Ogden tell me about. He kill one of Mister Chatterton shoats . . . that a baby pig what they take
away from the sow tit. He was caught and Mister Chatterton say, 'What you got there?' Nigger say, 'A possum.' The
master he take a look and seed it was a shoat. The Nigger
said, 'Master, it be a shoat now, but it sure was a possum
while ago when I put him in the sack.' Well, you is a
shoat that is playing you a possum."

Adela realized that Sukie had nothing to tell her. She
was as old-fashioned as any of the Kittredge or Lanier
aunts. Sukie was brought up the old way, and that's all
she knew. You were a lady or you were trash. She would
have to sort out things for herself. She wasn't going to live
the old way, but she was afraid of the world ahead of her.
For eight years she had only known war and the chaos
afterward. The world was changing fast, too fast for her to
find her bearings.

She'd heard about women like Victoria Woodhull,
women who traveled and lectured and lived the life they
pleased, women who preached against being slaves to
men, and who were open in their love affairs. A girl at
school had shown Adela a copy of *Woodhull and Claflin's
Weekly* that a Baltimore cousin sent her. It talked about
women suffrage, free love and socialism. Adela understood little but the spirit of the editorials. But she felt that
if she could escape Palmyra and her family, the ignorance
and violence around her, she could change, free herself.

Sukie had tried to make her ashamed of what she'd
done with Catlin and what she was going to tell him,
though Sukie didn't scold her for making love to Kortman,
where passion was the element. But Adela knew she was
right. She loved the old woman, who had risked her life to
help her. If something had happened to her, they would

have hung Sukie or beat her to death. Her father would have tried to prevent it, but there was no hiding anything in that town. And whatever happened, Sukie would never say a word. Adela thought she was old enough to do what she wanted.

There was different world to be tasted in the big cities. She could work, women worked and earned their own living now. But where? Memphis? . . . Atlanta? . . . *New Orleans!* The rich port city was almost untouched by the war, from everything she heard, just like a foreign city, more a French place than anything else, a city with restuarants and theaters and fine shops, beautiful cathedrals so unlike the grim brick churches in Palmyra. It intrigued her, but she began to think more ambitiously. The Yankee cities, so mysterious and remote and threatening for years . . . New York, Boston and Philadelphia. . . . She smiled when she remembered the story Sukie once told her, about the master who pretended he was going on a trip. He wanted to see what happened if the slaves thought he was away. He came around their quarters disguised as a tramp, face smutty and clothes dirty and ragged. They didn't recognize him and he walked up and begged for food. One negro boy said to him, "Stand back, you shabby rascal. If there be anything left, you get some. If there be none left, you get none. This is our time. Old Massa done gone to Philaneyork, and we having a big time."

She was tired of pretending to everyone that she was sweetly chaste, listening to the cant of town ladies full of swooning platitudes as if the war had never happened, their world changed forever. She thought that one day she might hunger for the big house in Palmyra, remember it as safe, peaceful, even domestic . . . try in some strange place to feel how she was often overwhelmed by the shadowy misted colors of the distant highlands, the calm solemnity of the countryside. But even the beautiful yellow poplars and white oaks were poison trees now. She would miss touching, as she often did, her German china dolls, the red and yellow hobbyhorse, her stuffed moneky figures with the eccentric legs, all the tangible memories. But to stay would be paying for the same dead horse over and over again.

Catlin came to dinner one evening, and afterward they sat on the veranda, holding hands, watching the moon emerge through smoke from a fire somewhere in the woods. She didn't know how to begin and let him take the lead, knew he'd be insistent on making plans.

"We could bring my family from Arkansas. It would be a good way to have a reunion, have everyone meet."

She pretended not to understand that he was talking about a wedding.

"My father will be happy you're from the South. I think he was afraid I might marry some stiff Yankee lady. He's about as hardhead South as you can get."

"I thought your folks were from Ohio?"

"It's like reformed sinners. They're the worst."

She took a deep breath as if girding herself for an enormous physical effort. "I can't marry you now." She was surprised that he took it so quietly. He gave her an ironic look and she thought she caught the meaning. "Now you think I'm wicked because I went to Gladehill with you when I wasn't sure."

"No. But I think you're doing this for some reason that has nothing to do with us, or for someone."

For myself, she thought, for myself. So I won't have to live the rest of my life at cozy socials, raising a brood, always introcuded as the handsome captain's wife. She wanted to tell him the truth, hated being a hypocrite, but he could never understand. "Anyway, I'm just excitable. I think I was born loony." It would make it easier if he thought he had fooled himself with a bad choice. But he was wise enough to know that when a woman mocks herself, it was because she thought it was the kinder rejection . . . *You are good and handsome and exciting . . . I am young and ripe but a silly little dunce, not good enough by far for you.*

"I don't want to give up." He couldn't help himself. Even the rustling of her dress provoked him, made vivid the slender springy body beneath, and he had been grateful for his outrageous good luck.

"I don't want you to." She wanted to tell him about Matthew so he would still protect them, but thought he knew all the Ku Klux in Palmyra and had never said anything. She felt sorry for him. "But we can't talk about marriage for a long time." She cared more for him because he hadn't made a scene, insisted that she keep her promise, force her into doing something rash. But when he kissed her goodnight on the cheek, she felt a core of misery in her because she'd made him unhappy, and he made it worse by glancing back from the foot of the stairs with a puzzled, reluctant look, saying, "If you need help. . . ." She went into the house thinking that once Matthew was safe, she might change her mind, but realized it was just balm for her guilt. The doctor said Matthew would be fine in a few weeks. Sukie and Jessie were changing the dressing on the wound when she came into his room. After they left she sat on the bed and fussed with the bandages to make them neater.

"I've got an idea."

He lifted the injured arm slowly, wincing a little. "I didn't much like the last idea you had even if it did save papa."

"Remember we talked about you going to school up north."

"And you said it was too late."

"I've been thinking. It isn't."

"Even if I would go, what good would it do. He talks about Princeton, says it's always been a place for Southern boys to get a good education. Hell, I can't even do the school here. Everything they stuff in my head is useless nonsense. I can't remember anything. They'd ship me right out of that Princeton."

"But that's because of the way things are done down here. They teach old-fashioned and they think the same way. You know you're not dumb. What if I went with you? Wouldn't that be fun? Don't you want to get away from here? She made it sound like he was a bored rustic dreaming of the big city, when it was a matter of his life that he got away.

"Maybe."

"Jesus, I can't stand it here anymore. When they killed Trask, that was the last straw."

"Why did the niggers moan like that? They moaned three days on Trask."

"That's niggers. White folks don't have fine funerals like niggers."

"Where is this Princeton?"

"In New Jersey state. Right near New York and Philadelphia." She thought she'd see him safe in school, then move on.

"If we went up there, they'd kill us."

She laughed. "There are Southern boys up there right now. You heard papa say it. And they were soldiers, a lot of them."

"I don't know. What about them?" He motioned to his parents' room. "You said they'd be in danger."

"Mama can take care of herself, you can be sure of that. And papa can't be any more worse off than he is now. You're just going away to school. You get better fast. You can't go there until the new school year, but we could go sooner, get used to things." She was caught between the here and there, an emotional physics that threatened to crush her and kill Matthew if they lingered too long in Palmyra.

A sergeant came into Catlin's billet one morning and said a man wanted to see him.

"What's it about?"

"He said he'd only talk to you."

Catlin was tired after a night chasing Ku Klux and wanted to rest. He blew breath out and rubbed his eyes. "Tell him to come back later."

"He said you'd want to see him."

"All right, send him in."

The man was short and crabbed-looking, hair almost to his shoulders, a seamed, weathered face with a long knife scar along his chin, and eyes that blinked constantly. He smelled of woodsmoke and whiskey and animal grease, carried an old musket with a powder horn slung across his shoulder and a butcher knife in his belt. Catlin noticed

that the man's face had little trace of the sun, and he had
been in the area long enough to know a mountain "Piney."
They rarely came out of the deep woods, only an occasional visit to a crossroads store to exchange pelts for
beans and salt and flour. Most of them had come out of
the Kentucky mountains, as did many Palmyra townfolk
and farmers, but they had stayed rooted, cherishing the
freedom and savage harshness of their primitive lives. Catlin knew they were people with lawless souls who fought
even the mildest curbs on their liberty. Instead of building
snug farms and bustling towns, they chose to stay hidden,
illiterate, rough and hard-drinking. They were the ones
who had cleared the Cumberland of Indians, hunting
them down with the same relish with which they tracked
and killed bears, for the fierce pleasure of the sport. They
were cynical, hard, lonesome and bitter people, and the
names they gave places told what had made them so:
*Stinking Creek . . . Devil's Jump . . . Hell Mountain
. . . Greasy Squaw . . . Massacre Mountain. . . .* Catlin
knew that some were Klansmen, though they rarely even
saw a negro, and wondered what the stranger could tell
him. They weren't people to make themselves important.

The man pointed to the iron stove in the center of a
wooden frame filled with sand. "Can I warm?"

Catlin nodded, thought he had come a long way in the
cold dawn. The man put his hands close to the glow and
rubbed them. Catlin was impatient but knew he couldn't
hurry him. Maybe he'd seen a Klan raid, something, and
wanted to talk. People like him might think the Klan was
just another threat to their freedom. If some had joined,
they had come into small towns on their own. No Klan
recruiter ever crossed the Cumberland or Sulphur Rivers,
went back into those woods and flat-topped mountains.
During the war they were left alone, shooting and knifing
and beating each other to death. Sometimes it had something to do with the war, but most of the time it was
because it was what they did best when they were drunk.

The small man turned and faced Catlin. "Name of Levi
Strachan." He took a clay pipe out, filled it, held the tobacco pouch out to Catlin who shook his head, took a

wood shaving from the floor, stuck it in the fire and lit the pipe. "You the Captain here?"

Catlin pointed to his bars. "That's right."

"I can tell you something."

"Good. What is it?"

"O know a Klucker."

"Only one?"

"This one here, he's a pup, not long off his mama's tit."

Catlin wondered why a Piney would come in to inform on one man. "How come you know him?"

"Never no mind, Yankee. He's a bad one."

Catlin warned himself to be careful. The South was a conquered, occupied country, and too often in times like that men were getting killed because someone didn't like their politics, had an old grudge to settle, wanted their woman, their business or land, or any of a dozen different reasons that had nothing to do with the war or the occupation.

"Where you from?"

Strachan vaguely waved north toward the mountains beyond Palmyra.

"Who's the man?"

"Name of Lanier?"

"The lawyer?"

"The son."

Catlin had suspected that Matthew was in the Klan. Too often at night, when he was visiting Adela, Matthew was away and his absence coincided with a raid. Catlin had often seen him with Billy Laidlaw, a known Ku-Klux. But he thought he'd have to arrest everyone in the county on suspicion if that was the case. He admitted to himself that he had never pressed it because of her. Catlin tried to fit things together . . . her reluctance to marry him, his insight that she might be trying to protect someone. But why would this ragged bastard inform on Matthew? Maybe it was the land Everett told him about, land purchased when he came to Palmyra, valuable timber and minerals, the reason he settled there. He wasn't able to develop it before the war, then afterward could do nothing because all legal titles to land were in question. But he often talked about the land, the future, how it would benefit the whole state. The land ran up into the Cumberland Plateau, and those people considered it their own preserve forever. They had killed the Indians for it, had murdered their own kin or outsiders to stay on the same land since they came spilling out of Kentucky and the western Carolinas.

"How do you know the son is Ku Klux?"

"I seen him."

"Do what?"

"I seen him kill."

Catlin was angry. "When the hell was the Klan ever in your parts?"

"I moved around. I seed things. I seed the killing."

"Where?"

"He killed the nigger Parton."

"You saw him?"

"That Jesus truth."

"You knew it was him under the mask?"

"Took it off, jabbering away at the nigger."

"That happened months ago. What took you so long to tell?"

"Winter." As if that explained it . . . holed up in the mountains, scrounging for game in the cold and snow to feed his brood, puffing his bright leaf and drinking woods whiskey, maybe shooting a lost trespasser near his rough cabin, or fighting in the shanty taverns along the Kentucky line.

"You see him do any other killing?"

"The courthouse in this'n town. Got a man name of Douthit." He scratched his head. "Nigger Trask too."

Catlin thought the man was shrewd enough to know what was going on, probably had kin in the Palmyra Den. But he thought it ludicrous that Strachan would try and implicate Matthew in three of the worst murders. Why pick on him? He suddenly remembered that Everett had the land surveyed only a month ago; maybe it was then that Strachan discovered it was owned by a town man, somehow got Lanier's name. The Piney probably thought that all the legalities and titles would disappear if he got the owner's son in trouble. Catlin wondered why Strachan and some cronies hadn't just ambushed Lanier the few times he'd traveled the winding, isolated trail into the mountains. Maybe he was making it too complicated. It could be only spite, the envy of people living on the edge. Matthew might be a rich man one day, could get marshals to push them out of their woods. He didn't think anyone had put Strachan up to it. A man like that wouldn't do anyone else's dirty work. Catlin wanted to get rid of him.

"I'll arrest that Ku Klux."

"I want to see that."

"What do you care if he killed a couple of niggers and a Southern traitor?"

"Niggers is people, and the white man he got no fair trial."

Catlin wanted to laugh in his face. Where the hell did Strachan hear that kind of talk. The worst Ku Kluxers were the ones that had little to do with negroes, the ones who suffered least when they were freed. It was all narrowminded spite and hate because they lived so hard . . . the bleak compatches, the wild turbulence of their natures, the women spent at thirty, their fear of the outsider, the new, the strange. They thought of themselves as the last splendid free creatures on earth, but didn't even have the restlessness and curiosity of the pioneers who moved on, always someplace different, confronting new dangers, using guts and guile to pull them through.

"You can go back home. I'll take care of it."

"I want to see."

"I can't just arrest a man in high day. I have to get more witnesses like you. I'll send for you when it's time for a trial."

"You don't put him in jail straight away?"

"No. You have to prove things first." Catlin felt as if he was talking to a child. He reassured Strachan that justice would be done and thanked him for turning in a dangerous, murdering Ku Kluxer.

"He gonna hang?"

Catlin winked and grinned and Strachan seemed satisfied. He gave a little two-fingered salute and walked out without telling where he could be found, as if Catlin would send a courier into the mountains and Strachan would be there, know it was time for a trial.

At first, Catlin wasn't going to do anything about Matthew, then thought he could pressure him for information. If Adela was concerned about him, he might be weakening, might be willing to talk. She'd hate him, think he was doing it because she'd made him foolish and lovelorn. But he had to know who the leaders were. General Evans commanding the Occupation troops had orders to cut the Klan's head off. General Forrest had denied any connection, though he voiced his sympathy with the secret society. In any case, Forrest was for all purposes only a businessman now, and Union authorities figured it would be bad business to arrest and humiliate one of the South's great heroes. It was the State and County leaders, even the local Dens. Cut off the head, take away their leadership, and the Klan might dissipate into outlaw bands without organization or discipline. He didn't think Matthew knew much beyond his own Den and might be too frightened to talk, but he had to try.

That afternoon he asked Adela if he could speak to Matthew.

"I'm sorry, someone's informed us that he's in the Klan."

She seemed relieved that it was in the open. Maybe something could be done to save Matthew now. "Didn't take the Pinkertons to find it out, did it?"

"I have to try and get him to talk. If he can give me some information about the Klan, we can get him out of the state quickly."

She told Catlin about her plan to go north with Matthew, how she had to convince him. "It's too late for that, isn't it?"

"Maybe later."

She seemed resigned, then her eyes were curious. "Why now? Why did someone just happen to inform now?"

"It had nothing to do with us. If you think that, I won't talk to him. I won't touch him."

She touched his arm and looked at him for a long time. "No, I don't think you're that kind of man."

When Matthew came home she brought him to the sun parlor. He was surprised to see Catlin and joked about lazy good-for-nothing Yankees who couldn't find any better business to do than court in the daytime.

"Sit down, Matt," Catlin said.

He looked at Adela and sat on a velvet ottoman. "What's all this?"

"Someone's informed on you."

"About what?"

"Stop it," Adela said. "He knows."

"You can help us and yourself."

"How?"

"Tell me who the leaders are."

"You got to be loose in the head."

"We're going to break the Klan sooner or later. You can save yourself a long sentence in the penitentiary, and save your family a lot of misery."

"That's all they'd have if I talked."

"We'll protect you."

He tried to show some bravado. "No one can do that. You think you know the Klan, but you don't. They're an army."

"Do you want to get out?"

"Maybe. Maybe it wasn't what I thought." But he was quick to insist that he'd held his own with dangerous men.

"Then help us. I can get you out of here with troopers . . . flag the train out of town."

"Shows how much you know. Damn engineer or brakeman or station agent could all be Ku Klux, anyone on the railroad. It ain't exactly like rescuing a prisoner in the war."

Catlin knew he was right. "Then there's only one good reason for you to talk—to stop the raids and killings around here, save innocent lives."

"That sure sounds noble when it ain't your skin."

"Matt, you know they would have killed your father and Judge Darcy if Adela hadn't warned them in time."

Matthew had a rueful smile and rubbed his arm. "You know she shot me that night? I was standing far picket."

Catlin was astonished, wanted to tell her how much he

admired that kind of courage, but thought it wiser to keep on Matthew. "I heard you got the wound hunting rabbits."

"I told them a rabbit started my horse and my gun went off and hit me. Good thing they didn't look at it, but they suer gave me the hee-haw."

"You know how many times they've warned your father. You saw what they did to Douthit because he tried to help negroes. Your father——"

"Damn you, Matt!" Adela broke in. "I should have killed you. Because someone's going to get you. A Yankee or the nigger militia, a farmer you're rousing or in some whorehouse. You might even get it from some Ku Klux who maybe don't like you just because you're papa's son. For God's sake, tell him something!"

"Where's mama?"

"Back in the garden."

"I don't want her to hear me. You promise you'll get me out of here safe?"

"Yes."

"What about the family?"

"I promise we'll do our best."

"It's only dangerous for me and papa," Adela said and laughed. "Mama would join them. You know what I mean . . . such a good patriotic Confederate plantation lady." She'd given Matthew the hint—Jessie knew Colonel Tyler, the Grand Cyclops, had convinced him to take Matthew when he wasn't old enough. Make Catlin put the pressure on her too. Make everything bad enough, stir things up, so they'd all have to get out.

But Matthew either didn't understand or refused. "I'll give you some names, but they won't be anything new. They're the bad ones, the kind the Klan didn't need. They do most of the rough work."

Adela didn't think he'd mention Kortman. She wanted to gloat a little at first, wanted him to take some punishment, be debased the way he did to her, learn that everyone in the world is vulnerable one way or another. He had never lost any of his damned lewd impudence, and she was suddenly crazy with the idea that she would be the one to kill him, blow his brains out. Put him to rest. She remembered

once asking him to stay and make love to her again. He
said, casually, that he had to go, but it wouldn't be too
long before they saw each other again. She gave him a
brilliant smile and asked him if he knew what he was. He
said no, what? She said he was a cruel son of a bitch. He
said he was too edgy to stay, and almost as an after-
thought said he loved her. She said he made it seem like a
crime and she was his accomplice. What was the difference who killed him? It wouldn't make his death any less—
or more—glorious to be killed by the Yankees than a
woman who hated him because he refused to love her.
However obsessed both were, he was the cannier of the
two from the start, knew that each might kill the other in
time. She would only make that fate come true . . . but
she would be the killer.

"Thevemow and Cissel, they're two of the worst," Matthew said. "Louis Chandler, Joe Hatton . . . Duryea,
Harry Evans, Duncan Padgett. . . . That's all I want to
say."

"What about the officers?"

He thought of Tyler, Fred Currier, old Graham Petit,
Morehouse and the rest. His own class . . . quality men
that maybe did wrong, but it wasn't what was in their
hearts at the first, they were just men who loved the
South. "I don't know any. They never unmask."

Catlin knew it wasn't true. Pinkerton detectives had in-
filtrated two Dens and described the meeting ritual. But
he didn't want to challenge Matthew. "Don't you recognize their voices?"

"No. They all sound like outsiders. Maybe that's the
way they do it. Send strangers in to give the orders." He
flushed, knew he wasn't fooling Catlin. Then he thought
of one man he wanted the Yankees to get, the Klud, the
gaunt Baptist preacher. He hated the man, always talking
against any other church, whipping the men up. Once a
new man came in and the Klud found out he was Church
of the Nazarene. The preacher got the Palmyra men to
think it was the devil's church, said the man was there to
put a curse on them, and most of the ignorant Kluxers
believed it. They took the man out one night and beat his

head in with barrel staves. "They got a Baptist preacher from Wyatt. His name's Aspinall. He gets them to kill so they can be Jesus-saved he says . . . that whorehouse in Cumberland, a lot of other times. You ought to put him in a crazyhouse.

It was useless, Catlin thought. He wasn't going to touch a preacher, not in that part of the country, and he could have arrested those others at any time. Padgett was the one man named who might be vulnerable, a middle-aged bank clerk with a large family. Pick him up, ship him east, slam him into a military prison and put the pressure on. Then Catlin thought that he might have compromised Matthew. He wasn't going to act on the information, but he'd been seen too often with Adela and visting the Lanier house. If Klu Klux riders were ambushed and began to take bad losses, if anything went wrong, the Klan leaders would look in their own ranks for an informer. Matthew might be too wary, too eager to put them off the track.

He regretted listening to Strachan, had been too anxious to see Adela again and used Matthew as an excuse. But the worst thing—what he didn't know—was that he had underestimated Strachan.

12

ONLY hours after he talked with Catlin, Strachan had his cousin Thevenow bring him to Hope Mills to meet the Klan officers.

"You got a traitor."

Kortman was suspicious. "Who sent you here, you weasel?"

"No one. But I seed the man talking to the Yankee captain."

"Who?"

"Lanier's son."

Blanton glanced at Tyler. "He's your man, isn't he?"

"I'd swear for him, any man we have."

"You're kind of quick to call a man a traitor," Kortman said. "How do you know they weren't just talking, passing the day?"

"I went to the Yankee to come up the creek because some niggers was trying to root there on my land. We was gonna kill them woolhead bastards, but they had them Bureau men with them."

"How do you know he told the Yankee any Klan business? Catlin's fuck-hard for the daughter. Maybe he was just buttering up the kid brother."

197

"I was standing just outside and hear them talk." He paused, careful, waiting to be prompted by questions.

"What did Matt say?"

"He was talking anmes . . . so many I can't know 'em all. But he said my kin's name"—he gestured toward Thevenow—"and most all your names."

Kortman didn't believe him. What the hell could Matthew gain by informing? He knew what happened to anyone who betrayed them. Maybe the Yankee just took a chance and squeezed him.

"I knew we should have killed that lawyer bastard a long time ago," Hoagland said, and looked at Kortman. "You always said it would be dangerous, said Lanier coudn't hurt us, we shouldn't touch the quality. Then his goddamn strip goes and tells on us. Maybe the lawyer had the idea for him. We gave him a hundred warnings. You think a man's gonna be scared when nothing happens. You were fucking down with the girl—that's why you wouldn't touch him."

Kortman's scarred cheek flamed. He knew the danger the moment someone in the Den questioned another's loyalty or dedication to the cause. His caution for the Klan had been genuine: Lanier was no threat, and Adela had nothing to do with it. But Blanton and Tyler were looking at him hard. Strachan moved away slowly by instinct. Kortman pulled his revolver and jamed it into Hoagland's stomach.

"You're going to die, you damn liar!"

Hoagland thought he was bluffing, putting on a show for the others. He grinned. "You kill me, you ugly bastard, there's three guns that'll take you on the spot."

Blanton tried to make peace. If Kortman killed Hoagland, he had no idea of drawing on the man. Hoagland was a fool. Throw mud on a man's honor and you deserve to die. Kortman was fast with a gun and might take them all if he thought they believed the loose talk.

"Put the gun up, Jim."

"I'll put it up his asshole and blow his damn shit out!"

He began to slap Hoagland, still holding the gun on him. Hoagland saw Kortman's eyes and began to mutter a prayer. Kortman suddenly raised his weapon to the head and fired pointblank. The shot sounded like an explosion in the cellar. Hoagland kicked back with a quick groan and dropped. Kortman stuck the gun in his belt and turned to Strachan. He was going to tell him to pack the body into the mountains and bury it, then had a better idea.

"Why don't we kick his face in some, put another couple of bullets in him, then string him up down the hill from Lanier."

Blanton thought it was needless, stupid, but was careful how he talked to Kortman. "Why do it that way?"

"A couple of things that are food for us. First, we show people what the Yankees do to a Ku Klux. We put a sign on him and make sure of that. Turn them against the soldiers. Another—if Matt talked, this'd put him off his guard. He'd know from something on the sign that it was Klan work on a traitor. He'd think Hoagland was talking too, and we found out and got the right man.

Blanton felt sick with the conspiracies, contortions, the eternal secrecy and plotting, the lack of trust or honor. He had felt honorable in battle. Like others, he thought the Klan was a way of fighting the war again. But all that he saw come out of it was brutes making more dead niggers and scared niggers, and whites killed for conscience or petty misdeeds. He thought he would command soldiers, but he was only the keeper of fanatics, like some murderous sect, men who'd kill like the church people in olden days if they smelled an infidel, then created infidels to keep killing in the name of some holy cause. He glanced at Thevenow, a near-cretin who took pleasure in it. And now Kluxers were killing each other. He didn't blame Kortman. If he had let Hoagland live, the talk would have made Kortman a pariah in the Klan, killed, ironically, by the same chilling zeal he ignited in the Palmyra men. If Matt Lanier was guilty, he had to die. Blanton believed in the sanctity of an oath and would stay to the end, but was beginning to think that they were doomed, that all of it was suicide. He could understand why someone like Matt would come to a poor pass and want to save his soul by betraying others.

Kortman told Strachan to get out and never show his face again. "You did us a favor. Now I'm going to do your kin a favor and let you walk away." He turned to Thevenow and pointed to the body. The big man kicked Hoagland's face in with his heavy boots, then stomped him in the groin. He pulled a .57 Springfield from a rack and blew holes in the dead man's face and body. Then he held the rifle by the barrel and smashed Hoagland's teeth with the gunbutt.

"Enough!" Blanton cried. "For Jesus' sake, enough!"

Kortman enjoyed the scene . . . how quickly everything turned. He'd been afraid that Hoagland had put the mark on him, that Blanton and Tyler would judge him. Now one man was dead, the General couldn't stand watching what he'd ordered Kluxers to do a hundred times, and Tyler was too afraid for his hide to do anything. Thevenow was *his* man because he knew how often to unleash him and some others and keep them happy. Blanton and Tyler and the rest, porky old snobs who let Kortman and the others do the dirty work. They went to Nashville to sit in overstuffed chairs in a hotel parlor, ate the best food with Forrest, smoked good cigars, bragged about their fierce riders, talked all the mumbo-jumbo at meetings, made out like the whole damn thing was collecting dues and selling uniforms and making rules and passing fines on any Kluxer who did something wrong. Always talking about the high ideals and politics, and it was him that had to do the blood. Stinking hyprocrites. He wasn't going to do their dirty work anymore. With Grant in office, it was going to be run-and-save-your-own-hide in a little while. He had little regret or guilt about anything he'd done. Most people the Klan attacked, had it coming, But he wanted to give the big men in the Klan, the inner core, a taste of his rage—and do it before they could swallow their spit.

"Matt Lanier goes into the Dead Book," Blanton said. "We're not going to waste any time bringing him in. And this time we're not going to fool around with Lanier himself. He goes too."

Tyler stroked his curly beard. "That seems the best." He looked at Kortman. "Better to get the lice before they infect more men, isn't that right?"

Kortman felt slick. They were going along because they were afraid of him. He was convinced of it now. He held the aces, had the power, could do with them what he wanted. He began to tease.

"What about the Lanier women?"

"We can't——"

Kortman broke in on Blanton, wanted to see how far he could go. "We get them all."

Blanton was aware of Thevenow standing near him, still holding the Springfield. "If you think it's the only way."

Kortman thought he'd show them up by making dressy plans for the operation—then warn the Laniers. The whole Tennessee Realm, maybe the whole Klan, would get on the Palmyra Den, ride their ass good because they let an informer get away . . . a trifling boy and a cripple and two women escaping a big band of riders. Blanton and Tyler wouldn't be invited to Nashville after that.

He had to time everything perfectly. Give the Laniers only a day. If he gave them more time, they'd be long out of the state before the Klan started after them. It wouldn't look bad enough unless he cut it that close. There was danger for the Laniers that way, but he didn't think he cared what happened to them. He was worried about Strachan. The man had been hanging around the Yankees, then came to them. Even if he was Thevenow's kin, how did they know he wasn't a double agent, or just a mean little treacherous bastard who'd turn anyone in for his own reasons. He couldn't leave anything to chance. If Strachan talked, Kortman knew he wouldn't be able to bluff or fight his way out another time. He pulled Thevenow into a corner. Blanton and Tyler thought they were discussing the traitor and sat quietly, riffling through papers, afraid to even pretend to leave in a casual way.

"Your kin," Kortman said. "I don't trust him." He hoped

he wouldn't have to say it, that the brute would understand from his look that they had to get Strachan.

Thevenow's red face looked like it was square-hacked out of a big clump of red cedar with an axe. His squinty pale eyes flickered once under the red eyebrows.

"He's no blood kin."

Kortman winked. "Go after him. Wait until you're up in the hills. Then get back here quick."

A meeting was called for the next night. Kortman hoped Matthew would show. If everything seemed normal, he could carry out his plan. But if he stayed away, Blanton, feeling cockier with so many men around him, might still have enough spunk to order the riders out that night. When he saw Matthew ride up, he thought that someone was giving the kid some good advice . . . *act as if nothing happened*. He greeted him and they went into the cellar together. Hoagland's body had been buried in the woods the night before by Thevenow and Cissel. Aspinall started the meeting with one of his hellfire sermons, putting some men into the "jerks," a kind of religious hysteria where they shook and quivered, eyes ecstatic, then fell to the ground in a faint. Blanton took over and said Kortman had something important for them.

"Inside the week, the Palmyra Den is going on its most important raid, something great for the South . . . something real interesting. Every man will ride. You're to be on alert every hour of the day."

Blanton wondered why Kortman didn't pin it down, was being so evasive, but didn't object. Some of the shopkeepers didn't like it. They were the men who took the negroes' money and acted friendly, and at night went to their cabins to whip and kill them. They thought a raid that big might upset things.

Currier reported that a married man named Bannister had fallen in love with another woman, burned his wife and three children in their house, then moved a few miles away with the woman.

"He says she just works around the place, but they're surely hard-fucking and both have to be punished."

Despite what he said about the alert, Kortman didn't want them riding for a week or so, knew they'd get lazy. But the Den was geared to furious periods of activity, and when they thought they had put fear into people, made the countryside quiet, they were quiet. There had been no raid for four days. Let them ride once more that night.

"What the hell would he be doing with a woman now?" said Kortman. "You ever see a man crazier than when it happened?"

"Woman's got nigger and Cherokee in her. Put a spell on him to do it."

"Her name Mary Duffield?"

"Yes."

Kortman had seen her helping Bannister clear his place two days after the fire. A formless girl, sagging, cheesy flesh. You couldn't tell she was other than white. A plain sallow face, faintly splotched, her breath coming with a slow and sad adenoidal murmur when she spoke. Who the hell would kill his family for a woman like that? He wasn't going to argue with Currier. They believed in Indian and nigger spells, let them. Let them do what they wanted to the poor bastard. He didn't want anything to snag his plan. Later he heard what happened. They caught Bannister and the woman in bed and axed them to death, cutting off his penis and her breasts, then torched the shack. On the way back to Hope Mills they decided to have some fun with a nigger family. They knocked on a cabin door and a boy about ten opened it slowly.

"Come out here, boy," Buckner said.

"Yessuh."

"Where's your pap?"

"He working off on the railroad."

"Your mammy?"

"She dead."

"Who else is here?"

"Old Aunt Lucy. She mighty sick."

"You been a good nigger boy?"

"Yessuh."

"Stand on your head."

The boy turned a few somersaults. They ticked him

around with their whips and laughed when he managed to stand on his head.

"Who lives down the road?"

"Man name of Nicodemus."

"What does he do?"

"Work in the field."

"Show us the way."

The boy ran fast across the field to keep ahead of the big horses. A tall skinny negro came out when the boy knocked and said "Holy Moses" when he saw the riders.

"What's your name?"

"Nicodemus."

"What do you do?"

"I farms."

"What do you raise, Niggerdemos?"

"Cotton and corn."

"Take us to see your cotton. We're just from Hell and we ain't got no cotton there."

Nicodemus took them to his crop and Buckner dismounted.

"What is that?" he said, feeling grass.

"That grass."

"You raise grass too?"

"No, it come up."

They gave him a whipping and warned that they'd be back soon and give him worse if he kept raising grass.

"You raise cotton and corn on this farm. Good nigger crops. But no grass, mind you."

By daylight Nicodemus and his family were out with hoes, scythes and knives cutting the grass. There wasn't a blade left on the place when they got through, and though the Ku Kluxers never bothered him again, there never was.

Kortman had to be careful how he approached Everett Lanier; he thought it better to speak to Catlin first. There was little time left. The next morning he saw Catlin ride out of the courtyard of the troop billet and cross the road, walking alongside the horse.

"I want to talk with you."

Catlin stared straight ahead. "We'll talk when I'm ready." Then he gave Kortman a quick glance. "Maybe sooner than you want."

"The Laniers are in danger."

Catlin had a sarcastic look and said nothing . . . *same old scare talk.*

"They're going to be killed. All of them. Believe me."

Catlin saw something in his eyes. He kept the horse walking slow. "Where can we meet?"

"Their house. Tonight. You get there early. I'll come through the field around the back."

"What is it?"

"We got to get them out of here." Kortman walked away quickly.

Catlin went to the Lanier house around seven. He breathed easier when he saw Matthew and Adela there. She seemed annoyed, but he quickly said that he was there on important business.

"You're in danger. The whole family," he said to Everett.

"What do you mean?"

"The Klan."

Everett gave a futile wave. "Why now?"

Catlin didn't want to tell him about Matthew. Let Kortman do it. "I don't know myself. But I've got good reason to believe it." He paused. "Someone is coming here. He'll tell you about it. Receive him—and listen to him." A few minutes later there was a knock at the back entrance in the pantry and Catlin brought Kortman into the parlor. Matthew wondered why he was there, but no one else betrayed any surprise.

"I've told them all I know," Catlin said.

Kortman took a deep breath. "I know you have no cause to believe me. But what I'm telling you now is the truth." He knew how easily he could inspire rage in any one of them for different reasons. "The Klan is going to kill you, and no fooling this time with warnings and bullcrap like that."

"Why all of us?" Everett pointed to Matthew. "I could

understand if it was only him, or myself." He was telling his son that he'd known for a long time.

"Because they're having trouble, and one of them wants to prove how powerful he is. You show weakness in a pack like that and they drag you under." He had that sardonic, twisted grin.

"Why would you help us?"

"To be honest, it's not so much helping you as getting at them . . . for my own reasons. But I don't hold with murder by the lot like they want to do."

"If the order is out, how can you help us?"

"Because I'm the one who's supposed to carry out the order . . . lead the raid."

"They're not going to drive me from my house."

"Mister Lanier . . . Captain . . . that kind of talk went out with the war. You still don't know who you're sitting down with. You'll have to leave—or I'm going to have to let that pack of dogs loose to kill you." He was shaken. He'd started the whole thing as a tease, a bluff to push himself to more power. But if he couldn't convince Lanier, force him out, he had a bad choice—kill the family or go on the run himself.

"You better leave for a while," Catlin said. "You can come back when it's safe."

"No, they can't ever come back as long as the Klan is around. They're going to burn this place down if they find you or don't."

"I can't believe this," Everett said.

"You better. And you better not push your luck too far."

Kortman thought about his own luck. He was risking his neck for them, and the odds were getting too long. But he wasn't sure he cared any more. The Klan was under fire, and a lot of Ku Kluxers now were swaggering kids who had grown up during the war and occupation. They learned truculence as a way to settle matters, saw lawlessness as honorable. Just sweet mean killers never plagued by memory of limits and decency that fitfully haunted Kortman. He had to mock them with an unsentimental wit, play it rough and crazy to keep himself from getting too morbid, from being prey because they'd kill him just for the killing, to simply keep on until someone gunned him.

"How can I believe you?" Everett's face had a rare hardness. Both Catlin and Kortman knew they were seeing the iron in the man, the cavalry officer, the man who'd defied the Klan. "One way or another you've poisoned everyone in this family."

Kortman was stunned that he knew and had never challenged him. Maybe the man liked to suffer, maybe what he knew about his own women excited him. Matthew was another story. He thought that a man like Lanier would have killed his son before he let him go Ku Klux.

"I want to go to Loretto," Jessie said.

"There is no Loretto!" Everett's voice rose. "Can't you get it through your head. That house is in ruins. There are negras cropping the land. Can't you ever stop dreaming?"

Jessie smoothed her apricot silk dress. "I won't go any other place. I never wanted to leave there."

"We'll do what's right, mama." Adela looked at Catlin. "Won't we?"

Kortman said he could give them three days at the most. He would give them their route. "When they come here and find you gone, I'll take them another way. You have to get to the Mississippi and get out of the state."

Everett didn't know whether to believe him. Why should a man like Kortman try to save them? What he said just sounded like bravado. Was it a trick to flush them out so it would be easier to kill them someplace else. If the Klan did anything like that in the middle of Palmyra, they were finished there. Town people didn't care what happened in the countryside on dark nights. People might not disagree with the Klan, but they would fight it out of sheer animal fear for their lives. If the Klan could do that to the Laniers, no one was safe. It had been his watchword from the beginning. He still believed in social ritual, yet he had warned others that no one was safe once the violence started . . . *"Don't be deceived by incidental virtue*. . . . He didn't hold on to the old world, the way Jessie did, but he understood her. Where would they go? There were relatives in North Carolina and Virginia. If

Kortman was telling the truth, he was right . . . they had to leave the state.

"Why go across the river? Why not into Kentucky? It's only twenty miles or so, and the state was Unionist."

"That's mountain country, near a damn wilderness all the way up into Kentucky. If the Klan don't get you, the mountain people will. They'd kill you for your horse, maybe just the leather in the rigging. You're going to have to go separate. Matt and Adela can ride. But you two go by carriage. You think you'd make it into Kentucky? Where the hell are the roads? Where would you go once you got there? If you did. My way is safer. I have friends all across this state."

"We could take the railroad"

"Don't you understand? I'm supposed to carry out this order. I have to pretend to keep you herded, tell people to watch the depots and roads. You and your wife could get out easy. A carriage, even in daylight. A ride to Aspen Hill or someplace else that won't rouse anyone. These two can ride out at night." He grinned when he looked at Matthew. "From what I hear, she can ride and shoot pretty good. Things get around." He wished Lanier would press Matthew, find out that he talked, gave names, that the Klan was told about it and that was why they had to run.

"Where would we go once we got across the river?" Adela said. "If we do."

"You can go to my family in Arkansas," Catlin said. "My father will take you in, I'm sure. You'll be safe there until you can come back."

"Where's your family?"

"Piggot . . . maybe eighty miles from Memphis. If they cross the river in the north part of the state, they can reach it across a corner of Missouri and cut the distance in half."

Kortman thought it was about 150 miles to Memphis from Palmyra, about 100 to the Mississippi through the northwest part of the state. *Piggot* . . . it sounded familiar. A Ku Klux from Piggot named Catlin who had been in the area a couple of times, the man with them in the courthouse when they killed Douthit. He had to be Cat-

lin's father . . . the same mean son of a bitch, a leader
in the Arkansas Klan. What a hellish joke. Right into the
bear's mouth. Catlin didn't seem to know anything about
his father, and he wasn't about to tell him. But they could
give the Piggot man a good story. People ran from the
Klan for different reasons. Or maybe have Matthew open
up that he was Ku Klux and had to run from the Yankees.
A loving family would follow the youngest. Kortman
thought he'd come up with something that sounded right.
He'd taken on too much just to warn them and get them
across the Mississippi. The hell with what happened afterward.

"That will put your family in danger," Everett said.

"My father's a good man. It's the one safe place, and I'll
know where to find you. As soon as Kortman gives me the
crossing, I'll telegraph my bother to meet you on the Tennessee side."

Kortman decided it would be safer and quicker to go the
north route. Fewer Klan Dens, and if they hugged the
Kentucky border, they could always try and get across if
there was danger.

"Get me a map of the state." Matthew brought a school-
book and Kortman examined the map for a long time.
"Right here . . . Phillipy . . . maybe thirty-five miles to
Piggot straight across the river and that patch of Missouri.
River takes a big bend right above it and steamers'll be
going slow. They'll take a hail. You get out of here by
Friday. That's four days. It's about a hundred miles to
Phillipy. Figure the carriage can't make it in less than
three days." He pointed to Matthew and Adela. "Don't
you two get any ideas of escorting them. You get out as
fast as you can. Wait for the carriage around the Phillipy
dock. There's always a lot of strangers and carriages and
freight wagons . . . no one will bother you. You just sit
tight and wait. Lanier, you don't push that carriage too
hard. You're just gentry out for a ride. Stop at hotels at
night. You can make it three days easy if you do it right."

Catlin was getting impatient, slapping his gauntlet on
his thigh. "Why don't I just get them safe across with a
military escort?"

"That's stupid."

"What are you talking about? That way they aren't separated, and they'd be protected all the way."

"Listen, we could have taken every man you have in the
area. There's that many Ku Klux. But it would have
brought the government down too hard, bring an army in.
We figured we could live with the troopers you have. Besides, you try and escort them, you'd have a battle on
your hands. Every Den in the west part of the state is
going to be alerted."

"What if we can't meet in three days?" Adela said.
"What if one or two of us don't get there?"

"You do it like a soldier. Catlin'll tell you I'm right. You
get out of here Friday. If someone's missing by Monday
midnight, you get on the first steamer that takes a hail. If
someone's held up, they know where to go and who to ask
for. If they're dead somewhere back on the road, it won't
matter if you wait a hundred years. I know it's hard to
think about, but that's the only way. Catlin, you tell your
brother to wait until someone comes and get them across
fast. Whoever gets there first can tell them how many
more to expect."

"He'll know what to do. I'll try to give him as much as I
can by the telegraph."

"What does he look like?"

"I haven't seen him since 'sixty-three, but he wouldn't
be likely to change that much." Catlin tried to remember
what might single his brother out. "First, he's thirty now.
Powerful-looking man, husky, about five foot eleven. His
face is swart, high face bones, dark hair, and if he's like
my father there'll be some early gray. His eyes take the
light strange, sometimes look blue or gray, handsome fellow. The best thing I can tell you is he's kind of showy-
looking, you pick him out in a crowd. When I saw him at
Mechanicsville in the war, he had a bad infected middle
finger on his left hand, and he thought the Yankee doctor
was going to cut it off. I don't know, but you can look for
that."

"The last thing. Ylu tell your brother—because he's
going to have to tell your father—that Lanier is accused of

stealing government money from the Radicals that was supposed to be parceled out to the niggers to get them to vote the right way." Kortman was pleased with himself. The story was reasonable and would make their way easier with the Piggot man.

"He won't take a man like that. My father's Bible, real stern religious."

Oh, yes he will, he'll kiss him, Kortman thought. "You tell him you think he's innocent, but the Radicals want to get him because they think he's a true pigheaded Southerner they have trouble with."

"Why do you have to say I'm a thief?" Everett asked.

"Because that telegraph message can be picked up anywhere along the line. Except for the military posts, the telegraph men are all station agents and they're mostly Klan." He caught Catlin's look. The officer realized that much of the army telegraph traffic had been picked up by the Klan; they knew where troops would be and raided in other places. This way, if the Klan gets it, they won't bother—not until they get the alert the next day." Kortman paused. "But we got to give your father a better reason why we sent the family to him. Adela, you tell the brother you're promised to the Captain, and he'll be coming home soon."

Kortman gathered everyone around the dining room table and pointed to the map:

"You first head west toward Mobley. The Tennessee's too wide and fast there, and rivers are going to be trouble all the way because of high water. Get south to McKibbon and the railroad bridge if you can't get someone to ferry you across. You still have high land about ten miles across the Tennessee. Keep north, try to follow the Louisville–Nashville tracks"—he pointed to the towns—"Big Sandy . . . Manlyville . . . Vale. When you get to Richland, you'll see the railroad turn southwest to Memphis. You go north, then you cross the middle and the north forks of the Obion. It's all flat after that. You circle around Tiptonville right up into Phillipy."

"I'll have a man make good maps for each one," Catlin said.

"Make yourself look different . . . something," Kortman said. "Lanier, you go skinhead. Ma'am, you wear something plain. Things like that."

"I know what I'll do," Jessie said. "I'll pull my hair straight back in a bun, take one spare dress like any respectable lady, and I have my Daddy's gun." She surprised Everett. He thought she'd insist on taking a trunk and they'd have to drag her away, protesting.

"Matt, I told you to grow a moustache or beard. Men might have taken you serious. We could have shaved it off, give you some specs and shoe-blacking in your hair."

"I tried. Nothing came out strong enough."

Kortman looked at Adela. "I don't know what the hell you can do. Pity to spoil anything. You have to cross about six counties, and I'll bet there's hot young bloods in half of them that heard about you." He rapped the table. "Anyone got a question, ask it now, because when I leave here, that's the last you see me." He had the wicked grin again. "Not unless I catch you."

Adela thought he was crazy and treacherous. Struts in to save them, then practically says he'd lead the chase and kill them if they were captured. She had the same uneasy feeling as her father. They'd be traveling the route he picked. He'd know where they were all the time. Was it just a bad joke? Only minutes before he said he'd take the Klan a different way. Was it a trick? Even Kortman couldn't be that pitiless, give a performance like that just to roust them out of their house and town. No . . . she knew him . . . it was just his way of pushing off any gratitude.

At first when she thought about the trip she was afraid, then, slowly, began to feel the excitement. She wouldn't have to rot in Palmyra where people said he was queer and outlandish and got on their 'narve strings.' She might wind up dead and rot someplace else, but, damn, she would have her adventure first. The fancy cities up north could wait. There would be plenty of time. She began to think about the West . . . Arkansas was called the dividing line. She felt shocked that she had so little feeling about leaving everything behind. *And I'm not promised to anyone* . . . She thought it was funny for Kortman to sound so courtly when he said it. He was ready to leave, gave a little two-fingered salute and started out. She had to talk to him, rushed past Catlin and led Kortman out on the porch steps in back.

"Why did you do it?"

"No noble reason. Depend on it."

"Aren't you taking a big chance?"

"As bad as you can think."

"You know, I once promised I'd kill you."

"For what? Making love to you? And that crazy bitch of a mother?"

"For not loving me, for not keeping Matt out of the Klan. I don't care what you do, you're a cruel bastard, maybe you enjoy it. But you weren't that way once."

"Do you know the hell I've been through?" It was the first time she'd ever heard self-pity from him. He touched his face. "Not just this. Plenty of men got worse. But no one comes out of a war the same way." He seemed to be trying to explain himself, as if he'd never see her again. "Everything's dead. It's going to take this land forty or fifty years just to recover from the battles. My father, friends . . . Shaddy . . . everything I cared for. It's all gone. I once thought it didn't matter that you lost, or what you lost. It only mattered how you lost and how you redeemed yourself. And whether you remembered the lessons. I thought we lost honorably, but I took the wrong way to redeem anything. You have to be lucky to cut your losses, not think of the past. I wasn't."

She grabbed his arms. "And you were going to take everything down with you."

"What the hell's the difference." He pulled away. "I'm not so different in some ways from your mother. I think about the old days too much. I stood for something then. I look at other people's lives and they seem whole, no matter how bad times are. It's always halfhearted with me. I try to invent faces I can love. That's the hell."

Adela thought she understood. All he was left with was rage, could only survive by denying, destroying.

"Do you know how many times I've walked these

streets and looked into windows where families were sitting at supper and eating quietly. I knew I'd never have a world like that. I'm always throwing bridges across rivers that keep vanishing."

"You could have had it with me."

"Don't fool yourself. You were just a kid with a lot of passion and not much else. The minute I turned quiet and kind, you would have been bored to death."

There was a loud rapping at a window that looked out on the porch and Adela saw the shadowed forms of her father and Catlin. She waved them away. "Could you have loved me?"

"Listen, you have to go on the run, and that's all you want to know." He was in control of himself again and laughed. "You know, you were the charm of this bustling town, and I was the pick of the fire-club set. You just got more charming and beautiful and delightful . . . and I was left somewhere back in the war. I never really came back. It really would have been hellacious, wouldn't it?"

"What?"

"The two of us together."

"I used to dream about it long ago."

"You want some advice? You're not so damned strong as you think. You meet up with the wrong kind of brute—and you're finished."

"What do you mean?"

"I just killed or ordered killing because I thought it was a way to keep fighting, a way out. But there are men who are really evil. They're strong and full of contempt. They'll wring you out to be the slut you want to be."

"You're an insolent bastard!"

"Listen close. To be a beauty, to be enchanting, isn't enough. What the hell does breeding or quality mean now? Life is a battle and you're weak . . . in the worst way a woman can be weak. You fall for someone who has the morals of an imbecile and you're done for. That kind of man smells women like you. I hear you talk about love, but that's only a freak of your imagination. You clutch at men. That's not love."

She couldn't believe it, not even the small eloquence he

showed. But she had to face her feverish version of love:
seething, repressed desire turned wild, lovers outcast from
society, broken vows, intercepted letters . . . a place of
dangerous dreams, a paradise of lust she couldn't be
driven from.

"I could have done what I wanted with you, but I only
needed that sweet touch of you sometimes. There are men
who wouldn't mind being hanged if they could strangle in
a woman's garter. But I didn't feel that for you, ever. A
nigger woman is a slave, but a time comes and she's free.
But you won't . . . you'll never be free. . . ." His voice
trailed off as he smelled the wild plums and crabapples in
the soft wind. He thought of the wet-wood smell of a
campfire, petals on nearby trees shaken loose by the
pounding of hundreds of horsemen and drifting down,
while their fragrance found its way to men enveloped in
dust and powdersmoke. "I have to go. Goodby and good
luck. Kill some of the fuckers if they get close to you."

"Jim—this Klan order?"

"It's true."

"You understand why I ask?"

"I don't blame you."

"Why don't you come to Arkansas. Get out of it."

"You still don't understand. I don't want to get out."
Then he was gone.

Adela was glad, suddenly tired of listening to him. She
went inside, thinking how funny it was, how everything
was changed from what she'd thought. Kortman had the
bright marbles all the time, and that wasn't the way she
thought it was at all. *The wrong kind of brute.* She knew
that when she made love, she never cared what satisfaction she had, mesmerized by a man who took her roughly,
enslaved by her needs, anxious only to please him. She
couldn't understand the split in herself—how quickly she
could be subdued, how submissive she was in passion—and
how blithe and certain she was about the world, how she
had strength to make everything her own peculiar confec-
tion. She often deluded herself that she sought fragrance
and gentility in love, but the gentility inflicted boredom,
used up too little of her furious energy. She was a romanc-

er who lied to herself for the love of it, but knew the
truth. Still, she couldn't believe Kortman. She wanted to
control her life. It was only when she was fuck-wet, when
she needed to be possessed by another life. . . .

Whenever her mother gave her another popular novel
to read, Adela was amused by the counterfeit romanti-
cism, as if Jessie was trying to turn her back to innocence.
Were there really chaste, sweet girls like those in the
books? Even the girls she knew in Palmyra were different
than that. Maybe some were too scared—of lovers, of family, of breaking the codes—to unleash themselves. But she
never knew anyone like those simpy heroines. Southern
women were all seducers anyway, she thought. They
might play the compliant or honeyed or doomed beauty,
but they ravished men, whatever their tactics. That first
time a young man at a cotillion cooed a song in her ear
between spasms of hot breath, how she wanted to run her
hands all over him, and never felt a moment of shock at
the idea. That night in bed she still felt the desire and
there was a wild zeal in her solitary love-making.

She went upstairs and tried to comfort her mother, as-
suring her that the bad times would pass and they would
come back. Adela felt some sympathy for her, knew how
Jessie loved the beautiful home, the family heirlooms and
elegant furnishings brought from Loretto. But Jessie was
still in control, nothing of the sobbing and recriminations
they all expected. Adela had a sly idea that her mother
had something of the same excitement she felt. Forced out
on the road, she could free her own passions . . . put beyond the law, she could be as wayward as she pleased.

Adela broke into tears when she saw her father standing
rigid at a window, staring into the darkness. She was sorry
only for him. Nothing had come out right. A wife that
treated him with the courtesy of custom, all the while
mocking him. His idea of the law as the spirit of civic
virtue, the town that he saw as a mecca of culture and
would end up just another backroads place, all a lost
dream now. He was like an elegy to the past. The worst,
because he never spoke of it, was the shame of his son.
She hated and pitied Matthew. Everything was lost be-

cause he was anxious to be counted among the men of the town. He had reveries of battles already lost, when exhausted warrior long thought of the war as a disaster. He was ignorant or stubborn about what had happened so recently, and because of it he defamed his own time, then was too frightened and soft to bear the violence. Maybe Jessie had encouraged him. But she was only stupid and lecherous, desperate to find her way in a new time.

Adela went to her room and lay on the bed in the dark. She thought she could face misfortune, unhappiness, and see and live beyond it, but she had little faith in any kind of innocent or comforting illusions. That would kill her, all of them. Maybe that's what Kortman was trying to tell her . . . *The wrong kind of brute.* . . .

That night she dreamed of pole-ferrets and antler spikes and hyenas and black wolves with gleaming fangs and cruel yellow eyes. She woke with a start, her heart hammering, looked out the window and tried to make the images vanish by thinking something gentle. How light fails in crossing a river and the current still shines deeply without it. A handsome man standing atop a hill across a river waving a white cloth at her. The air turned over one leaf and there was only one force in her arms, to swim to him, her loose hair straining. He stood motionless as she went into the water. Would she fail and go down to the sea? Should she call as she changed to water? She swam to overcome fear. One force was left in her arms, to come to him in glory. The current burned, but she loved that moving-to-him-love, and her fear flowed away to the sea she had never seen. The way to move upon water, she knew, was to work lying down, as in love. Her breath was humming in her ribs as she imagined herself stepping from the twilight water. They walked to a house where the moon opened wide on the floorboards. How should she perform? Then she knew that she would give him the fear-killing moves of her body.

13

THE house was quiet in the next days. Adela wanted the family to visit people, talk and laugh, live in a jolly crowd for a brief time so they wouldn't have to face the pain alone. But Everett stayed in his library, refusing yet to say goodby to his exalted sentiments, sick because he was too conscious of what had happened, suffering the melancholia of everything completed. Adela convinced him to take Jessie for a ride in the country so that people would be accustomed to seeing them out in the carriage. They drove into a lovely valley rimmed by gothic pine trees. When he remarked how beautiful it was, she replied, "I want to go back. I'm not interested in scenery, I'm interested in feelings." Everett knew she was a woman who had to extract personal advantage from things. Anything that didn't give her immediate gratification was useless. He turned the horses and whipped them up. Why should he demand more of her than anyone else? The sorriest little woman-chaser in town dreamed of Oriental queens. Jessie was like a sailor in distress, casting desperate glances over what she thought of as the waste of her life, seeking some distant white sail in the mists of the horizon. He was useless now, he thought, couldn't protect his family from a single suffering, and that was what exhausted him so completely.

Matthew seemed afraid of the others. He kept to himself and Adela often found him at a window in an upstairs hall. She tried to cut through his isolation with jokes and dirty gossip, pushed him to look on what would come as an adventure, then saying plaintively, "Don't blame yourself. These are bad times, bad things happening to everyone. But you've got to shake out of it. Weak nerves will kill you now."

"I should never have given Catlin the names."

"You think that's what did it? Catlin and everyone else knows who most of the Kluxers are."

"How long did papa know about me?"

"A long time." She tried to grapple with his confusion. "That's not what's driving us out. Someone wanted to put some mean on you and told Catlin. He had to make a little show, that's his duty. The Klan knows everything that goes on in this town. Maybe they heard. Maybe someone told them too. It could have been you or Billy Laidlaw or any one of a dozen young hotheads." He looked surprised when she mentioned Laidlaw's name. "Jesus and Christ! You see what it's all about? You thought it was all a big secret. People are just too afraid to talk. Where did so many men go at night—a coon show or a French opera or maybe a real uplifting lecture? Yes, they did not."

She thought that Matt was trying to make some sense of it, and saw how shadowy other people were. How little she understood him, even though they hadn't been separated for more than a day or two since he was born. She shivered a little. It was as if loneliness was the hard and final answer about life.

"We're going to a new place. There's hope."

He tried to hold her but she didn't want him desperate and clinging. "I'm so miserable."

"Well, hope is the only medicine I know when I'm miserable." She hated that kind of fatuous talk, but didn't know what else to say. She tried to make herself laughable. "I hope—but most of the time I'm scared to my bones."

"I don't think you were ever scared of anything." He pointed to his wounded arm.

"How is it? Will you be able to ride?"

"It's almost healed. Remember the times we raced. You'd take a jump a cavalryman'd think twice about."

"I just hoped. See? Listen, you're more like me than you think. You took chances because you loved something. I know you did. That's a kind of madness, but I've done madness for love. If love isn't madness, it isn't love. It's because I don't think anything out, just act because my nerves are always jumping too. Just like you. Maybe there's more Kittredge in us than Lanier."

He had a thin smile. "I sure got that part big, and didn't get any Lanier brains."

"Everyone's dumb when they're young. There can't be anyone who's done the dumb things I did."

He didn't believe any of it, but knew she was trying to be kind. "Is mama crazy?"

"If I tell you, you promise never to tell anyone?"

"I won't." He was more himself now, grinning because they wrre once more close and in conspiracy.

"She's just a dreamy, fading bitch that gets in heat too quick. I told you all that before. You know how she's always talking about love? That's because she gets the pleasure out of it, and not with papa. He's the one who gets the sadness. She's not crazy, not by half. She's just a glutton, a hog."

"It's more like they hate each other."

"You remember your Bible, little brother, the Song of Solomon? . . .'Love is as strong as death; jealousy as cruel as the grave.' "

"They never talk about Porter."

"That's part of it too. The way she pushed him off to the war." She said nothing about Jessie getting Matt into the Klan.

"Why did they stay together?"

"Like I said, she isn't that crazy. She knew what happened to Loretto, that she could never go back there. Papa was respected and made money, and he was important in town. She liked that, being queen bee again, the best society. Besides, she had a man to take care of her, just like her 'Darlin' Daddy,' as she called him, always did. And there weren't too many men around during the war, even a one-armed man like papa."

She remembered something that happened at Loretto when she was only five or six. Jessie took Adela and Matthew to the plantation for a visit. Her mother had died a year before and she took the children down every few months because her father was alone. Her two older brothers, later killed in the war, were often away. Everett rarely went and Porter stayed at home this time. The afternoon they arrived, a scrawny black woman took the children into a ground floor bedroom for a nap. But Adela was too energetic, too full of wonder about the mansion to sleep, and when she saw the slave dozing, she began to wander about. She walked the long halls, went through every room, full of awe at the mural on the ceiling of the ballroom, its gold-leaf decoration, the decorative wood carving along the walls and crystal chandeliers, the mirrors everywhere. She went into the library, bounced from chair to chair and settled in the oval-backed satin chair that was taken back to Palmyra. She looked through a book of paintings by Holbein called "The Dance of Death," but was terrified by the images and started up the long serpentine staircase. Wind banged through the big house and she was cold and frightened. She went along the second-floor hall line with portraits and heard strange noises from a room nearby. The door had blown open a crack and she looked in.

Her mother and grandfather were on the bed, moving and thrusting under a coverlet, and she thought something terrible had happened to him. She ran in and Jessie rose quickly, her heavy taffeta skirt dropping to the floor, grabbed the child roughly and took her out. Adela thought she would be punished and began to cry, but Jessie tried to calm her. She said that Grandpa was sick and she was nursing him. Adeal asked if they could write papa and tell him, and Jessie said there was no reason to worry him. When Lyman Kittredge came down for the evening meal, he gave her a ruby ring.

That was the way she remembered it. But she often wondered if her mother wasn't telling the truth, that over the years she had created the lechery only because she learned that things like that happened in families, made it a weapon to hold over her mother. She thought of the ring as a bribe, but her Grandfather had given her valuable gifts before that day. In the moments when she hated her mother, she tried to go back over the years to that murky light, the two figures on the bed, make certain she wasn't vilifying Jessie because of a memory contorted since childhood. That was one thing she would never tell anyone, though once when she was jealous of her mother, she almost told Kortman, but was canny enough to know that the perversity would only intrigue him, and later he would make good use of it in the town.

Catlin came for the last time on Thursday night and brought four army Remington .44 revolvers and ammunition. He had four copies of a small topographical map and quickly tried to teach them to read it.

"Kortman knows the state. When I got back and looked at our map, his description of the country you have to cross was very good. Do it the way he said."

Catlin thought it all happened because of him. He let Strachan twist him into interorgating Matthew . . . he believed Kortman's warning and brought him to the house. But it was better not to voice his own doubts. He saw how they wavered and questioned, as if he could rescue them at the last minute. He spoke to Adela after he said goodby to the others.

"I'm going to come for you. I don't care what you said."

She tried to be heartless. "I can't think about that now. But I don't think I'm going to change." She had been mildly, briefly, in love with Catlin, the way she could have fallen in love with any good-looking and warm-blooded man to fill the void. But the emotion was only a flash that burned quickly and died. It was a love that came too early—or too late—or was merely her imagination playing stunts. She was sick of love, or talk of love and people who loved hopelessly. She let him kiss her, but she felt only the tease that any man's flesh gave her. He began to talk urgently, how lonely he would be, how just the sight of her thrilled him.

"I'm leaving the army soon. I've done my share and I hate this kind of duty. I'll come to you in Piggot."

She thought it would be a mistake to be kind any longer. "There was nothing. You can't hold on to me. No one can." But she didn't believe it, and often dreamed of a master.

At first light on Friday, the family gathered in the kitchen and ate a big breakfast prepared by Sukie. A large suitcase had been hidden under the seat of the carriage along with a rifle and shotgun. Adela was to ride King Bruce, and a good fast chestnut look-a-like had been hired two days before for Matthew from livery stable in Glade-hill. They were all armed, Jessie concealing a twin-barrel Deringer in a handkerchief in her reticule tied to her wrist by a black grosgrain ribbon. Jessie started to walk through the rooms but Adela stopped her.

"That will just make it worse. There's nothing left to see, and nothing left to do here." She touched Jessie's hand. "We're good Reb soldiers. We're ready."

Jessie gave a rare sweet smile that Adela believed. "Your father's not up to all the driving. I'm strong. I'll help him, you'll see."

"You're learning, mama. This isn't the time to play the belle." She knew her mother had the same doubts they all had. *Maybe it was all needless.* That was the worst punishment, trying to sort out the truth, bear the tensions, believing that they might die if they stayed, or lose everything for no reason if they went. She and Matt had talked of doubling back to the house to see what happened. Maybe the Klan wouldn't come. But it might be the second night. Whatever happened, at least Matt would be out of it. Jessie insisted that Sukie make the beds and wash the dishes.

"If they're going to burn us out, they're going to burn a proper home."

Adela liked that. A nice flourish, a kind of private thumb on the nose and hand-wiggle to the Klan. Sukie had been dusting and cleaning for three days, and it was like old times having her sleep in. She was to leave first, walking up the road with a basket in the early morning to do her marketing as she did every day. When it was time, Everett gave her $300 in eagle coins. The old woman hid the heavy pouch beneath her skirts.

"I got so much waddle in my walking, no one gonna see that."

They all laughed and Sukie began to cry. "Excuse me Misters and Missers, but I got to say it—goddamn them infernal Kluckers!" Adela embraced and kissed her. Jessie held her for a long time, remembering how Sukie had come from Loretto with her so many years ago, had taken care of her all her life. Sukie did a clumsy curtsy before Everett and Matthew. "I learn that from the quality."

The parting was beginning and Adela felt a shudder, had an image of death. "You sure you know what to do?"

"I stays with my son in Gideon a spell. Then Judge Darcy he take me to his house."

"You know why you have to do that?"

"Cause they ask me where the family is, and if I don't tell 'em I don't know, which I don't, they gonna hurt me."

Sukie went out the back door and down the steps to the path that led to the road. She never looked back. Everett looked at his watch. It was the time Adela left for the seminary and Matthew for school. He and Jessie would wait until a proper-seeming time in mid-morning. Matthew said he'd go through the fields in back and turn out on the road to school about a half-mile up, Adela could go through town. He brought his horse from the stable and mounted, saw them watching at the window, the low sun bouncing off the panes and he could barely glimpse their faces. They looked tiny, fragmented, no longer real. He thought he could be man enough to give them courage, made his horse rear and waved his hat, made them think that it was going to be hallelujah all the way. He took a low fence and cantered across a long shallow slope in the field, then disappeared from the trees. Adela left with no more show than if she was coming home for lunch in a few hours. She gave her parents a casual peck, said "See you," and was gone.

Matthew rode to within a quarter-mile of the school, reined in at the top of the hill and watched the students going toward the building, a few on horseback. If Mr. Wendell sent someone home to ask about his absence, his parents might still be there and tell the messenger that he was sick. If they were gone, it didn't matter. With a sudden, wonderful sense of freedom he turned northwest for a while, then reckoned west by the sun and galloped across Yellow Creek into the wind-riven high country. He hoped the others remembered the Klan signals he'd taught them . . . the owl screech and cat cry, the trill of reedy whistles, the sound of a small bellows they carried, the clicks and clucks, the sequence of one shot followed by three more in rapid fire.

He passed a series of giant caves dug out by an underground steam and knew the Klan took victims there, often buried then on the spot. Sometimes they just holed in and got drunk for a couple of days. The sun was coming up fast in a chalky sky as he pushed his horse. By early afternoon he was hungry, but told himself to go as long as he could without food. He rested the horse for an hour in a deep nest of brush along the bottom of a ridge. It was a good mount, Arab for speed, Morgan for bull strength. At night he found shelter under a natural rock bridge and stayed awake for a while. He figured he was in Houston County now and watched for any signs of riders. He saw two lights, maybe torches, moving slowly in the distance. Each suddenly flattened out in the night mist. He thought it was somewhere near Mobley, but knew how tricky a faraway light could be, a hundred yards or a mile off.

Sometime in the night he was awakened by a burst of gunfire. After a long interval he heard a single shot far off, like a distant cough. He scanned the perimeter of dark trees and hills but saw nothing. He saddled the horse, waited, then decided to get out. He heard horses and saw a band of Klan riders. They were passing at a canter when Matthew's horse began sniffing and neighing. One rider turned and poked his mount into the brush near the rock bridge. Matthew lost sight of him and thought he was gone. He wondered if they had been alerted earlier and were looking for him. A big cat growled and in that instant Matthew knew the Kluxer was signaling the others. He reached for his gun but the rider was on him before he could fire.

The hooded horse was plunging past Matthew. He leaped and dragged the rider from the saddle. The Kluxer lost his gun in the fall and pulled a big buffalo knife. Matthew lurched up and drew his own knife. Both began slashing the air and Matthew fell. The Kluxer tried to get behind him, jabbing the air with short slicing strokes. Matthew pinwheeled on his back, kicking up dirt, keeping the man to his front. The knife flew out of his hand but he recovered it and got to his feet. Ducking under a thrust, he locked both arms around the bigger man's chest to keep the man's knife-arm raised, trying to jab his weapon into the back, but he was wrestled to the ground. Matthew scooted away, sucking air from fear. But the Kluxer was badly wounded, had taken a deep cut in the face through the hood as they hit the ground. A bloodstain was spreading and Matthew kicked it. He felt the bones break with a soft squashing sound. A nerve pulsed in Matthew's face when he heard the riders shouting from far off. He jumped the man and cut his throat. For a second he wanted to see the man's face, see if he recognized him, but left the hood on.

It was the first time he had ever killed. He mounted and galloped north, off-course, but knew they'd be looking for a stranger when they found the body. He wondered how many men they'd kill before they were satisfied they had the right one. He didn't understand irony, but thought it strange that he could kill hand-to-hand when he was running from the Klan, and could never even whip someone without flinching when he was desperate to prove himself to other Klansmen, how often he was taunted for being squeamish or, worse, a coward. He reached for his carbine but the scabbard was empty. He suddenly remembered taking it out to keep by his side as he slept. It was there, with the dead man.

By dawn thunderheads piled up in front. He whipped the horse, praying for a storm to cover him. Before he'd gone only a few miles, a hard slanting rain lashed the hills and cut into his face. Matthew knew that kind of storm would move fast. He kept slapping his mount, shouting, racing the storm to the foothills of the Highland Rim. It was still raining when he took the horse up a long steep incline. The chestnut was skittish, pawed the ground, kicking rocks over the side. Matthew came out on a flat-topped hill along a rust-colored wall. The rain began to pass and he saw a lone rider starting up from the valley toward him, hailing with a high arm. Matthew waved his hand and started down . . . probably a local who could tell him the quickest ride to Mobley.

A shot cracked, whined and splintered against the rocks. The rider had a carbine leveled and was firing as he came on. Matthew pulled his revolver but realized the man was out of range. The rider's horse went to its knees and he hung by a stirrup. Matthew spurred his mount, trying to gain ground before the man recovered. He dismounted on the run and took cover behind a small hump. The rider was coming on again. Matthew held the horse in his sights a long time before he fired. He missed and pulled off another shot. The horse dropped, but the man went prone in deep grass and brought his weapon up. Matthews sidled along the ground to where the hump began to level out. They lay there for minutes, neither man daring to make the break. The storm was beating south but it was still dark. The other man's nerves broke first.

He came up the slope, firing with one hand, the other bracing his body against sliding on the wet grass and rock. Matthew fired into the gunflash. The man tried to level the carbine with both hands but began to slip and Matthew fired twice. The man rolled a little way and lay huddled in a lifeless heap. Matthew went for his horse and rode down the slope to the dead man. He picked up the carbine and took the ammunition belt off him. When he examined the weapon he saw it was his own. The man's horse was standing nearby and Matthew looked in the saddlebag . . . a Klan uniform. There were others around, he was sure, looking for him, anyone they thought killed their man.

He slipped the carbine in the scabbard and was about to leave when he thought he might just show them who they were fooling with. He lifted the body across the saddle, ran a rope under the horse's chest and tied it to the dead man's arms and legs, then tacked it to the rigging rings and stirrups on both sides. He gave the big bay a smack and the horse galloped off toward Mobley. It was the first time Matthew was convinced that Kortman was telling the truth. Mobley was only thirty miles from Palmyra, plenty of time for a fast rider to alert the Mobley Den. Matthew was sure the men he saw the night before were looking for him. He looked at the map and thought it didn't much matter which way he took. It was Saturday, and by now there must be Ku Klux search parties everywhere. Maybe it was best to follow Kortman's route; he said he'd lead the Klan from that area. But they'd have a description of him and the others, and he warned himself to be careful. If they were looking for him, the house was already burned. But he felt confident, a real killer, and playfully put his horse into a showy strut for a few yards.

He turned away from Mobley, heading for the Tennessee River, riding along the bank for miles but saw no ferrymen. The river was running fast and high, heaping up in gray slabs that slipped up with dirty white edges. Matthew knew Adela could take care of herself in bad country, but that whole part of the state was drained by the Mississippi and other big rivers. If it was wet ground all the way, what could his parents do in a carriage. Beyond McKibbon, heading for the railroad bridge, he came on a camp of negro refugees, crazy rotten shacks under a dull metal sun, flimsy boards, sacking, branches, discarded army tents, tattered and rotting away. He saw mostly old faces, scrofulous and grizzled, yellow-veined eyes, clawhands, gray flesh dry in the palms reaching out to beg food from a group of white people standing around, sick faces staring out beyond the crowd, at nothing. There were babies with skin tight on the skulls like big gourds,

the necks not even strong enough to hold up the heads,
the bellies swollen. Matthew wanted to keep out of trouble, but couldn't stand the sight of the misery and walked
his horse through the crowd. He took some food from his
saddlebag and threw it to them. The whites began to hoot
and press around the horse. Matthew swung the reins
back and forth across the horse's neck, alternating each
motion with his gentle spurring and the animal began to
prance side to side, clearing a path. He wondered what
the hell they were so mad about. Shared, the food wasn't
more than crumbs.

"You wasted your vittles, sonny!" a man shouted. "We
gonna burn 'em out!"

"What did they do?"

"Ain't them. It's the bucks that left 'em here to go with
the nigger militia. All we got around here now is a lot of
dirty sick niggers and stealing."

"I never saw such miserable niggers. If it ain't them,
why you gonna burn them?"

"Teach them nigger militia a lesson."

Matthew felt sick in his stomach. The same thing, he'd
been doing the same damned thing. Maybe his idea was
right . . . maybe he wanted glory but picked the wrong
way. What he'd done wasn't so much different . . . feel
a hardship from someone and blow it up so you could
burn or murder without thinking twice. He tried to drive
it from his mind. *When you're young and make a mistake,
you think: it's all right, I'm learning and I won't make that
mistake again.* But he wondered if he'd ever be forgiven
for that mistake, allowed another chance. All the talk he
heard in Palmyra, all he thought, was that niggers were
riding high, sassed and bedded white women, had all
the spoils and were robbing whites of what was rightfully
theirs . . . savage niggers who didn't even do their
church proper. But the truth was in front of his eyes. Even
the niggers in Palmyra. Most of them, the best they did,
was become poor farmers, croppers who were still cheated
and half-worked to death. It was no sudden revelation. He
always admired the ones who tried to raise themselves
once they were free, dressed their children neat and sent

them to the new schools, the hard-working men who opened shops or took the best crops out of the land that could be grown. God, it wasn't even the niggers. He loved Sukie, and maybe a dozen others, more than he did his own parents.

What was he trying to do when he joined the Klan? What was he afraid of, the changes everyone talked about? But he'd heard enough talk by the men who came to see his father that the power was still in the hands of the same men, North and South. The niggers were just used in the voting to give white men power. There was no new world for anyone, least of all the ex-slaves. The Ku Kluxers were men made crazy by the fear of change and went to terror to save the world they knew, save what little they had. They didn't want to change anything, they wanted to stop change, and their strength and brutalities made people's anxieties into real fears. He often wondered why a man like Kortman would hang around with men no better than town bums, the ones who lived on the edge with massive hates and grievances.

Matthew had always been smaller and slimmer than his schoolmates, a quiet boy rarely admired, thought a poet because he liked to be alone. He knew, despite each family member's possessive memory of Porter, that he felt the loss hardest, but never thought it was a tragedy to be killed honorably in battle. The terrible thing was to be the one left alone, his protector gone. He was afraid of the burden of being the only son, the expectations, afraid of failure, humiliation, being the object of ridicule—and his defenses and fears often made him ridiculous. Many times he thought his father's ordinary, customary silences were a subdued rage directed at him. He lost himself in long rides, reading tales of chivalry and conquest and splendid lost causes, a boy stuck in yesterdays, in sentimental ignorance, but afflicted with the idea of the cathartic effects of violence. If he experienced an emotion, he was depressed at his inadequate performance, and lured the inevitable—living vicariously as a romantic, but without the necessary intensity and morbid poetic nature the pose demanded.

The ground began to rise and he saw the wooden spider trestle that crossed the river. A freight train was starting its slow grinding climb. Matthew didn't like the idea of walking his horse along the narrow railbed that lay on wood braces. The trestle was about a hundred feet up and he could see open spaces all along the rails. He rode alongside and hailed the engineer:

"Can I get a ride?"

"We're heading for Memphis."

"Just want to get across. Horse a little lame."

"Can't stop now. Got to get power up." Matthew started to fall back, when the engineer said, "We got through a cut about two hundred yards up. See?"

"Between the red rock and fence?"

"Right. Get up there. Charlie"—he pointed to the fireman—"will get them to open the empty in front of the caboose. You can just jump in from there."

Matthew galloped toward the high ground alongside the cut. The fireman went up the ladder of the tender and walked the top of the other cars to the caboose. A brakeman came out with him and shoved open the door of the empty car. Matthew saw the brakeman waving a red flag. The train still labored slowly, the wheels slipping, then there was a steady slow rocking sound as the train neared the top of the grade. When the empty car was a few yards off, Matthew took the horse back a ways, then turned and went fast for the open door. The horse took the ten-foot jump and landed almost in the middle of the car, slipping on the straw floor, hurtling into the far wall. The brakeman stood back as Matthew leaped off and soothed the animal.

"That's a hell of a horse!"

Matthew stroked him. "Goddamn he is."

"Engineer told Charlie you can't get off right at the crossing . . . not unless you want to jump him down."

"Where's the first stop?"

"We take water at Eva. Only a short way."

Matthew looked at his map. It was only about ten miles south of Big Sandy, the same distance from Vale, the next town that Kortman marked.

"Where you going, young fellow?"

"Up to Phillipy." He tried to sound like a country man. "See my kin up to Missouri."

"That spit of a town."

"Hear they got a lot of riverboats put in there."

The brakeman shrugged. "You get off at Eva less you want to end up in Memphis."

From Eva, Matthew passed through Vale and Richland, crossing Carroll and Weakley Counties. He tried to keep track when he crossed a county line. Some Klan Dens were small, and only rode occasionally. But he couldn't remember much he'd heard about the Weakley Ku Klux as he crossed a shallow ford on the middle fork of the Obion River. According to Kortman, it was about fifty miles to Phillipy. The high land was behind him and he was making good time. Because of the ride on the freight he would be far ahead of the others. He tried not to think about where they were, or whether they'd had any trouble. He thought his parents would be all right, but was worried about Adela. A fine-looking young girl like that riding alone. . . . He saw the lights of Sidonia a long way off and slept in a hotel there Saturday night, thinking he'd push for Phillipy all the way the next day. Maybe Catlin's brother was waiting and he could find him, prepare for the others. He had a picture of a bustling river town. In the hotel he heard some men talking about Klan trouble in Clayton, a big town across the north fork of the Obion. He decided to head west from Sidonia and hit the Mississippi, then ride north to Phillipy. It was a longer way around, but safer.

His first sight of the great river from high up on a limestone bluff was astonishing. It was almost two miles wide, and a steamboat coming down-river looked like a beetle skimming the water. Clouds had blown over, leaving the sky a frigid blue. In the middle-distance, the river smoked with toppling pillars of mist which softened the light. Smoke from a half-hidden steamboat hung over an island of Gothic pines. The air was inert and the surface of the river was as finely patterned as a fingerprint, each twist and eddy of the current showing up as black pencil curlicues on the water.

Matthew saw wild turkeys and buzzards, dozens of different birds along the sandbars and chutes and coulees of the river . . . purple martins, crested flycatchers, ruby-throated hummingbirds, redwing blackbirds and passenger pigeons. They were all moving to new shelters from the maple, ash, cypress, tipelo, live oaks, wild pecan trees and brush to find summer homes far north. Migrating water-fowl rested near the willow-fringed shore and in still pools and sloughs. Then he was startled when the ducks and Canadian and blue geese suddenly rose in a wild flutter of wings into a formation that streaked up the Mississippi flyway. White herons came undulating by the hundreds through the cypress and willows.

Deer passed in the brambles and forest thickets and Matthew heard wild boar rooting in the underbrush as he rode north. He saw mounds built by ancient people, like earthen snakes. The river had been life for the Confederacy, moving cotton and corn and manpower, but Matthew saw it differently now . . . a wild place where wolves and buffalo and black bear had wandered. The sun beat on the water, cleaving the mist, and making the orchard blossoms shine like diamonds, casting shadows in the farm furrows. He felt a tingle in his blood when he thought about crossing the river. It divided the country, and beyond was the West, empty land and savage Indians . . . the Spanish lance dipped into dark flesh.

He stopped to watch a man jug-fish. "Looking for crappie or bream," he said, "but get mostly catfish." The man placed empty, gaudily-painted gallon jugs on the water, floating and dangling a heavy cord and hook and smelly bait from its corked mouth. The fisherman's boat followed lazily. When a fish struck, usually only a big catfish, under went the jug and fish and both stayed there until the fish's strength was gone. Then both erupted into the air and the fisherman approached to haul in his catch.

He heard the dry snapping sound of rifle fire in the forest but figured it was hunters. The river became wider

as he pushed north, a great, intricate drift of dark water
more than three miles wide, spooling and crumpling as it
went. Just past the big bend at Ridgely, he found a narrow blacktop road lined with pine and hickory trees and
kept the river in sight. Sunlight made dappled yellow pat-
terns through the leaves. Islands thickened, buoys marking
out a narrow, wriggling path between them. He could
hear the river through the tindery rustle of the leaves. He
climbed to a high bank and saw a torrent of yellow mud
rushing in a narrow strip alongside the calm water. It was
floodwater from the wild Missouri River that joined the
Mississippi about 200 miles north.

Matthew passed canebreaks and fought mosquitoes,
once drowsing while he sat the horse in the scant shade of
some tall brush. Passing through Wynneburg, he saw
rough river men from the keelboats, coal barges and
timber-rafts, drunk and brawling, taking over the small
main street. Matthew pulled his black slouch hat down on
his windburned face, and thought with his long dirty hair
he could pass for a backwoods man. He stopped at a tavern and talked with the men, mentioning "that big river
town Phillipy" where he had to get a boat.

"Hell," a riverman said and laid his pipe down. "Your
old granny's telling you tales. That ain't nothing but a
pissy little place. Once a day a cheap packet comes down
from St. Louis, and another up from Memphis."

Matthew bought the man a drink and said he didn't
rightly know, he was a hunter from Henderson County on
his way up to Missouri. He talked about the mountains,
riding all night in cold rain and pitching a camp and
sleeping in wet blankets to rise the next morning and
hunt. Oh, he got bear, but would as soon shoot a doe or
fawn as a buck, wild turkeys to feed the dogs, all but the
breast.

"You ever see a city?" the riverman said.

"No."

"Everything you want in a city like St. Louis. Fancy
places, streets, and at night they look like day with gas-
lights. All the women you want. You ever get there, just
ask where Mrs. Dalene's place is."

Matthew rode the twelve miles into Phillipy, keeping an eye to his right toward the south end of Tiptonville Lake, his heart beating fast, hoping he might find Adela there because of his detour. He knew he was close when he began to smell barbecue smoke. People in river towns smoked and dried meat and sold it to be served on the boats. The smell made him think of a mahogany table in a cousin's house in Palmyra where he once saw Yankees butcher steers during the war. Then he saw the spire of a church over the lip of a hill.

14

PHILLIPY wasn't much of a place, a white town drowsing in the sunshine of a late spring afternoon. He had expected busy wagon traffic to the docks, but the streets were almost empty, one or two clerks sitting out in front of the Water Street stores, their splint-bottomed chairs tilted back against the wall, chins on breast, hats slouched over their faces, asleep. A sow and a litter of pigs loafed along the sidewalk, stopping to eat watermelon rinds. Three or four piles of freight were scattered above the levee, a pile of skids on the slope of the stone-paved wharf, with a man who looked like the town drunk asleep in their shadow. The Mississippi shone brassy and Matthew saw dense forest far off on the Missouri side. The river at that point looked like a sea as it turned a gigantic loop so that it lay both in back and in front of Matthew, the town isolated as though it were on a point of land. He walked Water Street but no one gave him notice, and he saw no one resembling a well-dressed city man. There was no hotel, only a small boarding house and he didn't want to do any asking about his family. He knew they'd be out on the street if they'd arrived.

A film of dark smoke appeared far off. A negro who drove a freight wagon, famous in town for his quick eyes

and booming voice, lifted the cry, *"Steamboat a-comin'!"*
The town stirred to life. The drunkard sat up, the clerks
woke, a clatter of wagons came toward the wharf. What
looked like a dead town was alive and moving. Wagons,
carts, men, boys and dogs, all hurried to the wharf. They
fastened their eyes on the St. Louis packet, long and sharp
and trim. She had two tall fancy-topped stacks, with a
gilded device of some kind swung between them, a big
pilot-house all glass and gingerbread perched on the Texas
deck. There were two other decks, hurricane and boiler,
all three fenced and ornamented with clean white railings.
A flag flew from the jack-staff. The furnace doors were
open on the boiler deck and fire flared.

Passengers crowded the upper decks, waving. In the re-
cess of the main deck, back of the engines, in the open
shed roofed by the boiler deck, there were mountainous
piles of hemp bales and bacon fletches and whiskey barrels and tobacco hogsheads, and pens of sheep and swine,
most of it bound for Memphis and New Orleans. The
black smoke rolled and tumbled out of the stacks, created
by bits of pitch-pine burned just before arriving in a town.
A broad plank was run far out on the bow. A deckhand
stood with a coiled rope as steam screamed through the
gauge-cocks. The captain rang the bell. The giant paddlewheels stopped, then reversed, churning water to foam,
and the steamboat eased into the wharf. One passenger
debarked, some freight was taken off and barrels loaded
aboard, and the steamboat was into the river within
twenty minutes.

"That the only southbound?" Matthew asked a
freighter. The man knew he was an inlander. No one on
the river ever said it any way but *"down-river."*

"You looking for any special boat?"

"No. I'm going to Missouri to see my granny."

"Hell, you can get a skiff across. Only cost a dollar." He
pointed. "That's Missouri."

"I know where damned Missouri lays. I got to wait for
people. We figure to get down around Cooter."

"That's the best you got to take. And you can't be sure
the master'll stop there for you. He ain't got no business at

Cooter, he got to get to Memphis so he don't put in too late. Freighters they don't like to sit around."

"Any boats take a hailing?"

"Maybe some old ladies in the day. Not by night. Not unless they're crazy. It's either robbers or someone running from the sheriff . . . worst, maybe the Klan. They stopped boats a couple of times looking for people."

"What they do?"

"They dragged them right off. Master wouldn't do anything to risk his own skin."

"Happen around here?"

"No, Klan in Obion County's not much. Happened down in Dyer. Two men was grabbed at Wynneburg and found strung up next morning." The driver climbed up. "You best take the *Kentucky Belle*. She'll be the one down-river the same time tomorrow."

"Eevry day?"

"I already told you. One boat down-river, same time every day, less there's a storm and they got to lay in someplace."

Matthew walked the town, then hung around a waterfront tavern, but saw no one from his family, or no man who resembled Catlin's description of his brother. He slept in the boarding house that night.

Adela came in early the next morning, looking as bright and fresh as the moment she left Palmyra. They met as she entered the boarding house to get breakfast. Matthew introduced her to the proprietor, who looked at them suspiciously and thought they were no more kin than she was to a nigger. Some funny business she wouldn't hold with. Feed them slop and get them out fast. "You're late. I'll see what I got." She prepared a meal of rancid boiled bacon, half-boiled snap beans, boiled white corn, and sour buttermilk taken from a churn.

Adela whispered, "Now this is what I call real hospitality. She must take those Velpeau's French Female Pills."

Matthew proudly told her of his encounter with the Klan.

"You think they got it over the telegraph?"

"Maybe. I didn't see anything the rest of the way. What happened to you?"

She started to laugh. "I was treated like the Queen of Sheba all the way. Every young man with a carriage insisted I ride with him, and we tied King Bruce on behind. One fellow he had a carriage, you never saw anything like it . . . rubber-tired wheels with shiny brass rims, brass lamps decorated with big glass rubies, a patent leather dashboard, even the wood shafts were polished and varnished. Well, this fellow brought me home to his family. I wanted something good to eat, and I stayed there the night.

"They had a friend with a big boat and he took me across the Tennessee. The family gave me a note to some kin in Manleyville, and the kin told a Yankee officer that a young girl shouldn't be traveling alone like I was. So he put me on a wagon in a convoy that was bringing horses down to soldiers in Dyersburg. King Bruce made a lot of friends, and I had the Yankee protection all the way. When I left, the officer gave me a gun and said a sweet young thing like me should be careful. I said"—she put on a simpy voice—"'I'm awful afraid of those nasty Ku Kluxers,' and he said they weren't much in that part of the state." She put her hand over Matthew's. "Maybe we're going to be lucky. If only mama and papa would come." She looked out the window of the dining room. "You see anyone that looks like Tom Catlin?"

"No. And if he's half as flashy as his brother says, you couldn't miss him a mile away in this town."

They were walking along Water Street at noon when they saw the familiar carriage. Everett saw them in almost in the same instant and made little motions. They knew they meant for them to act easy and greet them further down the street near the wharf. When the carriage stopped and Everett helped Jessie down, Matthew walked over slowly and the two men shook hands in a perfunctory way. The women pecked each other on the cheek, a customary greeting for even casual friends. Everett said their journey was uneventful, and smiled.

"I don't think your mother liked it. People treated us

like we were an old respectable couple out for a spring ride in the country. Either of you have any trouble?"

Matthew told him about killing the two Klansmen and thought he had to convince him. "I really did, papa. But I didn't see anything after that. Adela says a Yankee officer said the Klan was pretty quiet in these parts."

"You feel better now? You know. . . ."

"A whole lot, papa. I'm sorry."

Everett didn't want to dwell on it. "What did you find out about the boats?"

"One up-river and one down-river a day. Driver said most boats won't take a hail, especially at night."

"We can't stay around here too long. It's a smaller place than I thought."

"Same fellow said we could get a skiff across."

"How many does it carry?"

Matthew shrugged. "The way he talked, it was an ordinary thing to cross that way."

"If we have to, we could do it two by two. Catlin's brother was supposed to be here by Sunday night the latest."

The boat from New Orleans and Memphis was steaming around the bend and the town came alive again. The wharf was crowded and they felt less conspicuous. If Thomas Catlin didn't show that day, Everett thought, they could get on that boat the next day to Cairo, all river traffic stopped there, then work their way back to Piggot. At least they'd be together this time.

As the steamboat was slipping into the wharf and the milling and excitement were high, Adela saw a man approaching and knew it was Tom Catlin. He was a flamboyant-looking man, very much the dandy, and she wondered how they'd missed him. He looked like a city man, fine muted plaid trousers cut close, glistening boots, red waistcoat with a mesh gold chain, opulent linen, black coat and black hat, a red tie with the sun red on it.

But when he came close, Adela noticed something else, the peculiar wideness of the grayish-blue eyes in the ridged face, staring eyes that seemed committed only outward, implying little feeling or inward life inside the iron scan. In that instant, she believed she saw a man more corrupt than she could ever guess, sensed a certain vague moral dinginess about him, but his impact on her was physical. She wondered if it was love—or conquest—at first sight . . . a hundred years in a second. He began to sing a song that Matthew knew was a Klan recognition:

> *"There was an old soldier*
> *And he had a wooden leg.*
> *And had no tobacco, no tobacco could he beg.*
> *Another old soldier*
> *Sly as a fox,*
> *He always kept tobacco in his old tobacco box.*
> *He always kept tobacco in his old tobacco box."*

When he finished he tipped his hat with a flourish and a splendid grin. "Thomas Catlin."

"Everett Lanier, Mister Catlin."

"Call me Tom. My brother is a Mister Lanier or Captain Lanier. I've been waiting for you."

"I've been here since yesterday," Matthew said. "I didn't see you."

"You don't walk around a smelly little river town in clothes like these two days running. I was on the wharf when you got here yesterday." He shook his head. "You talk too much, ask too many questions. And don't try to sound like someone from the woods. No one does anything for anyone they think is lower than them."

"Why were you singing that song?" Adela said in a low vioce. "A lot of negras were looking at you."

"So were any Kluxers if they're around."

"If a Kluxer dowsn't like the look of things," Matthew said, "he sings that old tune so people'll know he's on the right side."

Adela thought Tom Catlin was smart and mean, the kind of man who could outwit someone or take the bark off them. But how did he know the song? She noticed how his strong nose started from the depression between his eyes, a small hump, then a straight line like a minia-ture rifle butt. The lips of a sensual sphinx, the close shave that made his cheekbones shine and seem to quiver in the light. She felt magnetism, strength and a divinely wicked man. When he spoke, he stretched his chin upward as if he wanted to free himself from his collar, his body.

"We're going to start out of town after dusk," Catlin said. "I found a place about two miles north of town, a point of land that juts into the river. A packet can see a hail a long way off, and a master can make up his mind. We can tell whether he's coming in or not. If he don't, there are good hiding places. Nothing around, no farms, just river land with a lot of brush and canebreaks." Matthew started to talk but Catlin stopped him. "I know all about the hailing. I heard you talking. That freighter didn't know there are different signals. He was thinking you meant waving a torch like in a parade. A river captain'll answer distress signals. He's bound by law. And there's one special signal some answer. The Ku Klux. Some of them belong. But I don't know it."

They passed some time in a general store. "Buy something," Catlin said. "Nothing makes the heart of a storekeeper friendly to strangers more than buying. A spit of a town like this, we're going to stick out because another boat won't be in here today." He bought some cassimere, twilled woolen cloth, for a suit; Adela and Jessie, old-fashioned dress shawls; Matthew, ammunition; Everett, a pipe. Catlin walked outside with Everett.

"You carrying the money you stole?"

For an instant Everett didn't know what he was talking about was about to object, then suddenly remembered his role: a man who stole Yankee money. He recovered quickly.

"No. I thought it would be too dangerous for the road. It's well-hidden near Palmyra, in a barrel marked for tallow, ready to be delivered when I send for it."

"That was smart. There's a bunch of young thugs riding this country. They don't stop at nothing. Money ain't safe anyplace, not even a bank. They even held up a railroad. And you got every kind of crook and swindler riding this river or hanging around these river towns."

Everett found himself enjoying the game. "I pray you won't be offended, but I intend to be generous to you for helping us."

"Hell, I'm doing it for my brother. You give him some?"

"He wouldn't take it. Too stiff a man."

Tom Catlin smiled. "Sounds like him. I won't take any offense, you can make sure of that."

At least the man was straight, Everett thought. You could always trust an honest scoundrel better than a respectable hypocrite. He wondered if Catlin would be there if he thought they were fleeing the Klan or a family feud or because the Yankees wanted him for political reasons. No . . . he was in it for the money. Everett had enough to pay him off when the time came. Catlin took them to the boarding house and rented rooms for the night and paid in advance to avoid suspicion. He told the woman they were going to visit friends in Clayton, a few miles away.

"Ain't my business where you go. Just be in by ten. I close up and don't heed no knocking."

"We'll be back by then. You got a meal?"

Adela and Matthew looked at each other and she raised her eyebrows. But Catlin seemed to work magic with the woman and the meal was excellent: fish, shrimp and okra served over rice, potato soup, fried cornmeal balls, fried chicken and deep-fried clam bellies. Catlin produced cigars and the men lit up. In a little while, at his signal, they drifted away from the table and went upstairs to one of the rooms where he briefed them:

"You'll be able to take that carriage in only a little ways. After that you ride double." He glanced from Adela to Jessie. "You got to play sick," he told Jessie. "No one's gonna believe she's got anything wrong. You ain't an old woman, but you got to look old and sick. We're going to hail that boat to get you to kin in Piggot before you pass away on us. Get all that rouge and fixing off your face." When she hesitated, Catlin grabbed the end of the shawl and wiped her face roughly. "Damn, if I tell you something, you do it." Everett made no protest, and Adela warned herself not to tease the way she liked to test men. Catlin told her to do what she could with Jessie.

Adela mixed some face powder into the luxuriant hair and pulled it into a severe bun. "Mama, you got to strap your bosom and get into a plain dress." Jessie took her clothes off and Adela wrapped the shawl tight around the breasts. Jessie said it hurt and might damage their shape, but Adela said it wouldn't be for long. She thought it was funny. If she could make her mother look like she had no breasts, she could do tricks like the conjurers she saw in carnivals. She selected a plain black dress and ripped the fancy-pleated collar off. She threw her paisley shawl on the floor and rubbed it across the floor with her foot, then put it around Jessie, who started to look in a mirror. Adela stopped her.

"Don't look, mama. Give me a whiny sick look. You know, like Aunt Martha."

Jessie tried to look wan and pinched, sucking her cheeks in, her eyelids drooping.

"That's a mighty fine sick look, mama." She pulled some strands of hair loose, brushed some of the powder off, thinking no one would notice it at night, and gave Jessie a large, handkerchief. "Now, remember, you got the consumption and you cough a lot. That way you can keep it to your face. Make yourself shrink a little." Adela bent and drew her body in. "Like that. You're still too handsome a woman to fool anyone for too long. Whatever happens, you don't act any different, even if you hear guns. You don't raise from the near-dead. God knows you've seen enough people pass off slow like you're supposed to be doing. And do whatever Catlin says."

Matthew went downstairs first, signalled that the woman was in the kitchen and the transformed Jessie could come down safely. There were only a few people about outside. One old woman offered to help when she saw Jessie half-carried to the carriage by Catlin and Matthew. Catlin gracefully declined and said she was a good old soul and would she pray for his mother. The woman assured him she would, she was known as the prayingest woman in Phillipy and had worked miracles for the sick.

Catlin led the way out of town. They rode silently under a humpbacked moon and soon the road meandered into woods and ended. Catlin and Matthew took the carriage down a hill through thick brush and put the anchor out. The horses had had their bag of feed only two hours before and would stay there until they were hungry. "But they'll have a hell of a time getting up through that brush," Catlin said, "with the iron dragging and twisting." He gestured to Everett's stub.

"Your wife has to ride with me."

Jessie was lifted to his horse and sat side-saddle in front of him as he braced her with one arm. When they'd gone only a few hundred yards, Catlin glanced back and saw the others keeping the proper distance he'd ordered. He let his hands stray to her breasts.

"Pity to strap them down. I bet they're beauties."

Jessie thrilled to the touch but was coy at first.

"What makes you think I won't call my hisband?"

"You won't do that."

"You're pretty sure of yourself. You think I'm some slut or something low?"

"No, I think you're ripe . . . always liked them that way." He kept rubbing her, searching for the nipples and trying to twist them. "You like that?"

"Yes." She thought it was a good thing she hadn't looked at herself in the mirror. She still felt desirable, beautiful.

Catlin, who had been sitting far up the cantle to give her room, jammed forward and she felt him hard against her thigh. Then he took one of the saddle's loose-hanging leather skirt strings in his hand. She reached to touch him, but felt a sudden lash of the leather on her buttocks. It was a light touch, a promise.

"You want more?"

"I don't know. I've heard about such women."

"You do like I say."

She felt his strength as he pressed his hand into her stomach, rubbed it, and let it drop to her groin. She slowly turned one thigh higher than the other and opened herself to him and he shoved his finger in. She tried to help him, but he said, "Don't move, you bitch, they can see us. They can't see what I'm doing." He licked her ear and whispered, "I could get us some time now."

"No. Not now. Later . . . later." She was too much in herself to hear Adela ride up, but Tom was alert, pulled his hand away and smoothed the skirt.

"Please. Please. Don't stop. I'll go crazy."

"Someone coming."

Jessie was breathing hard, flustered when Adela came alongside. She put the handkerchief to her mouth and coughed. "I've been practicing." This was one she wasn't going to share with Adela. Jessie was convinced that her own sins were penance for being cursed with too much love and emotion, an impassioned soul who had never known a requited love. Adela was the real Kittredge, a devil with bad blood. All the Kittredge women back through the years, every one of them notorious in Lawrence County. Her own mother crazy before she died . . . a history of mistresses to important men, even a president, raped children put out with the niggers, blood duels and suicides and murders of passion . . . fathers and daughters. . . . She often wondered if Adela had understood what she saw that day long ago at Loretto.

It wasn't her fault, Jessie thouthe. Her Daddy had forced her, said it would make him happy. He loved his beautiful Jessie, he told her, and all of Loretto would be hers. But she remembered the thrill of the secrecy, the forbidden trysts, the Labyrinthine plans to escape mother and brothers, the furtive touching at a dinner table or at cotillions with dozens of people around, the pitiful way he shook and shuddered when he became old . . . and the first time she felt ashamed and startled—the moment when she knew she had the power and didn't stop when he begged for her bed. There was no tradition of virtue to remember for her to survive the horrors of that darkness.

Maybe she would have turned out differently, placid and faithful, if Everett hadn't been wounded. He was different when he was young, a serious man always, but an ardent lover. In her way, she traced her need for voluptous pleasure, the cheating, the shameless affairs, everything, back to the war, his wound and the ruin of the country, to the boredom of life. Only the Klan had opened her again to excitement. Maybe they were barbarians, but they brought her to life. Now she had to run from them, her beautiful home in ashes, every fragment of the past destroyed. But she no longer cared. Loretto hadn't stood there forever through heavenly creation. Ancestors, tough and taking men and strong women came over the mountains to build it and work it. She had lingered there too long in her mind. It was built and was in ruins now, and everyone that ever lived there except her was dead. That was the way the world worked.

She looked forward to the new life. She had lived by strict custom, codes and conventions, despite her indiscretions. Even the love her Daddy demanded from her, she thought, was often custom in that place in that time. A man owned an empire of land and an army of niggers and overseers and his wife and children, and he could do goddamned well as he pleased with any of them. She had to sneak and lie to quiet the rage in her body, but it didn't have to be that way anymore. She could live the way she wanted. In time, she would tell Everett and there was nothing he could do. When Adela dropped back, Jessie leaned her cheek against Catlin's stubble of beard and rubbed it up and down like a lascivious cat, smelled the tobacco and clothes, the whiskey breath, the overwhelming man-smell of him. But Catlin was already bored, figured the old bitch would be good for his father. He was thinking about Adela.

Kortman had kept his promise. After the Klan burned the house, he quickly sent a strong body of men southwest, said the fugitives would probably head for Mamphis, where Lanier had a brother and friends. They alerted Dens all along the way to watch railroad depots and patrol the roads. Buckner, however, insisted that Kortman call on the Dens in the north and west—Stewart, Henry, Weakley, Dyer and Obion Counties—to watch for the Laniers. Kortman didn't object, didn't think it was the time to challenge anyone. Since he'd killed Hoagland,

General Blanton and Colonel Tyler had given up any direction, though they remained in office, and Buckner had grabbed more power. He was a big untidy man, an ego stuffed with cleverness and daring, a type useful for work like the Klan's, cynical and fanatic, a deadly mix.

Kortman had always felt bored and restless all the time the Klan rode unopposed. But man like Buckner and the others accepted the depravity and operated on a different plane, accepted the bad dream. But unlike the few like Kortman who felt some little remorse, stomach fluttering after a raid, they didn't seem to want to wake. A town man once described them as "the kind of people who had owls for chickens and fox for yard dogs." Everything was in anarchy and Kortman wanted to redeem himself for what he'd done. But he was sharing power and could do no more than suggest. Men who had followed him without question were now rigid and fearful, thinking that the threat was real, that Matthew's information had given the Yankees the proof and excuse they needed to round them up. Kortman throught it ironic that he was going to get himself killed if any Kluxers found him out and thought he was helping the Laniers as an act of chivalry. But he thought he could only exorcise the past by opposing the fates. It had little to do with the Laniers, and there was nothing sentimental prompting his betrayal of the Klan. It was one thing to know you weren't a coward in the conventional sense; quite another to be afraid that you didn't have moral courage. He could never erase what he had done. His life was lost, either way. He only regretted the waste, the constant assault on his emotions for so long. He tried to snatch at any random emotion that would have been appropriate, but felt nothing.

Where could he go afterward if he got away with it? The West. In those times, that was the escape route for everyone, the new beginning. Thieves, the poor and desperate, clerks, dreamers, scoundrels, anyone seeking to be anonymous, to start fresh, to lose their old lives in a country that offered hope and a chance, and perhaps suffering of a new kind that was at least better than the old life in dying towns and on blighted farms, the political turmoil and the memory of the war. It was a place that made merchants dream of being princes, former slavers plot with politicians to use the Indians and work them, dirt-daubed farmers have visions of great spreads of fruitful land, men have visions of great cities. They saw its immensity on maps and gravures, listened to tales, and thought it was a paradise. But Kortman had seen it, knew it was desert and mountains, most of it, and it would stink with death and loneliness in time because an entire nation was deluded.

Dens in the northwestern counties asked about the prescence of strangers coming from the direction of Palmyra to the Mississippi. They heard about a beautiful girl riding a chestnut with white stocking legs, a stranger, who stayed with a family in McKibbon, then was seen with a Yankee officer near Manleyville and rode out with their convoy. The Houston County Den reported the killing of their two men. Klansmen talked to trainmen on every freight crossing the trestle over the Tennessee. One brakeman said they had a kid ride with them to Eva, and the fireman remembered the kid saying he was going to Phillipy and up to Missouri to see kin, remembered him because he was a hell of a horseman. In Eldridge in Obion County, they heard about a couple traveling by carriage at a local hotel. The proprietor gave them a detailed description of Everett and Jessie. He said they'd come from McKenzie and he'd especially remembered them because he didn't get quality folk like that too often. He'd even offered to buy their fine carriage and throw in a serviceable rig, but the man wouldn't sell, said his matched blacks wouldn't budge for a seedy old rig like that. The hotelkeeper said he thought that was a stinger and took it the right way because the man gave him a friendly smile and a nice tip.

Samuel Miksell, the Obion County Grand Titan, wired the information to Buckner and Kortman at Milan, half-way between Memphis and the northwest border. Buckner drew circles on a map at places where strangers, or anyone resembling the Laniers had been seen. There were three distinct routes, all differing a little, but all leading north and west. He sent a telegram to Obion and Dyer

Dens. They were to split into four patrols and take watch on river towns in that area . . . Ridgely, Wynneburg, Tiptonville and Phillipy. Meanwhile, he would have men watch all the way down to Memphis.

"You get on the railroad and take charge up there," Buckner told Kortman.

"Will they take my authority."

"They'll take what we damn say. We're the strongest in the state, and after we get these skunks, we're going to take over the whole Realm. I been talking to people."

Kortman knew what it was going to come down to. If they found the Laniers, he was going to have to kill them—let himself be killed—or run until the Klan cut his heart out. He couldn't stall any longer and told Buckner, in that cold flat voice that impressed Kluxers, that he'd get them, follow them right across the damned river if he had to. He took the morning Louisville & Nashville train to where it crossed the Gulf, Mobile & Ohio tracks and rode north to Wynneburg, arriving on Sunday morning. He hade contact with the local Dens and thought they were a sorry lot. So much the better. But he gave them a fiery speech and said they had to kill the Lanier bastards, the stinking traitors. They'd heard of the Palmyra Kluxers and were roused by Kortman, impressed that he was leading them. He thought he could take them every point of the compass and they'd follow. But he knew Buckner was friendly with Miksell, another ambitious Kluxer, and the Obion man would have someone in there watching him.

Kortman began to forget any plans of escape. Blunders, absurdities, brutalities, anger . . . that was the past he wanted to flee. He was at that murky point where pride and boredom had vanished, no longer isolated his soul. He had broken through the barrier of loneliness. Death was only death—it was only the indecision that made him miserable. The Klan was a pestilence that he had to come to terms with. Ego and melancholy had been the enemies of his nature, his intelligence. He had to let go of everything, go where he was taken by circumstance. He didn't want to think that the future belonged to masses of men like the

Ku Klux, or to men who gave them simple explanations for everything that happened in the world.

He led the band north, gathering men in other towns, leaving someone to watch the wharfs, then linked up with Miksell in Washburn. They commanded forty-five men as they passed through Tiptonville, heading for Phillipy. Miksell told him about the great loop the river took there, and said it was the likeliest place. The Laniers could get into Kentucky easy or get across to Missouri from there. Kortman's grim sense of irony became a simple wit. He would sound like all the men who pleasured in killing, figured Miksell for one.

"I want to cut those bastards up when we get 'em."

Miksell wasn't impressed. "Just get 'em. We're bringing them someplace to be talked to."

"They're from Palmyra. They give the Palmyra men the hoot. I'm gonna cut up those bastards and string up the parts like a butcher shop."

"You do, you'll have to answer to people. Buckner says some important people want to talk to them. There's orders from Nashville they don't get killed." Miksell suddenly realized that Kortman didn't know, that Buckner hadn't trusted him for some reason. He was going to keep an eye on Kortman . . . one false move and he'd kill the sonofabitch. Maybe do it anyway, get the credit for taking the Laniers. Kortman'd have a secret burial with all the honors and be out in the Book of Noble and Chivalrous Dead, and they'd be done with him.

They rode the foot of low crumpled ridges along the river, and saw the lights of Phillipy. Kortman began to give orders and Miksell said nothing, waiting to hear him say something slippy. But he was impressed by the quick, smart way Kortman dispatched the band. He sent riders to scout far north above the town, near the Kentucky line, another group to come in from the west and head for the wharf, the rest to proceed up from the south and block off the town. Miksell thought Kortman would make some manuever to separate himself from the group, but the man surprised him. Kortman said they'd ride together, the two

of them heading straight through town to link up with the
scouting party north of town. They stopped in the dark to
put on their robes and hoods.

People saw the night riders coming in and quickly
headed for home or a tavern. But it didn't take the Klansmen long to get information. A party that answered Kortman's description had been in town and stayed at the
boarding house. There was a flashy-dressed man with
them. The landlady said they had an early supper and
went out to visit kin. She told Kortman they said they'd be
back before ten. But he knew they weren't coming back
and wondered who the stranger with them was. They had
a three-hour start. Maybe they were a long way into Kentucky by now, or on a steamboat. He felt calm as he rode
north through town into the dark woods. If they caught
up with the Laniers, he'd blow Miksell's head off, then
take his chances. It was the least he could do for a Grand
Titan . . . make him die in Christian glory chasing traitors.

15

Thomas Catlin led them between the big bend of the river where it looped north for almost ten miles, then west for five more before it resumed its journey south. They came out of the scrub onto loamy land that jutted into the river that lay on both sides.

"They have to take it slow around that bend, the current's always changing. Boat needs more stream going up to keep speed, but most captains don't like to waste the coal unless they're way off schedule."

The moon passed in and out of wispy clouds. Everett stood out on the point and could see miles up- and down-river. They saw a coalboat and two big keelboats, the kind that were disappearing from the river. Catlin assured him that there were at least four big boats passing that night, two bound south for Memphis, two coming up from New Orleans and Vicksburg.

"Are you sure your father will take us?"

"He didn't much like the idea of you being a stealing man, but Dan's letter said you were innocent. Course, I didn't believe it for a minute. Fine lawyer man like you, he wouldn't run if he was innocent."

"What kind of man is your father?"

"He's a heller for slaves and the South. Like any good Confederate."

"Daniel said you came from the north."

"Pap liked what he saw once he got to Kansas. Talks about owning land all the time. He couldn't buy nothing but a rock farm up north. He even run guns into Missouri in all the fighting there. He used to say, real hallelujah-like, 'Sharps rifles can persuade a man's morals a hell of a lot quicker than the Bible.' But don't get me wrong. He's Bible and Christian all the way. Sisters and brother that stayed with him, they're the same. Everett saw his grin in the darkness. "I slipped away from it. He's after me all the time. But as soon as I get to Piggot, I'm thinking of getting out, maybe to Texas."

"You have night riders there." Everett didn't want to use the name, Catlin might think he was sniffing around.

"Ku Klux? Hell, yes. At first, there wasn't much, but they was strong in Texas because a lot of niggers ran there, and some of the boys came up and organized everything. They're talking about spreading it all over the West. They figure get some men in with the cowboys driving herds north, get the word out. There's talk they're going into all the Territories. Some army men and Indian agents, they're in cahoots. Someone's got some crazy idea about using Indians like niggers. They figure if they can't work nigger slaves by law anymore, no one's going to give them a whistle for savages. Course they got to get them all penned up on reservations before than do it, but the army's got the word.

Everett wasn't too surprised. It was like a new dark ages, chaos and decay, a reign of terror. A new breed was taking over—schemers and bureaucrats, speculators, mad dreamers, little men who controlled things no better than scum. Men who made selfishness and greed rampant virtues. It had all passed too quickly, his age, when survival demanded skill in combat, and poets and philosophers praised courage and honor. It would go beyond the Klan who were hungry for nigger blood, or the army in the West that spilled Indian blood. It was going to be intrigues for profits with the Yankee factories, bribes, and more and more hypocrisy about a pure race to keep the system alive. The Rebellion, he knew, had its roots in a pathetic but honorable cause. This could be worse, much worse. Anarchy and crooked legislatures, connivers, an underhanded struggle over an empire for the taking. There were fortunes to be made.

Railroad barons and the northern money men had already stolen millions, taken millions of acres of land on a railroad's right-of-way. The railroads would soon connect east and west and make it easier. What had begun a hundred years before as an agrarian paradise, a vision of a classic Republic, a saga of the deepest human experience, would end in the passion of mobs and old fears, like some dark legend that loses its potency in the telling. He no longer believed that Americans could be as various and human as the poets sang. He no longer cared whether he lived or died. But he had to stick with his children, get them somewhere safe.

Adela and Jessie huddled together while the men kept watch along the river. After two hours, Matthew saw a smudge of light in the distance. The smudge became a blaze as the steamboat came down-river. According to the schedule, Catlin figured she was the *Grand Turk*, bound for Memphis and New Orleans. He decided to wait until she was in the first turn of the loop and had to buck the current. He took the torches from his large saddlebag, three pieces of soft pine wrapped halfway from middle to top with cotton soaked in orange dye and turpentine.

"Just pray there's no dangerous shoals around here or the pilot won't turn her in."

But he saw the river was brimming full, the waters lapping high ground, the heavy spill from the Missouri and Ohio rivers gentling out. There were no lantern-beacons bobbing anywhere in sight along the loop they later found was called American Bend because it passed through three states. The waters must be safe, enough draft for a big boat. Catlin estimated that the steamboat was still ten miles or so distant, and the fastest boats only did fourteen or fifteen miles an hour. There was still time to light the torches. Dark shapes passed up and down the river . . .

one of the small trading scows that peddled from farm to farm, a lumber raft, two coal barges, a broadhorn freighter, all running close in to shore to give the steamboat right-of-way, riding high water right under the overhanging trees. As the steamboat turned into the bend, they saw her outlines, the pilothouse a sumptuous glass temple riding high above everything . . . the long gilded saloon with tiny figures passing under prism-fringed chandeliers. It was an outward-bound boat and had flags still flying at the jack-staff and the stern verge-staff. She had eight huge boilers on the second-story deck, the fires fiercely glowing from a long row of furnaces, the red glare lighting up the river in great shimmering patches as the engines drove her into the bend, big brass bells ringing out a warning to other craft as the pilot took her into a channel near shore. Firemen, deckhands and roustabouts were moving up and down the deck.

Catlin pulled his gun, fired two shots into the air and quickly fired a third into one of the torches and it blazed. Matthew and Everett lit their torches and the three men waved them in a rhythmic swing back and forth over their heads. Catlin saw some deckhands and passengers running to the rail. Faces were pressed to the window in the pilothouse. He quickly told the others to swing the torches from sky to earth and keep time with him. If she was going to take the hail, it would have to be in the next few minutes. They heard the engines still roaring, the side and rear paddlewheels slapping at good speed. The resin and pitch-pine she burned before leaving port as a sign of preparation was still giving off tall, ascending columns of coal-black smoke trailing to stern. The party on shore watched, forlorn, thinking she would pass. Suddenly there was a jangle of engine bells and the engines answered, shooting white columns of steam high out of the escape pipes. Slowly, almost too slow to notice at first, the boat turned toward them, the pilot manuevering because, as he said later, he "smelled a bar." Foamy ridges spread from the bow, the turn became sharper and created a great swell. The wheels began to slow, hitting the river with a snapping sound. The pilot fought the current as the engines stopped, searching for the fine lines on the surface that indicated reef, trying to miss the ends but run her close. He was going to take her onto the bar that lay under every point and had just enough drift. The boat came to a stop about ten feet offshore. Deckhands ran the gangplank out, passengers crowded the upper rail, and the captain came down with his first mate. He was a bright-eyed old man, long and bony and horse-faced, wisps of mouse-colored hair under his cap and no upper teeth.

"You folks got trouble?" The accent was way up-river, maybe Iowa.

"Yes, sir, Captain," Catlin said. "Woman here's got the consumption. She's about ready to go and prayed she could see her eldest in Missouri before her time came. Daughter couldn't come to her because she got a big brood and no man to take care."

"Why didn't you just take her across in a skiff?" the mate asked.

"You be quiet, Sim," the captain said. "A dying woman should have a fine boat like the *Grand Turk* take her across."

"Thank you, Captain. Poor soul she never been on anything like that boat."

The captain gestured to the others. "Who are they?"

"Man's her brother. Did good service for the Union like you can see. That's his boy." He took Adela by the waist. "This here's my wife."

Adela wondered if he had thought up the story long before, or said it at the moment. But it sounded right. The captain ordered two men to carry the sick woman aboard and put her in his cabin, then looked over their heads.

"What in hell is that?"

They saw a torch flitting through the trees, then heard the pounding of horses.

"Might be Kluxers!" Catlin said.

"What do they want around here? Nothing but river."

"Maybe they're going for someone on the boat."

The captain looked hard at Catlin. "They coming for you? They don't ordinary bother anything on the river."

"We ain't done nothing."

The bank of hooded riders were coming out of the forest onto the flat stretch of the point, the man in the lead holding the torch high.

"Get everyone aboard!" the captain shouted.

Jessie was rushed up by the two deckhands and Adela ran alongside. The mate and the other three men drew weapons. Catlin fired first and the torch-bearer's horse went down in the mud. Another horse stumbled over the fallen mount, throwing its rider.

"Start back!" Catlin yelled. "Me and the kid'll hold them off!" The captain and mate ran up the gangplank. Everett hesitated, then followed. The Ku Kluxers began to spread, coming at them from three sides. "Get away," Catlin said and Matthew backed off, still firing. Catlin turned and ran, hitting the gangplank just as deckhands started to pull it in. But it was too late. Riders plunged into the water and grabbed it. Two riders galloped up the gangplank and ran down a deckhand, making the others back off. The riders in the water stood in their stirrups, reached up and climbed aboard the main freight deck. A passenger on the saloon deck pointed down to where Catlin and the Laniers stood.

"There! There they are! Glory to the Ku Klux!"

Some of the crowd took up the chant, but others rushed inside. One Klansman rode up the slippery plank and held his gun on Lanier. The captain rushed between them.

"This river is run by the United States of America government . . . the Union government. Now you rebel scum, you get the hell off my boat. These people ain't done nothing."

"You stringy old bastard, you get back or I'll blow you to kingdom come. We're gonna take 'em."

The captain asked the mate for his revolver. As he started to hand it over, the Klansman fired and he fell to the deck. The captain calmly picked up the gun and leveled it at the rider.

"You're going to hang for that."

"Throw him over!"

Two men rushed him, but the captain fired, hit one man in the shoulder and the other stopped. The mounted

Klansman spurred his horse at the captain, pinning him against a bulkhead.

"One more move like that, I'll let the horse kick your brains in. Can't hang me for that."

"I give you a last warning. Anyone I take on board this boat is under my protection and I'm the master of everyone and everything aboard. You're getting the hell off here or I'll have the army on you." He wanted to kill the man, but was afraid they'd slaughter the Laniers on the spot. "You yellow-striped bastard. Take that hood off. Let them see what a stinking skunk looks like."

The Klansman saw that the mate was still moving. He pointed to the captain and wounded man. "Throw them over!"

Men went for them and the captain fired at the mounted man but missed. The two officers were thrown into the dark river on the far side. The Laniers and Catlin were disarmed and men began to tie their hands when shots were heard in the distance. The Klansman ordered men into a picket line, afraid it was negro militia. But only two riders emerged from the forest, Kluxers, whipping their mounts. It was Miksell and Kortman, alerted by the shot moments after they spotted the lights of the *Grand Turk*. They rode through the line of Klansmen and went up the gangplank.

"You got them?" Miksell shouted.

The Klansman pointed to the group.

"Where's the captain?"

"Threw him and the mate over. They fired on us."

"Damn fool." Miksell turned to Kortman, who remained silent. "That them?" Kortman nodded. "Get those men out of the water." Kortman led four men right past the prisoners, glancing down at Adela. She knew instantly that it was him. He was lying all the time, wasn't anywhere near Memphis. Kortman came around with the Kluxers holding the captain, threading his horse carefully around the stacked cargo. The negro firemen, deckhands, barbers, waiters and roustabouts that worked the ships were loyal, proud of the jobs that gave them standing in the river towns. They slipped around back and armed themselves with rifles passed down from the Texas deck, led by an ex-slave named Wikky. He was a Koromantine, the fine-looking, brave negroes admired on the plantation. It was said that even when they were branded before being loaded on a slave ship, they drove their chest on the hot brand-iron and laughed. Once at a negro ball in New Orleans, a man thought Wikky was putting on too many airs and challenged him:

"Who is you, anyway? Who *is* you? That's what I wants to know."

Wikky swelled his chest and boomed out: "Who *is* I? I let you know mighty quick who I *is*! I wants you niggers to understand that I fires the middle door on the *Grand Turk*. That's who I is!"

Wikky split the men into groups. He knew there was still steam up and sent the "Texas-tender," the negro boy who served the pilot and officers during the watches, to the pilothouse.

"You tell him to tell the engineer to back off fast he can do. They ain't no ropes holding and we can just let the plank drop. Then when you hears the engine, you ring that bell like the devil coming." That was the signal to open fire. Most of the Klansmen were still on shore. Only Kortman, Miksell and about six others were aboard, all grouped.

"Mate's drowned," Kortman told Miksell in a low voice.

"You're all going to hang for this," the captain said.

"Take it easy old man. Man here was too short tempered. We don't mean you no harm, or any passenger. These here are desperados . . . thieves. We're just upholding the law. Not let 'em go with no more trouble"—Kortman cocked his gun—"or you won't be around to see us hang."

The captain shook his head. "This here's piracy. You boarded my boat under arms. You'll have to kill me first to take them. If they're what you say, they'll get the law from Union men."

There was a sudden hiss and the loud pulse of engines as the boat started backing off. The noise startled Miksell's horse and it reared and threw him. The bell clanged and Wikky's men opened fire, killing three Klansmen in the first volley. They came out from behind the engines and hemp and cotton bales, firing as they advanced. The plank was dropping into the river. Klansmen leaped over the side and struggled to shore, but Kortman held his skittish horse, then threw his gun down and moved forward so that he could no longer escape.

Everyone stood silent as he pushed his horse through and stopped in front of Adela. The Klansmen had missed the Deringer in Jessie's reticule and she had passed it to Adela who had it palmed behind her back. Kortman was helpless now. She quickly brought the gun up. Kortman said nothing, but she understood. He seemed to be beseeching her to kill him. She had once promised herself she would, but it was different now. She was flooded with pity, believed that he had tried to save him. He held the pommel with both hands, then suddenly made a movement as if going for a hidden gun. Adela fired point-blank into his face. He slumped forward in the saddle and started to slide off. Adela rushed to hold him up, but she sagged under the weight. The captain ordered two deckhands to throw Kortman over the side. Adela went to the edge of the deck and saw the body floating in the shallow water, rump up. *I'm sorry, Jim Kortman, she thought, I'm sorry for you.* The captain came up to her and said she was a brave young lady.

"He got what was coming to him."

She wanted to say, *"Didn't you see him just sit there and drop his gun? What I did was mercy in cold blood. . . ."* Was there such a thing? She never understood why she killed him. Maybe because they had been linked so close and so long, and she understood him, the only one to know his facets, the one person who never saw him as pathetic or plaintive, never pitied him until that moment, had only loved and hated him. He had to know it if he selected her for his executioner, begged her—and he did, she insisted to herself—to explode the life out of him. He understood that she had felt the passions that made him human, not just an ugly remnant of the war. She could never connect the Kortman she knew as a young girl with the man who hung around with sullen, desperate ex-soldiers and town bums. She was aware of his reputation for cruelty in the Klan . . . but maybe it was all a kind of suicide.

"I don't figure," the captain said to Everett, "that anyone the Klan wanted did anything bad."

"No, it was like we told you. My sister wants to see her daughter and grandchildren before she goes." He wanted to tell the truth but Catlin was nearby and he had to think about the future, the time to spend in Piggot until he could make other plans, get money he'd sent to his brother in Memphis. It would be wise to stay with the Catlins for a time, but he was determined to move the family north, get his children away from the terror.

"Where do you want to get off?"

Everett hesitated, but Catlin spoke quickly. "It would be real convenient if you touched at Caruthersville. It's only a way from there to Wardell where we're going." He thought it was better to make it sound like they had a town destination in mind instead of asking to be put off directly across the river. His brother Lewis was waiting there with a large rig.

"I put in there quick to hitch the thirty-cord wood-boats in tow. We been burning fast."

It was full fifty miles down-river and might take four or five hours, the captain said, and they could rest in the cabins. Jessie and Everett were taken to his quarters, and Adela and Catlin kept up the masquerade and went into a cabin as husband and wife. Matthew wandered the boat for a while. It was truly a floating palace, he thought. The main cabin was at least 200 feet long, a resplendent tunnel separating the cabins and serving as social hall and dining room for the passengers. Elaborately-carved brackets supported ceilings covered with ornament. Light from stained glass clerestory windows fell on varicolored Brussels carpets. Imported chandeliers, paintings, rich draperies, plush-covered furniture, and a grand piano were reflected in the towering, gleaming mirror at the end. There was exuberant gingerbread decoration everywhere. There was fine silverware, china and linens. The bill of fare had fourteen courses—four types of fish, six broiled meats and six kinds of roasts, eight entrees and nine cold dishes, five types of game, and thirty-six different desserts.

The captain said Wikky and his boys had done good and deserved a drink. Most of the passengers had retired and the bar was closed but the captain opened it. Matthew noticed that the bartender gave him some excellent brandy, but mixed complicated and picturesque drinks for the negroes. When they returned to work, Matthew asked the bartender why he didn't give them the brandy.

"Because the niggers won't have any other. They want a *big* drink. Don't make no difference what you make it of. You give a nigger a plain gill of half-dollar brandy for five cents—will he touch it? No. Ain't size enough to it. But you put up a pint of worthless rubbish, and heave in some red stuff to make it pretty—red's the main thing—and he wouldn't put that glass down to go to a circus."

In the cabin Tom rested on the bed, while Adela stood looking out at the river, wishing she could sail all the way to New Orleans. A waiter brought food and wine and they toasted their escape and talked for a while, edgy and mocking each a little. They were both a little drunk when Catlin put his arms around her and they started to dance. He kissed her on the neck but she thought he was only being playful and didn't mind. She was damned, she thought, if she'd lose control so easy this time. She was tense and excited, but thought it had to do with the confrontation with the Kluxers, the gunfire, the disturbing vision of Kortman's body sagging. . . . She thought she had almost pushed him out of mind already and felt ashamed. Once when they danced past the mirror, Tom turned her and stopped, leaned his chin on her shoulder and they smiled at the artless contrast of her lucid color against his dark heavy features. She saw his eyes change and he touched her breast. He head went back and she closed her eyes, but she broke away.

"No! Goddamn it, no! Who the hell are you?"

But she wanted him, puzzled because it was all mixed together . . . the horrid desire she knew she wouldn't resist . . . murdering the love of her youth . . . the hot-house mixture of the erotic and the deadly. She felt a lush despair when he held her again and kissed her. She didn't move when he started to open the buttons at the back of her dress, but pushed him away when he tried to slip the dress off. They sat apart on the beds and Tom lit a small cigar. She laughed when he offered her one, but took it and they smoked, tensed like shrewd combatants, the slowly-revolving ovehead fan curling and spreading the smoke in wisps.

They repeated the sneaky disrobing ritual twice before she let him strip her, everything but her amber necklace. A believer in the magic moment, she was afraid that once it passed, she'd change her mind, try to be sensible, make fun of him, and she helped him undress, her face grave, and arched toward him. But he forced her to suck him and she was voracious and giddy. She whispered gratitude as he mounted her for "freeing" her, encouraging that perversity that frightened and possessed her. She turned over him and began to sway, her breasts rolling slowly. He grabbed one and made a slicing motion as if he could easily cut it off and never think twice, grinning all the time, heaving up and sweating. She had a crazy grin, felt as if she was dying, didn't care what happened. Then her eyes rolled back and her breathing began slowly, mounting in tempo, until she pleaded with almost spastic hands and he jammed his finger into her asshole and she came, a silly smile on her face, as if she had played a trick on someone. She rolled over and lay gasping.

"Tell me . . . *tell me*. . . ."

He mocked her. "Tell you . . . *tell you*. . . . What?"

"That you love me."

"Oh, Christ. Don't get any ideas."

"You can be cruel to me—but don't be a son of a bitch."

He kissed her and said he loved her. She locked her arms around his neck and pulled him down on top of her.

"The way you say it, you make it sound like it's a crime and I'm your accomplice. Don't leave me. I'll do terrible things."

"You forget already? I seen you do bad. Who the hell would think you could blow a man away, even a Kluxer."

"I don't mean that. That's easy." She thought she be-lieved it. That's all she'd heard and seen almost half her life. Everyone's life was balanced too shaky. She was al-ready years removed from the life in Palmyra. She had felt a ferocious attraction for Tom the moment she saw him, tried to rationalize it away, but thought now that he was the man she was searching for . . . smart and sensual and just enough mean to always keep her anxious and crazy for him. Adela suddenly began to sob when she re-membered Kortman's warning . . . *the wrong kind of brute.* Tom paid no attention to her tears, lighting another cigar, and she felt more lust because of his indifference, because he allowed her to drift between emotions without any rules or lectures or punishments or attempts at senti-mental comfort. If he scanted her in that moment, she was confident she could always pull him back. They were, she thought, in perfect confluence, and when they made love again, she was sure. He began to laugh and she tried to squirm out from under him but he was too strong.

"I was thinking about poor bastards that had to fuck someone with a scraggly ass, and I got this sweet soft mar-ble to play with."

"You spoiled it. Get off!"

"I'll do like I damn please. And I'll do with you like I damn please. Don't forget that. Or I'll feed you to some Kluxers who'll cut you hind to front right up that sweet hole you got."

She was afraid of him and wondered if it was the prom-ise of his power, or the threat that might turn real. She wouldn't give in that easy.

"You know why I'm sweet on you? Because you like to play the tough man."

"Sweet on me! You got the nerve, you bitch. You broke into a sweat the first time I touched you back in Phillipy. You think I didn't see that. *Sweet on me!* You say that again, I'm going to get real mad. You just sweet on me?"

"No, I love you. I'm mad for you." And she couldn't deny it was a lie because she didn't know what it meant. It *was* a madness maybe, and maybe that's what love was. But she knew how gluttonous she was and expected little

virtue from herself. She wanted a lover's romantic ca-
resses, but she also wanted his pinch and rough hands and
abuse that hurt but were needed. The lamp was sputtering
and the shadows grew long and danced in crazy-quilt pat-
terns. Tom fell asleep and she dressed and walked out on
deck.

A storm was flaring, running northeast, and the river
looked like molten lead, tumbling heavy in dirty swells.
There was an iron-gray gap that joined river and sky
through the horizon and the rain came. In that moment
Adela felt an insolence toward life and reveled in the danger, then began to have misgivings. She was afraid of that
morbid, wicked part of him, but more afraid that she
would never get free of him. Was she crazy, or stupid?
When a man was inside her, she could promise her life
away, force him into saying things he didn't believe, nor, in
the end did she. Maybe that was her real talent, dirty little hidden encounters, and dazzling self-betrayal to prove
how worthless she was. She felt drained, but knew it was
only her will to make the guilt fester and that would pass.
But even that was part of the excitement. She thought she
was cursed because she often dreaded, more than desired,
that solemn moment when hope in love was exchanged for
certainty. She thought of her father and tried to translate
his constancy and wisdom and intellectual serenity into
something useable, thought of glowing rooms with polite
women in powdered entente, damask, cut glass, sweet
songs and Mozart. But none of it worked. She could find
nothing in the memories to protect her.

She returned to the cabin and looked down on Tom and
hungered to see the strange slate eyes, how opaque they
became in sex, a shadow of deadness, as if the eyes were a
screen that isolated him. He wouldn't do with her as he
pleased, she promised herself that, but she wasn't ready
yet to give him up. At least she wouldn't end up like other
women, once lovely and curious girls who were bored
with the local gentry and never had the gumption to fly
beyond that circle. She might be incapable of making the
right decisions, or any real decision at all, but she was all
too aware of her weakness, and that was a kind of

strength. She wouldn't live with delusions, only feelings, act only if she was touched or obsessed to do so. Everything girls like her had been brought up to believe in was so much mash, and she wondered whether she would have a glorious or shabby future because she saw things clearly.

She thought about Kortman to see if she suffered any regrets, or remorse, and felt no shock when he seemed like someone she'd known long long ago. The linen hood splotched with blood . . . the way he slumped, his face still hidden from her. That might be part of the answer. She was delighted, thought she was being profound. Everything in him had shriveled after his face was ruined. The Klan hood was a way to hide from the world, more than in just a simple, literal way. She tried to drive it from her mind, tired of the lurid tricks memory played.

Catlin was awakened by a soft, suffused feeling when she sucked him to hardness again and was straddling him, stroking his face, saying that she would never be trouble to him, that she understood. Afterward they danced to the storm-noise until they were wild, grabbing for each other, Tom merciless in the way he handled her, Adela tricked by a hazy scheme of love and tormented by its imminence, trying to have the strength that impudence and arrogance always gave her. But whatever she held back from Kortman and others, she would give to him. And the more she thought about it, the lovelier the bargain seemed. For a time . . . until she could decide what to do, where to go.

She understood that she had never been anywhere or done anything, and couldn't know what she wanted, except from others' secondhand stories. But she thought that was better than what she saw in older people who had experienced the world. Their ability to choose was maimed as well. Having seen or done too much, there was an abundance to choose from, a known variety that could make the head spin—and, she thought, being ignorant of life or burnished by it, everyone started from the same place. No one really planned or decided how they'd live their life. Passions and luck and superstition determined fate.

A friend of her mother's once said that the war had

destroyed illusions, particularly for men. She began to understand it. Men had to face a hapless fact of life, that some things are irreparable. They had undergone a change in the way they labored and made a living, while women performed tasks that had hardly changed for centuries. It was men who became lost, who had no bearings—even the Ku Kluxers who were only mad dreamers of another kind—whose place in the world became fragile and strange, who were abruptly severed from their true evolution. She told Tom what she was thinking, was she silly?

"The trouble with you is like all women. You think men drink and are savage to women. That they close themselves away . . . don't give women the stingiest privilege."

"Well, you don't. At least Southern men. You treat women like they're dolls, a toy, a prize to show off." But she had seen it in the town, in her family, how most men, except for outsiders like Kortman and Tom Catlin, were made docile and dull by defeat, how men had to suppress the best in themselves.

"It was men who were twisted by the war," Catlin said, "not women."

"But all the women and girls I know—if they have any imagination—they're hungry for the life of men. A man's life is whole. A woman's is all shrunken and disguised. You never see her real nature, it's hidden."

"Hell, you silly bitch, men are the only victims. And I don't mean the battles. They still have to try and be something, support families." He had a mocking look. "Be *manly.*"

Adela understood what he meant: stifling their best instincts, being potent behond fantasy, still trying to achieve and succeed when it was hopeless. If she were betting on who would survive in her family, it would be she and Jessie, not the men. She smiled "If you look at it a certain way, a man's life is fearsome territory, isn't it." She meant that they were the true romantics, the dreamers who believed in heroes and lost causes and excellence in all the valiant, transient, menaced things. Women, Adela knew, were the true survivors. Men could be spurred and tricked, commit gaucheries and ignorant crudities . . . while all the while women just claimed superior natural virtues. She didn't have to be afraid of his domination. In her way she was exercising power, making the "dominator" obey—making the erotic response on her own terms. She tried to imagine him in a workaday way and asked what he did.

"No special thing. I'm here and there."

"But how do you make your money?"

"I'm in with my father."

"I can't see you clerking in a hardware store."

"No, we got other business."

"Is it interesting?"

"More promising than interesting."

"Why all the mystery?"

"It's nothing."

"You said he was a Ku Klux. I can't see you doing that."

"The Klan? Hell, they're going to be finished off soon. Government's getting too hot about them. What I do is bigger, me and my pap."

"Come on, you're busting to tell me. Maybe it's just a lot of lies. You're trying to sound like a big man."

He gave her a playful slap. "Don't ever say that to me. I'm in it for the money, but my pap, now he's gonna be a big man, as big as the railroad men or the money people back East."

She didn't know whether he was boasting, being sly, or teasing her. His look told her not to pursue it any further. She began to feel tired, almost regretted what she'd done that night, the waste, the constant assault on her emotions. They heard shouts. The boat was pushing through the rain, turning into the wharf at Caruthersville. The noise was deafening as the engines reversed and the pilot fought to keep from slipping back into the current.

16

IT was still dark when the *Grand Turk* tied up. They thanked the captain and Tom led them along the cobbled warf to a hotel. Two men were waiting for them, standing alongside a big rig with three rows of spring-seats. They went inside and Tom introduced his brother Lewis, young and lank-haired. Adela saw a passive-looking face without guile or strength and beautiful dark eyes.

"He's the pup in the family," Tom said "This here's Simon."

The second man was a negro. Then Adela remembered what Tom said about him being a breed. Simon had black wooly hair and negro features, but his skin had a copper cast and he had light eyes. He looked to be in his thirties, but she could never tell a negro's age, she thought, and was struck by the quiet, intelligent, brooding air of the man when he said that his name was Simon Hooper. It was a subtle demand to be treated with dignity. This was no Uncle Billy or Little Willie. Lewis said be brought him along because he thought there might be trunks, or someone would need help.

Jessie insisted on taking a room to change her clothes and do her face and hair, said she wouldn't go another step looking that way. Evertt looked embarrassed, as if he was guilty for her vanity. The men joined a group sitting around the lobby stove, Simon standing back at the entrance. Three looked like locals, weatherbeaten faces and rough clothes, but the other was a well-dressed English traveler. They were arguing about slavery. The Englishman said that his country had abolished it peacefully by law more than twenty years before. There was no reason for the war or scum like the Klan. A man with big fumbling farmer's hands spit on the stove.

"How the hell you come here and tell us about niggers, you sucking bastard! The Kluckers'll ride you under a big tree with a rope and teach you what-for."

"What the hell were you doing in Africa?" Tom said. "You sold niggers and you're still nigger-holders. I know what's going on. You work the niggers in Africa and other places, and then you take the cotton or wood or cane, or whatever the hell it is, and make something for cheap and sell it around dear."

"It seems that you forget that it was we who helped the South during the war. We ran the blockades——"

"Just because you were hungry for cotton. No other reason. Now you don't need us . . . least that's what you think."

"You bloody self-righteous Americans. You're still butchering your natives, or bunging them onto reservations unfit for the plow or anything else. We developed. You slaughtered. Remember, these Africans have been in trees for donkey's years." He seemed unaware of Simon's presence.

"We never killed them before," said a second man. "Only if they was trying to raise the others to mischief, or laying with a white woman. Hell, I know a nigger woman and she says, 'They say bad whipping was the old plantation way, but my master he whip only once, cause some bad nigger steal his favorite pumpkin that he was saving it for the seed.'"

"No, we didn't kill them because they were worth money to us," Everett said. "Back where we come from, a white woman was found with a buck. She was killed, but

the negra was sent back to the fields because he would
work like three men."

"Well, they ain't worth nothing now. Cost money to
work niggers now."

The third man rested his elbows on his thighs and
looked at the ground before speaking. "You speak right,
brother. But you can't go around killing niggers like the
Kluckers do. Not for nothing. Niggers I got, they work
hard."

"Hell, they're killing niggers cause they're gonna kill us.
We're the chickens now and they're the foxes. The Yankees seeing to that." He recounted talk he overheard in his
barn, when two negroes thought they were alone:

"We got to learn to fight."

"I can fight. I can whip any man."

*"You dumb mule. I mean we got to learn to kill with
guns. Somes learn in the army."*

*"We free now. What the hell we got to fight any
more?"*

*"Cause they got to pay us, and I sees how afraid they
be. You think they gonna give us land like it was nigger
Christmas?"*

"We gonna get the land. The Yankee officer he tell us."

"Them Kluckers don't care what the Yankees say."

"That just old woman talk about the Kluckers."

"Them ain't no old womans riding the night."

"When did you hear that?" Everett asked.

"A while back."

"How far back?"

"What the hell's the difference? That's what I heard
them niggers say."

"It had to be a long time ago. Negras already got land.
And the vote. The Yankees kept their promise. Sure nigras
killed white men"—he couldn't shed his lawyer's stance—
but it was mostly in self-defense. I'll tell you that for every
white man killed, there was a hundred negras or more
dead." He wanted to tell them that it was other white
men, Southerners, who kept them living poor, them and
the negroes, but thought better of it.

One of the men was about to challenge Everett and

seemed to notice the stub for the first time. "Well, the Lord spared the fitten, and the rest he seen fitten to die." But he thought the man sounded like a stinking scalawag. Tom wondered why Everett was so hot about niggers for a crook who stole money meant for niggers. What the hell did he care, he had his money. The men he talked to so high and mighty, maybe one of them had a slave or two before the war, but they just sounded mean because they were bitter, maybe did niggers's work now just to keep their families going. Lanier was a crook for all his fine talk. Maybe, Tom thought, he'd have to find out where the shoe pinched. It wasn't poor bastards like these that Lanier had to worry about, it's other people that he'd never dream were mixed up in it.

While the men argued, Adela spoke to Lewis. "I hope we're not going to be trouble for you."

"No trouble."

"I hear you have two sisters."

"That's right."

"It'll be nice to meet other girls."

"Might."

"I know your brother Daniel. He's the one who sent us here."

"I know."

She thought he was just one of those rustics stingy with words, or bashful . . . or someone had warned him. She suddenly felt war, a restlessness and nervousness she couldn't shake.

It was first light when they piled into the rig. Lewis and Simon were up front, with Everett, Jessie and Matthew behind them, and Adela and Tom in the third row. The countryside was heavily-wooded and beautiful in the tipping sun. But Adela thought the people they passed looked worn and frightened, the farms tumbledown. The rig passed through Haytio and they stopped for the night in Kennett. In the morning they were across the Missouri boot into Arkansas. Simon whipped the horses up at a crossroads and turned north for Piggott. Catlin called the names of towns as they passed through . . . Rector . . . Nimmons . . . Greenway . . . but they all looked the

same: clusters of false-front frame buildings of raw wood
and shingles and a two-story brick building or two around
a square, horse-droppings and swarms of flies, deep ruts
in the dusty road from wagons, a livery stable, pigs slop-
ping around mounds of garbage, a church, and people in
homespun or cheap store clothes glancing suspiciously at
the rig.

"Piggot like this?" Adela asked.

Tom laughed and reached two rows to poke his brother.
"Hear that? Tell her what Piggot's like."

"Nice place."

Adela whispered in Tom's ear. "He a little simple?"

"Couldn't ever figure it out. Never says much. Maybe
he's simple, just simple enough so we get no trouble from
him, but not so simple he gives us any trouble." He
pointed to Simon. "Now that one, he's cold smart. Maybe
the blood mixes good."

"What kind of Indian you say he is?"

"Shawnee. Warriors . . . but that was a long way
back."

"Where did you get him?"

"My pap picked him up somewhere in Missouri. He was
a kid, running around town doing odd jobs and sleeping in
a livery stable. He loves my old pap."

"I always hear about how niggers loved their masters in
the old days. They sure showed it. The minute they were
free, they ran from home and friends and master and
joined the Yankee army, or just followed to do what they
could . . . hungry and in danger so they could stay free.
Damned strange people, niggers."

"Not Simon. He's a humble, obedient fellow. He stayed
with us because pap saved his life. Once when he was a
kid the dumb breed says 'Howya Sis' to a white lady.
Some men were going to string him up, whip his hide off
at the least, but pap saved him."

"Ku Kluxers?"

"No, it was long before that."

"I thought if it was Kluxers, you pap, like you call him,
wouldn't have any trouble, since you said he was one of
them."

"I say that?"

"You did . . . all those plans he had."

"I was just trying to fool you."

"A regular clown. Just wanted to bumfuzzle me." She wondered if he thought she was stupid, or was it a contempt for all women. She didn't like him. He was fiercely beautiful and just the right kind of cruel. If only he was stupid along with it, they could enjoy each other. But he wasn't. He just laughed, never warned her not to mention it to his father, pretended to be whispering and all the time sucking and licking at her ear. She didn't like the furtive touching, but couldn't resist him, or was afraid to. He took her hand and placed it on his pants. She squeezed hard and knew he was enjoying it. God, he was wonderful to play with, a lovely toy with bewitching smells and surfaces. She watched the back of her father's neck and thought how sad he would be to know what was happening to her. Jessie kept talking about how excited she was and started to turn. Adela pulled her hand away, thinking she was crazy to do anything like that in broad day.

"What are your sisters like?"

"Yes," Jessie said, "it will be nice to have other women to talk to."

"One's a little beauty. Other's a little worn."

Adela poked her head toward Lewis. "You're beginning to sound like him."

"They're nice, good women. One takes care of my pap since my mother died. She don't mind, wants it that way."

Adela thought he was hiding something, or proving her right, had never noticed them much. How could he say anything reasonable about women, especially sisters. To a man like him, there were nice women, good women or bad women. Adela thought she was the perfect choice for him, the nice woman he could turn bad. But would he have the same passion for her then?

"You all right, Matt?" She was worried about him. He'd hardly said a word since they left Phillipy.

"Fine."

"Tom says there's good hunting up his way."

"That true? Country around us was just about shot out. People too hungry."

"Best shooting country you ever saw," Tom said. "Good bird eating, quail, pheasant . . . deer, wild hog, big cats, bear, everything."

"What do you use?"

"For big game I like the Enfield the English sent here in the war."

"We found out later they sent it to us *and* the Union," said Everett.

"I also got a Bench rifle, the kind the snipers used. It's got a telescope sight. You could kill a bear with it at six hundred yards. Small game I use a Sharps carbine."

"Never got my hands on one," Matthew said, "but my papa carried one in the war."

"You can use mine. Even got me a Remington Sporting Rifle Number One when I was in Dubuque once. You like a shotgun?"

"Ain't real sporting, is it?"

"Young fellow, you go out to kill something, you better not think about sporting. You just get yourself a good double-barrel percussion shotgun. Nothing's better. Hell, that's what they used in bloody Kansas and Missouri."

"Enough of that talk!" Everett said in a firm voice.

"Old soldier like you shouldn't be scared of gun talk."

"Listen, I killed men in the war, more men than you ever gave an angry look. But I don't want to hear any more talk about killing or guns or the like. I've heard enough for a lifetime, and I don't want my son——"

"We're just talking hunting, papa."

"No—you were. He wasn't."

Tom thought he was a preachy old bastard, first in the hotel and now. Didn't think anything was wrong with scooping up the good Yankee dollars, did he? Where the hell did he hide it? He was going to have to talk to him serious real soon. When they got to Piggot, Lanier wouldn't talk that way if he knew what was good for him, not in front of Isaac Catlin. Not in that sermonizing voice. But he heard the cavalry officer in the voice, thought he better talk more amiable, said he was sorry and hadn't

meant anything. Everett accepted the apology with a
grudging nod but said nothing. They rode in silence and
after a while Catlin saw a burned barn at the side of the
road.

"We're near Piggot. Maybe three miles."

It was starting to get dark after the long twilight. The
sunlight gave way to red and purple and blue, and the
shadows grew long. Sukie once told Adela that it was the
hour called "the time between the dog and the wolf,"
when all that was natural and familiar and safe changed
into the unnatural, the strange and frightening. Foxfire
danced in the woods and the trees lining the roads made
forbidding shadows. They saw a glow, then lights just
ahead and rolled into Piggot. Maybe he isn't lying, Adela
thought. It looked like a prosperous town, far different than
anything she's seen since leaving Palmyra.

There was a square in the center of town with a second-
generation courthouse, a square-brick structure with a
peaked roof capped by a cupola. The main street had a
great variety of stores, two hotels, four churches, and just
beyond were a cotton gin, flour mill, a printing shop and
two small factories. Some streets were graded and lined
with shade trees and the new gas lamps. Adela wondered
at that; most cities up north, she heard, didn't have them.
The people looked well-fed and clothed, and a few called
out a pleasant greeting to Tom and Lewis. Adela had
thought of the escape as an adventure that would free her,
but when she saw the people she knew they were the
same kind she hated in Palmyra—all respectable, indus-
trious, God-fearing, early-to-bed-and-early-to-rise, heedful
of their neighbor's good opinion, bent on making moeny
and avoiding alien ways.

A negro boy about twelve ran alongside the rig and
tugged at Simon's arm. "You bring me something?"

"Scat . . . tell you later."

Adela thought he was too young to have a son that age,
but knew niggers weren't like whites, didn't wait for no
proper age or regular marriage. They just did it. That was
one of the reasons so many whites hated them, men and
women. They were tied tight by custom, and when they

saw all the devilment and pleasure, they thought niggers had to be worse than them because they could enjoy life even when they were so miserable. Tom pointed out his father's hardware store. It was a big-well-lighted place on a corner, taking up half the street on each side.

"Is he there?" Adela asked.

"No, he don't hardly go to the store. I told you he got other business. He likes the land. That's what he's dealing now. My sister Abby takes care most days."

Simon whipped the horses up at the edge of town, turned into a pasture that was going to scrub and guided the rig along a narrow lane up a hill. A Victorian Gothic mansion stood at the crest. It had an arcaded veranda that curled around the first floor and rested on thin gingerbread columns, a grilled iron railing around the second-floor balcony, and a large porte-cochere. Jessie was thrilled at the sight of it. She'd thought she was going into a wilderness, and here was a house with something of the grandeur of Loretto. What kind of man could build a house like that in raw country? What kind of man wanted a house like that? But Adela thought it was too new and haughty. In summer, when the grass was soft and bright, with a flower border and rose trellis, it might appear pleasant. But in the cold, fallow months it would look bleak and naked and arrogant.

There was a flurry at the door and two negro women came out to help. The Catlin sisters stood in the doorway. When Adela went up the shallow steps to the veranda, she saw them clearer. The one called Metta was in her twenties, small and fine-boned, with delicate cameo features, yielding dark eyes and dark hair worn in a soft bun. She liked her on sight. The other, Abby, was the oldest Catlin child, in her thirties Adela judged, but looking older. She seemed agreeable, but couldn't pacify or change what people saw . . . a tall, parched, haunted-looking woman with the trace of a once-handsome girl. She tried to be friendly and hospitable, but she was awkward, unlike Metta, who had a natural grace.

"We just got a message from Daniel. A Yankee soldier brought it. He says he hoped your trip was easy and will see you in a month or two. You know, he's leaving the army."

"No, I didn't." Adela tried to sound guileless.

"You should." Metta held her arm. "He sent you a special greeting. I'll bet the Yankees on the telegraph had their big laugh." She glanced out to the rig "That Simon. He'll wear those horses thin the way he drives."

Adela thought she was going to scold Simon, but saw them talking quietly for a few seconds before Metta took her inside. They passed through the main door fitted with beveled glass panes into the vestibule that had a lantern of jewled glass mounted in brass. There was a staircase on the right, a low ceiling formed by the staircase leading above, a coat closet, and a door leading to the kitchen. They went through an archway into the parlor. On the wall was a large painting that was a copy of a daguerreotype hanging alongside. It was a woman with a round face sagging in the cheeks, a low forehead with hair drawn back and a wide-eyed stare. Adela thought it was a severe, reproachful face, had the smell of camphor and religious fervor.

"Is that your mother?"

"Yes," Tom said. "Scary ain't it. Tallowy-looking bitch."

"Don't talk like that!" Abby said.

"Come on, you're glad she's gone."

"She was hard on me because I was the oldest. We didn't get along. No, I didn't weep for her, but that was long ago."

"Well, you took her place real good."

"Someone had to care for Father." Aedla noticed that there was no easy going "Pap."

"That's right, Abby. You're a good woman." Tom turned to the Laniers. "Sacrificed everything to keep the family together. It near broke her heart when Daniel left to join the Yankees."

"Not because he went with them. I love him. He's the nearest to me."

"Then I came along and spoiled it."

She tried a small smile. "You're a scamp, you always were."

"Stop teasing her, Tom," Metta said.

"Where's papa?"

"He'll be down soon."

Lewis was gone and the others sat in the parlor. In a few minutes Isaac Catlin came into the room. Adela was surprised. He was Thomas grown older, a rough-hewn face, muscular, with a shock of thick graying hair that made him look like a Roman senator. She thought he was the kind of man who, with a stare, could give her a sense of her own unworthiness. Matthew thought he looked familiar, and at first had the same impression as Adela, that it was the resemblance between father and son. Then he suddenly remembered where he'd seen him . . . the man in the courthouse when they strangled Douthit. They'd walked right into a Klan house and he wondered why Daniel Catlin had sent them there. But Isaac Catlin seemed different now, polite, even a little ripe in his manners, flattering the Lanier women. He expressed regret that they had to flee Palmyra, a town he knew well and admired. He didn't press any questions on Everett.

"I haven't seen my son for a long time. We had a hard quarrel at the start of the war. But I admired him because he followed his own conscience." Isaac seemed anxious to allay any fears they had. He seemed to be talking to Adela. "Did you know him long?"

"Oh, they're promised," Jessie said.

Adela glanced at Tom, who winked. She wondered whether her mother said it maliciously, or because she remembered what Daniel said and was trying to help. "That's right."

Metta, who seemed the soul of sweetness, rushed to Adela and embraced her. "I'm so happy. Daniel had his share of everything terrible." But she seemed almost rueful when she said, "It's wonderful to see people free to love."

"What kind of mistress of the house are you?" Isaac said to Abby. "When will you feed these tired people?"

"Right away, father. We waited for you."

They sat down at a table lighted by a candle chandelier, the flames reflected in glass and silver, linen and china. Jessie's hair caught the light and turned dark reddish, while Adela's blazed. The talk was genial and relaxed at first. Everett commented on how nice and solid a town Piggot was, but said nothing about nearby places they saw. He said he had tried to make Palmyra a center of culture.

"I remember the splendid opera house," Isaac said. "But we are bent on other things first here. This will be the entrance to a new America, a great and shining city." They thought he was going to indulge in windy rubrics and sentiments about the Union being joined again, but he began to talk about a new American empire.

"The country east of the Mississippi is finished. The war did that. A terrible mistake. But there is more land and riches lying west of here than you can dream of. And few people. This time, the right people will come."

"Isn't most of it desert and mountains?" Everett said.

Isaac shook his head. "No, there are great plains of grassland, hills of silver and gold for the taking, big rivers for commerce."

"There are farmers and ranchers there already. Are they your new people?"

"That's the beginning."

"Of what?"

"A grand prosperity."

"For who?"

"The right people. For one, the Chinese must be driven out. They served to build the railroads. Now it's time to ship them back."

Matthew, fascinated by Indians, asked what would be done with them.

"The federal government has the right idea this time. If a white civiliaztion is to flourish, they will all be herded onto reservations. It's only a question of time."

"And negroes." Everett pronounced the word properly as a challenge.

"The *negroes* as you call them, will be free citizens as the government dictates now. I have nothing against them. But the Indians are savages and must be tamed if the country is to expand and grow. They stand in the way of progress."

"I would hardly call negroes free, even now." But Everett said nothing about the Klan. On the surface, he thought, there seemed nothing wrong with what Catlin was saying, though he seemed a wonderful talker who had the art of telling you nothing but a great harangue. Most Americans felt that way about strange races. Negroes were tolerated to a point because they were Christians, Protestants like the old American stock, and aspired to the same things white people did, had long been a part of the country's fabric. But he'd heard tales about the slaughter of Chinese in railroad towns and San Francisco, knew what the army was doing to the Indian tribes.

"We want the good stock, that's all I mean. The northern people of Europe. We need them. They were the first to have the character and courage to come here and build, go beyond the Mississippi to clear the land and fight the savages."

"It seems to include a lot of different people . . . Germans, Swedes, Polish and Russian, Hungarians, English and Irish. . . ."

"All descended from the noble Knights who met under the great German oak."

"I think the railroads will carry Hottenots west to keep their franchises, and all the land they stole. The Homestead Act of sixty-two gives a quarter-section to anyone who'll cultivate it and live on it for five years. Anyone— native stock, immigrant or baboon. It's the government that's changing things in the West—not adventurers or dreamers."

Everett had heard that nonsense before, how the noble ideals of the white race came down almost a thousand years from a band of Teuton warriors. It was the kind of talk that captivated boys like Matthews, hearts racing, secluded in some corner of a house with a book of history that was nothing but fable. They read and believed, fascinated by the woodcut illustrations: storms and mythic creatures, iron shields and swords . . . bearded knights,

stern and handsome, who wore the cross on a tunic over
their chainmail . . . great fires and oaths taken to Christ,
fealty sworn to a Society of Christian Knights . . . all under the great stout tree that symbolized the root and
flower of white men and their religion.

"Later, men discovered that it was a pathetic travesty of
the truth, a swindle. But the tales shaped generations,
gave them memories of a splendid long-ago past, and memory was the one paradise people couldn't be driven from.
When people grew and learned the world, they might suffer crises of nerves, adopt other values to survive, become
cynics and sinners, but few ever wholly outgrew the wondrous mixture of blood and battle and piety, made it diffi-
cult to relinquish dreams of glory, or resist the stupidity
and waste of war fought for "noble" causes.

It was incredible nonsense, even dangerous. Everett was
a part of his time, believed in his heritage. But he had
placed his faith in the law and learning, believed in sci-
ence and the new. He didn't want to challenge Catlin
openly, but thought that it was more of the same that
caused suffering all the way back to the war's prelude in
Kansas and Missouri, when anti-slave "Jawhawkers" and
pro-slave "Kickapoo Rangers" and "Doniphan Tigers"
raided and killed each other. It was a time of fanatics
. . . John Brown, the self-appointed "Messiah" of negroes,
killing innocent people in the Pottawotami Massacre, slavers burning whole towns. . . . It was the history of men,
Everett thought, that they killed because someone else
claimed moral or religious superiority, because someone
wanted power and riches.

Talk like Catlin's could only brew a slaughter that
would make the war pale by comparison. First the Orien-
tals and the Indians, and after the West had been cleared
of them, what of the Mormons who had been killed before
for their apostasy. Would the old American stock then
set upon the Russians, thought to be heretics from their
own church. And the true Catholics were hated. Twenty
years before, the Know Nothing Party wanted Catholics
driven out, believed the Irish a sub-breed, the Germans
free-thinkers. They were Protestants who formed the se-

cret "Order of the Star Spangled Banner," and when questioned about their activities, members said, "*I know nothing.*" The Know-Nothing slogan was "America for the Americans." No one except a native-born American of Anglo-Saxon stock, and no Roman Catholic, could hold office, and no immigrants were to be given land. This time, Everett knew, anyone who was different or thought inferior, anyone who threatened that mythical pure American race would be prey.

Catlin was ignorant. Was he just another kind of fanatic, spouting old superstitions and hate in the guise of progress and racial purity, ideas that could have the same hideous result as before. What was his place? Was he just a merchant hungry for land, blowing about gold and grass? The Southern cry that "Slavery follows the flag" had ended in tragedy. Who could talk now in the same terms and mean it, believe that the mass of Americans could be ruled by a commercial or gun aristocracy, or some deadly combination of the two. *Only a Ku Kluxer?* In that instant Everett connected the name to something, a name that sounded so familiar for a long time, but one he never linked to dark deeds because Daniel Catlin was such an admirable man and Adela seemed to care for him. One of the names Pompey overheard in Chatterton's house . . . one of the men who killed Douthit, and maybe Trask. Daniel Catlin had been away too long, estranged from his father, and probably knew nothing about it. Everett was suddenly afraid for his family, thought he had pushed Catlin too hard, maybe aroused suspicion. He smiled and lifted his glass of wine.

"Allow a grateful guest to toast a fine and visionary man, a lovely family, and the great state of Arkansas."

Matthew wondered what his father would say when he told him about Catlin. For a moment Everett thought he had been too hasty in judging the man. Catlin, any man, could express perverse opinions and not act on them. But he was certain he remembered the name correctly, some mention of a connection to Arkansas, and regretted never pressing Matthew about the Klan. He knew he had been too passive, despite accusations of scalawag against him and his occasional public stand. He'd avoided too much that he saw, knew what was happening, not just politics and the Klan, but to his women. He had to face it. They were little more than courtesans, whores of a kind if he wanted to be cruel. He had used his wound, his loss, to turn away from conflict, content enough just to practice law where he found the only order in life, or read books where he found the only perfection. He maintained appearances, when every night when they sat down to supper their world fell around them. He was bitter because his own dream had faded and vanished along with the ruin of the state and the town. He glanced at Tom Catlin, Was he just a cheeky, charming rogue, or the same kind of man as his father?

Catlin and Everett toasted each other. They rose from the table and shook hands, Isaac with an arm around Everett's shoulder. He said it was a pleasure to talk to an intelligent man, to have his mind challenged and honed. Everett said that he found Catlin interesting and would like to talk to him at length, find out more about his ideas about what the West would become.

Abby and a servant led the way upstairs to the bedrooms. The house became quiet. Adela lay in bed, trying to sort out what had happened at the table, what would happen to them, when they could leave. She heard someone on the balcony outside her window, knew it was Tom, happy that she wouldn't have to think any more. Her face was an elixir of fate and fascination. She was discovering that she loved lassitude, being able to succumb to mood without guilt, eager to surrender to pleasure. She lay quietly, like prey in a trap, waiting for him to undress. He bent over her.

"Come with me," he whispered.

Puzzled, she followed him out on the balcony and they stole to a window toward the front of the house. She saw two figures kissing by a dim lamp, a man's rough hand mashing the woman's breasts. She was suddenly swung back years to another place, the forbidden things she'd seen. Isaac Catlin and Abby were embracing as the burly man took her dressing gown off. Adela felt excited, captivated by the act, and wanted to watch them make love, but Tom pulled her back to her room.

"Why didn't we stay?"

"You saw enough."

"Why did you show me?"

"So you wouldn't believe anything righteous she tells you about me."

The exchange between the two in the parlor . . . he was trying to tell her then, also warn Abby to remain quiet about something.

"When did they start?"

"Since she was fifteen, maybe. She was a hell of a looking woman for a long time. Now she's no better than a slave. But she likes it that way. She's the lady of the house . . . that's the way he shows her in front of people. I was only a kid, but I used to see them go into my mother's room and pretend how bad they felt. Pap kept giving her one of those medicines that put people in dreams and sleep most of the time. Then they would go back into his room carrying books, like he was teaching her. I used to hide and see them close the door. I didn't understand it for a long time. Then I listened one time and I damn well knew what it was then."

"What about Daniel, did he know?"

"He never saw and I never told him. He'd never believe it anyway. He and Abby were too close. She made him a hero and raised him after my mother died, even though she was only five years older."

Adela wondered if she should tell him about Jessie, then felt conspiraterial and told the story about the afternoon at Loretto. "Two of a kind, huh?" They felt giddy about the shared secrets and it made their love-making more wicked and delicious. Afterward he lay on his back, a hand outstretched and idly straying over her stomach. The moon speckled her body and she tried to curve into him again.

"I'm no bull!" he said and rolled away. "Let me be."

He made her feel like a wandering old crone, desperate for human touch, serving anyone who would favor her begging. But that wasn't the way she thought of it at first. She had lived in a morning world, often an imprudent,

frivolous girl dallying at pleasure. But now it was all dark
and frost. Pain fretted her heart, but she thought it wasn't
the pain of love. It was a moment of revelation . . . that
the passion she dreamed, sought with unfocused fear,
could subdue her, make her feel squalid. To survive, she
had to think of him as dangerous, a phantasm, a hellish
messenger who brought momentary torment and a trance
of frenzy . . . but only that.

In the weeks that followed, Adela rarely saw Matthew.
He sometimes went out early and rode into the countryside, but spent most of his time in town. Everett sat in his
room a good part of the day, morose, and came out only
for meals. He said nothing when Isaac took Jessie to town
or showed her land he was buying. Adela tried to keep
busy, but there was little to do and she often sat out on
the veranda waiting for Tom. He often was gone for days
but never told her where he went or how long he'd be
away. She talked with Metta to pass the time and was
jealous of the girl because she seemed to touch everyone
with her goodness, rarely showing an emotion beyond
compliance, acceptance. They became good friends and
shared innocent secrets. On nights when Tom was gone,
Adela liked the warmth of holding Metta, found excuses
for them to be close. Sometimes they slept together, Metta's head resting on Adela's breast while she stroked the
delicate woman's hair.

But Adela was curious, eager to find out something
else. She often saw Metta and Simon talking. It always
looked proper, but she sensed some strong connection between the two. She noticed that they were both often
gone at the same time. One afternoon Adela was in Metta's room. For the first time the girl looked nervous, vulnerable. Adela thought that Metta was near tears, was tan-
talized by the idea of something forbidden and probed
slowly. But Metta began to chew at a handkerchief.

"What is it? Tell me. Maybe it will make you feel better."

"I can't."

"If you keep everything to yourself, you'll bust. I know how that is."

"Father's going to Nashville. He's taking your mother."

"I know. Papa thought it would do her good, get to a city and enjoy hershef." She laughed. "Living out in Piggot's not exactly the high road to adventure, now is it?"

Metta couldn't help herself and giggled. "You're so good, Adela."

"It bother you that your father's taking my mother?"

"Only that he'll be gone."

"You mean you miss him that bad?"

"No. But something could happen that wasn't planned." Adela pretended exasperation and started for the door but Metta stopped her. "Can I trust you?"

"Of course." Then to show the girl she meant it, she said, "It's something about you and Simon."

Metta's face went white. If a stranger could find out so quickly, her family must know, waiting to catch her. "How could you know?"

"Because I see your beauty, how your face changes when you're near him, just that little bit that I can see. Because of the way he seems to protect you, even from a distance. I think I saw it from the start."

"I loved Simon since I was a little girl, when my father brought him home. I'm not ashamed of it. He's the best man in the world. We've been lovers a long time."

"How did it start?"

"It just happened. I think I was fourteen. Come with me."

She took Adela out to a path that went along the yard fence, between the fence and the woods across the field, and then on back past the chicken runs and the woods until it was lost to sight where the woods bulged and cut off the back field. It led back through the woods to a swamp, skirted the swamp where the big trees gave way to sycamores and water oaks and willows, and then led to the river.

"Nobody ever goes back here except to gig frogs in the swamp," Metta said, "or to fish or hunt. And most don't ever come too far because father and Tom don't welcome them. They had dogs out here to howl a warning. If they thought strangers were only sportsmen out for a day, they left easy. But if they had any suspicion, they just poked their rifles back in the direction of Piggot and everyone skedaddled." She pointed. "Our old house used to be back there. One day, father sent Simon to get something from the old house when the new one was built. I followed him. It started then." She showed Adela the entrance to a root cellar through a tangle of charred wood and weeds. "That's where it happened. Then when father burned the old house down, we knew we had our hiding place, our love place we called it, and knew we could never be found out if we were careful. We only went in the day . . . never had more than an hour together."

"What has this got to do with your father going away? I'd think you'd be happy."

"Because we've been planning for a long time to run away to Oregon. Simon wants to go now, says we'll never have a better chance."

"Then go."

"I can't. I'm afraid."

"If you don't do it now, you never will. You'll get stuck here. That's what I was always afraid of, just growing old in the same place." She took Metta's shoulders. "I envy you. I wish I had a man that strong for me."

"I'm not afraid for myself. I'm afraid of my father and Tom. If they catch us, they'll kill Simon. And I know them, they'll chase us from here to hell."

"Your brother doesn't seem to care much about anything except his pleasure."

"You don't know him." She saw Adela's look, knew what she was trying to tell her, and quickly said, "No, you don't. Don't ever trust him—about anything. God, how I wish Daniel would come back. He was the only one who could control Tom or stand up to my father. You knew him, you saw how strong he is."

"Yes. I even thought I loved him. Or maybe just grateful because he heldped us." She tried to fight any regret. "I'll help you." She thought how dismal it would be without Metta, no one to talk to, nothing to do, just sit and wait for that arrogant bastard to take her. She began to curse, looking like a madwoman, thinking that someone like herself who needed punishment should be sacrilegeous. Sex and pain, sex and death. That was all she'd learned, that you paid for the pleasure, one way or another. She knew she was incapable of loving anyone the way Metta did, a dogged, soft and steadfast love. She got control of herself.

"If you don't take a chance now, you'll die here, just wither and dry up, trying to steal an hour here and there. And you'll tell yourself that one time long ago there was a chance to get out. What's the difference if you die on the road? At least you'll be together. That's what's important. You'll be doing what *you* want, be with whom *you* want. And your chances are good. Don't miss it. I'm younger than you, and I have so many regrets. . . ."

Two days later Isaac Catline left with Jessie, and Tom said he'd be away for a while. After an early supper, when it was growing dark, Metta and Simon hid behind the seat of a carriage driven by Adela. She got them past Piggot and they climbed into the seat with her. When they reached Bledsoe, Adela stopped in the darkness a short way from the railroad depot. Metta kissed her, then, impulsively, Adela kissed Simon, wished them good luck and preteneded to turn back to Piggot. But she watched as Simon, walking in front like a proper servant, carried Metta's hand-trunk and hatbox to the train. She was helped up the steps of a first-class coach, and he went back to the car for servants, still called the "niggar car." Adela saw Metta at the window in the glare of the bright lamps. She waited until the train started, gave a tentative little wave, and turned the team around.

She took the carriage into the stable and hoped Abby hadn't seen her. What did it matter anyway? They'd be discovered missing tomorrow morning at the latest. There would be hell to pay whatever she did. She went up to see how Everett was. He seemed a little more buoyant than usual.

"I've decided to open a law office in Piggot."

Her heart beat wildly. "I don't want to stay here."

"Why not? It's as good a place as any I've seen. A prosperous place. I have to think about Matt. He's doing the same thing he did back home, hanging around town, no idea or say of doing anything proper with his life. He could read the law with me and set up here with me in an office."

She thought of all her fanciful dreams . . . the big cities and foreign places, the theaters and museums and stores she heard about. She said to Everett that she was going to leave soon, but didn't believe it. She felt drained, as if she'd never have the energy again to do what she wanted . . . what she thought she wanted. She hugged her father with desperation and began to cry.

"Come, come, what's wrong?"

"I just thought everything would be different. I thought once we left Palmyra things would change."

"They have. We can have our own house again. My brother will send the money. Catline even offered to lend me some to get started again, but I didn't want to feel more of an obligation to him." He paused. "Strange man. All those crazy ideas, then he's so kindly. I've already written to Memphis."

"Don't you worry about Mother being with him?"

His face was a ruin. "I gave up your mother years ago." Adela knew it, but was surprised he would bend enough to confide in her. "She's a woman who needs a different kind of man. Always told me I was too stingy with my passion. She was my bad bargain. But you were pleasure enough to repay me." He smiled. "But I can't be a godly man and say Matthew's been the same."

"He'll settle down, papa."

"I wonder sometimes. If he was plain wild, I could understand it. But it's something else, a damned kind of stubbornness when he gets an idea. You know, the other day he had the gall to tell me that maybe he was wrong about the Klan. Can you imagine? Said the more he saw of what was happening, the more he thought the Klan was right. I think he still sees himself as some kind of savior of the way we lived. I said it was already gone, had gone with the war, that it was doomed anyway. I said that even his mother had accepted it, was resigned to a new time. But I think he's got some idea he can redeem himself with the Klan. Be a part of it again."

"Papa, this is a Klan house."

"I know. I didn't want you to know and be upset. I was hoping to get us out of here before anything happened. Matthew and I both knew something about Catlin, some killings back home."

"And that didn't change his mind?"

"You know him. Tell him one thing one day, he believes it and you can't tell him anything else. Tell him something else the next and he'll believe that. First Catlin seemed to scare him, but I think he's been talking to Matt, twisting him around."

"Tom told me some things that made me think it was Klan. He never came right out with it, just talked about big things that were going to happen."

She knew that he was aware of her and Tom, was ashamed and worried for her. The moment they stepped off the boat, she could have stopped pretending that she was Tom's woman. But she thought he'd never be able to talk about it to her.

"Maybe we should have stayed in Palmyra," Everett said. "Dan Catlin would have protected us."

"Papa, it's all past."

"Why couldn't you love him? He asked for your hand, said he did it because he liked the old ways."

She took a breath. Tell him once and for all what she was. "For the same reason mama couldn't love you."

"Well, at least there's no humbug in you."

She was smoothing her father's hair, when she heard noise on the steps and Tom came into the room.

"Get the hell out," he told her. "I want to talk private."

Everett gave him a reassuring look and she left, thinking that he might devour her, but she wasn't going to let it happen to her father.

17

Tom slammed the door shut. "Where the hell's the money you promised?"

"My brother in Memphis is sending it."

"That was smart, hiding it with him."

"It seemed the best way."

"Listen, you damn cripple! There ain't no money, and there ain't no brother. There's a plague in Memphis. The Yellow Fever. And if he had any money, he don't any more. He's dead. Adela told me about the brother. I was going to give you one chance. If you weren't a damn nigger-lover, then you really stole and put the money somewhere safe. I did a little asking around down there. I got a lot of people with a lot of ears. He died maybe ten days ago. They burned his house."

"Then the money went with it." He thought of Malcolm, poor Malcolm, smitten with art, a man of scant talent that he supported, the brother who would often paint until darkness and then sit in front of his easel for hours, alone, bothered less by the absence of light than the presence of light or other people.

"You know why I'm going to blow your head off? Not because you tried to shivvy me. I don't blame a man who looks for the advantage. But because you're a damn nigger-lover. You work for the Yankees. Someone gave you a wrong story to tell. The minute I saw the Klan at Phillipy I knew it. If you stole from Yankees and niggers, why the hell should they be chasing you?"

"My son was attacked. They were looking for someone, but it wasn't him. He had to kill two of them."

Tom ignored it. "I tried to figure out which one they wanted, but it didn't matter. Then I thought maybe you stole from the Klan. That wouldn't be so much. Klan's like anything else, someone always looking for quick money. Then we got an order. You, everyone in your family, are in the Dead Book. But pap decided to wait a while. Maybe if you told us the true story, we might have helped you. Everyone makes mistakes. He's a powerful man in these parts. The things he got going, he needs smart men. He could have protected you, maybe brought you in." Tom suddenly walked to the door and opened it. There was no one in the hall and he closed it slowly and sat down. "Now I'm going to tell you something that'll ring your ears. And if I tell you, it's too dangerous to let you live. You get that?"

"What about your brother. He believes the Klan is wrong. He fought with the Yankees. Would you kill him?"

"When the time comes, I'll blow his head off just as easy."

"Suppose I told you I was Ku Klux, sent here undercover by General Forrest because he suspects some of your Hydras of being traitors."

"That's a good one, a real nice fairy tale." His voice grew sharp. "Where the hell do you think my pap is right now? He's with the Grand Wizard in Nashville. A holy old sonofabitch like you Ku Klux? Not when I got to hear you argue the first night we came. I could see you busting to tell him to go to hell." He drew a revolver and tapped Everett's knee with the barrel. "Listen, he organized everything west of the Mississippi. He's Grand Dragon of the Arkansas Realm, and he's got his own men in at the top in Texas and Missouri. We're the ones who blew up those steamers carrying Yankee troops to here and Texas a couple of months ago. We're bigger than the whole Confederate army ever was, and better organized."

Everett had heard it many times, like a litany. "They were beaten."

"We're not going to fight a war. We don't have to. We got millions in the central treasury. You'd be surprised where that money comes from. It don't come from no dollar entrance fee and fifty cents every week for a ghoul."

The teacher in Everett made him try to explain to Tom about the North, the spurt of manufacture brought by the war, the new developments, while the South and West were still agrarian places, everything predicated on the earth, grass for cattle, soil, for crops. "This time they could crush you—us—years quicker. They learned."

"You don't want to understand. It's all done different now."

"Don't you fear the government?"

"The *government*? Hell, we're part of the government now, and going to *be* the government. We control lawmen, judges and juries and legislatures from here to the Carolinas, even with the niggers in them. We got a governor in a free state, people in the damn United States Congress—right now! We got everything set up in the Territories for when they become states."

Everett knew much of it was true, and accepted the rest. In those times, the ordinary could become the nightmare. But he pretended shock and a grudging admiration. The man was aching to tell him more.

"We got generals out West in our pay. Fucking Yankee bastards think they won the war. They just made it better for us in the long run. We're going to have all the land we want, and all the cheap workers for it . . . Indians and niggers. Pap already owns hundreds of miles. The railroads are tied up in it. They ain't railroad companies, they're land companies, taking millions of acres. You know how many quarter-sections of 160 acres that makes? You think it's those night-riding backwoods skulls that counts? No more. Whole damn country's rotten to the core. A lot of powerful people decided to make their own country.

You think them Russian kings got the riches? That ain't pigspit to what we're going to get."

"Then why did you kick up such a fuss about the money I promised?"

"That was for my little pleasures. Money in my hand right now. But you sure slicked me. I admire a man that can do that, so I'm going to do you a favor." He poked the gun into the stub of the missing arm. "I'm not going to get you tonight. But don't get any ideas. There's people watching the house. Tommorrow morning, you come back up the path with me to the swamp. Nice and quiet. You'll just get sucked under. That way Adela won't get no shock. And Abby'll be in town at the store."

Everett gazed at the fraying edge of his shiny black coatsleeve. He had a feeling of sadness that was no longer like pain. He had raked the muck this way and that, but it was still muck. The years he had brooded, set himself aside, he could have been stringing pearls for the delight of heaven. He had trusted wisdom and reason and ended up mangled and betrayed. But only a god goes woundless all the way. Life had become coarse and base. For the first time he understood his women. They were erotic because they substituted action and feeling for thought. And that was much like the violence Matthew was drawn to. His illness was that he was too conscious of splendid possibilities, without the energy to act on them. Blunders . . . pride . . . regrets . . . the corridors of his brain haunted.

He could never tell anyone how he felt to see a great idea like democracy taken over by inexperienced clumsy hands that dragged it out in the streets and shared it with other fools . . . then coming on it in the junk market, un-reconizgable, grimy, without a sense of proportion, without harmony, used as a toy by stupid brats. *Let Catlin take him.* The future belonged to men like him, and the speculators and confidence men and politicians who'd trick the masses of people and democracy.

"Wait until my wife returns," he said. "There is something I must tell her, apologize for. I promise you no trouble. Afterward, I'll say we're going away on business."

Catlin believed him, but had contempt because Everett insisted on a gentleman's code to the end. He agreed and left with a warning—one suspicious move and he'd kill the whole family—then went back to Adela's bedroom.

Hours later Everett was still awake, looking out at the stars that seemed to crackle and burst like sunstarts on a stream, when he heard the door open. He sat up with a start, thinking that Catlin had lied and was coming for him. But it was Adela. She sat on the bed and put a finger to her lips, her face close to his, whispering.

"He's sleeping drunk. What happened?"

"He threatened me."

"What do you mean?"

"He's going to kill me. Told me their plans and said I knew too much."

She had to decide in that moment. Thomas Catlin was a walking idea that she came to terms with, and like much joy it was ugly. There could be others. She suddenly couldn't face the exhileration of freedom, the end of her Palmyra world. "We can kill him."

"What about the others?"

"Metta's gone. I'll explain later. There's only Abby and her room is downstairs."

"Catlin's a strong man."

"Damnit, he's going to kill you. Don't sit there like you always do, find excuses." Everett remembered his self-reproach only hours before and didn't resist any longer. She took his right arm. "It's strong, papa. Wait here."

She returned in a few minutes with Matthew. "He'll help." Everett reached out and Matthew took his hand and started to say something but she told him to be quiet. She sat a while, then told them what to do and went back to her room.

Tom was breathing heavily. She gently put a pillow over his face and he didn't move. She opened the door and Everett and Matthew, both barefoot, came in. At her signal they grabbed the pillow and pushed it down into Tom's face, smothering him. His feet twitched in reflex, but there was little struggle. They threw the covers over his face on top of the pillow and Adela jammed a revolver underneath against the temple. The shot was muffled, but Matthew went out on the landing. The house was quiet.

"Once more to make sure," Everett said. He took the revolver and put it against the head and fired. He threw the covers off and lifted the pillow. "His skull's blown hollow." He began to feel crisp again, like a soldier. "Wrap him in the blanket and put him in the closet. We'll take him out tomorrow. He said Abby was going to the store. Matt, take anything bloody and hide it in your room."

Adela got fresh linen from a closet in the hall. She forced herself to look at the pulpy, gaping wound but no longer recognized Tom, felt nothing. That night she slept in the room with the dead man, feeling no remorse, happy that she had broken the spell.

After Abby left in the morning, Matthew brought Adela the big cotton sack he'd taken from a storehouse along with a coil of rope. They stuffed Tom's body in and lashed it tight. Matthew rode into town in the afternoon. He returned at a gallop toward dusk and said Abby was still there, that she told him she'd be another hour or two. Adela said she's keep the servants busy in the kitchen. Matthew brought his horse around the side of the house, and he and Everett went upstairs to Adela's room. Matthew looked out the window.

"It's all in shadow down there."

He made a noose and slipped it around the top of the cotton sack. They dragged it to a window, lifted it over the sill, then began to lower it slowly. It bumped twice against the house and Matthew thought he felt the noose slipping.

"Get down there quick!" Everett said. He held tight with one arm, feeling his muscles beginning to tear, but the rope slipped off and he dropped it and rushed downstairs.

The sack landed a few feet from Matthew's horse and it shied. He soothed the animal, then tugged the sack upright, threw it across his shoulder and lay it over the saddle, then mounted, sitting behind the cantle. He walked the horse around the back of the house. When he found the path, he spurred the mount and galloped into the woods toward the swamp.

A servant heard the horse running. "Where that boy going? Where Miss Metta? Miss Abby don't like to wait on her supper."

"He's just going to tell the Keith boy about a party tomorrow."

The negro woman laughed. "That for young folks."

"Do you like to dance?"

"I likes, but I can't do it no more. Feet swells like a bug with the blood."

Adela saw Everett in the kitchen door, casually lighting his pipe, and knew it was safe to go to her room The bed held no terror for her and she lay down . . . the linen fresh and clean . . . the bloody mattress turned. She felt free and relaxed for the first time in weeks. It would be easy to explain Tom's absence. He came and went at quirky hours. They only had to wait for Jessie, keep pretenses for a while, then leave. She began to think of marriage, how intricate it could be, its near boundless possibilities. Any marriage, happy or unhappy, suddenly seemed infinitely more interesting to her than any romance, no matter how compelling and passionate. She thought she was very wise when she decided that a romance leaves off at the point of "They lived happily—or miserably—ever after." But a marriage was about that decisive "after." And as quickly as she felt smug, she knew she could change her mind in an instant.

When Abby returned, she sent for Metta and waited impatiently. The maid said she wasn't around. Abby sent the girl to ask the field hands if they had seen her. She came back and said no one had seen her all day—and Simon was gone too. Abby rushed to Metta's room and found clothes and the hand-trunk missing. She wrote out a message and gave it to one of the men she called into the house.

"Take his to the telegraph in Piggot. Tell the agent it's from me and he's to send it immediately."

Adela knew she was sending for her father in Nashvile. "Where is Tom?"

"You know him. Comes and goes as he pleases."

"My father will crucify me."

"She's probably visiting friends. She'll be back soon."

"Are you crazy? Without a word? Bag and baggage gone? She's run off with that nigger."

Adela wondered why Abby didn't seem more shocked . . . as if she'd known about them all the time. Everett knew they had to give Matthew time and he tried to convince Abby not to worry, said that Adela often went off like that on a whim.

"You two think I'm blind or stupid? That little whore's gone for good."

Matthew came sauntering into the house. "Where is everyone? When we gonna eat?"

Adela knew from his face that everything was all right.

"Something's happened. Metta's gone. You go out along the road to every house, go into town and see what you can find out."

"No!" Abby shouted. "Think we want the whole town to know it? That little simpering nigger-lover thinks she's going to get away free, she's crazy. My father-owns this country. He'll find her, and he'll lock her up in a cellar for the rest of her life . . . if he doesn't kill her."

Isaac Catlin and Jessie returned the morning of the second day. Adela thought that something had happened between them. Jessie hadn't wasted any time. She looked handsome in new clothes, flushed, her breasts pouting, the hazel eyes bright and eager again. Adela knew the look too well. Abby took her father into the parlor and shut the sliding doors. He was quiet when he came out and called the Laniers together.

"You know anything about this?" When there was no response, he turned to Adela. "You two were always twitting around like a couple of birds. She tell you anything?"

"No. She just seemed like a happy girl. I never saw a girl so content."

"Where's Tom?"

"You know about as much as I do. He doesn't tell me anything." Her heart skipped. She almost said, *He never told me* . . . .

For days Catlin rode the countryside, sent messages to army friends, klan officers and lawmen that a nigger had put his daughter under a voodoo spell and kidnapped her. They were to be found and brought back. He wanted the nigger alive. But each passing day lessened his urgency. It was more the insult, the challenge to his authority, than the loss that maddened him. He never had any use for Metta . . . not for his flesh-sins or plans of empire.

In time, Everett surrendered Jessie to him, almost willingly as if it had been decreed. Abby faded to nothing, a drudge, a sparrow figure walking between rooms. Isaac and Jessie spent long hours alone and soon slept together openly. They talked of slaves and the South and the Great West, land to which there was no boundary . . . black and red men to serve them. Each was fascinated by the other, social opposites; the once-great beauty and aristocrat, the plantation queen, and the uneducated, harsh, virile, tyrant-in-the-making. Jessie seemed to drift through the house, scarcely speaking a word to anyone, between bedroom and parlor. She became even more lunatic in her visions than Isaac and drove him to give her a barony. He had made careful plans, wanted to wait, but together they drifted into a kind of madness. She said she couldn't stand the sight of Everett any longer . . . he was plotting against them. Isaac believed her and said it would be done. She opened her dress and offered her breasts to him, an ecstatic look on her face. Isaac twisted them and drew his revolver.

"Where is he?"

Her eyes were still closed. "Somewhere upstairs . . . somewhere."

Everett saw Catlin come into the room. He made no move to escape. He would die like a gentleman. A gentleman had to be brave, show no sign of panic or cowardice, meet death without flinching. He knew it because he had learned the code of the gentleman in many different ways . . . by example, by advice, by what he had been taught at school or by his parents, and by endless stories of perfect knights. He found it ironic that what he thought rubbish and romantic morbidity in his son was the last thing he would impose on himself.

Adela was walking down the veranda steps, feeling the first rush of hot wind. She saw a rider a long way off and watched as he approached. She thought it might be Matthew returning from town, but the figure never seemed to materialize. Then she recognized the forward-leaning style, the lean cavalryman's body. It was Daniel. Her eyes brimmed. If she ran to him, just touched him, she could be saved. Everything had started in a dark poetry, in boredom, like most sin and melancholy. She had surrendered to languid, tainted pleasures and wasn't sure she could live any other way, that she needed the outcast, parching, brutish mating that Daniel could never give her.

She heard a shot from the house and knew immediately. She was like stalked prey, running this way and that, turning to Daniel and then to the house in eccentric circles. She saw herself looking at her dead father, pleading with him to understand that he had been killed by the times, by all of them, Catlins and Laniers and the Klan . . . by lost dreams and every kind of greed and passion.

EPILOGUE

ADELA and Daniel Catlin brought Everett's body home to Palmyra for burial and were married soon thereafter. Daniel was appointed head of the Tennessee militia and the Catlins stayed in Knoxville, the capital, until Daniel was elected to Congress and served for fourteen years in Washington. When he died, Adela remained as a leading hostess and mistress of a President. When scandal drove her out of town, she settled in New York City, where, in her forties, she became the center of the new artistic and social circles that emerged prior to World War I. She was the friend of writers such as Edith Wharton and William Dean Howells, and her salon in Gramercy Park became famous. She died at age 81, surrounded by friends and admirers.

Matthew Lanier, after living with Adela and Daniel in Knxville and attending the University of Tennessee, went West in search of his destiny. He became a surveyor, then a Division superintendent for the Union Pacific railroad. He died in his early forties in a dispute over gold claim in Cripple Creek, Colorado.

Isaac Catlin and Jessie Lanier never married but stayed together until Jessie died in an influenza epidemic at 53. Isaac's fortunes declined along with the fortunes of the Ku

Klux Klan, and he suffered a stroke and died in 1878. Abby Catlin regained her place with Isaac and nursed him in his last illness. After Isaac's demise, Abby and Lewis Catlin ran the hardware store until 1901, when Abby died in an old-age home and Lewis was committed to an insane asylum, where he died in 1914.

Metta Catlin and Simon Hooper, posing as mistress and servant, ran a successful restaurant in San Francisco, had a son in secret, and lived happily into their sixties, passing the restaurant on to their child. Before her death, Metta told the son, Ezra, of his true parentage.

The "Night Riders"—the Ku Klux Klan—faded into obscurity after 1870, when President Ulysses S. Grant sent a message to Congress decrying the existence of the KKK, after which a series of bills were passed outlawing the organization.

In folk-say and racial memory, the legend of the Klan grew larger then life. The seed would lie dormant for almost fifty years and then burst through the soil again, still firmly rooted in the hatreds of the old days.

The Ku Klux Klan had its modern resurgence in 1915, reached a new peak of influence in the 1920's, and still exists today, but without any significant political or terrorist power.